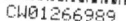
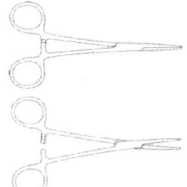
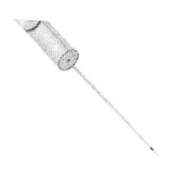

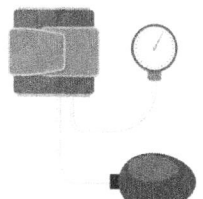

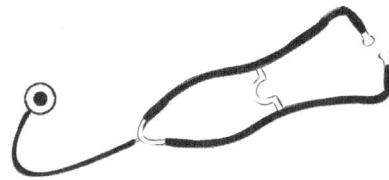

Total *Pressure*

By Rob Lederer

Copyright © 2024 Rob Lederer

All rights reserved

The characters and events portrayed in this book are fictitious. Any similarity to real persons, living or dead, is coincidental and not intended by the author.

No part of this book may be reproduced, or stored in a retrieval system, or transmitted in any form or by any means, electronic, mechanical, photocopying, recording, or otherwise, without express written permission from Rob Lederer, author.

ISBN: 9798871842645

Cover design by Christine Lederer
Printed in Canada

Front Cover Photo: Alex Azabache
Back Cover Photo: Paolo Chiabrando
St Andrews Roundabout: Natalka Krusche

To Peaches and Keen

For My Mother and My Aunt

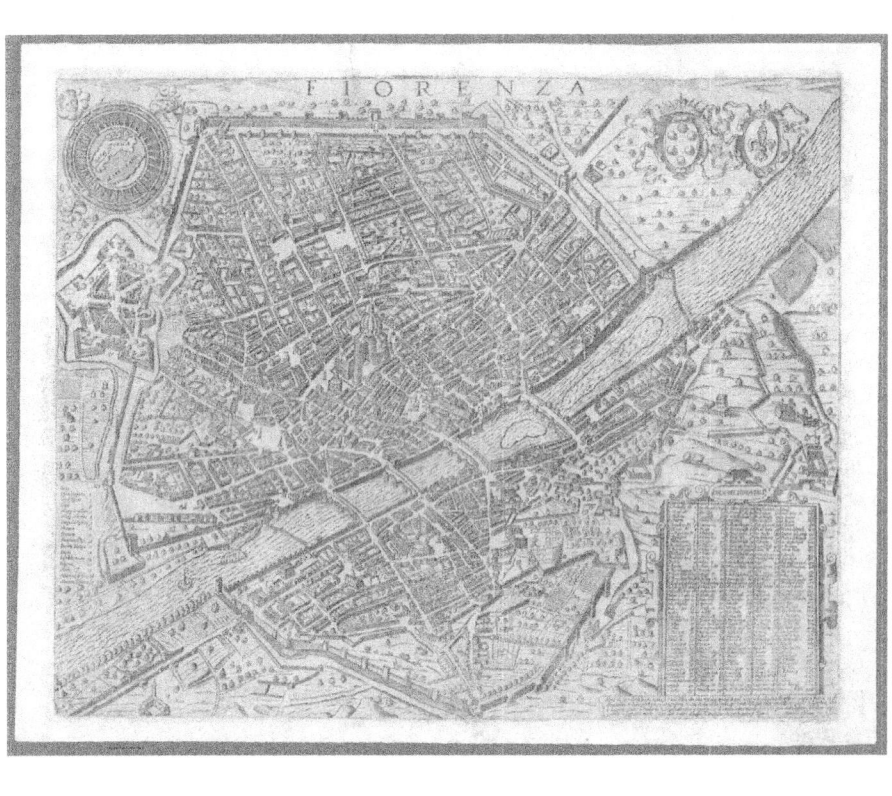

The grey clouds of the mid-autumn sky gathered from two directions to converge on the little village. The wind increased its intensity, displaced leaves from the chestnut trees, and scattered them to the northeast. The tall grass bent, recovered, and bent again to the gusts that swirled in the valley. Organic debris was lifted up in columns, strewn about, and deposited on the forest floor in random fashion. Completely random, except for one small thing.

The twice-folded piece of paper that had materialized from the fuzzy light of the tunnel entrance tumbled out from between two honeysuckle bushes. It was caught in an updraft and lifted out of the valley. It glided along on a current of air high above the little village. Then, as if released from flight by a Guiding Hand, the paper descended gently into a back garden in the village of Butte-aux-Cailles.

Madeleine Laurent was removing the last of the laundry from the clothesline as the storm intensified. She grabbed at the bonnet and blue shawl she was wearing that were attempting to take flight, and stuffed them into the laundry basket. Then she made her way to the back door of the house.

It was just a little piece of paper, barely noticeable, but it caught Madeleine's eye. She picked it up from the stone step and put it into the basket. Madeleine then closed the door behind her with no small effort, as the wind whistled through the doorway.

While her husband, Jean, secured the last of the storm shutters on the windows, Madeleine and the children folded and put away the clean clothes. When they were finished, Madeleine took the basket to the back door and placed it in the washtub. She noticed the little piece of paper in the basket. Madeleine opened the first fold of the paper and read the words that were written boldly by a sure hand. She stood at the back door for a long moment, looking at the paper.

It was a message that was written just for her, she thought.

Madeleine brought the twice-folded paper to the sitting room and took the small, leather-bound family bible off the shelf. She tucked the paper inside the front cover and replaced the bible. Just then, her husband came in from outside.

"It is quite the storm approaching, my dear," he said, struggling to close the front door. "I hope the house can manage the stress."

"I am certain we will be kept safe, Jean," Madeleine said. "I have a good feeling all will be well."

Chapter 1

"Could I get a bit more suction here, please? And doctor, could you give me a half dozen more turns on the retractor so I can get a better view."

The lead surgeon continued cauterizing the incision as the scrub practitioner and assistant surgeon performed the requests.

"How's that?" asked the assisting surgeon.

"Perfect right there," replied the lead surgeon. "I'm going to finish peeling back the pericardium, now. How are the patient's vitals?"

"All good," answered the anesthesiologist. "Blood pressure normal, breathing normal."

"Great. Okay, there we go," the lead surgeon said upon exposing the beating heart. "Aorta looks good, superior vena cava looks good." The lead surgeon moved a free hand along the vessels. "I don't feel any plaques. How's it all look to you, doctor?"

"Considering the patient's age and weight, it all looks normal," said the assisting surgeon. "Ready to harvest the left internal mammary artery?"

"All set for LIMA," replied the lead surgeon. "Forceps, please." The surgeon began to gently pull up on the endothoracic fascia with one hand, while using the electrocautery with the other.

"A quick *peru*sal indicates all is going well with the patient," said the assisting surgeon. Then, after a pause, "Get it? I did a *Peru*sal during the LIMA harvest?"

"Ugh," went the anesthesiologist and scrub practitioner.

"Tough crowd," said the assisting surgeon. "Time for anticoagulant administration, doctor?"

"It is," replied the lead surgeon, handing off the used forceps. "Doctor, could you administer 2500 units of heparin, please?"

"2500 units, right away," the anesthesiologist answered, injecting the dosage into the patient's IV line.

Beads of perspiration were forming on the lead surgeon's brow. The scrub practitioner alertly dabbed off the sweat with four surgical sponges attached to a Rampley holder. The lead surgeon turned slightly to receive the pat-down.

"Thank you. These surgical lights are pretty hot, aren't they? Okay, here's the artery. I'm going to clip off the anterior portion, now. Forceps." The scrub practitioner had the instrument in the surgeon's hand in 0.3 seconds. The assisting surgeon applied suction to the area of the chest wall with a steady hand and began humming a tune.

"I know that song," said the anesthesiologist. "My dad used to play it a lot."

"It's a great one," replied the assisting surgeon. "It's Moondance, by Van Morrison. I was thinking of the patient's chordae tendineae. His heartstrings are playing soft and low right now."

"I'd prefer that you give us a chorus of Don't Go Breaking My Heart," kidded the anesthesiologist. "It might be more in your vocal range."

"I couldn't if I tried," said the assisting surgeon with a wink.

"Ugh," went the scrub practitioner and anesthesiologist again. But they were smiling under their surgical masks, their squinting eyes giving them away.

"Perhaps you could *try* a bit more suction along this incision, doctor," chided the lead surgeon, with hands quivering ever so slightly. "I've almost got this artery harvested."

"Roger that," the assisting surgeon replied, just as a beeping noise came from the ECG monitor.

"Doctor, we have a drop in the patient's blood pressure," said the anesthesiologist. "But nothing really outside of nor…" The beeping noise picked up its cadence. "Hold on…"

"What is it?" asked the lead surgeon, stopping the extraction procedure and turning toward the monitor.

"Tachycardia. We've got a big jump in pulse," replied the anesthesiologist with a worried tone. "Respiration rate increasing…"

"Patient in distress, doctor," the assisting surgeon said, looking across at the lead surgeon.

The doctor looked back at the assisting surgeon with widening eyes, hands quivering more than a bit, now.

"Increase O₂ level," the lead surgeon said anxiously. "Prepare to do an IV push of 6 milligrams of adenosine."

"Yes, doctor," replied the anesthesiologist.

"Heart rate now dropping, doctor. Blood pressure dropping, too," said the assisting surgeon.

"Administer the adenosine, but make it 12 milligrams."

"Patient not responding, doctor. Heart rate decreasing."

The lead surgeon stood frozen for six long seconds, with hands starting to tremble. The assisting surgeon broke the silence.

"Doctor…we're losing the patient. It might be time to pull out the big guns."

The lead surgeon stared at the assisting surgeon across the operating table for a short moment and then replied, "Yes, right. Prepare for synchronized cardioversion, doctor."

The scrub practitioner moved quickly and rolled the defibrillator next to the lead surgeon. The doctor was handed the electrodes. The lead surgeon just stood there, staring down at the patient's chest, hands noticeably shaking.

"Doctor?" said the assisting surgeon.

No response.

"Doctor, you've got to apply the electrodes, now."

"I just…"

"There's no time!"

"I'm not…"

"Dr. Campbell!"

The monitor went from beeping to a steady tone. The surgical lights cut out. The operating room went dark.

The lights came back on in the operating theatre. The lead surgeon, assisting surgeon, anesthesiologist, and scrub practitioner removed their surgical masks. The patient lay motionless on the operating table. As always.

"Well, it wasn't a complete disaster," said a voice from above. "Aside from the patient dying, of course."

Dr. Raven stood up from his chair in the gallery that was directly above the operating room, his hands buried in his lab coat pockets. Eleven medical students were sitting behind their Surgical Skills instructor, notebooks in hand.

"Let's start off with the positives," Dr. Raven said softly in his South-West Irish accent. "Ms Lombardi, your responses to the lead surgeon's directives were quick and decisive. If you were to drop out of medical school, you would make a fine scrub practitioner."

"Uh…*grazie*?" replied Marianna, looking up at her professor from the operating room floor below.

"Ms Banes, your anesthesiology work was acceptable."

"Ah…thank you, sir," said Holly, also not quite sure of what to make of the comment.

"Mr. Munroe, you had even more to offer your lead surgeon, today. You can't be reluctant to speak up when you encounter difficult situations in the OR."

"Yes, Dr. Raven," Mark replied.

"And in the UK operating theatre, Mr. Munroe, we would not say 'Doctor Campbell' we would say 'Ms Campbell', correct?"

"Ah…yes, Dr. Raven, sir. No…I mean, Mr. Raven, sir."

"And about the Van Morrison in the operating room…"

"Yes, sorry, Sir Raven…um, Doctor Sir," Mark said sheepishly. "It won't happen again."

"I was going to say, 'Keep up the good work'," Dr. Raven said with a smile. "Though I would have preferred his song, When Heart is Open."

Chuckles from the gallery.

"Now, Lead Surgeon…"

"Yes, Dr. Raven…I really blew it today," said Natalie Campbell, not looking up.

"You only blew one thing today, Ms Campbell, and it didn't cost the surgical dummy any more life than he didn't have already," the professor said, matter of factly. "I credit you for your correct procedures throughout the exercise. The one step I had issue with was enough for me to launch the distress program from my seat." Dr. Raven pointed to the ECG monitor.

"But I was so nervous," Natalie said dejectedly. "I didn't handle the stress very well when things went sideways."

"No one does the first time, Ms Campbell. That's why we practice our practise," replied Dr. Raven. The instructor turned to the students in the gallery. "All right, everyone. That'll do for today. Complete breakdown of each group's first surgery on Monday morning."

The students rose up and exited the theatre. Marianna, Holly, and Mark began undoing their surgical garb as they walked to the door. Natalie stood over the surgical dummy who was staring straight up at her from the table.

"I'm sorry," she said quietly. "I'll do better next time, I promise."

The four friends met in an empty first-floor seminar room at the St Andrews School of Medicine. Mark was the last to arrive, with a tray of paper cups of tea from the café across the hall.

"Four céilís with milk," he said, placing the tray on the table in front of the women. And then, passing a cup to Natalie, he added, "And one with sugar, because she's not feeling sweet enough."

"I'm not sour, Mark, I'm just disappointed," Natalie said, elbows on the table and head resting in her hands. "I felt like I had no clue about what was going on in that simulation surgery. I let the pressure get to me."

"You're being too hard on yourself, Nat," said Holly, looking up from her laptop screen. "Dr. Raven thought you did fine. He said there was only *one* thing he didn't like."

"And now he's left me to stew about it," Natalie grumbled.

"Stew? What is mean, this stew?" asked Marianna. "He make-a you hungry?"

Marianna Lombardi was an international student from Milan, Italy. Like her three friends, she was a second-year student at the Scottish medical school. Her two girlfriends at the table were Canadian: Holly Arnott from a big city in Ontario; Natalie Campbell from a rural hamlet in Alberta. Mark Munroe was a Scotsman, from the quaint seaside village of Rockcliffe, though his heritage was more heard than seen; the lilt in his voice said Scottish, but his wardrobe screamed Hawaiian. Mark wore brightly-coloured aloha shirts. Every day. Without fail.

"No, not hungry, just in a lather," Natalie replied.

"Ah, he make the *lather*!" exclaimed Marianna. "In Italian we say, *schiuma*! It's-a like *scum*."

"Ooh, I wouldn't associate Dr. Raven with that," smiled Mark. "He's difficult at times, but he's not a lowlife."

"My granddad called it 'being in a tiz-woz'," added Holly.

"Tiz-a-woz-a?" asked Marianna.

"Now you're both speaking another language," said Mark.

"In a tizzy," Holly clarified. "Agitated."

"Ah! *Agitazione*!" declared Marianna. She looked at her friend. "Natalie, you are *agitazione* over the surgery?"

"That's it, Marianna. It's got me all *agitazione*." Natalie took a sip of her tea. "Why did he put our patient into cardiac arrest? What did I do wrong?"

"What did *we* do wrong, Nat," corrected Holly. "We were a team in there today. Just like the Maple Leafs."

"And we lost the game," Natalie sighed.

"Just like the Maple Leafs," Holly repeated. Mark looked over at Holly's laptop screen.

"You're doing your ice hockey pool stuff, again, I see."

"Not *ice* hockey, Mark. Just hockey. I'm a Canadian. Don't say ice hockey to me unless you're looking to get cross-checked into the boards."

"I have no idea what that means, but it sounds positively painful." Mark looked over at Natalie. "A blood clot could have caused an arrest."

"I thought about that," Natalie replied, "but we administered heparin when I started to electrocauterize."

"2500 units," Marianna added. "But why you not-a say 5000 units?"

"We were told in the handout that the patient was on an anti-coagulation protocol." Natalie produced the pre-operation information paper given to the group by Dr. Raven and placed it on the table. "See, the dummy was on aspirin prior to surgery."

Mark studied the sheet carefully for 34 seconds. A smirk came over his face, and he slapped the sheet back down on the table.

"I think he got us, right here," said Mark, pointing at the sheet. He read, "'The patient said *yes* when asked if he was taking aspirin.'"

"Riiight," said Natalie. "So?"

"So, the *patient* provided an answer to a potentially nebulous question. The dummy could have been saying, 'Sure, I take aspirin…sometimes.' He may not have been on a pre-operative protocol at all. And if he wasn't, we needed to administer 5000 units to prevent a clot from forming during the operation."

"He sandbagged us!" cried Holly.

"We play in the beach?" asked a confused Marianna.

"He tricked us, Marianna," said Natalie. "Dr. Raven was testing us to see if we were paying attention to the details."

"That's for certain," said Mark. "And I'll bet if we had given 5000 units of heparin, he would have put the dummy in distress because we administered too much."

"A no-win situation," Holly smirked, crossing her arms. "Like a nuclear-arms standoff. Or that Star Trek simulation thing…"

"You mean-a the *Kobayshi Maru*!" Marianna interjected. Her three friends looked at her with surprise.

"What? We watch-a the Star Trek in Italia, too, you know!"

Chapter 2

Natalie and Marianna hooked up with the St Andrews Circuit via Station Road, turned right, and headed south on City Road. They walked past Molly Malones and were tempted to stop at Chariots of Hire for a rickshaw ride, but Marianna thought that the 4K loop should be walked today. 'Too much of a-standing around and not enough of-a the-moving in the OR', she had said.

It was an overcast Friday afternoon in St Andrews – when wasn't it? – when the young women set off. It would stay that way for the entire hour-long hike. They were dressed for the cool, late-autumn weather: Marianna in her lined, water-proof rain jacket and wide-brim rain hat; Natalie in her soft-shell jacket and water-resistant toque.

"Thanks for suggesting the walk, Marianna," said Natalie, as the two turned left onto South Street. "I needed to clear my head in the fresh air."

"*Prego.* What are the roommates for, ah?" Marianna responded, giving Natalie an elbow nudge. "I can't-a believe how much-a real the surgical dummy is. It have-a the beating heart, it leak-a the blood, it even-a make the funny noise when you put pressure on the chest."

"That funny noise was coming from me," Natalie groaned. "I didn't handle the pressure of the OR environment very well."

"You must not-a be so hard on your body, *mia amica*. Like Holly say, we are a-teammates, no? And it was our first-a time!"

"We're teammates, yes. And I suppose for a first time, it wasn't so bad." Natalie offered a weak smile. "Mark sure was composed, though."

"Compose, like-a the music?"

"Composed, as in he had it all together."

"All together like he make a collection?"

"He was very calm and not worried."

"Ah, *sì*. He was very composted!" Marianna agreed. "Maybe he will become a surgeon for the specializing."

"I think he does want to specialize in surgery later on," said Natalie. "He has the right demeanour for it."

"I don't-a think Mark is a mean man."

"No, no…he's not mean. He has the right…um, *attitude* for being a good surgeon."

"*Sì*. I understand-a this," Marianna replied. "You are so good for helping me make-a my English nice."

"And you're helping me learn more Italian, everyday! Did I tell you that my mom speaks Italian fluently?"

"I thought-a she was French?"

"French Canadian, yes. But she learned Italian in school. I think. One of her jobs is to translate apps."

"She must-a be very smart to do this job, eh? And she is so nice when we do the video chat together."

"She's nice and smart, yes," Natalie mused. "And she's my best friend, too."

"Aw, that's-a nice," Marianna gushed, as the women approached South Castle Street. She grabbed Natalie's arm. "Come on. I buy you a *gelato* at Jannettas' and we take to the castle, ok?"

"If you insist!" Natalie exclaimed with a smile.

After the two had purchased their ice cream treats – two double-scooped, chocolate-dipped cones of *Stracciatella*, the flavour-of-the-month – they walked straight up to North Castle Street and crossed The Scores. They showed their membership cards at the gate, entered the castle grounds, and found their favourite bench along the tallest wall of the ruins, with their backs to St Andrews Bay.

"Thanks, Marianna, I needed a treat," Natalie said, biting into her ice cream. Not licking it, because the *gelato* wasn't exactly melting in the cool sea air.

"It was a stressful day, today," her friend replied. "We need-a something special."

The women sat silently, eating their ice cream and enjoying the tranquil surroundings of the courtyard. Natalie was first to disturb their reverie.

"Do you have strategies for handling stress, Marianna?"

"Eating the *gelato*!" she answered with a laugh, crunching into the cone. "No, really, though, my father taught-a me when you feel, ah…like-a this…" Marianna clenched her fist twice.

"Tense?" Natalie offered.

"*Sì*! When you are a-tense, you stop-a what you do, you take-a the deep breath, you close-a your eyes, and you see your heart…"

"See your heart?"

"*Sì*, see. You make a picture in your mind of your heart beating, and you imagine it to slow down."

"And does that work?"

"It work-a for me. I think it just-o make-a you concentrate on something else. Itta calm-a your brain."

"Visualization," said Natalie, with a mouth full of *Stracciatella*.

"It-a work on-a the autonomic nervous system. I think there is research to show that-a the parasympathetic system can be controlled just a-illa bit."

"But only *un poco*," replied Natalie, with her thumb and index finger showing only a small space.

"*Sì, sì…un poco*," Marianna nodded in agreement.

"Here, take my vitals," Natalie ordered her friend, as she held out her left wrist. "I'm going to visualize my heart and slow it down." Marianna quickly found Natalie's pulse. Natalie closed her eyes and took a deep breath as Marianna set her cellphone timer. The women sat quietly for 46 seconds.

"Ooh, it's-a going down," said Marianna. "One-a beat less every 10 seconds." Then, after another 11 seconds, "One less, again…Oh, is that-a Mark over there?"

"Where?" said Natalie with a startled jump on the bench.

"Oh, oh! A rapid-a pulse increase, doctor!" Marianna chortled. "Shall I administer-a the beta blocker?"

"What are you talking about?" barked Natalie, yanking her arm away. "Rapid pulse increase my eye!"

"Now, now, calm-a down," Marianna smiled. "Your eye look-a fine. Though the lady doth-a protest-a too much, methinks, eh?"

"He's nice. We're friends. That's all."

"If-a you say so."

"I say so!"

The women sat quietly for two minutes looking straight ahead, finishing their gelati.

"He has-a nice eyes," said Marianna, breaking the silence. Natalie smiled and smacked her friend on the leg.

The women left the castle grounds and continued their walk along The Score, past Martyrs' Monument, turning left at The Royal and Ancient Golf Club of St Andrews.

"Nice Shakespeare reference back there," said Natalie, as they crossed over to Links Crescent. "Who said that?"

"Lady Gertrude, in-a *Hamlet*. She was making a comment about-a the play in-a the play."

"Speaking of plays, you've seen all of Shakespeare's, haven't you?"

"You know-a my love for all theatre and opera, *mia amica*. And I am-a so excited for-a the play tomorrow night!"

"Me, too!" Natalie enthused. "It'll be a nice trip into Edinburgh. We could all use an evening out."

In four minutes past the roundabout, the women arrived at their student residence, Agnes Blackadder Hall. Natalie opened the front door and waved Marianna in first.

"After you. After all, you're cooking tonight."

"It's-a my turn again?" Marianna complained. "I hope-a you like beans on toast."

"That's not very Italian of you, Ms Lombardi."

"You don't-a like my cooking?" Marianna smiled. "Then-a visualize!"

Natalie propped up the pillows on her bedframe and placed her laptop on a pillow on her lap. It took three rings before her call was answered.

"*Ah, bonsoir, ma fille! Comment ça va?*" her mother chimed as she repositioned her cellphone on the kitchen countertop. Michelle Campbell was up to her elbows in flour.

"*Qu'est-ce qu'on mange ce soir, maman*?" Natalie asked, continuing the conversation in French.

"Your brother asked for a good starchy meal tonight, because he was going on a long run after school with Angus and Graeme. So I thought I would make a sugo and we'd have gnocchi with it."

"Oh, no way! We had gnocchi for dinner, too!" exclaimed Natalie, her dinnertime being seven hours earlier. "Marianna said we were going to have beans on toast, but she changed her mind. You won't believe this: she made the gnocchi with dehydrated potato flakes!"

"*Mamma mia*! She could lose her citizenship if the Italian government found out!"

"I know, right? But they were pillowy soft, just like yours! And they only took ten minutes to make!"

"It's a very tempting idea," Michelle said as she kneaded the dough on the cutting board, a puff of flour on her nose. "But I do like my old recipe."

"On our walk this afternoon, we were talking about how you speak Italian. I told Marianna that you learned it in school, but I wasn't sure. Did you take an Italian course?"

"*Non*, we didn't have that class in our school," said Michelle, rolling the dough into long strands. "I had some Italian friends growing up, and I learned it from them."

"But you're so fluent, Mom."

"They were good teachers, Natalie. Plus, it's easier learning another Romance language."

"True enough. I find that my brain accesses the French side when I'm figuring out an Italian translation. It's been fun having a roommate from another country this past year and a half, and…"

A loud banging noise came through Natalie's computer speaker, interrupting the conversation. Michelle turned her head toward the hallway.

"Hello, you clumsy cat burglars! Welcome home!" she said in English.

Natalie could see her dad, John Campbell, and her brother, Connor, stroll and bound into the kitchen, respectively. John gave his wife a kiss on the cheek. Connor grabbed two mandarin oranges from the table and the phone off the countertop. Natalie watched him prop her up on the dining table.

"Hey sis, you're up late again!" Connor said, peeling the orange. "You need to congratulate me."

"What did you do this time?"

"I just drove me and Dad home through my first snowstorm! It started right after our run!"

"Whoa! How'd you do?"

"Well, we're home," John Campbell said, entering the picture. He held his fists up to the camera for inspection. "How do my knuckles look, doctor?"

"Pretty white, Dad," Natalie answered. "Your hand muscles look to be in tetanus from gripping the dashboard all the way home."

"I was in the back seat, clutching my briefcase in front of my face."

"Hey, I only went into three uncontrolled skids!" the teenage driver said defensively. "Maybe we need snow tires."

"The car *has* snow tires on," said Dad.

"Then maybe we need new ones," said his son.

"I bought them two months ago."

Connor paused. Natalie watched him lean toward the camera. He whispered, "Maybe we need a new car…that's just for me!"

John Campbell moved his son's head away and looked at his daughter. "After today, I'm going to buy your brother a tank, Nat."

"Safety first!" said Natalie. "But you're getting a reward for your courage today, Dad. Mom's making you gnocchi!"

"Sweet!" Connor exclaimed. "I'm going to clean up before dinner. Later, sis…gotta go!" Connor's head grew larger in the laptop frame until his lips filled the entire window. "Mwah!"

"Mwah to you, little brother," Natalie replied in kind. "Don't go too far! Remember what happened last time!"

"I'm home for good, Nat!" Connor said, no longer in the picture. "My TT days are in the past!" Natalie could just hear him as he bounded up the stairs. "Ha! In the past, get it? In the *past*!"

Natalie smiled. Then she saw a jumbled view of the kitchen ceiling. Her mother came back into focus as the cellphone was placed again on the countertop. John Campbell was putting a big pot of water on the stove as Michelle cut the strands of dough into small pieces.

"How's Connor doing this week?" Natalie asked.

"Much better," said Mom. "He was really missing France this past month. He did make some close friends, there."

"I'd say he's pretty much back to his old self," added Dad. "Well, not his *old* self. More like his old, more-current self, I guess. He's busy at school and that helps a lot."

"Did you miss you transtemporal trekking friends when you came back home for good, Mom?" asked Natalie.

"Of course! They will always be special to me!"

"Ah, yes! Those special people from…from…?"

"Natalie," Mom said, shaking her head while cutting the gnocchi, "I told you that you and your brother will learn everything about my TT at Christmastime, next month. All will be revealed soon enough!"

"But I want my present now!" Natalie whined, a fake-pout forming on her lips.

"Patience, my dear," said Dad, wagging his finger at the screen. "Your mom and I have our reasons for our closed-lippiness." And then, changing the subject, he said, "We're getting all amped up for our trip tomorrow!"

"I still don't get it, Dad. Why are the two of you going on a canoe trip at this time of year?"

"Because we've never done it!" Mom exclaimed. "It's going to be an adventure!"

"A cold one, that's for sure," said Natalie, eyes rolling.

"We're bringing our woollies," Mom said as she dropped the gnocchi into the boiling water.

"And you're going to such a remote area. Aren't you nervous about being incommunicado for a whole week?" Natalie inquired, projecting her own anxiety with the question.

"No stress, here," said Dad. "We're completely prepared. If we get into any trouble, we've got the sat phone. And speaking of stress, how did your mock surgery go today?"

"About as well as could be expected," said Natalie, not telling the whole story in a truthful kind of way. "Practice is going to be the key going forward."

"One way to handle high-pressure situations is to commit the outcome to someone other than yourself...wherever, and even whenever, you are," said Michelle. Then, to her husband, "Could you call your son down for dinner, please." John went to the bottom of the stairs and barked out orders for his son to get a move on.

"And when you can't practice, visualize!" Natalie added. "That's Marianna's dad's advice."

"Very wise," nodded Mom. "Do you want to stay for dinner?"

"No, I'll just fall asleep watching you eat and start snoring, or something," said Natalie. "I'll let the three of you have dinner in peace."

"See you later, my girl," Dad said with a wave, taking the cutlery to the table.

"Bye, Dad. See you in a week."

"Eight days, Natalie," Mom corrected. "Please remember to check-in on your brother every so often while we're in radio blackout, okay?"

"No problem, Mom."

"And, Natalie?..."

"Yes?"

"*Je t'aime. Et soyez prudent, d'accord?*"

"Sure, Mom. But you're the ones who need to be careful!"

"*Bon nuit, ma chérie.* I'll see you soon."

"*Bon nuit, maman.*"

Natalie waved and closed the laptop lid on her mother's unusually wistful face.

As Natalie got ready for bed, she thought about her family back home in Canada. She thought about her brother, Connor: how he had undergone the most incredible adventure you could ever imagine – time travelling back to the 1700s to meet Marie-Anne and Antoine

Lavoisier – and how he had become a better person for the experience. She thought about her Dad: the stoic patriarch – kind, loving, and wise - who gave the best advice with the fewest words. And she thought about her Mom: her bright, sunny, full-of-life best friend. Michelle Campbell had been a time traveller, too, though her children were sketchy on the details. Natalie thought about her mom saying that all would be revealed soon. That made Natalie want soon to come even sooner.

As she began to drift off, Natalie thought about how nice it was that she had never felt dislocated from her family. She was half-a-world away at her med school in Scotland, but modern technology kept her close to them. Sure, she was on the outside of the time-travelling experience, but her family always kept her in the loop. She was too far away to contribute to their home-life every day, but she became an important part of Connor's TT undertaking – having been in France at just the right time to perform just the right operation when her brother needed her the most. She gave a little prayer of thanks for all of this.

And she even gave thanks for the stressful difficulties in her day, knowing that a little tribulation would have its perfect outcome in learning some much-needed patience.

Chapter 3

Saturday night at Edinburgh's Pig and Thistle Pub - down the road from The Royal Lyceum Theatre - was alive with music and conversation. Tears for Feargal, the live band, kept the small dance floor busy playing a mix of traditional Celtic music and 80's new wave - it was all there in the name, of course. The bar area was packed with standing patrons, and extra chairs had been brought out for the tables that were arranged around the perimeter of the premises. The high, timber-framed ceiling and plastered walls gave the pub a cozy feeling. The band's double-time, synth-powered version of The Bonnie Banks o' Loch Lomond ensured that cozy never became sleepy.

At a table opposite the stage along the back of the dance floor, Mark, Holly, Marianna, and Natalie were recounting their evening at The Lyceum.

"I thought *Wicked* was just wicked!" Holly exclaimed, straining to be heard over the band. "I loved the costumes, I loved the sets, and I thought the story was really clever!"

"A far happier ending for the Wicked Witch!" Mark said loudly, after taking a sip of his Guinness. "I didn't see the trap door coming!"

"It would not-a be a trap-a door if you could see it, eh?" Marianna said with an overly-raised voice, combatting the noise level but mostly giving in to her slight inebriation. "The music was-a so wonderful, it make-a me happy! Did you like, Natalie?"

"Honestly, I thought the music was nothing special!" Natalie shouted. But her booming reply came out just as the band finished their song. A good number of the pub customers turned a curious look at the brunette with the funny accent.

"Well, it might be a good time to take a break, then," the guitarist said into the mic, with a smile. Natalie brought her hand up to cover her face. Her friends burst out laughing.

"Nice one, Nat," said Holly, giving her friend's shoulder a squeeze. "Another glass of wine?"

"It appears that one is enough for me!" said Natalie, embarrassed.

"What? So, you did no like-a the musical?" Marianna asked her with a slightly offended tone.

"It was okay, but it wasn't exactly *The Wizard of Oz*, you know? Nothing too memorable for me."

"Maybe you have to see *Wicked* ten more times, like we all did with *The Wizard of Oz*," said Mark.

"Yeah, maybe," Natalie replied. "But to be really memorable, a work of art has got to speak to you. It's got to, I don't know, inform your life. Speak to the human condition."

"Well, I think that *Wicked* is about friendship," said Holly, twirling the stem of her wine glass. "And about personal identity, too."

"*Sì, sì* ...the identity!" Marianna agreed, slapping the table. "Iz about who we are and how we stand up-a for what we believe!"

"Hmm. I can see that, I suppose," Natalie pondered. "But I think that's a bit of a stretch."

"You need-a to stand up? I stretch with you!" Marianna rose from her chair and raised her arms up. "I sit-a too long!"

"And you *drink-a* too much," Holly smirked.

"Eh! Just-o two *compari* and-a ssoda so far!" Marianna replied, slurring her soda and sitting back down.

"No one's driving tonight but the Shuttle service," said Mark, referring to their ride back to St Andrews via passenger van. "So Marianna can have another *compari* after we order something to eat."

"*Sì! Dobbiamo mangiare!*" said Marianna a bit too loudly, pointing at the ceiling.

"I'll get us some menus," said Mark, standing up and moving toward the bar.

"So, iz-a Filip coming tonight, or-a what?" Marianna asked her friends.

"I think he'll be here pretty soon," said Natalie, lifting up her phone and looking at the time.

"*Va bene*! He make-a the party become alive!"

"He is the life of the party, isn't he?" Holly agreed. "I wonder what he's majoring in this week?"

Filip was an integral part of any outing for this friendship group. He spiced up the conversation, laughed at everyone's jokes, and found ways to agree with you and challenge your notions at the same time. And that was the thing about Filip – he had a hard time deciding about anything, so he ended up doing just about everything. Filip was introduced to the gang the previous autumn when they were all in first year medical school together. But he quit three weeks before Christmas and found work as a turbine-technician assistant on a wind farm in the North Sea. Finding a lack of mental stimulation in the job, he left it to attend the University of Edinburgh for the winter term, majoring in Pharmacology. By summer, the switch was made to English and Scottish Literature. But before the fall semester started up, his designs were on Landscape Architecture as his degree program of choice. The girls all agreed that Filip was going to end up in school for the rest of his life. Mark thought Filip was the coolest guy in Great Britain.

"Well, speak of the angel, there he is now," said Natalie, looking towards the door. "Filip! Over here!"

"Ah! Hello, all!" Filip called out, lifting the case in his hand as a wave. Everyone turned to the young man at the door.

"Filip!" the *Cheers*-cheer rang out from the Pig and Thistle patrons. Filip made his way to the table and set his case down beside an empty seat.

"Whaddya say, mate?" said Mark to his friend, as he returned to the table with the menus and a glass in his hand.

"I'd say Stàinte Mhath if that pint was for me," Filip replied, accepting the glass of Guinness from Mark and taking a sip. "Love the coconut trees, bud!" he also said, pointing at Mark's shirt. "Every day should be Aloha Friday!" The two young men sat down.

"I say the Slan-ja-va to you, too!" toasted Marianna with a giggle. "We miss-a you at the show tonight."

"Sorry I missed it, too," said Filip. "How was it?"

"We all had a good time, except for Natalie," Holly answered for the group.

"Now stop it!" huffed Natalie. "I never said I didn't like it! I just thought it wasn't up to *Wizard of Oz* standards, that's all."

"I think you would-a like it if-a you only had a brain!" offered Marianna.

"Nice one, Ms Lombardi! Ha!" exclaimed Filip, giving Marianna two fist bumps, the tipsy Italian having missed the first one by a considerable distance.

"I don't think she's missing a brain, or even a heart," Filip winked at Natalie.

"No, but if you saw me in the OR yesterday, you'd have said, 'If she only had the *noyve!*'"

"Ah, ah...we're not in Kansas anymore, Dorothy! No reliving that scene!" chided Mark. He looked over to Filip. "She was actually very good in the mock surgery."

"Of course she was! That's our Natalie we're talking about!" said Filip, raising his glass to her then taking a sip. "And I agree with her that *The Wizard of Oz* sets a high-bar for excellence. It's so deep!"

"Deep?" Holly questioned. "After 'there's no place like home' it doesn't exactly play out like an ode by John Keats."

"Not John Keats...Carl Jung," said Filip. "*The Wizard of Oz* is a treatise on the yellow-brick road toward self-enlightenment."

"Come on," dismissed Mark.

"No, really. Think about it. Dorothy is the innocent dreamer, and her three companions represent the three stages of Jung's idea of Animus..."

"Who is-a this Animus?" interrupted Marianna. "Iz-a the Cowardly Leone?"

"It's not an animal," corrected Filip. "Animus is the male-personality aspect that resides in the human female. The fourth stage of Animus is the emergence of the 'spiritual messenger', who, of course, is represented by the Wizard."

"Oh, brother," said Mark, rolling his eyes.

"The Good Witch is the Jungian mother figure, Toto is the trickster, and the flying monkeys are..."

"Don't tell me...the embodiment of the inner dark-side of one's personality," Mark interjected.

"No," said Filip, matter of factly. "They're just a bunch of monkeys." Natalie's laughing spit-take caused Marianna to lose it, as well.

"I'm not sure about this whole Carl Jung, 'I've got a man inside of me' idea," said Holly. "I've never felt the urge to do typical guy-things, like embarrass myself in public. Or, you know, eat a chocolate bar with Dijon mustard on it because someone said, 'I dare you'."

"Hey, I was provoked into that action!" said Mark, defensively. "And it wasn't all that bad, just saying."

The guitarist for Tears for Feargal stopped at their table on the way to the stage. "Hey, Filip! I see you've got your case with you. Not your guitar this time, though?"

"No, you've got the six strings covered, Luke. I thought I'd only bring four this time." Filip lifted the case from the floor.

"Brilliant. Come up now and start off the set, will ya?"

"Love to."

"But be careful what you play," said Luke, pointing to Natalie. "This one here is a terribly harsh critic."

"Oh, no...I, " stammered Natalie.

"Ah, I'm only pulling your leg, my dear," smiled Luke, making his way to the stage.

"Pulling the leg is-a no good," said Marianna. "You can hurt-a the patellar tendon!"

"All right. Here goes nothing," Filip said as he unzipped the case, took out the instrument, and bounded to the bandstand. When he reached the stage, the patrons gave Filip a hearty cheer and a round of applause, like they always did every Saturday night.

"This one is for my friend, Natalie, who celebrated her twentieth birthday just last week," Filip said into the mic. Natalie smiled and blushed. "I hope no one thinks this mash-up is too irreverent!" He turned and gave some instructions to the band. They all nodded.

When Filip put the bow to the strings of his violin, it only took two bars for everyone in the pub to let out a sigh of recognition. The plaintive strains of The Braes of Balquhither filled the room and set everyone to swaying where they were sitting or standing. Slowly, the people began singing along softly to the well-known melody,

Let us go, lassie, go
To the braes o' Balquhither
Where the blae-berries grow
'Mang the bonny Highland heather

By the second go-round of the verses, the two Canadians and the Italian in the crowd had the lyrics down, and joined the locals in a pleasant daydream of the wild mountain thyme that perfumed the moorlands of Scotland.

Then, right after the final line of the chorus was sung,

Where glad innocence reigns
'Mang the braes o' Balquhither…

Filip stamped his foot, the band kicked in, and the tune morphed into a spritely reel that got everyone up and dancing. Mark grabbed up Natalie from her chair and the two made sweeping three-step circles about the dance floor for a good four minutes, only bumping into one other couple along the way – Marianna and Holly, trying to figure out who should lead.

When Filip came back to the table after the set, he gladly took the napkin that was offered by Holly and wiped his brow.

"Did you recognize the tune, Nat?"

"I did! It was Going Home, wasn't it?"

"Theme of the Local Hero, yes!" Filip exclaimed. "You had mentioned last month that you loved that movie, remember? You sent the DVD to your parents. I was curious, so I watched it, and I fell in love with the theme song."

"I've been to Camusdarach Beach, where they filmed that movie back in the 80s," added Mark. "It's a nice scuba area. Pretty scenic." True to his choice of apparel, it was no surprise that Mark was an avid diver.

"Is it far from here? Can we go sometime?" asked Holly. In three seconds, Marianna had the map up on her phone.

"It's-a three hours by car, four if we take-a Filip's hippy van."

"I'm in," said Filip. "There's a cairn or two around Fort William that I've been wanting to see for a while."

"How about we go a week this Monday on our mini-break?" Natalie suggested. "Will that work for you, Filip?"

"I've got the same school break, so it works for me fine," Filip replied. "What say ye, fellow pilgrims?" Everyone at the table clinked their glasses in approval.

"Then it's settled!" said Mark, picking up a menu. His friends followed suit. "Now, let's order something. I'm feeling peckish."

"Me, too, Mark!" Marianna said, parsing the first page. "Now where is-a this chicken?"

Her tablemates all smiled into their menus.

Natalie always enjoyed the walk from her residence to the Byre Theatre. Most days, she could do it in fourteen minutes at a fast clip, book bag included. But on this pleasant, somewhat sunny Sunday afternoon, she slowed her pace and enjoyed the easterly stroll down North Street.

There were lots of other places on campus where one could study, but there was something about the Byre that appealed to Natalie. Maybe it was the welcoming façade of the building, with its tall, A-framed barn roof and picture window rising above its surroundings. Maybe it was the architectural juts and jags of the interior that constantly revealed another special social space around the corner. Maybe it was the charm in the incorporation of the theatre's humble beginnings as a cattle shed in the 1930s, where a look out the window would reveal a quaint, stone-built garden wall and vennel. Maybe it was the relaxed atmosphere of the Byre Living Room, which had its own manifesto that welcomed those who were mindful of noise-levels, those who were conscious of cleanliness, and even those who had well-behaved pooches. In the end, it was all of those things that Natalie loved about the Byre. But today, what appealed to Natalie the most was the small conference room, hiding just down from the 220-seat auditorium.

Natalie entered the theatre from the main doors, stopped at the BrewCo at the Byre for a cup of tea, and brought it to her quiet space on the second floor. The room was furnished with a good-sized table and six chairs, a white board, and, curiously, a 1.5-metre-tall shelf with dusty old books on display. As Natalie walked past the shelf to take a seat on the long side of the table, she tucked in a little leather book that was sticking out past its neatly arranged companions. She placed her book bag on one of the chairs and began removing her study materials. In no time, the table was covered with texts and binders and highlight markers. Natalie sat down, took a sip of tea, and started her afternoon review session.

Immunology was first up. They would be starting a new sub-unit on parasitology tomorrow, so Natalie did some advanced reading on the topic. The pictures in the text reminded her of when she studied invertebrate zoology in Mr. Mason-Ivy's high school biology class. She reminisced about how much he loved teaching his students about spineless creatures, with lots of inspecting and dissecting going on in the lab room. Natalie smiled as she remembered the day that unit ended, and Mr. Mason-Ivy made them all lunch: he fried up calamari, baked escargot, steamed clams and oysters, and dared his students to join him in eating some pickled 'cephalopod'. Natalie enjoyed the calamari, tried the escargot, slurped an oyster, but avoided the pickled 'head-foot' creature. She cringed all over again at even the thought of octopus tentacles on her tongue.

After looking at some medical diagrams for Tuesday's Anatomy class and re-writing some notes for her Blood and Gastrointestinal class, Natalie checked the time on her phone. Four o'clock! Time flies when you're having fundus! She giggled at that one, thinking her brother would like that awful science pun. As she was about to put her phone in the front pocket of her bag, the picture on the homescreen caught her attention. She looked at it for a long moment: Natalie and Mom with big smiles, wearing their sunhats, on their hike in the mountains last summer. Michelle wearing her favourite top that exposed the scar on her right arm, Natalie wearing a silly grin that exposed her goofy side. Natalie looked back and forth between her and her mother in the picture. She thought: Nope, I can't see the resemblance. I look way more like my dad than my mom. Connor looks more like Mom, that's for sure; he has her blue eyes. If it wasn't for me and Mom both having a pinched right earlobe, you'd look at this picture and think we were two people that just met on the trails.

Natalie packed up the rest of her belongings and started back to Agnes Blackadder Hall. She felt good about her study session, feeling better prepared to take on the coming week's deluge of information. The accelerated medical program at St Andrews was just that, accelerated. It was like the course material was being sprayed at you from a disgruntled fire hose, wanting you to share in the pressure it was under. Natalie wondered if the constant flood of facts and details wasn't just for the next exam, but also a test of one's ability to handle the stress of becoming a physician. If that was so, then she was going to need some assistance to keep her head above water. Her feeling of failure over the mock surgery only highlighted the greater issue of not making it as a doctor at all. As the rain started to fall just before she arrived at her residence building, Natalie decided a visit to her faculty advisor was in order, first thing in the morning.

Dr. Blanco had always been a reservoir of calm in the roiling sea that was med school.

Chapter 4

Natalie set her watch for the walk from her residence to the School of Medicine Building. She took the long way around, past the School of Management, to get in an extra few hundred steps of exercise. She cut a diagonal across the grassy roundabout and entered the northwest door of her med school. Natalie took the stairs to Dr. Blanco's third-floor office, doing one at a time in quick succession, thereby maximizing her work effort and step count. She checked her watch at the top landing: 702 steps in 5 minutes 3 seconds, 46 calories burned. Not as good as last week, but she took it all in stride.

Natalie knocked on the door at the end of the hallway. There was no response, but she could hear music on the other side – that David Bowie and Queen song, she was sure – so Natalie knocked again, loudly. The door sprang open 6 seconds later. Dr. Blanco, wearing a black and yellow checkered jacket with green and grey striped tie, was wide-eyed with surprise.

"You're early, Ms Campbell. You caught me in the middle of my breakfast!" Dr. Blanco said with a mouthful of scone. "Care to join me?" He offered Natalie one of the pastries off the plate he was holding.

"No thank you sir. I just ate."

"You don't know what you're missing. My wife makes a mean scone! Soft inside, yet with a crumbly exterior." He set the plate down on his paper-strewn desk and brushed back a dishevelled lock of hair from his forehead. "Perhaps not unlike your advisor, what?"

"I don't see you as soft at all, sir. Crumbly, yes…but not soft."

"Fair enough!" said Dr. Blanco, clicking off the music in the middle of the last line, right after the word *under*.

"A cassette player?" Natalie remarked. "Was that here last week?"

"No, I just bought it! Isn't it a beauty?" Dr. Blanco smiled and gave the component a gentle dust-swipe of appreciation.

"I'm not an authority, but it does look nice in a retro sort of way."

"I saw it a shop window down the high street the other day, and I just had to have it. I was pretty young when these were all the rage in the audiophile world, but I always wanted one."

"And now you're living the dream," said Natalie with a smile.

"I am!" he exclaimed. "But the problem now is finding the blasted tapes! I've played this one so much the past five days that the band should be giving me royalties. I don't suppose you have a few cassettes kicking around the dormitory that you could lend me, what?"

"I'm afraid not, sir. But my dad has a pretty big collection back home."

"An analogue man, I presume."

"The analogiest. He's got a big record collection and my brother's into it now, too."

"The Campbells are my people!" Dr. Blanco took another bite of scone and washed it down with a big slurp of tea. "Now, what can I help you with, Natalie?" He pointed at the chair next to her as he sat down behind his desk. Natalie removed the paper pile and running shoes from the seat and sat down across from her faculty advisor.

"Well, on Friday during mock surgery…"

"Were you the lead surgeon?"

"Yes. During the surgery I had…"

"Were you performing a bypass?"

"Yes. I was finishing the harvest of the left…"

"And all of the sudden your patient went into cardiac arrest, you performed the necessary steps, and it was still lights out?"

"Literally. The lights went out in the theatre."

"Ah, Dr. Raven and his flair for the dramatic! I love it!" Dr. Blanco exclaimed, banging his hands on the armrests of the chair. "He didn't follow up by pulling a Major Burns, did he?"

"Um…ah, I don't think so," said Natalie blinking, with an accompanying headshake. "Who's Major Burns?"

"You don't know? In the movie *M*A*S*H*, Private Boone comes back with the wrong needle for a patient, who then dies. Major Burns says, 'You killed him'."

"That's terrible!"

"It is! But Trapper saw the whole thing and punched Major Burns, so at least he got what was coming to him. You didn't punch Dr. Raven did you?"

"No!" Natalie exclaimed.

"He didn't accuse you of killing the patient, then?"

"No, of course not!"

"Well then, there's nothing to be worked up about, Natalie."

Natalie took a deep breath. "How did you know that I've been stressed out, Dr. Blanco?"

"Because it's about that time for most second-year med students, young lady," he said, with elbows resting on his desk, chin on his folded hands. "The work is piling up, the course material gets more challenging, you get less sleep, you get more anxious. It happens to us all, Natalie."

"*Us*, Dr. Blanco?"

"Oh, I was a basket-case in my first two years of med school! Walking around campus like an extra in that movie, *Invasion of the Body Snatchers*. Seen that one?"

"No, sir."

"Don't get out much, do you lass?" he teased. "The original from the 1950s was better, but the late 70s remake is really good, too."

"Sir, I was born in the 2000s. My movie references only go as far back as *Clueless*." Then Natalie sighed, "Which is how I've been feeling lately."

"We've all been there," said Dr. Blanco. He stood up and walked over to the tape machine. "Now, are you getting enough exercise?"

"I walk every day."

"Distance?"

"I'm always over ten-thousand steps."

"Good. Three squares a day?" He removed the cassette from the machine, placed another into the door of the player, clicked it closed, and pressed rewind.

"And a fruit snack in the afternoon," nodded Natalie.

"Tossing and turning, or sleeping relatively well?"

Natalie thought about that for a moment. There were some sleepless nights recently, worrying about her brother and his TT exploits in France, but that all worked out just fine. "Much better of late," she answered.

"Great. When encountering times of stress, taking care of yourself physically is of primary importance." Dr. Blanco sat back down and looked directly at Natalie. "Do you use any stimulants or antidepressants?"

"Apart from a coffee in the morning, no sir."

"Fine. What are some of your diversions?"

"Well, I haven't had time to pursue any hobbies, lately. I do like to travel, though. I'll be going on an excursion next week with my friends."

"Where to?"

"Camusdarach Beach, on the west coast."

"Where they filmed *Local Hero*! Love that movie!" He leaned back in his chair. "Have you seen it, Natalie?"

"I have. It's a favourite of my parents."

"When you go there, make sure to be on the lookout for injured rabbits," Dr. Blanco said with a smile. He rose up from his chair and looked out the window, his hands folded behind his back. "When I had a crisis of confidence back in my med school days, my faculty advisor knew exactly what I needed. And since you're presenting with the same symptoms I had back then, I'm going to prescribe the same antidote." He turned and faced his student. "Practice."

"Practice?" asked Natalie.

"Practice. You're a bit of a perfectionist, Natalie, with tendencies toward anal retentiveness."

"I am?" Natalie said, incredulously.

"How many steps to my office this morning?"

Natalie sighed. "Seven hundred and two."

"Time?"

"Five-o-three," she said demurely. "Not as fast as last week."

"Uh huh," replied Dr. Blanco. "I can relate to perfectionism, though you may not think so by looking at me or my office." He swept his hand over the room. "But perfectionists take on many guises."

"So how do I get the practice?" Natalie asked.

"You come to Victoria Hospital in Kirkcaldy for the next four Friday afternoons. That's when I'm on call in the surgery. You can assist me."

"I can do that! Thank you, Dr. Blanco. That would really help."

"Of a certainty. It helped me when I was your age."

"What was that crisis of confidence you had back in the day, if I may ask?" said Natalie.

"You may ask," replied her advisor. "I had a bad case of atychiphobia."

"What's that?"

"The fear of failure. It's a big problem for many doctors. Straight A's to get into med school, but now keep it up! Mistakes? Mistakes aren't allowed - this is someone's life we're talking about! Is the patient getting better? They have to get better! Have I done everything I could? What if my best isn't good enough?" Dr. Blanco sighed. "Stuff like that."

Natalie squirmed in her seat. She saw a lot of herself in that description.

"So, you're saying that the best way to conquer that fear is to not shy away from pressure situations?" she asked.

"So you can gain the necessary experience to handle those situations, yes," Dr. Blanco answered. "When you find it becoming easier, you're winning! And you will win, Natalie, trust me. You're very good at this."

Natalie smiled at her faculty advisor. She did trust him. He always said the things you needed to hear, at just the right time.

"Thank you, Dr. Blanco. That means a lot." The tape machine finished rewinding and shut off. Natalie rose from the chair. "Well, I'm off to class."

"What's first today?"

"Immunology."

"I hope you're *ready* for it!" said the advisor. "Get it? *Ready* for it?"

"Um...no, I don't," admitted Natalie.

"You will soon enough," he laughed, getting up from his seat and pressing play on the tape machine. The sound of an acoustic guitar leapt from the bookshelf speakers. "Do you like Traffic, Natalie?"

"I try to avoid rush hour, sir."

"Ha! Good one, Ms Campbell! Good one! Ah, wait for it…wait for it…" As the band kicked in, the faculty advisor hit the air-snare with his air-drumsticks.

"See you later, sir," said Natalie, closing the door behind her.

"Later, lassie!" said the faculty advisor, switching over to air-piano.

That was a good visit, Natalie thought as she made her way down the stairs. Yep, she was definitely Feelin' Alright.

"I can't look at that again, it freaks me out!"

Mark backed away from the dissecting scope, shaking his head in disgust. Natalie repositioned the specimen and took another look.

"I think the hooks on the scolex are a feat of engineering," marveled Natalie.

"I think the head of that thing looks like every sci-fi alien's pet monster," said Mark with a shiver. "Why are we doing this again?"

"Because every GP is going to eventually encounter intestinal parasites in their practise, Mr. Munroe," said Dr. Silver from behind her student.

"You weren't supposed to be there to hear that, Ma'am," Mark said sheepishly.

"You seem to be better with the tapeworms than your friend, Ms Campbell," the professor remarked. Natalie was stringing her gloved hand down the length of the cestode.

"I remember studying them in high school biology class, Dr. Silver. My teacher had jars of tapeworms and nematodes and flatworms all around the lab room. What are these bumpy sections called again?"

"Those are the proglottids," answered Dr. Silver, taking hold of the other end of the specimen. "Each one contains both sex organs for self-fertilizing."

"That seems rather, um...efficient," commented Mark.

"Oh, they're all about that," said the professor with admiration. "Utilize the scolex for firm attachment to the intestine; dispense with circulatory, respiratory, and digestive systems by absorbing all nutrients directly from the host's food sources; detach proglottids to release thousands of tapeworm embryos into the environment to be ingested by a series of hosts. Oh, yes, these are very efficient creatures, Mr. Munroe, with much to admire."

"From a distance, Ma'am," replied Mark.

"Oh, Dr. Silver?" said Natalie as the professor was moving to the next group. "Dr. Blanco asked if I was *ready* for this class today? I think he was trying to be funny, but I didn't get it."

"It does seem you are *Redi* for this class today, Ms Campbell, given your affinity for the invertebrates! As in, Francesco Redi!"

"Who's that?" asked Mark.

"He was one of those 17th century Italian geniuses, and a principal founder of pretty much everything biological!" exclaimed Dr. Silver with admiration. "He was a medical doctor, toxicologist, parasitologist, experimenter extraordinaire. He was even a philosopher and pretty decent poet. He wore a lot of hats!"

"But did Italians back then wear brightly-coloured Aloha shirts?" said Mark, panning his hands down the coral reef scene on his top.

"They probably invented them," replied the professor.

"Francesco Redi. I'm sure I learned about him in high school," said Natalie. "He did some really important experiment, didn't he?"

"He disproved spontaneous generation with an elegant investigation where all he used was a set of jars, some rotting meat and cheesecloth. Then...BAM!..." Dr. Silver clapped her hand together. "...the idea that living creatures can arise from dead things was crushed like a flatworm!"

"Ew," grimaced Mark. "Nice simile, Dr. Silver, but I prefer crushing, say, grapes to flatworms."

"Redi did as well, as he was quite the oenophile." Her students remained silent. "A proponent of potables? Master of mead?" She was playing with them now. "He really liked his wine?"

"Ah!" the med students replied together.

"You know how it's important that we use 'controls' in our science experiments?" asked Dr. Silver. The students nodded. "Well, Redi was probably the first to employ them in research."

"This guy did it all!" said Mark, impressed. "A real Renaissance man!"

"Almost literally," noted the prof. And with that, Dr. Silver moved to the next group.

"You want to have another look?" Natalie asked Mark as she placed the tapeworm back into the dissecting tray.

"No thanks. Just the thought of touching that thing makes me lightheaded."

"Your fears may be overcome with practice, you know?" she said, employing some Dr. Blanco wisdom.

"I'll let you know when I'm Redi," Mark said with a wink.

Natalie entered the seminar room across from the café with her book bag on her shoulders and cake pan in her hands. Holly and Marianna were busy on their computers while Mark was cleaning out the respirator on his scuba mask.

"Teatime, everyone!" she pronounced. "Anyone care for an afternoon treat?" She placed the pan down in the middle of the table and her bag on a chair.

"Me, me!" cried Holly, slapping down her laptop lid. "You've been busy I see!"

"I'll get the tea," Mark said, rising from the table.

"No need," said Natalie, unzipping the bag and producing a large thermos with paper cups. "I've got that covered, too!"

"You are-a my favourite Natalie in-a this room today!" Marianna announced. She looked at the cake. "That is a-gorgeous. What is-a that design you make? I never-a seen anything like-a this before!"

"That's a *fleur-de-lys*," Natalie replied. "It's on the flag of Quebec. I was in the mood to celebrate my French heritage."

"I like the powdered-sugar effect," said Holly. "You made a stencil, I take it?"

"Yep. I cut out a paper *fleur*, put it on top, went crazy with the icing sugar, lifted the paper, *et voilà*!" Natalie placed napkins on the table and produced a scalpel from her bag. "Who wants to make the first cut, doctors?"

"Allow me," said Mark. He turned the pan toward him, lengthwise. "A transverse incision across the patient's *fleur*, yes?" His three colleagues nodded their agreement. Holly passed out the tea, Marianna handed out napkins of vanilla cake, and the friends partook of their midday snack.

"Were you studying?" Natalie asked Holly from across the table. "You looked like you were engrossed in something important."

"I *was* studying...hockey stats! Did you know that Bobby Nystrom is tied for sixth for most playoff overtime goals, with four? Pretty amazing."

"Incredible!" Mark shouted with exaggerated emphasis. "I mean, come on! How did he do it?"

"Do-a what?" asked Marianne.

"I haven't the faintest," Mark replied with a chortle.

"Laugh it up, Sweaty, but it's a notable accomplishment," said Holly.

"How so?" asked Natalie.

"Bobby Nystrom played in the NHL for 14 seasons. He averaged less than twenty goals a year. He was far from being a star, more of a grinder..."

"He grind-a his teeth? That's-a no good."

"...but when it came to the playoffs, he was one of the Islanders best players."

"So, he thrived in pressure situations, is that it?" asked Mark.

"Exactly. Some people just have a knack for rising to the occasion."

"Oh, like-a Osmano in-a the opera *L'Ormindo*!" added Marianna, excitedly.

"That's exactly what I was going to say!" Mark interjected with a smirk.

"*Silenzio*, Sweaty! Any-a-way, Osmano, the captain of the army, is-a told by the king to poison the lovers in-a the story. But Osmano, he think-a fast and switch-a the poison for sleeping potion." Marianna took a bite of cake and a sip of tea.

"And...?" asked Holly.

"And everyone kiss and sing and go home happy," Marianna shrugged. "It's a very old Italian opera, what-a can I say?"

"Well, after my chat with Dr. Blanco earlier today, I'm resolved to responding better to stressful situations with added practice," Natalie chimed in. "I'm going to be the next Bobby Osmano!"

"Good-a for you!" Marianna exclaimed. Then, after some cake-eating silence, "Holly, why-a we call Mark, *Sweaty*?"

"It's an old cockney nickname, Marianna. Sweaty, as in sweaty sock, which rhymes with Jock. And a Jock is a Scotsman."

"I-a see," said Marianna, not a-seeing at all.

"It's not exactly a nice thing to say," said Natalie to Marianna. "Mark is really more of a cloaca!"

"Hey, I remember embryology class, Ms Campbell," Mark said, insulted. "That's not very nice at all."

"Relax. The cloaca is just an opening, which is another way of saying drain, which rhymes with pain."

"Ah! So, Mark is a pain!" said Marianna.

"Exactly," said Holly.

"Okay, that's better," said Mark, returning his attention to the scuba mask. Then, five seconds later...

"Um...HEY!..."

Chapter 5

Natalie plonked herself down on the sofa and sent a text to her brother. Connor replied in 18 seconds with a video alert, and the siblings were chatting in no time afterwards.

"I'm going to my locker to get my lunch," were Connor's first words as his face popped up on the screen. "You eat dinner yet?"

"Just finished. We had leftover ditalini. But Marianna threw in some sausage and put the whole concoction on top of some shredded cheese in the fry pan and called it a *frico*."

"Okay, that sounds way better than what I'm about to have." Connor opened his locker, his eyes looking up from the screen and right arm reaching upward. "See?" The picture on Natalie's phone showed the inside of a cloth bag that contained a bunch of snack bars and an apple."

"At least you packed some fruit, brother dear. In a hurry this morning?" Connor's face returned to the screen, and he closed his locker.

"Kinda. Mom and Dad started off on their trip pretty early. My timing got all thrown off because I didn't have to drive Dad to work."

"I'm afraid our boy was a tad too leisurely this morning," came a voice from over Connor's shoulder. "He missed our Great Hall confabulation on Worst Movies Ever!"

"Hi, Will," said Natalie. Connor moved the phone to his left and Will appeared on the screen with a wave. "What was your pick?"

"Hi, Natalie. Well, at first, I said *Plan 9 From Outer Space*, but Angus kiboshed that selection." The boys heads were bobbing up and down in the picture. Probably heading to the cafeteria, Natalie thought. Will continued, "He said the rules were you couldn't pick a movie that was so bad it was actually good…"

"Like *The Room*," Connor interjected.

"Or *Attack of the Killer Tomatoes!*" Natalie added.

"Right," said Will. "It has to be the kind of bad where you'd never watch it again, because it was such a dispiriting spectacle. Angus gave *Star Wars Episode 1: The Phantom Menace* as an example."

"Yeah, but as disappointing as that was, you're going to watch it again, because it's *Star Wars*," said Natalie.

"Well, that's what I said, Natalie," responded Will. "I told him that one day you're going to watch the whole saga from start to finish, and you'll have no choice. Mobo took Angus's side and said that the right to choose was an essential freedom for all mankind. But Derek countered that statement with his take on determinism that he learned in Phys Ed class.

"He learned about determinism in PE class?" Natalie interrupted.

"He couldn't play dodgeball because of a sprained ankle, so he was reading *Legends of Tomorrow* in the bleachers."

"Is that some existentialist literature?" she asked.

"No, it's a comic book," Will replied. "Once you get past the time-travelling Time Master tedium, it's a pretty deep read."

Connor and Natalie coughed in unison.

"Regardless, that's a pretty big step-up for Derek," said Connor.

"I'll say," Natalie agreed. "Learning about determinism in Grade 11!"

"No, I meant reading *Legends of Tomorrow*," said Connor. "It's a DC comic. Derek is strictly a Marvel man."

"*Was* strictly a Marvel man," corrected Will. "Anyway, after a brief metaphysical discussion, the whole Great Hall conversation came to a screeching halt when Graeme said that *The Longest Yard* was the longest movie he ever endured. That made Chris mad, and he chased Graeme down the hall."

"You don't insult anything related to football around Chris," Connor said to his sister, "unless you can run the 40 in less than 5 seconds."

Natalie smiled. "Ah, good old Renfrew School. The only place where you'll find Jean-Paul Sartre and Peyton Manning in the same huddle."

"I hear Sartre threw a pretty tight spiral," said Will, with a grin. "Bye, Natalie. I'm off to math help. Can't keep Ms Choi waiting!"

"Bye, Will!" said Natalie with a wave. In another 9 seconds she was propped up by her brother on a two-seater table at the back of the cafeteria.

"See, now I would have picked *Bill and Ted's Excellent Adventure* for worst movie," said Connor, unwrapping a snack bar. "Everyone knows that you can't do transtemporal trekking from a phone booth. Whatever a phone booth is."

"No one knows that but you, brother dear. So, aside from your late start this morning, is everything good?"

"I know Mom and Dad want you to check up on me, sis, but they've only been gone for a few hours. Did you get the text Mom sent? The picture at the picnic table with them pointing?"

"Yep. That wooden outhouse is still right there."

Almost every summer growing up, the Campbell children were taken on a British Columbia road trip by their parents, always stopping at the same rest area for lunch. On one occasion, a seven-year-old Natalie found a way to lock herself and her four-year-old brother in the outdoor commode. It took 22 minutes for John Campbell to get the door open without breaking it down. Connor thought the whole thing was an adventure; Natalie, not so much. Her aversion to using pit toilets was strong to this day.

"I still can't figure out how you managed to lock us in there," said Connor.

"If it wasn't for Dad, we'd probably still be trapped," Natalie replied with a smile. "I'm trying to learn how to be cool under pressure like him."

"You know, I've been thinking about that for the past month or so."

"What, latrines?"

"Ha, no. About what I learned about myself in France. In some tough situations, I just ran."

"Like your encounters with the lady in the blue shawl."

"Right. Running away seemed to be the best thing at the time. But in other circumstances, like when I threw the lance onto the *HMS Friendship*..."

"When you were in Dover..."

"Uh huh. When I did that, I was thinking on my feet. I got inspired and acted in the moment. But in retrospect, I realize that I was being prepared for that instant in time. Things I had practiced my whole life up to that point I got to put into action."

"I got some advice from Dr. Blanco today along the same lines. He told me that to get over some OR anxiety, I needed more practice to gain confidence. So, I'm going to assist him at the hospital on Fridays now."

"Okay, wow, that's awesome!" Connor exclaimed, drawing looks and smiles from Stella and Sadie three tables down. "By the way, sis, I've never thought of you as an anxious person. You just want to do things right, and when you don't, you take it hard. Like Mom."

"Yeah, Mom's like a dog with a bone, sometimes," Natalie agreed.

"Yep. And you're definitely her puppy." Connor's eyes looked up and over. "Oh, hey, Mr. Mason-Ivy! Look who I'm talking to." Connor turned the phone to the science teacher, who produced a big smile.

"Natalie Campbell, med student extraordinaire! How are you, my dear?" DMI took the phone from Connor.

"I'm great, Mr. Mason-Ivy. I hope you are, too!"

"I am! You know you can call me Don now, right?"

"I'll never be able to do that, sir," Natalie said, shaking her head. "You'll always be my biology teacher."

"I suppose you're right, there. I saw my old English teacher at the mall last week and I had to call him Mr. Hanevy. My brain gave me no other choice."

"That's incredible," said Connor, off-screen. "You went to the mall?"

"I did. And later today, I may even go to the bathroom, Mr. Campbell."

"Ah! TMI!" Connor exclaimed.

"No...it's DMI," replied the teacher. "But only to Natalie."

Natalie smiled. Suspicion confirmed after all these years: Donald Mason-Ivy *did* know that his nickname at school was DMI.

"You'll never guess what we did today, sir!" said Natalie. "We were looking at intestinal parasites in the lab. It brought back memories of Grade 11 at Renfrew School!"

"I didn't know you had tapeworms in Grade 11, Natalie," DMI winked.

"Only in your class, sir," Natalie smirked. "Some of my friends in the med lab were grossed out, but I was in there like a dirty shirt, touching every parasite in the place."

"So, I prepared you well to *handle* that situation, Ms Campbell?"

"As always."

"You're too kind, my girl," said the teacher. "Okay, back to hallway supervision now. I have to *worm* my way through the student body. Bye, Natalie."

"Bye, sir!" Natalie waved. Connor's face came back on-screen.

"I'm off, too, sis. I have to help Mr. Dyson set up a demo for chem class this afternoon."

"Blowing something up, I take it?"

"Mr. Dyson said we're going to light paper on fire...by using water!" said Connor with raised eyebrows. "That can't be possible."

"Said the boy who travelled back in time."

"Shhh!" Connor admonished in an exaggerated tone. "Not so loud! You want to blow my cover as the guy who brought the word *cafeteria* into existence?"

"It was *restaurant*, Time Master."

"Cafeteria, restaurant...whatever," dismissed Connor with an eye roll. He kissed the screen. "Love you, Nat."

"Love you, bro," said Natalie, waving.

Natalie could hear the twins give out an 'Aww...' from three tables down, as Connor's face turned red before the app window closed.

Tuesday afternoon was open time in the Anatomy Lab, and the room was abuzz with medical student activity. Toward the back of the room students were working with cadavers, carefully examining them to discover cause of death and identifying disease sites. Near the front of the room some students were reconstructing a human skeleton, while some others worked with models – turning them this way and that – to analyze muscle and ligament movement. In the middle of the room Mark and Natalie were practicing suturing techniques: Mark on a silicone model that replicated intestinal layers with colour-coded mucosae; Natalie sewing away on a pig's foot. Marianna and Holly, stationed next to their friends, were taking each other's blood pressure.

"Your bites are really nice and straight," said Mark, looking over at Natalie's work. "Very even spacing of the stitches. Your future patients will really appreciate that you learned how to *sow*. Get it? *Sow*? As in, 'oink, oink'?" Natalie and Holly groaned; Marianna laughed out loud in a way that suggested she didn't get the joke.

"Hogwash," Natalie replied, pulling on the thread.

"No, no...I'm sure they'll *squeal* with delight," Mark countered.

"Ugh...stop!" said Holly. "You're *boaring* me to death!"

"*Sì*, bàsta!" Marianna exclaimed. "*Dovete tagliarlo tutti*!" Her three friends turned to look at her. "You all need-a to *chop* it!"

"Ahh," replied the trio with giggly appreciation as Dr. Raven stopped by on his rounds.

"What's all this frivolity in the lab?" he barked with his hands on his hips.

"Sorry, Dr. Raven," said Mark. "We were lightening the mood with some pig puns."

"Let's see if your patients think you're that funny when you botch the closing of their incision, Mr. Munroe."

"Sorry, sir," said Mark, demurely. All smiles were returned to straight-lip position.

"Much better." Then Dr. Raven declared, "No more of these un-*porcine* circumstances."

It took five seconds for three of the friends to laugh as one. Zero giggles from Marianna, not wanting to get into any more trouble. The students resumed their work.

"Very nice needlework, Ms Campbell," said Dr. Raven over Natalie's shoulder. "A little more perpendicular to the skin on insertion." Natalie straightened the needle and pushed. "Now, rotate your wrist to pass the needle atraumatically." Natalie rotated, and performed a smooth return bite into the tissue. "Very nice, indeed."

Dr. Raven turned his attention to Mark's specimen. "How do you like working with the silicone?"

"I really enjoy it for two reasons," Mark replied. "No smell, and no fear that I'll encounter a nematode."

"Ha! Did you have an unfortunate experience with one of Dr. Silver's parasites, then?"

"Let's just say I couldn't *slither* out of her lab fast enough."

Dr. Raven smiled. He then looked over and down at Holly and Marianna seated behind him.

"Ladies, your blood pressure taking leaves much to be desired." The young women looked at each other, perplexed.

"First of all, I don't trust these digital things as far as I can throw them." Dr. Raven took the apparatus to the side cabinet and returned with a different set up. "I want you to get used to the most reliable device for measuring blood pressure: this, young people, is an aneroid sphygmomanometer. This instrument has an eight percent greater reliability than a digital device, measured against the gold standard of the mercury sphygmo." The instructor handed the apparatus to Holly. "Stethoscopes out!"

Holly and Marianna reached into their bags and pulled out their 'hearing aids'. Then Holly strapped the cuff onto Marianna's left bicep and began to inflate it using the attached bulb.

"One-sixty?" Holly asked her instructor.

"That should do nicely," replied Dr. Raven.

When the needle on the pressure gauge read 160 mmHg, Holly positioned her stethoscope in her ears and on the crux of Marianna's elbow, and gently turned the release valve.

"The first sound you'll hear as you deflate the cuff is Phase 1 Korotkoff, Ms Arnott. Record that in your head. That's the systolic pressure." The needle on the gauge began to lightly flick and Holly made auditory confirmation with a nod.

"Phases 2 to 4 are the whooshing and thumping sounds of blood fighting its way past the cuff. As soon as you get the Phase 5 silence, record diastole." The gauge needle stopped flicking, Holly gave another nod and opened the valve all the way to deflate the cuff.

"135 over 73…not bad for a heavy smoker," Holly said to Marianna with a wink.

"Very funny, but I no laugh. I think I have-a the 'white-coat syndrome', eh?"

"But I'm not a doctor yet," said Holly.

"No, but-a he is," replied Marianna, pointing at Dr. Raven. The professor smiled.

"Apologies for flummoxing you, Ms Lombardi. No need to cower before me, I can assure you." Marianna returned an uneasy smile, not sure if she was being called an ox, a cow, or both.

"Dr. Raven, what is this unit of pressure on the dial, here," asked Holly, pointing.

"Millimetres of mercury."

"I know that one. But what's this one underneath." Holly raised the gauge toward her instructor and pointed to the lettering in parentheses.

"Oh, that's another way of saying millimetres of mercury. That 't-o-r-r' is torr, in honour of Torricelli," said Dr. Raven, making an ess sound in the middle of the name.

"Ah, *mi scusi, professore*," Marianna interrupted. "His-a name is-a pronounced, Torri*ch*elli. Is-a 'ch' sound in Italian when-a the cee come-a before the e."

"I *cee*!" said the instructor with a grin. "So, if I asked you in Italian 'Where's the ocean?', I would say?…"

"*D'ovè l'ocheano?*" Marianna replied with a 'ch' sound.

"But I thought two cee's in Italian was 'ch'" said Mark, turning to the conversation.

"It's-a not a 'ch' sound like in-a the word *cucchia*. It is-a more of a longer 'ess'. *Cussia*."

"So, then, the word soccer would be pronounced 'sosser' in Italian."

"It's-a not 'sosser', silly. In Italia, we say *calcio*…because it's-a called *foot-a-ball*. Soccer! Bah! What is-a that, eh?"

"Is calcio spelled c-a-l-c-i-o?" Natalie asked Marianna.

"*Sì.*"

"So why did you pronounce the first cee as a kay and the second one as a 'ch'?"

"Because-a the first cee is in front of an a, but-a the second cee is in front of-a the i."

"Well now, that clears it up!" announced Mark, shaking the cobwebs from his head.

"Dr. Raven?" Holly interrupted. "Getting back to reality for second, who was Torricelli?"

"Only one of the greatest scientists of the 1600s!" beamed the instructor. "He was a student of Galileo, you know. Torricelli invented the mercury barometer, came up with an important fluid dynamic law that I really don't understand, and pretty much invented calculus."

"I thought that was Leibniz," said Mark.

"Leibniz gets the recognition for being the Father of Calculus, but Torricelli deserves a lot of the credit," said Dr. Raven. "It was Leibniz himself who said that." The professor heard his name being called from the cadaver station. "Ah, that's me. *Ciao*, everyone. Did I say that right, Ms Lombardi? *Cheeow*?"

"*Perfetto!*" Marianna replied with the 'okay' hand gesture as Dr. Raven left. Natalie and Mark returned to their stitching. Marianna strapped the sphygmomanometer to Holly's arm.

"Let's check-a your Torricellis, Ms Arnott," she said. Then, with a smirk, "You want-a to have a smoke first?"

"You mean, does Holly want a *ch*igarette?" asked Mark. The three young women turned their heads to him.

"What? They're your rules, Ms Lombardi, not mine."

The horse stable was burning to the ground. Thick, black smoke curled upward before being whisked off by the strong southerly winds. A child's wagon lay overturned at the side of the road, its front wheel rotating gently, making a squeak every half turn. The front door of the house at the end of the street was wide open, banging repeatedly against the overturned table in the sitting room. The clothesline to the right of the walkway had been cleared, save for a lonely blue shawl that was flapping in the breeze. No one from the village was there to save the stable, to pick up the wagon, to close the door, or to collect the blue shawl. There was no one in the little village at all.

A man in a tattered red and white uniform appeared from over the hill. He ran down through the tall grass, taking a tumble just before he reached the bottom. He rose up quickly, grimacing in pain. He had no time to search for his Swiss Guard hat; he could hear the Provincial Fédérés coming fast along the main road from Paris. The man hobbled toward the village. Knowing he couldn't go much farther before being seen, he struggled up the walkway, entered the house at the end of the street, and closed the door behind him.

How had it come to this?, the Swiss Guardsman thought to himself. All was calm at the Palace yesterday! The commander made it sound like all the troubles with the angry mob were being worked out. It would end up being a quiet August, he said! And now I am running for my life from revolutionaries!

The Swiss Guardsman looked out the window and saw the approaching band, armed with sabres and muskets. He knew he was trapped. As a last resort, he limped to the back room of the house and scurried under the bed. As he lay quietly, his hand brushed up against something. He ran his fingers over the leather-bound object. He brought the book up to his face. A little family bible! He clutched it to his chest to steady his racing heart. He began to pray.

The Swiss Guardsman heard the front door open, the sound of footsteps in the sitting room, the sound of feet kicking at furniture. And then he heard the breathing of someone standing close by. He could see the scuffed boots of a Fédérés stopped at the bedroom door.

"Pierre!" a voice called from outside the house. "We found a hat in the grass nearby! We think the scoundrels are on the other side of the hill!"

"Bon!" answered the Fédérés at the bedroom door. "Let us get after them quickly!" The boots disappeared from the door. The sound of the rowdy band of revolutionaries grew fainter as they tore off over the hill.

The Swiss Guardsman lay motionless for over an hour before he emerged from his hiding place. He sat on the bed, a smile coming to his face. Then he let out a chuckle. Then a belly laugh.

As he stood and placed the bible on the bed, a slip of paper fell out from inside the front cover. The Guardsman unfolded the paper once and read the words that were written boldly by a sure hand. He smiled again.

It was a message that was written just for him, he thought.

He placed the twice-folded piece of paper in the breast pocket of his coat, patted it in place, and left the house. He walked gingerly on his bad leg down the main road back to Paris. Whatever the future held in store, the Guardsman now felt unafraid. He had a good feeling all would be well.

Chapter 6

The picture on the screen at the front of the class was certainly a micrograph of a cyst. It had the telltale multilayer encasement surrounding a lighter-stained jumble of developing tissue. Anyone paying attention in Immunology Class the past two weeks could spot that. Identifying *where* the cyst was located was a trickier proposition for the med students.

"No one?" asked Dr. Silver. Then, looking to the students in the third row of the lecture theatre, "What do you think, Ms Arnott?"

Holly scratched her head. "Well, my guess is that it's intramuscular."

"And if that were the case, how would an infected patient present?" the prof continued.

"There might be some subcutaneous inflammation, so maybe a warm red spot on the skin? " Holly answered.

"Warm...kinda like me right now," Mark whispered to Natalie, looking uncomfortable while pulling at the neck of his ukuleles-and-mangos aloha shirt.

"Very good," said Dr. Silver to Holly. "You would expect a fever and elevated eosinophil count as well. Now, what if I told you the patient was presenting with headaches and dizziness?"

Marianna raised her hand. "Then-a the cyst is maybe neurological?"

"And the patient would be experiencing...?"

"Ah, dizziness and-a headaches?" Marianna replied with a shrug.

"I'm feeling lightheaded again," whispered Mark.

"And if the patient was also experiencing seizures," said Dr. Silver, clicking to the next slide, "then this is where the cysts would be."

The med students groaned at the picture of a human brain dotted with dark lesions.

"I think *I'm* about to have a seizure," Mark said to Natalie, as he slumped down in his seat.

"Dr. Silver, how does a tapeworm larva get to your brain?" asked Natalie.

"The oncosphere will burrow through the intestinal wall and enter the bloodstream. From there, it's onto the muscles or brain. Or even your eyeball!" The professor said this while wringing her hands, villainously.

"Okay, I'm out," said Mark, excusing himself as he made his way past the other students in the row. He bounded quickly up the stairs and out the door. Natalie showed a concerned look; Holly and Marianna supressed a chuckle.

"I only lost one today?" Dr. Silver asked with a sly grin. "Usually, I get two or three attacks of psychosomatic neurocysticercosis."

"What would the treatment be for those brain cysts, ma'am?" Holly asked.

"Steroids to reduce inflammation and albendazole to deal with the problem," replied Dr. Silver. "Surgery, if all else fails."

"What about the adult tapeworm that attaches in your gut. What's the treatment there?" asked Holly.

"Albendazole or PZQ. Not fun. As always, prevention is the best cure. Wash your hands if there are pigs around, and employ rigorous meat inspection protocols."

"How did-a they treat the tape-a-worm before we have-a the drugs?" asked Marianna.

"Like in the renaissance days of Francesco Redi, perhaps?" said Dr. Silver as Mark made his way back to his seat. "So glad you asked! Ever heard of wormwood?" The doctor brought up a picture of a greenish-grey coloured plant. "This antihelminthic has been used on intestinal parasites since the first century. Very effective, too, though diarrhea is a nasty side effect. Still, much nicer than the alternative treatment…"

Dr. Silver clicked to the next slide. The drawing was labelled, *Strassburg, 1497*. It pictured a man being suspended upside-down from a rope-and-pully contraption, a large tapeworm being drawn from his mouth by someone in a physician's smock.

"Apparently, this patient was treated at the local clinic," smiled the professor. "Far too much equipment for a house call, wouldn't you say?"

"Ugh," was the collective student response. Marianna, Holly, and Natalie all looked down the row toward Mark. His hands were covering his eyes.

"Should we tell you when it's over?" asked Holly.

"I'm just playing hide-and-seek," Mark answered. He turned toward the women and uncovered his eyes. "Redi, Arnott…here I come!"

He got a good smack from Natalie for that one.

The sky looked beautiful, not a cloud to be seen. The fir tree needles were a bright yellowy-green colour, setting the montane forest aglow. The river water, coursing clear and noisily through the polished stones, was sparkling in the midmorning sun. Natalie felt a sudden pang of homesickness, but covered the feeling with a Mona Lisa smile as her mother's image came back on the screen.

"Now that's a Canadian morning in the mountains, Mom! It doesn't look as cold as the clothes you're wearing, though." Michelle Campbell was sporting a down jacket, deerskin gloves, and a lamb's wool toque.

"Looks can be deceiving, my dear. It's just below freezing today. Your father has his electric socks on already." Michelle panned the phone toward her husband who was packing up their campsite after breakfast.

"Gotta keep those toes warm!" John Campbell smiled at his daughter. "What did my old coach always say?"

"You can't think when you're cold!" Natalie and Dad said in unison.

"Since when do you have to think when playing hockey, Dad?" Natalie smart-alecked.

"Actually, it was my high school football coach who said that. It got pretty cold in November during playoffs. You couldn't shut your brain off playing wide receiver with all the audibles we ran!"

"What's an aud...?" was all that Natalie got out before the phone image swung back to her mother.

"Don't ask your dad sport's questions unless you have an unlimited data plan," said Mom to her daughter. She changed the subject with, "How was your day at school, *ma chèrie*?"

"Pretty good. We finished up a little subunit about parasites in Immunology that Mark didn't handle very well..."

"Neither would I," Dad said off-screen.

"...and then I had a GI class, a Dermatology class, and now I'm home for dinner before I go to the theatre tonight."

"What are you seeing there?" Mom asked.

"My textbooks," Natalie answered. "The Byre Theatre is where I like to study. It's quiet and no one can find me there, so I can get in some good review time."

"Craigie Hall, sixth floor, cubicle next to the window. That was my study spot in university," said Michelle.

"Mine was the Fine Arts building," said John, appearing in the picture behind his wife. "No one could ever find me there. I always spread out on the same third-floor table, the one with my all-time favourite graffiti written on it."

"Okay, I'm ready," Natalie winced.

"It was...*Back in five minutes. Signed, Godot.*" John Campbell produced a silent, head-bobbing laugh à la Kermit the Frog. "Get it? Godot! He never shows up!"

"Ha, ha...yes, I get it, Dad," Natalie said with a bemused eye roll. "Actually, that's pretty good. Not your typical dad joke."

"I'll take that as a compliment, my girl," said John, leaving the picture.

"Okay, I'm going to give you a big kiss now, Natalie," said Mom. "Good luck on your upcoming Immunology exam!"

"That one's not 'til the 27th," corrected Natalie. "I don't remember telling you about that. Were you just fishing for information right now, to see if I'm keeping up on things?"

"*Qui, moi?*" Mom smirked. "Anyway, I'll wish you luck on the 26th, when we're reunited. In the next few hours we won't have any cell coverage for a quite few days."

"Too many days, Mom. I was just thinking this afternoon, I've never *not* talked to you for a whole week before."

"I know. We've been talking since you've been talking." Michelle smiled and took a deep breath. "*Je t'aime beaucoup, ma chèrie.*"

"Love you lots, too!" said Natalie, blowing her mother a kiss. "Love you, Dad."

"Right back atcha, my baby girl," Dad said with a wave. "Oh, hey, here's another one for you: How many surrealists does it take to change a lightbulb?"

"How many?" Natalie grimaced.

"A fish!" John Campbell exclaimed, holding up the skeletal remains of last night's dinner with a goofy smile.

"Splash Dad with the paddle for me today, okay, Mom."

"Will do! *Au revoir, Natalie!*" Mom gave her a big, screen kiss.

"See you soon," said Natalie waving.

"*Oui,*" said Mom with glassy eyes that were not missed by her daughter. "*Je te verrai très bientôt…*"

Natalie strolled down the hallway that lead to her favourite study room in the Byre Theatre. The sun had been down for over two hours, so the building was quieter than usual. She stopped at a glass-panelled railing that overlooked the first-level seating area and took a sip of her hot tea. She saw a young woman at a window table take a break from studying to scratch her dog behind the ears; a couple talking animatedly, yet quietly, directly below. Aside from the barista at the BrewCo there was no one else in view. Not a busy place on a Wednesday night.

As she continued her leisurely walk, Natalie whistled the catchy tune she had heard on STAR, the campus radio station, that afternoon. The DJ sent it out to all the med students, a Robert Palmer song called Bad Case of Loving You from 1979. She didn't know a lot of songs from back then, but she was sure that her Dad knew it. He probably has the record in his collection, she thought.

Then Natalie thought about how things were falling nicely into place. Her stress levels were up lately, sure, but she was getting lots of good advice from different people. She thought Marianna's dad might be onto something with that visualization thing. She could see how that could work for her. Ha, *see* how that could work! She liked that one. Meeting with Dr. Blanco was a great idea, too. His advice about practice was spot-on, and she was thankful he was giving her the opportunity to shadow him in the surgery this Friday. That would help put her mother's stress advice into play: prepare yourself for all possible outcomes!

Natalie arrived at her quiet room, opened the door, and reached for the light switch on her right. She flicked it up, but nothing came on. She toggled the switch a few times. Still nothing. Other than the moonlit image of the window on the far wall, everything was dark. Looks like someone needs to change the light bulb, Natalie thought. Now where were those surrealists when you needed them? She smiled to herself. Pretty good one, Dad.

Natalie was about to leave when she spotted something near the bookcase. She looked carefully. It wasn't so much near the bookcase as *around* the bookcase; a soft, pulsating glow. She looked over to the window and traced the moonlight into the room. No, it was still landing on the far wall. Letting curiosity get the best of her, Natalie entered the room, aided by the light from the hallway. That is, until the door closed behind her, and Natalie was encased by sudden darkness. Feeling for the table with outstretched hand, she parked her tea and bookbag and turned toward the bookcase.

The pulsating glow was more pronounced in the darker room. Natalie took out her phone and swiped from 6:31 pm to Face ID to the apps on her homescreen. She tapped the flashlight icon and pointed her phone at the bookcase. The faint glow disappeared in the bright LED output; everything looked normal, although the book that Natalie had previously tucked into place was sticking out again. She rectified that annoyance and smiled: anal retentive said Dr. Blanco, and boy was he right! She moved the phone light up and down, inspecting the bookcase. It looked okay. When she turned the light off, the soft glow instantly re-emerged. Where was that coming from? Was there a night-light behind the case?

Natalie placed her phone on the table. She turned to the bookcase and placed her hands on either side. It moved rather easily on the tile floor. Must have those felt pads for feet, Natalie thought. She slid the bookcase to her left, exposing a metre-tall, oval-shaped opening. Natalie stepped back, bumping into the table.

The opening had an opaque appearance and emitted a fuzzy light. Natalie bent and peered into the space; she could faintly see some objects on the other side. A chair, perhaps? A table? Natalie stood up straight. Logic dictated that she was looking into the room next door. But why would someone stretch cellophane across this opening?, she thought. Natalie reached out to touch the film, but her hand kept going through. She didn't retract her arm.

It was decision time: cancel the operation or continue with the procedure? The med student took a deep breath, bent down, headed straight...

...and went to the other side.

Chapter 7

The room next door looked like the set from a period movie. The wall on the left had a stone finish that appeared rough to the touch. The wall on the right had an off-white, textured-plaster appearance. Old-fashioned furniture occupied the middle of the small, 4x4m room; two straight-back wooden chairs on one side of a rectangular table with ornate legs, and one fancier chair with armrests on the other side. A Renaissance-type painting was hanging from a peg in the plastered wall. It depicted a young nobleman on horseback and an entourage of red-capped, serious-looking old men making their way down a road from a castle on a hill. The deer were jumping, the horses were prancing, the birds were flying this way and that. There were lots of orange trees. The scene was rather tranquil, certainly quaint. The only problem with this painting was the colour; it was far too vibrant for a medieval work of art. It looked like it had been painted only yesterday.

But there was an even bigger problem. The room was illuminated by a semicircular window on the stone side, where the sun was casting its light on the door straight ahead. The sun. Not the moon, like in the room next door. I gripped the back of the armchair and took a deep breath. Then I said out loud, "Toto, I have a feeling we're not in Kansas anymore."

I turned around. The opening to the other room in the Byre Theatre was still there, glowing fuzzily. I bent, stared into it, and could just make out my book bag lying on the table. And there was the cup of tea, sitting next to my phone. I didn't dive straight back through the hole, but I did take a seat in the armchair to catch my breath and steady my nerves. I was shaking like a leaf in a Chinook wind.

I had a good feeling about what was happening. Or was it a bad feeling? Feelings aside, I was going to confirm my suspicions and take the next logical step. I got up from the armchair and walked to the door. My hand was shaking as I lifted the latch. I opened the creaking door slowly and stuck my head out...into a sunny courtyard with statues and columns and arches. I closed the door, leaned against it, and tried not to hyperventilate.

Confirmation achieved. This was not the Byre Theatre.

I looked over to the opening in the wall. It was still there, and still glowing. I went around the table and stood in front of the hole. I stretched my leg out into the opaque film. It went in unhindered. I lowered my head and stepped completely through...

With one elongated stride, Natalie was back in the quiet room on the second floor of the Byre Theatre. She turned to the opening and gazed into it. She saw the three chairs and the table, albeit fuzzily, and with a squinty effort she could even make out the picture on the wall.

Natalie sat down and took a shaky sip of tea. Hmm, still hot after being gone a few minutes, she thought. She was feeling hot as well, so she took off her outdoor jacket and placed it on the table. Then she looked at her phone. The screen said 6:31 pm. 6:31 pm?, Natalie thought. She hadn't actually been gone at all.

Natalie shook her head in disbelief. This was exactly what her brother had experienced just over a month ago. The fuzzy light, the lack of elapsed time, the – what did Connor call it? – feeling of confuddlement? Yes, that was it...an emotional state of perplexity mixed with wonder...confuddlement! Natalie made a mental note to push for the acceptance of this disorder as a bonafide medical condition.

There was no doubt about it, Natalie thought: she had just experienced her first TT. She was transtemporal trekking!

Natalie continued to stare at the opening, sitting relatively calmly at the table, drinking her tea. What do I do now?, she pondered. She would call her mom and dad, of course! But John and Michelle weren't reachable by phone at present, paddling their way through the Canadian Rockies. She would call Connor, of course! But it was before noontime at home, and his phone would be turned off while he was in class. That left Natalie alone at the moment with the fuzzily lit opening in the wall. She could come back to the hole later, she thought, after getting some advice on how to proceed. Or she could do a little exploring right now, just to get a feel for where and when she was, when she wasn't where she normally was.

And it wasn't really the toughest decision that ever was. Natalie stood up, noted the 6:41pm display on her phone screen, and went through the hole.

It was cooler on this side of the wall, and I rubbed my arms to get warm. I didn't notice the temperature when I was here last time – one second ago, I assumed – but that's no surprise…I was flop-sweating! I looked around the room again and noticed everything was the same: the picture, the table, the three chairs, the light from the window hitting the door. All the same. I now noticed that the table had nothing on it. This room was pretty stark.

As I was tucking the armchair in so I could get by, I noticed that the tabletop had a slender drawer underneath. It wouldn't really be snooping to pull it out and have a look inside, would it? Isn't it more of an information-gathering strategy, like performing exploratory surgery, say? Made sense to me. I sat in the chair, pulled out the drawer, and was presented with an oversized book with a green cover. I pulled it out and placed it on the table.

After dusting off the cover, I opened it to the middle. The pages were heavy, almost like parchment, and were about the same off-white colour as the plaster on the wall. There was writing going down the lefthand side of the page, with the same two words starting each sentence, *Caddy detto*. Well, that's what the words looked like; it was all in fancy, cursive handwriting that was hard to read. I realized pretty quickly that these weren't really sentences so much as *entries*, because there were numbers at the end of each line. The numbers all descended in a left-side column, leaving a blank column on the right. My first guess: this was an accounting ledger. I tried to make out some more of the words, but it wasn't easy. Second guess: this wasn't English.

In the middle of the page I found some words that looked familiar, so I tried my best to sound them out.

Caddy detto Setteciento cinquantadue p[20] filippo alamany   752   ____

Sette...seven. *Ciento*...hundred. *Cinquanta*...fifty. *Due*...two! Seven-hundred fifty-two! And there it was, 752, in the number column! Third guess: this was Italian! I went back and reread *ciento* and *cinquanta* with a 'ch' sound at the start. Marianna would have been proud of me using proper pronunciation.

I flipped to the first page, which looked to have come from a printing press. In the middle of the page was a large family crest: a horse rearing up over a shield, a crown hovering over its head. A wreath of ribbons and flowers and some other weird things made a circle around the shield. There were words above the crest, which looked a lot like Latin to me:

AD COSVM
MEDICVM
FLORENTINORVM

And the words below the crest helped to confirm that theory:

Bononiæ apud Alexandrum Benaccium

But the letters below that...

M D C X L V I I

...made me freak out! I double checked my left-brain memory for all the Roman numerals I had stored there. It kept coming out the same...one thousand, five hundred, one hundred, ten, fifty – no, make that forty – five, one, one...one-thousand six-hundred forty-seven...Sixteen forty-seven! 1647? That's impossible!

Impossible? Natalie, you're time travelling! Sheesh.

I closed the ledger and put it back in the drawer. I stood up and arranged the armchair back to the way it was. Then I made my way to the door again, lifted the latch, peeked my head out, and had a good, careful look around.

The courtyard was aglow in the midmorning sun. At least it felt like midmorning; it was slightly cool out, and the shadows were elongated. Along the wall to my left there were four nooks with ornate archways. Each nook contained a statue of a man on a pedestal. All the statue-men wore long, flowing robes. Directly across the ten-metre stone floor was an arched entryway leading to another part of the building. It was crowned with a stonework of some nude babies flying in the air. What do you call them? Cherubs? They were holding up the drapery for the archway, but the drapery was made of stone, too. Very clever.

And speaking of nudes, on either end of the courtyard there stood two rather tall statues. The nearest one, to my left, was a stone figure of a man looking off to the side with his hand resting on the head of his dog. The farthest one, to my right, was a bronze sculpture of a long-haired man wearing a strange-looking hat, who was holding a sword in one hand and a rock in the other. It must be a temperate climate in these parts, what with all the nakedness. The cool morning *was* having an effect on these two works of art, though, as could be seen from the, ah, anatomical shortcomings on display. Clinically speaking, of course.

As I was counting the number of pillars around the courtyard that held up the three-story structure, I failed to notice three men enter through the archway straight ahead. A tall man on the left was carrying a bucket and what looked like a toolbox. A short man was carrying a wooden ladder. A man with a straw hat had a large sheet under his arm. All three men were wearing rumpled brown slacks and white shirts. I froze in place, my head sticking out of the door, as the four of us locked eyeballs.

"*Cosa ci fai qui, signorina?*" the tall man called out from across the courtyard. I understood the signorina part, but nothing else. My mouth started to move, but nothing came out. I gulped and finally got some words out.

"*Sì, sì!*" I answered, not knowing what I was saying yes to. The men put their equipment down and began to approach. I slammed the door and in a panic and ran around the desk to the glowing hole in the wall. I could hear their footsteps just outside the door.

I ducked my head and literally jumped through the wall.

Natalie landed on the tile floor of the quiet room. Her momentum thrust her forward, but she caught herself on the table, her face hovering over the 6:41pm display on her phone. Natalie turned toward the hole in a crouched stance, ready to bolt in case the two men were hot on her heels. But nothing happened. No one came through the hole. She stared into the fuzzy light, and only saw what she had seen before: the three chairs, the table, and the faint appearance of the picture on the wall. Natalie sat down and exhaled deeply, like she was measuring her vital capacity on a spirometer. She took a sip from the cup and smiled.

The tea was still hot.

Chapter 8

"What's up?" asked Connor, goggles dangling from his neck. "This better be good. You're taking me away from an amazing lab."

From the picture on her cellphone, Natalie could tell that Connor was standing in the hall outside of chemistry class.

"What are you doing?" she asked.

"Transferring coloured water from one graduated cylinder to another with soda straws," Connor replied with a smirk. "Not exactly riveting science. Mr. Dyson promised that we could blow something up later if we do a good job."

"I remember that lab. It explains equilibrium pretty well. You'll be impressed with the results. Balancing matters, you know?"

"So I've heard," said Connor with a raised-eyebrow nod. "Now, what's going on? Are you walking somewhere right now?"

"No. Why?"

"Because your picture is bouncing up and down."

"I'm actually sitting down," said Natalie from the floor in the hallway outside the quiet room.

"Well you're shaking so much that you're either freezing or you've got to go to the bathroom. If it's the bathroom, please call me back."

"Something's happened that I need to tell you about."

"Is everything all right?" asked her suddenly worried brother.

"It's nothing bad. Sorry, I don't mean to sound alarmed."

"Okay, then calm down, and take a few deep breaths," Connor instructed. Natalie took the breaths.

"Now, tell me what's happened," said Connor in a soothing tone.

Natalie swallowed and said, "I've just come back from a TT!"

"YOU WHAT?" Connor's shout echoed down the hall. Natalie and Connor both shushed each other on-screen with fingers to lips.

"What do you mean you've TT'd? That's impossible!" Connor whisper-shouted.

"Why is it impossible, aside from the fact that time travel is impossible? *You* did it!"

"Yeah, I know, but...well...I don't know but what, but it's just a but, that's all!" Connor brushed back his mop of hair and exhaled audibly. "Did you just wake up from a dream?"

"I haven't been sleeping. It's just after dinnertime."

"Did you bonk your head?"

"No."

"Did you take any medication?"

"I'm not on anything."

"Were you just at the pub?"

"No! I haven't been drinking!"

"Are you experiencing a case of transtemporal-trekking envy?"

"What?"

"TT envy! It's where you wish *you* had been the one selected to go back in time and not your little brother."

"Did I ever display symptoms of that condition before, Connor Campbell?" Natalie employed the death-stare on her little brother.

Connor looked back at his sister for six seconds and then said, "No. No, you've never been envious of my TT. You were only supportive. And you were pretty necessary to the whole operation." He took a deep breath. "I take it you've called Mom and Dad."

"First thing. But I couldn't get a hold of them because they're on that canoe trip."

"Right. They're in commando, now."

"*Incommunicado*, Connor!" Natalie corrected with a chortle. "Mom and Dad are definitely wearing underwear in the mountains today!"

"No wonder when I said Mom and Dad were going commando to the gang this morning, Will spit up his breakfast tea. Now, *where* were you on this TT? And *when* were you?"

"I don't know the answer to either question definitively, but here's what I think: Italy. In 1647."

"Come on! This is too much!" Connor exclaimed. He then turned his head and called back toward the lab room. "No, everything's okay, Mr. Dyson! I'll just be another two minutes!"

"You need to go back to class, and I need to go back to res," Natalie said.

"Where are you right now?" Connor asked. "Where's The Portal?"

"It's right here in the Byre Theatre, in a little room on the second floor. I'll show it to you." Natalie got up from the floor in the hallway.

"Well, you won't be able to show me," Connor replied.

"What? What are you talking about?" Natalie scoffed as she went into the room. The fuzzily-lit hole was right where she left it. "See, it's right here." Natalie pivoted the phone so Connor could have a look. As she turned her wrist, the fuzzy light disappeared.

"Told you," Connor smirked. "Now turn the phone back." Natalie obeyed, and the fuzzy light reappeared.

"It's back!" she said, stunned.

"Sure it is. Now do it again."

Natalie turned the phone; The Portal vanished. She turned it back; The Portal popped back up. She spun her wrist even quicker; The Portal disappeared even faster.

"Hey, you're making me dizzy," said Connor.

"Sorry. Why's it doing that?"

"Don't you remember when I tried to show my fuzzy light to Angus and Graeme in the tunnel?" Connor explained. "They couldn't see it. As soon as they weren't looking, it came back right away. I'm pretty sure it has to do with how the act of observing can influence the outcome of an experiment. It's supposed to be a quantum-level effect, but it seems to be a feature of TT-ing, too. In the end, The Portal is for your eyes only."

"Incredible," said Natalie, sitting down across from the glowing hole. She was trembling even more than before, and she knew her brother could see that, as well. "It's just so *incredible*."

"I know, right? You're handling it better than I did, sis. I think I had pretty much fainted twice by this point in my TT experience. You need to go home and relax. Have a bath, clean your dissecting kit, that kind of thing."

"I will. I will right now," said Natalie, reaching for her book bag. "Thanks, bro."

"I'm here for you, Nat. Right after I finish this super-exciting straw lab, that is. I'll call you tonight when I get home. Think you'll be up at midnight your time?"

"Think I'm going to ever sleep again?" asked Natalie.

"Oh, you will. Like a baby," Connor said with a wave. "Like a time-travelling baby."

"So, how would you say, 'What are you doing, girl?' in Italian?"

"You would-a say, '*Cosa stai facendo, ragazza*?'"

"Hmm…that's not quite it."

Natalie was grilling Marianna at the kitchen table. They were having a late-night snack from a leftover munchy box: kebab meat, chow mein noodles, naan bread, and coleslaw. It was an international smorgasbord of take-away delectables. If you ate it with your eyes closed.

"What-a you mean that's-a not quite it?" asked Marianna, slightly perturbed.

"I mean, it's not exactly what I'm looking for. The *cosa* sounds right, though." Natalie was trying hard to remember the exact words of the tall man with the bucket and toolbox. "How would you say, 'What are you up to, miss?'"

"Is-a almost the same, '*Che cosa stai facendo, signorina*?'"

"All right," Natalie paused for a moment, taking a bite of kebab. "How about, 'What are you doing here, miss?'"

"That's-a different. You would-a say, '*Cosa ci fai qui, signorina*?'"

"That's it!" Natalie exclaimed, pointing her naan bread to the ceiling. "*Cosa ci fai qui, signorina*!"

"Okay, that's-a good. Now, who ask-a you, 'What-a you doing here, young lady?'"

"No one I know, yet," Natalie said, truthfully. "I'm just preparing for the past…er…future."

"I see," said Marianna, but not really, thinking there must be something lost in translation.

"I'm going to my room now," Natalie told her friend. She licked her fingers, stood up from the table, and started to clean up. "You might hear me talking to my brother for an hour or so."

"No, no…I'll-a clean up," ordered Marianna, "You go and talk-a to Connor. Is-a he missing his mamma and papà already?"

"I think so. I'm going to make sure he eats a proper dinner tonight, and not some terrible junk food."

"You mean he should-a eat more like-a we do?" Marianna smiled.

"Exactly," said Natalie, dipping a final bite of naan bread into the coleslaw. "I want to make sure he's eating all the important food groups!"

"So, what was the tone of his, 'What are you doing here, young lady?'"

"What do you mean, 'the tone'?"

Natalie was sitting cross-legged on her bed, with her laptop displaying her sibling and her cellphone at the ready. Connor was doing likewise, an ocean and continent apart. They were engaged in some TT studying together, preparing Natalie for the sights and sounds on her trip to 1647 Italy.

"I mean, did he sound mad like he was going to turn you over to the police," Connor continued, "or did he sound like he was curious about you being there, like 'Hey, whatcha doing here, girl?'"

"More like that, yeah," Natalie replied. "He didn't really sound angry. He sounded like he was a bit surprised."

"Surprised. But not startled, right?"

"Right, but why are we playing Guess the Expression?"

"Look, it's important to know what those two men are thinking before you go back through the hole…"

"Portal," Natalie corrected. "I'm calling it The Portal, now. I liked it when you called it that before."

"Oh, um…great," said Connor with a tinge of satisfaction. "Anyway, as soon as you go back through The Portal, you'll be back in Italy…"

"In Florence, actually," Natalie interjected.

"Isn't that in Italy?"

"*Sì.*"

"So, when you get back to Florence, *Italy*," replied Connor with teeth clenched on the country name, "you'll arrive the very instant that you left. Were the men about to open the door when you, ah, *portaled*?"

"I think so. I think they were, maybe, two steps away. I don't think they were running."

"Okay, good. That fits with the 'surprised but not angry' theory. So, when you get back to the room…"

"I pretty sure it's an office."

"An office? Why do you say that?"

"Because when I searched online for the statues that I saw in the courtyard, I found this!" Natalie held up her cellphone to the laptop so Connor could read the caption on the picture.

"Pal-a-zo Med-i-see…" Connor butchered.

"*Palazzo Medici*," corrected Natalie, putting a 'ts' sound for the zz's and a 'ch' sound for the letter c. "I think my portal is in a palace!"

"Beats crawling through a dirt tunnel, that's for sure," said Connor, recalling his TT experience. "What's a Medici?"

"Who, not what. They were one of the most powerful banking families in all of Europe. They essentially financed the Renaissance!"

"That explains the ledger you found in the drawer, Nat."

"Yep. But by 1647, the Medicis moved their principle residence to another palace. Only the younger family members lived there then."

"Boy, that'd be rough, eh? Being banished to the other *palace*," Connor smirked.

"Here, look at these pictures, bro." Natalie sent a text to her brother. He opened the photos eight seconds later. "That first picture shows you pretty much exactly what I saw, except that the colours today are more vibrant than they were back then, believe it or not."

"Restoration work?"

"That's what I'm thinking. And that restoration was starting in 1647. I think those men outside the door are working on the building, to get it ready for sale."

"A sale? When would that happen?"

"Twelve years later, in 1659."

Connor took a moment to analyze the pictures. "It's a three-story building?"

"Family residence on the second level, servant's quarters and kitchen on the third level, banking offices on the first floor."

"Got it. The Portal is in one of the banking offices."

"Right," said Natalie. "And that picture on the office wall that I told you about? It's a reproduction of the *fresco* that's in the chapel down the hallway!"

"Who's The Fresco?"

"*Fresco*…it's a wall painting. And this one's famous. It's called Journey of the Magi." Connor scrolled to the last picture in the text.

"Very colourful," he said. And then, with a smile, "Are you going to Florence to see it?"

"I will, if I can get past the restoration crew that's about to open the office door."

"Okay, I've got an idea about that," said Connor. "Are you ready?"

"Shoot."

Connor spent the next 6 minutes going over the plan. He spared no detail, and repeated various steps for emphasis. His strategy came with a back-up scenario in case things went sideways. When he was done, he concluded with, "…and that should leave you free to roam!"

"Florence, not Rome," Natalie smiled.

Connor rolled his eyes.

"Baby brother, that is one fine plan. I think it'll work great. I'm going to get started on it first thing in the morning!"

"Just remember, there's no rush. You don't have to go back until you're absolutely ready."

"Got it."

"In fact, you don't have to go back at all," said Connor. Natalie read her brother's concerned expression.

"I know what you mean. Here we are, making plans for me to go on this trip, and not even talking about why I'm doing this in the first place. But I'm feeling like you did, Connor…I'm feeling like there's a reason why this is happening, and I need to find out what I'm supposed to do. I *have* to go back and find out."

"Do you feel the Guiding Hand, Natalie?"

"I do. I really do."

"Then you have to go and find out what the mission is, and what your job is going to be. Simple as that."

"Right," Natalie nodded. "Thanks, bro."

Connor nodded in return. Then he said, "I'll still be worried, though. Now, are you sure the year is 1647?"

"That's what the ledger said, so I'm going with that right now."

"And there's no war going on in 1647? No, like, French Revolution, where people are running for their lives?"

"Ha, no. No revolutions to worry about."

"Okay. Call me before you go through The Portal. And, then, right away when you get back!"

"Okay."

"No, I mean *right away*, the literal second you get back. Cuz if you don't…"

"I know…I remember," Natalie swallowed. "If you don't come back in a second, you don't come back at all."

"But you will…"

"Of course I will…"

"Because, you have to…"

"Don't I know it…"

"I mean…you're my sister, and…"

"And I have a responsibility to be here for my brother?"

"Exactly!" Then Connor sighed, "I'm glad you feel the same way, sis. I'll talk to you later." He gave Natalie an air kiss.

"Mwah, Connor. *A demain*."

Natalie closed the laptop lid and let out a big breath. She reached out and picked up the small, metal tin on the top of her dresser. The metal tin that she dug up in the cemetery when she was in Paris. When she helped Connor on his TT. She opened the tin and carefully removed the old, faded newspaper with the date 1771 circled in pen. She unfolded the paper once more and read the words, 'Dear Natalie, Enjoying Paris? Love, Connor.'

She certainly did. On both counts.

And now it was off to Florence.

Chapter 9

The aroma of something delicious baking in the oven greeted Marianna as she groggily entered the kitchen. She reached around Natalie for the espresso percolator.

"And I thought-a that I was up early this-a morning. What-a you make me for a treat today?"

"This will become cupcakes for our snack after Dermatology today," Natalie replied, stirring a bowlful of batter on the countertop. Then she nodded toward the cake cooling beside the stove. "And that's a special treat for another time." Another time. She couldn't resist that one.

"Ooh! For a special-a someone perhaps? Does he have-a nice blue eyes, maybe?"

"Does Mark have blue eyes?" Natalie asked disingenuously.

"How did you know I was-a speaking about Mark, eh? *Beccato*, Natalie!"

"What does that mean?"

"I think in-a English, you say, 'Gotcha'!" Marianna smiled. "I make-a you a cup of espresso, too? Not like-a you need it this-a morning." She looked over the culinary combat zone that was their small dormitory kitchen.

"I don't think I *need* one, but I'd like one anyway," Natalie replied.

"Ah, spoken like-a real *Italiana, mia amica*! I no make-a too strong, okay?"

Natalie finished up her bake fest and put the bowls into the sink, while Marianna made the coffee and got breakfast ready. In 9 minutes the two young women sat down to toast and jam and demitasses of espresso.

"If I wanted to say, 'I was sent here to give this to you' in Italian, what would I say?" Natalie asked between bites.

"You would say, '*Sono stato mandato qui per darti questo*'."

Natalie repeated the phrase three times. "And would that be the way to say it if I was speaking to someone in a more formal setting?"

"Like at-a fancy dinner party?"

"More like someone from another century."

"*Sì*, I suppose-a so," Marianna replied with a curious look.

"Okay. And how would I say, 'I don't understand, my Italian isn't so good'?"

"*Non capisco, parlo poco italiano.*"

Natalie repeated that phrase only twice. "Does that sound all right?"

"*Sì*, but it's-a strange that you are-a being sent somewhere, and you cannot speak-a the language," Marianna replied. "Very *mysterioso!*" The timer dinged, and Natalie got up to take the cupcakes out of the oven.

"*Posso aiutarti?*" said Marianna, asking if she could help.

"*No, grazie*, I've got it." Natalie placed the cupcakes next to the cake on the cooling rack. "There. Now I can start my day!"

"Start? You are already on-a your next day! It's-a like you are going to put-a two days into one!"

"Two days into one?" said Natalie, taking out her cake stencil. "You know, I think I'll try that!"

Natalie had just over one hour before her first class of the day. Enough time to whip down to the charity shop on Bell Street and have a rake around. It took her only eight minutes by foot, cutting down Doubledykes Road off of North Haugh. A friendly bell sounded overhead as she opened the door to the store.

"Good morning!" a voice called out from the back.

"Hello!" Natalie called in return.

"Can I help you?" the voice asked. Still no body present to match the sound to.

"Well, yes. I'm looking for a dress."

"Oh, aren't we all, my dear!" said a lady that finally emerged from behind a rack of jackets. She looked like a recently-retired elementary schoolteacher that was putting in volunteer hours: she wore a blue skirt, peach-coloured top with a white ruffly neck, and sensible shoes.

Her grey hair was pulled back gently and kept in position with rhinestone-encrusted hair clips. "Anything specific?"

"Actually, yes, ma'am" Natalie replied. "I'm looking for something that's full length, with an old-fashioned look."

"Call me, Ava, my dear. Like you're going to a 1960s cocktail party?"

"More like a 1660s barn dance. Call me, Natalie, please, Ava."

"All right, Natalie. I may have just the thing for you! Come with me." Ava led Natalie to the back of the shop. She slid a dozen dresses down the rack on their hangers and pulled out a stiff-looking gown.

"Something like this?" Ava asked, sizing up the dress under Natalie's chin. "It's a peasant dress. Very bohemian, don't you think?"

Natalie took the hanger. "It doesn't really flow, does it? The material seems rather rough."

"It's a *real* peasant dress," said Ava. "It's made from 100% recycled peasant fabric!"

"Peasant fabric?"

"Burlap!"

"So, this is essentially a potato sack?"

"The latest in agrarian chic, Natalie dear!" Ava exclaimed delightedly. "Nothing says rétro couture like wearing a sack! It captures the essence of rural existence, don't you think?"

"If by essence you mean odor," Natalie said crinkling her nose. She rehung the dress. "I'm sorry, Ava. I think I'm looking for something different. A bit…"

"Less environmentally friendly, perhaps?"

Natalie nodded.

"How about this one, then? It's a tad milk maiden-ish, though." Ava presented Natalie with a brown, short-sleeved dress with a lace-up corset.

"Now that may be just the thing," said Natalie. She took the dress and measured its length down her front. "Would you wear a white blouse underneath it, then?"

"Oh, yes. That would complete the bucolic presentation. Let me find you one while you try it on." Ava half-turned and pointed. "The change room is right over there."

Natalie emerged from the change room three minutes later wearing the dress and a blouse that Ava had found in no time at all.

"What do you think?" asked Natalie with a twirl.

"It looks divinely earthen, Natalie. And the flats you're wearing today go with it perfectly, too. I'd say you're ready for any Renaissance runway!"

"Thanks, Ava. I'll take them both."

Natalie changed back into her 21st century outfit and paid at the front of the store.

"Thank you for your help, Ava," said Natalie on the way out.

"My pleasure, Natalie! Let me know if you change your mind about the burlap dress! I've got some great accessorizing ideas!"

The slide on the screen showed the leg of a poor, unfortunate soul that was covered in blue spots and blotches. The students gazed intently at the picture from their lecture theatre chairs, leaning forward and squinting in concentration. Dr. Blanco, standing at the front of the room with arms crossed, broke the silence after a good 22 seconds.

"I'll give you all a hint. This could have been the leg of a sailor back in the day."

"How about an infected shark bite?" said Mark from the third row.

"Do those little dots look like they were made by shark's teeth, Mr. Munroe?"

"Uh…maybe they're from a baby shark?" Mark replied.

"Baby shark?"

The lecture theatre was instantly filled with the sound of 35 medical students singing, *"Do doo, doo-doo, doo-doo"*. Dr. Blanco let out a chortle; his own children had serenaded him endlessly with that earworm when they were younger, too.

"Yes, yes…very good. But it's not a bite from any size of shark. This colouration is not from a single traumatic event. Think deficiency."

Holly put up her hand, which was acknowledged by the prof. "If this is a picture of a sailor from the past, could it be scurvy?"

"It could be, and it is!" exclaimed Dr. Blanco. "Well done, Ms Arnott. This is one of the symptoms of ascorbic acid, or vitamin-C, deficiency. A patient that presents with this blue mottling would also have fatigue, muscle weakness, joint pain, and bleeding gums. So, if you notice you're losing your teeth one day, don't worry, it's just scurvy."

The students chuckled. Mark absently checked the sturdiness of his eyetooth with his thumb.

"Ms Lombardi?" The professor caught the attention of the Italian in the room. "What do you call scurvy in your native language?"

"Ah, I think it's-a called *scorbuto*," Marianna replied.

"It is. And another symptom of vitamin-C deficiency is called scorbutic tongue. It presents itself as red, inflamed, and generally sore."

"Dr. Blanco?" asked Natalie with raised hand. "What is the pathology of scurvy?"

"You need ascorbic acid for the production of collagen in your body. Without that protein, you can't make and repair bone, muscle, skin, cartilage, and connective tissue. You'll have fragile capillaries, and that means bleeding and haemorrhaging. You'll have lousy bones and teeth, and that means you're breaking them more often." Dr. Blanco took a breath. "So, what do you think the treatment is?"

"Bed rest and lots of vitamin-C?" Holly offered.

"Precisely that," replied the prof. "It's a slow recovery, but highly effective. If left untreated, it's fatal, of course. The Royal Navy expected that half of any long-voyage crew would die of scurvy! That was before the mid-1700s, when a Scottish surgeon found you could treat scurvy with citrus fruit."

"Slàinte!" Mark exclaimed in a cheer for his country. "Is that why the English sailors were called limeys, sir? Because they sucked on limes onboard ship to prevent scurvy?"

"Indeed! Nowadays, it's hard not to get your RDA of vitamin-C. One doesn't need to supplement if you have a balanced diet that includes fruits and vegetables. Broccoli, peppers, and even potatoes have plenty of ascorbic acid in them to keep us healthy. And, of course, there's camu camu."

"Of course!" Marianna exclaimed.

"You know about camu camu?" asked Dr. Blanco.

"Um…no. I just-a want to help you make-a the point," Marianna replied sheepishly.

"Well…" said the professor, eyes looking this way and that. "Anyway, camu camu is a rainforest fruit that contains almost 40 times the amount of ascorbic acid than a similar serving of citrus fruit! If you think lemons are sour!"

"Pucker up," Mark whispered to Natalie. She was this close to leaning over for a kiss, were it not for her quick grasp of the context.

"That's it for today, all," said Dr. Blanco as he clicked off the visuals on the screen. "Chapters 22 to 24 for next time."

The med students exited the lecture theatre. Natalie turned to her friends, holding up a plastic container.

"Shall we retire to the seminar room for some treats?"

"Oh, oh, lemme see!" cried Holly. Natalie opened the lid for a peak.

"Cupcakes!" Mark exclaimed. "Brilliant! What's the flavour of the icing?"

"That's an orange glaze," Natalie answered.

"How appropriate," said Mark. "The sugar that will rot our teeth will be combatted by the vitamin-C of the orange! You thought of everything, Natalie!"

"Oh, she's-a always thinking," said Marianna. Then, giving her friend a nudge, she whispered to Natalie. "Always thinking of-a you, Mark…"

Marianna got a pretty good nudge in the ribs in return.

After the last class of the day, Natalie nipped back to Agnes Blackadder Hall to pick up the oversized shopping bag she had packed earlier in the morning. It was mid-afternoon by the time she arrived at the Byre Theatre. Natalie made her way to the quiet room on the second floor, ducking in to see if it was empty and that The Portal was operational. Check and check. She then went to the ladies' room down the hall and changed into her new blouse and dress, examining herself in the mirror for fit and finish. Check and check, again. Natalie peeked out the door; there was no one in the hallway. She made the dash from the bathroom to the quiet room in 6 seconds and closed the door behind her.

The light switch was still dysfunctional, but the afternoon sun gave the room sufficient illumination. Natalie placed the bag on the table and reached in to remove…argh! Natalie pulled out her dissecting kit, remembered why she had packed it, and smacked herself on the head. She peeked out the quiet room door; there was no one in the hallway. She made the return dash to the ladies' room in just under 6 seconds. Then she removed her blouse and dress, took out the scissors from her kit, and cut out the clothing labels from her outfit. Connor had made that step in the procedure very clear – don't forget to get rid of the labels! On his own TT, Connor had been very fortunate that the French police inspector believed him when he explained that the translation of 'machine washable' on the tag meant 'of the highest quality'. Natalie put the outfit back on, and rechecked herself in the mirror for peasantness and primness. Re-checked and double-checked. She glanced down the vacant hallway, and then ran the door-to-door diagonal in just over 5 seconds.

Returning to the bag, Natalie removed the large plastic container and opened the lid. She gently removed the cloth-wrapped cake, turned to The Portal, and took a deep breath. Her brother had luck with the hot dogs he brought for some French dogs when he had a TT quandary. Now it was time to see if Italian workmen appreciated something a little bit sweeter.

Natalie composed herself, bent down, and stepped through the fuzzy light.

I stood up straight behind the desk, put on a charming smile, and waited for the office door to open. It took all of 3 seconds. The three men that had spotted me from the courtyard burst into the room; the tall man with his toolbox in hand, the short man without his ladder, the other man still wearing his straw hat.

"*Buongiorno, signori!*" I exclaimed.

Now for the big moment.

"*Sono stato mandato qui per darti pesto!*" I said, utilizing the first of my practiced lines.

I uncovered the cake and held it out to them. I could see that the three men were taken aback by my assertiveness; I thought it would be best if I went on the offensive in this potential stand-off. The man with the straw hat gave me a curious look.

"*Pesto?*" he said. Then he turned to the tall man. "Antonio, *ha appena detto 'pesto'?*"

Antonio looked back at the straw-hat man and replied, "*Sì, Alfredo, ha detto 'pesto'.*"

Their curious looks had my head spinning. I went through the sentence again in my head. They weren't taken aback by my assertiveness at all. It was my asininity that stunned them.

"*Ah! Non! Non 'pesto',*" I corrected myself. "*Questo! Darti 'questo'!*" I was holding a cake in front of them, not pasta in a basil sauce!

"*Una torta?*" Antonio asked me.

"*Sì, Sì!*" I answered. *Torta* sounded like cake to me.

"*Per noi da mangiare?*" asked Alfredo.

I answered with two nods. "*Pare noey da manjaray!*" I said, or something like that. I placed the cake down on the desk. The three men exchanged furrowed-brow glances.

"*Che ti ha mandato, signorina?*" asked Antonio.

"*Kay tee a mandato?*" I repeated. I wasn't really sure how to answer that. I got even more nervous. I looked behind me. No portal to duck into. Of course not…other people were present, so it wasn't there!

"*Era la Signora Medici?* Alfredo asked.

Now that sounded familiar. I think he was asking if it was Mrs. Medici that sent me. I couldn't think of anything else to say, so I said...

"*Ah... sì?*"

The workmen looked down at the cake.

"*La torta è molto bella,* Andrea," said Alfredo to the short man.

"*Sì, Sì, molto bella!*" replied Andrea. "*Tagliaci un pezzo,* Antonio." Antonio took out a knife from his toolbox and cut a piece of cake for each of them. Then he picked up a slice and looked at it discerningly.

"*Sembra schiacciata!*" he remarked.

"*È schiacciata, signorina?*" Alfredo asked me. It seemed as though they were commenting on the thickness of the cake, so I said...

"*Sì, una torta schiacciata!*"

"*Una torta schiacciata!* Ha!" exclaimed Andrea. It seemed that he was delighted by my answer.

The three men both bit into the cake and chewed appraisingly, like they were judges on a baking-show panel. Antonio smiled and looked at me.

"*È delizioso! Adoro l'arancia!*" He said this while shaking his wrist with the tips of his fingers pressed together. How very Italian!

"*Sì, l'arancia fa bene!*" Alfredo nodded in agreement.

"*Grazie,*" I said, being pretty sure that they were enjoying the orange zest I added to the vanilla cake recipe.

"*E adoro il simbolo di Firenze fatto con lo zucchero!*" Andrea said pointing to the *fleur-de-lys* design I had stenciled onto the cake with powdered sugar. *Simbolo? Firenze?* My *fleur-de-lys* looked like the symbol of Florence? Okay!

"*Il simbolo di Firenze!*" I proclaimed. I must have said it right, because the three men raised their piece of cake to me and said...

"*Saluti!*"

"*Saluti!*" I replied. That produced quizzical looks from the workmen.

"*Scusi moi, singnori...SaluTO!*" The quizzical looks continued.

"*Moi?*" asked Alfredo. He looked at Andrea. "*Non è Francese?*"

"*Sei Francese, signorina?*" Andrea asked me with a puzzled look.

"*Oui...*er... *sì, signoro,*" I admitted. I guess the *gatto* was out of the *sac,* so to speak. They figured out I wasn't Italian; they thought I was from France. I couldn't very well say I was from Canada since there might not even be a Canada yet. So I said, "*Sono Francese.*"

"*Beh non saprei dire!*" Alfredo exclaimed, smiling. "*Il tuo accento Italiano è eccellente, signorina!*"

"*Lei è totalmente Italiana,*" added Antonio with a nod.

I think that the men totally liked my Italian accent!

"*Merci beaucoup!*" I answered. "*Grazie mille!*"

"*Ha…grazie 'mille'!*" Andrea chortled. "*Questa è nuova!*"

"*Mi piace molto!*" declared Antonio, slapping Andrea on the back. "*Grazie mille, a tutti! Ha, ha!*"

"*Grazie MILLE, Antonio!*" replied Alfredo, slapping him back.

I had a bad feeling that I just introduced a new way to say thanks into the Italian lexicon…a thousand times over! Now it was time to make my exit.

"*Devo partire adesso, signori,*" I said, reciting another one of my practiced lines. Then I told them to enjoy the cake. "*Godita la torta!*"

I made my way out to the courtyard through the open office door.

"*Arrivederci, signorina!*" Andrea, Antonio, and Alfredo said together.

"*Racconterò agli altri dell atua delizioso torta schiacciata!*" Antonio added.

"*Arrivederci!*" I called back as I turned left and exited the Palazzo Medici.

The sun was shining brightly, not a cloud in the sky. I stood in the middle of the flagstone-paved street and made a full three-sixty turn. I saw the grand archway of the Palazzo Medici through which I had just passed, with the bumpy Medici coat of arms directly above. I saw a big building with a tall clock tower just down the street. And I saw a massive domed church that dominated the skyline only a few blocks away.

I took a deep breath of the crisp morning air and couldn't help but smile from *orecchio* to *orecchio*.

Wow! I was in Florence!

Time to explore!

Chapter 10

I almost pulled my sternocleidomastoid muscle checking the time outside the old palace, the Palazzo Vecchio. That clock was easily 60 metres straight up, and the tower had at least another 30 metres to go! There was only one hand on the dial, on purpose, but it wasn't too tricky to read. The arrow of the hand was pointing halfway between IX and X. It felt like 9:30 am, too…on a cool, autumn day in 1647. At least that was my guess.

The imposing stone wall façade of the palace was decorated with coats of arms set in oval windows that were positioned one story from the top of the main building. I counted four more stories going down, where each level alternated between having large, rounded windows and small rectangular windows across the 50-metre width of the building. Five steps led up to the main entrance on my right. It was decorated with an impressive, round arch.

But the man standing in front of me was even more impressive than all of this. He was handsome, with long, wavy hair and chiseled features. He had large hands, big feet, and boy was he ripped! He was looking off to the side, striking a pose like a male model on the cover of *GQ Italia*. Michelangelo's *David* was a sight to behold; all five-plus naked metres of him!

Two older ladies in black dresses and black cloaks approached as I was admiring the Renaissance masterpiece. They stopped next to me and looked up at David.

"*Ha bisogno di indossare un cappotto!*" one of them said. "*Sembra freddo!*" She was saying something about him being cold and needing a coat.

"*Sì. Oggi si è rimpicciolito,*" her friend replied with a sly grin, holding her thumb and index finger two centimetres apart on the last word. No translation necessary there.

"*Signorina?*" the first lady asked me. "*Ti piace David?*"

"*Sì,*" I answered. I liked him a lot. Then I tried, "*Mi piace molto!*"

"*È troppo vecchio!*" her friend said to me. "*Ha centocinquanta anni!*" Then they both laughed and went on their way. I pieced it all together and smiled. They were right; at 150 years old, David *was* too old for me!

I stood there admiring David for another ten minutes or so, but since he never returned my affections – his head was turned away from me the whole time we were together! – I continued my stroll up the left arm of the w-shaped square.

I stopped to have a look at a bronze statue of a battle-ready soldier with a sheathed sword on his hip and a baton in his hand. He was riding a muscular horse that was prancing on its pedestal. The inscription said Cosimo I. So, this is Cosimo Medici, the Grand Duke of Tuscany! The same man I saw in pictures back home on my laptop, only shinier! This Medici didn't look like a banker, though…more like a warrior. Maybe he was from a different branch of the banking family. Ha, different branch of the banking family!

I turned around to make sure I had my bearings before venturing further. There was the Duomo, the enormous domed church, off to the left – more precisely, to the north, judging by the morning sun on my right. I had passed by it as I walked down the street to the Palazzo Vecchio. The Palazzo Medici, where The Portal was located, was a little more than half a K northeast of the Duomo. That church was proving to be the ideal landmark for my exploring; it was centrally located and super tall!

I walked east for about 400 metres and turned left onto Via Roma, being helped by the street signs on plaques that were attached to the sides of the buildings…very convenient for this tourist from the future! Another quick right and then a left led me to where all the noise was coming from – it was a huge outdoor market! I saw people bustling here and there, from one kiosk to another. There was lots of excited talk and shouting going on. I decided to venture in further.

As I strolled down the main market lane, I was assaulted in the most pleasant way by the sights, sounds, and smells of 17th century Italy. I saw young women in long dresses and decorative cloaks socializing animatedly with friends; I saw older ladies bickering and bartering with the merchants, smelling an apple here and turning a nose up at an onion there; I saw young men dressed in baggy pants and puffy shirts with vests, laughing and carrying-on like young men do everywhere in any age; I saw little children holding their mother's hands and chewing on sugary treats that looked to be made of honey and nuts. I didn't see a lot of older men until I got to the far end of the market; they were sitting at small tables, drinking from tiny cups, and talking a lot with their hands. The words you could hear the most, above the general din, were *Duka Ferdinando* this, and *Casa dei Medici* that. They were talking politics over coffee. That sounded about right.

I was very pleased that my outfit wasn't drawing any attention. I seemed to be fitting in outwardly without any issue.

As I was standing next to a vegetable stand, I began eavesdropping on a conversation between a vendor and his customer. I concentrated hard on understanding the dialect. I was translating fervently in my head, and was quite pleased that I was actually getting most of the words being spoken. It was quite the jumble of Italian and French tossing about in my left frontal lobe, though!

The customer pointed at a basket of ripe tomatoes.

"Vincenzo, are you selling these *pomodori* or giving them away?" the lady asked with a disgusted look.

"These *pomodori* are *molto buoni, Signora Rossi*!" Vincenzo replied with defensively-shrugged shoulders. "They are from the *migliore fattoria di pomodori* in *Tuscano*!" It was a really good tomato farm. "They make a *sugo fantastica*!" A great sauce!

"They are too old for the *prezzo*!" said Mrs. Rossi, not happy with the price. "I want a *sconto*!" She was demanding a discount, I think.

"*Non posso muovermi* on the price." He wasn't budging.

"I can get them down the *strada a meno*!" Mrs. Rossi countered, pointing down the street. I think *a meno* meant 'for less'!

"But *signora*! My *pomodori* are the Caravaggio of *pomodori*!"

"I do not care if they are the Leonardo da Vinci of *pomodori*, I am not *spendendo* one *quattrino* for a *libbra* of *vecchio pomodori, signoro*!" She wasn't going to waste her money on a pound of old tomatoes, Vincenzo!

"*Uno quattrino*? Did I say *uno quattrino, signora*? No, no…these *pomodori* are only one *baiocco* for a *libbra*!" Vincenzo was making a price reduction on the fly.

"That's much *meglio*!" said Mrs. Rossi, pleased with the 'better' price. "But I am not *convinto*."

"*Eh, dai*!" Vincenzo exclaimed, frustrated. Then he looked at me. "*Signorina*! Do you like *l'aspetto* of these *pomodori*?"

"*Um…sì*," I stammered. I thought the tomatoes looked fine. A little ripe, but fine. Mrs. Rossi humphed at my answer and handed over a *baiocco* to Vincenzo. He placed a half-dozen tomatoes in Mrs. Rossi's bag and wished her good day.

"*Grazie, signorina,*" Vincenzo said to me after his customer left. "You deserve *una ricompensa* for getting me a good price for the *pomodori!*" Vincenzo gave me an orange and a big smile.

"*Grazie* to you, *signoro,*" I replied. Then I tried out a new phrase. "Is this orange a Caravaggio, too?"

"My oranges are as *dolce e succoso* as Botticelli's Venus!" Vincenzo said with a sly wink. I smiled demurely, backed away from the stand, and headed down the market lane.

Sweet and juicy like Venus? Oh my!

I found a bench to sit on near the entrance to the market. I peeled my orange, placed the rind in my dress pocket, and ate a section. Okay…it *was* sweet and juicy. I'm not sure about the Venus thing, Vincenzo, but it was a really fine orange. The sun was rising higher in the sky, and it was getting warmer. The streets were livelier; Florence was becoming a busy city. A mid-morning fruit snack and a rest for my tired feet was just what this future doctor ordered. So I had another section of orange and started a people-watching session from my vantage point on the Via Porta Rossa.

After a fourth orange slice, my attention was diverted to a slight commotion up the street to my right. A woman was shouting at a young man that was walking behind her. She was turning around every five steps or so, gesturing for him to hurry up. The young man wasn't moving too quickly, and he stumbled after trying to pick up the pace. The woman grabbed his arm to pull him along, but the young man stumbled again and this time he hit the pavement. The woman bent down and tried to lift the young man. He didn't respond. But I did. I stuffed the fruit into my pocket and dashed across the street, just missing being hit by a horse and cart coming fast on my left.

"Lorenzo! Lorenzo!" the woman cried, patting the young man on the face. He was conscious but not responding. "*Svegliati,* Lorenzo!"

I bent down next to Lorenzo, opposite the woman. I said, "*Signora, posso,…posso…?*"

"*Posso aiutarla?*" the woman said, helping me with the phrase, 'Can I help?' Then she said, "*Sì, signorina, grazie.*"

We lifted Lorenzo up, each of us taking an arm, and dragged him onto a grassy patch off the side of the road. I placed the young man flat on his back and elevated his legs to support blood flow to his brain. The woman looked at me curiously as I checked behind Lorenzo's head and down his body for any signs of injury. After I was satisfied that nothing was broken or bleeding, I began the struggle of asking the woman some questions.

"Are you a *madre* for Lorenzo?" I asked in my broken Italian.

"*Sì*, I am his mother, Isabella," she replied. My brain was choppily translating, utilizing three different languages. Then she asked, "You are not *Italiano*?"

"*No*," I answered. I was understanding, but it was slow going. Then I asked, "Do you *parli* English or French?"

"*No, signorina.*"

"Lorenzo...has he been *malade*?" I used the French word.

"*No*, not *malato*, but he is very *affaticato*," Isabella said. I took that to mean fatigued. "And his *ossa dolore*." She was saying something about his bones. I felt Lorenzo's elbow, and he let out a moan. He did the same when I squeezed his knee. By now, a small crowd was gathering around us. People were murmuring, gesturing, and looking concerned.

"Has he, ah...*mangiato* this morning?" I asked, putting my collected fingers to my mouth.

"He ate some *prosciutto* and some *pollo*," Isabella answered.

"Only meat?" I asked in Italian.

"He only eats *carne*. He says he is 18-years old and *e mangarà quello che vuole!*" Apparently, Lorenzo was old enough to eat what he wanted to!

I was getting a picture of the patient. I needed to check on two more things.

"Lorenzo?" I said to the bleary-eyed teenager. Then, glancing at his mother, I said in French, "*Ouvrez la bouche*?", pointing at my open mouth.

"*Lorenzo, apri la bocca!*" Isabella said to her son.

When he opened his mouth, I could see that his tongue was very red and inflamed. The crowd gave out a collective 'Ooooh!'

I looked at Isabella. "I need you...to...to..." I had no words for the last instruction. "*Mi scusi*," I apologized as I reached down and rolled up Lorenzo's pant leg. The crowd gasped, probably at my impropriety. I rolled down Lorenzo's stocking and exposed blue blotches and spots on his leg. The crowd gasped again, with a few *'Mamma mia'*s thrown in for good measure.

"Lorenzo has scurvy, er...*scorbuto*," I said to his mother. "He must see a *medico* right away."

"*Sì, sì*...a doctor right away!" she answered back.

Lorenzo was starting to come around now; he was blinking furiously and smacking his lips. A man in the crowd handed his mother a pitcher of water, from which she gave the boy a drink after we had propped him up.

"Here," I said to Isabella, handing her the contents of my dress pocket. "You must make him eat oranges!"

"*Arance?*" She looked at me in disbelief.

"*Sì. Arance e patate e broccoli!*" I insisted. "These are *importante mangiare* for *curare* the *scorbuto!*" Isabella took the rest of my orange as the two of us stood up. Two men in the crowd helped Lorenzo to his feet and brushed him off.

"*Grazie* for your help," said Isabella. "*Come ti chiami, signorina?*"

"My name?" I answered back in Italian. "My name is Natalie."

"*Grazie, Natalia!*" said Isabella as the crowd dispersed. Natalia? Hmm, it seemed appropriate enough considering the setting.

"*Prego,*" I said. Isabella took her son by the arm and the two of them walked slowly down the street. In an instant, I was left alone on the side of the Via Porta Rossa.

Well, not completely alone.

"*Mi scusi, signorina,*" said a voice from behind me. "*Posso parlare con lei?*"

I turned around to see the person who asked to speak to me. It was a young man that looked to be around my age. He was sharply dressed in a tan overcoat lying overtop of a similarly coloured waistcoat. His trousers extended to just below the knee, where silk stockings took the ensemble down to his black-leather shoes sporting slight heels. His shirt was ruffled at the cuffs, and he had a white ascot around his neck. That had to be a wig he was wearing; the flowing, brown ringlets of hair descended generously down past his collarbone. Real or not, it was the most hair I'd ever seen on a man.

"*Buongiorno, signore,*" I replied. "*Mi vuoi?*"

The young man chuckled and made a face that crinkled the thin moustache on his upper lip.

I went through that last sentence in my head and quickly figured out the issue: instead of saying, 'What do you want?', I asked him if he *wanted* me. Not a good first impression.

"*Mi scusi*…my *italiano* is not very *buono*," I stammered.

"*Sì, posso dirlo,*" he agreed. He cleared his throat. "*Parlez-vous français, mademoiselle?*"

"Ah…*oui,*" I replied. "*Pouvez-vous, monsieur?*"

I had just asked him if *he* could speak French! Well, duh. Nice one, Natalie.

The young man broke into a wide grin. "*Oui, je peux,*" he answered. We continued our conversation in French after that awkward introduction.

"I was watching you attend to the distressed boy lying on the grass," he said. "A very impressive intervention, I must say."

"Um…*merci,*" I replied, feeling my face begin to flush. "I was just trying to help."

"That you did! Elevating his knees to encourage blood to the head! It is not something that many would know to do in that situation." He said this with tilted head and raised eyebrows.

"Well…I had seen it done before…back home where I am from," I said. Not a word of a lie, there.

"The attention given to inspecting his body for potential injury was undertaken skillfully," he said.

"My brother back home is always getting into trouble and hurting himself, so I have learned how to carefully examine." A bit of an exaggeration there.

The young man put his hands behind his back and stepped forward. "Your diagnosis of scurvy was a masterful deduction based on the evidence you uncovered."

"I have seen photogra…er…drawings of someone with scurvy. The boy's leg looked very similar to that." I was grasping now.

He took another step toward me. "But the recommended treatment of fruit to combat scurvy! Such a bold prescription, not to mention controversial." He looked directly into my eyes. "How do you account for your knowledge of this remedy?"

"Um...I happen to know a sailor?" Well, my dad *was* paddling down a river in the Rockies right now, in the future. So, not exactly a lie.

"Putting all of this together has led me to a conclusion," said the young man, arms now crossed.

"*Oui?*"

"I sincerely believe..."

"*Oui?*"

"That, you, mademoiselle..."

Gulp.

"...are the most fascinatingly stunning woman I have ever met!" He took my hand in his and gave it kiss. "My name is Francesco, but my friends call me Ciccio." He pronounced his nickname with two 'ch's.

"It is a pleasure to meet you, ah...Francesco," I said, putting my free hand to my chest and gushing like a little med-school girl. "My name is...Natalia."

"Natalia! A name to make my heart dance!" Ciccio exclaimed, still holding my hand. "*Natale Domini*! It speaks of a new birth! How fitting since I feel reborn from this chance-encounter today! Mark the date, all you of Florence! Monday, October 14, 1647, is the day Ciccio was born anew!"

I didn't know what to say. I was flattered and flabbergasted all at the same time. I just stood there, smiling dumbly at my smitten new friend.

"Well, it was nice to meet you, Francesco," I said, turning the hand-holding into a handshake.

"Ciccio, my Natalia," he corrected, looking confused. Maybe handshakes weren't a thing yet. "Must you go? Can we not become better acquainted? I must introduce you to my father, the physician! He would be so pleased to meet you, to discuss your scurvy! Well, not your scurvy, of course...your scurvy treatment! Perhaps we could have lunch? Oh, Natalia, you have my head spinning like a *strùmmolo!*"

My head was spinning like a top, too. I managed to get something out. "I could meet you later, perhaps. I...I have to go to The Portal...er...down the Porta Rossa, now. Yes, that's it! I must go down the Via Porta Rossa...to...to..."

"Meet someone?"

"*Sì. Oui.* To meet someone on the other side of the wall…er…other side of the street…" I really had no idea where I was going.

"Will it take very long?" he asked.

"Oh, no…only one second," I said truthfully without thinking.

"Wonderful!" Ciccio shouted. "Meet me at the David in the Palazzo Vecchio at noon! I will take you to lunch!" I hesitated, but Ciccio seemed persistent. "As a reward for helping the boy this morning!"

I exhaled a sigh of defeat. "Very well. I will meet you there."

"Until then!" Ciccio kissed my hand again and then looked into my eyes. "You have such beautiful eyelashes, Natalia! *Ciao, bella!*"

And with that random utterance he was off, almost skipping down the street.

I headed north on Via dei Calzaiuoli toward the Duomo, which would take me back to The Portal at the Palazzo Medici. I had to admit, there was a lightness in my step. I was glad to be of help to the teenaged boy and his mother. And it was a real ego-boost to be fawned over by an Italian gentleman. He thought my eyelashes were beautiful! Now that was a…

Argh! Natalie! Come on, girl…what were you thinking! I made a mental note to bring make-up wipes to the quiet room before my next trip.

Ciccio may have been the first man to ever see mascara on a woman!

The smoke cleared, the dust settled, and the sound of cannon fire was no longer heard on the plain. The din of artillery reports had been replaced by the agonized cries and moans of the prostrate soldiers strewn about the battlefield. The British infantryman, his red coat tattered and stained black, looked down and around for his shako, but it was no use. His headgear could have been any one of the hundreds that lay on the ground on that terrible Sunday near Waterloo.

The infantryman rested his Brown Bess musket by his side, holding the barrel just under the bayonet, and surveyed the scene. There were hundreds, perhaps thousands, of men from the French and coalition sides lying dead on the scorched earth. The injured were being attended to by the beleaguered medical personnel who were having difficulty knowing just where to begin. Trees blasted apart and on fire, the ground pockmarked with craters, buildings reduced to rubble. A torn French flag lay ripped and trodden down in the mud.

The British soldier felt no pride in the outcome. Yes, the odds were not in their favour. Yes, it had taken courage and determination and discipline to emerge victorious. But no, there was no feeling of accomplishment today; just a hollow feeling in his chest and overwhelming relief that he had been spared while so many comrades had perished.

Off in the distance, a group of officers on horseback were surveying the damage, the plumes of their bicorne hats sullied from falling ash. A hatless figure in a dark overcoat stood out amongst the red jackets of the officers. The infantryman bowed his head and then gave a hand salute to his commander, the Duke of Wellington, showing respect for the man who had steadfastly led his army into battle. The soldier began his trek back to what was left of his camp. The mournful calls of the bagpipes of the Scottish regiment filled the smoke-laden air.

As the infantryman walked past a band of fallen French soldiers, he noticed a piece of paper tumbling toward him. It was a strange sight, since there was hardly a breath of wind at that moment. The paper stopped right in front of the soldier. He picked it up and opened the first of two folds on the paper. There was a message on it, boldly written by a sure hand. The soldier read it and mustered a faint smile. It was the right word at the right moment. A message that was written just for him, he thought.

The infantryman placed the twice-folded paper in the breast pocket of his red coat. He would show it to his friends and family in England for many years to come. A memorial from a historic day he was hoping to forget.

Chapter 11

"Yeouch!" Natalie cried, pricking her finger with the sewing needle. She was making some small alterations on her brown dress as she sat on her bed that evening. Her brother's laptop face gave a grimace from half a world away.

"Maybe you should let a professional take over, sis. Oh wait…you *are* a professional!" Connor cackled. "Or do you just use staples in the OR, now?"

"Actually, glue is my go-to," Natalie smiled. "But if the wound has to be sutured, I can always use my fall-back strategy."

"Which is?"

"Look at the assistant surgeon and say, "Would you close for me, please?'" Connor laughed. He liked that one.

"So, was it hard to get back through The Portal?" he asked after eating a forkful of penne that he had made for supper.

"When I got back to the Palazzo Medici there was no one around at all," replied Natalie after flipping her dress around to fix part of the hem. "The nice thing is, there's no door to the entranceway into the courtyard. It looks like I have free passage to The Portal whenever I need it."

"And did you check the office door, like we talked about?"

"Yep. There's no lock on that door, inside or out. Hey, that's funny…" Natalie was rummaging through her dress pocket.

"What is it?"

"I had orange rind in my pocket in Italy, and now it's gone!"

"Oh, it's there all right."

"Well, it's not. See?" Natalie held the dress up and showed her brother the empty pocket.

"When you go back to Italy, that rind will pop right back into place."

"Oh, right," Natalie remembered. "I can take things *in* through The Portal, but I can't take anything home."

"Correct," Connor said with a mouthful of food. Then, after a swallow, "Now, about this Chickio dude…"

"Chee-chio is how it's pronounced, brother dear. Try again."

"Okay, Cheee-chee-oh," Connor exaggerated. "Are you really going to see this guy?"

"He seems perfectly harmless, bro. I'm interested to learn more about the Italian people of 1647."

"Uh huh. Seems like you're more interested in learning about the Italian Ciccio's of 1647."

"Don't be ridiculous, Connor," Natalie protested. "I'm treating this encounter as research."

"I'll bet *he's* not," Connor stated matter of factly. "How many times did he kiss your hand?"

"Twice."

"Twice! Oh, man!"

"What do you mean, 'Oh, man!'?"

"He kisses your hand once, it's 'How do you do?', he kisses it twice, and it's 'When's the honeymoon?'"

"Okay, stop!" Natalie huffed. "He's a nice young man, and we're just going to have lunch."

"And meet his parents?"

"He mentioned meeting his father, yes."

"Did he mention the wedding date?"

"Connor!"

"Natalie! These single guys from back in the day move fast!" Connor stabbed at his penne with audible vigour. "Lavoisier proposed to Marie-Anne in less than a week! Count d'Amerval arranged a marriage in a day and a half!"

"Okay, okay, I get it," Natalie said calmly. "You want me to be careful. I'll be careful."

Connor gave a sigh of resignation. "I want you not to be distracted, Natalie, that's all. The reason you're on this TT may have nothing to do with this Ciccio guy."

"But it might," she replied, making a thread loop to end the stitch. "And I'll know more after we have lunch. Anyway, I know that the main reason I'm TT-ing wasn't only to help that boy with scurvy."

"How do you know?" Connor asked.

"Because after I returned through The Portal, I went to the bathroom, changed back into my regular clothes, and did some studying in the quiet room."

"And The Portal was still there, of course."

"Right next to me, the whole time. I think it likes me." Natalie said this with a wink.

"I think Mr. Ciccio does, too," her brother answered with a wink of his own.

The medical school cafe was alive with therapeutic chatter on Friday morning before the start of classes. Natalie and Marianna were enjoying their second cup of coffee of the day, Holly was sipping her fruit smoothie from a paper straw while engrossed in the latest NHL results on her phone, and Mark was starting his second meal of the morning: a two-egg breakfast burrito washed down with a large cup of tea.

"How did your Leaves do last night, Holly?" asked Mark. "Did they score a lot of pucks?"

"They're the Leafs, and they scored four goals, Mr. Munroe. Two on the power play."

"The power play! How militaristic! Were your Leafs able to assert their influence in battle and gain a victory?"

"They lost in overtime to the Ducks."

"Ooh. It must be embarrassing to lose to a Duck."

"Tell me about it," Holly sighed. "We've got problems between the pipes this season. Specifically, the five hole."

Mark took a sip of tea and contemplated a response. "Nope. I'm not going to touch that one in mixed company, Ms Arnott. Nice try."

"Nice stickhandling, there, Mark," Holly smiled, returning to her scores.

"Top o' the morning to Lecture Theatre Row Three," said a cheery Dr. Silver as she walked past with a breakfast tray. "I hope everyone is ready to be grossed out again today."

"As long as there are no worms on the agenda, I'm all ears, nose, and throat," replied Mark.

"Please join us, Dr. Silver," said Natalie, pulling out the chair next to her.

"Thank you Ms Campbell," said the prof as she sat down.

"Dr. Silver, can I ask-a you a question?" Marianna enquired. "It's about what-a we covered in-a the last class. About typhoid fever."

"Yes?" replied Dr. Silver between mouthfuls of oatmeal.

"Is-a there a vaccine for this?"

"Yes, there is. And it's a pretty effective one, too. It's been around for over a hundred years, in fact."

"Is it part of our childhood vaccination program?" asked Holly, as she put her phone away.

"It's not part of the 6 in 1 vaccine, no. It's not a very common infection in the developed world, what with public sanitation being in vogue these days." The doctor said this with a grin. "But medical people volunteering in developing countries get a typhoid shot before venturing off. And since most of you indicated that you would like to volunteer someday as well, we gave all of you that shot in Year One, remember?"

"Ah, now I recall-a this!" said Marianna, rubbing her arm in remembrance.

"So, the chlorinating of drinking water has helped decrease the spread of typhoid, right?" Mark asked the prof.

"It's probably the greatest impact on our well-being from a public health care perspective, Mr. Munroe. I know a lot of people don't think putting chlorine and fluorine into our water is particularly tasteful, literally and figuratively, but in my estimation it has been indispensable to our salubrity."

"Hey, *salu*brity! Now that's-a word I think I understand, Dr. Silver!" Marianna remarked. "*Salute* means health in *italiano*."

"And that's what salubrity means…health!" replied the doctor. Her English-as-a-first-language students at the table nodded in agreement, though never having heard the word before and maybe never again.

"In class, you said Cipro was the antibiotic of choice," said Natalie. "Is that because the bacterium is becoming more resistant to the traditional antibiotics?"

"Penicillin would have done the job well back in the day, but the bugs today are getting clever." Dr. Silver had a sip of her coffee. "What will we tell our patients in the future, future-doctors?…"

"Finish your prescription!" they all chimed in, though Marianna's last word was *prescrizione*.

"Exactly!" the prof exclaimed. "It's the best way to ensure antibiotic effectiveness for the next generation…of people and bacteria!"

"Speaking of penicillin, Dr. Silver," said Mark. "I've been reading online about some people that are making their own, preparing for the zombie takeover, I guess. Is that really a thing?"

"The zombie takeover? I sincerely hope not."

"No, ha…I mean making your own penicillin. Does that work?"

"I don't think manufacturing your own antibiotics is as easy as pie, or even moldy bread, but it could work."

"Who needs a laboratory when you have a bread box!" Holly laughed.

"An old sandwich a day keeps the doctor away!" Natalie added.

"But professor, homemade penicillin would be dangerous!" Mark interjected. "There would be issues of purity, sterility, and even dosage. How would you even administer it? Orally? By injection?"

"Well, you could do what Dr. Imhotep did," answered Dr. Silver.

"Who's that?" asked Holly. "One of your colleagues?"

"A very old one," Dr. Silver replied. "He lived over four thousand years ago in ancient Egypt. We think that he combatted infections by making a poultice from moldy bread and then strapping it onto the open wound of the patient. There you are, homemade penicillin!"

"Do you think that really works?" asked Natalie.

"Egyptians are still around today, aren't they?" Dr. Silver replied with a smirk. "I'm really not sure, but I wouldn't discount some degree of efficacy in that treatment."

"Still, I wouldn't want to meet my professional Waterloo by prescribing *that* home remedy," Mark asserted.

"Agreed," said Dr. Silver, rising from the table. "Now, are we all prepared to learn about battling mosquito-borne malaria in today's class?"

"Can't wait!" Natalie declared as she and her friends got ready to leave. "Is there a home remedy for that, too?"

"I hear the ancient Egyptians had an effective preventative for it," said Mark. He began moving his head in random circles and making a buzzing sound. Then he looked straight at his arm and gave it a smack.

"Non-invasive *and* drug-free," said Dr. Silver with arched eyebrows. "Bonus marks for you, Mr. Munroe."

Natalie gave Mark a swat of her own.

I showed up at the Palazzo Vecchio a few minutes past noon. I didn't want to seem too eager, of course, and I certainly didn't want to be there before Ciccio!

It was going to be a busy Friday for me in Scotland after Immunology class, but I decided that I could comfortably get away to Italy for a Monday lunch and be back in no time at all! I had to wait quite a while in the bathroom across the hall before I could get to The Portal today; there was an elementary school tour happening at the Byre Theatre and a frantic teacher was trying to herd a litter of kindergarten kittens to the exit for over 3 minutes. Once the trailing parent volunteer scooped up two misplaced jackets and an errant boot, the coast was clear for me to scamper off to the continent. But only after firing off a quick 'see you in second text' to my brother.

As I made the left turn into the plaza, I saw Ciccio waiting by the Statue of David. He was bouncing up and down, looking this way and that. When he looked this way again, he spied me amongst the thin crowd of people in the square and darted to meet me halfway. Just before reaching me, he turned his sprint into a fast walk. I think he was trying not to look too eager. Epic fail on that.

"Natalia! It is so wonderful to see you again after all this time!" Ciccio exclaimed in French kind of loudly - as in, They-Can-Hear-You-in-Milan kind of loud. He kissed my hand, of course.

"It has only been a few hours, Francesco," I replied.

"*Only* a few hours?" he burst out. "Dear Natalia, the seconds were as minutes, the minutes became days! My heart says I have not seen you for many years!"

"Well, your heart-clock needs winding, Francesco," I said with a smile. Then I changed the subject. "Now, where are we off to?"

"Please, call me Ciccio. I am treating you to lunch at my favourite *osteria*, Natalia! It is down the road, this way."

"*Grazie*," I said, a bit relieved that Ciccio said it was his treat; I had no 1647 cash on me!

We began our stroll to the tavern at a leisurely pace along the Via del Proconsolo, not saying too much, mostly exchanging shy smiles. After a quick left on the Via del Corso, we arrived at the *osteria*. A stout, balding man with an upturned moustache greeted us at the door.

"*Ah, Ciccio! Come stai?*"

"*Bene, Carlo, bene. Hai un tavalo per noi?*" Ciccio asked if there was a table for us.

"*Sì, sì! Vieni da questa parte, per favore.*"

Carlo led us to a small table near the back of the *osteria*. It was a fairly large room, but it was cozy. Rustic would be a better word. There were twelve tables with wooden chairs arranged in three rows in the centre of the room, with two benches running on either side. The walls were made of brick, except for a large space on the left-side wall that displayed a fresco of what looked to be the Tuscan countryside. It was a warm atmosphere, made even more comfortable by the smiles and head nods of the other patrons as we were led to our table. But the most inviting thing of all was the aroma emanating from the kitchen: an enticing blend of garlic, onions, herbs, and freshly baked bread. I didn't realise I was so hungry!

"*Il solito?*" Carlo asked Ciccio as he pulled out a chair for me. We sat down.

"*Sì, per due,*" Ciccio replied. "*E due bicchieri del miglior Chianti, per favore. Rufina…Sedici quarantuno.*" Carlo nodded his head and left for the kitchen. Looks like we were having the usual with a glass of wine!

"Now, tell me all about yourself, Natalia," Ciccio asked in French. "Where are you from?"

I knew I was going to get grilled at the restaurant, so I had prepared some answers ahead of time.

"I am visiting from another country. From the Kingdom of Scotland."

"The Kingdom of Scotland! How exotic! Do you also speak Gaelic? Or Scots?"

"Actually, my first language is *anglaise*." Then I said in English, for my own amusement, "I'm a pretty clever girl, don't you think?" Ciccio didn't understand that, but he looked impressed, regardless.

"Ah! This tells me much about you," Ciccio said, wagging his finger. "Your father is a diplomat, *oui*?"

"Well, *non*…"

"A banker?"

"*Non*, he designs clothing." How else could I say that my dad is a chemical engineer for Dupont that specializes in the fabrication of personal protective equipment?

"I see. And your mother?"

"Well, she works at home." No lie there. Mom has a degree in software engineering and now specializes in translating technical information for computer applications. In her home office.

"Of course she does!" Ciccio declared, as Carlo set two glasses of wine on the table. "Siblings?"

"I have a brother, Connor. He is still in school. As am I."

Ciccio almost did a spit take on the *tavolo*. "How can you be in school? You are a grown woman!"

I had emotionally prepared myself for a lot of tongue biting beforehand, so I calmly answered, "*Oui*, and I am engaged in medical studies at the moment."

Ciccio looked at me as if I had just told him I was from Mars.

"You are studying medicine?" he said, incredulously. "To become a doctor?"

"That is the idea."

Ciccio took a moment to respond. "Well, Natalia, this only proves that I am not prone to exaggeration. When I said before that you were fascinatingly stunning, I was actually understating your splendour!" He said that last part in a dreamy sort of way that caught me off guard. Luckily, the food had just arrived.

"*Ribollita e pane*," Carlo announced as he placed the dishes in front of us. We tucked into our heartly vegetable and bean soup with ornate silver spoons and continued the conversation.

"Now, how is it you speak French so well if your family is from Scotland?" Ciccio asked.

"My family is not from there. I am only studying in Scotland. We are from La-Nouvelle France." Another way of saying Canada, before Canada was actually called Canada.

"So, you are visiting from the Kingdom of Scotland, but you are originally from overseas!" Ciccio said, impressed.

"*Oui*, you could say that."

"Is it a long voyage from your home to Florence?"

"Not as long as you might think," answered the girl with The Portal pass. I changed the subject with, "This soup is marvelous!"

"It is my favourite here at the Marchesi House, next to this…"

Carlo had just arrived on the scene, this time with plates of polenta topped with cheese along with sausages and more bread.

"*Godere!*" chimed Mr. Marchesi. Well, what's *not* to enjoy!

"So, Francesco, tell me about yourself," I said, cutting the sausage with the sharp, pointed knife and two-pronged fork.

"Oh my, there is not too much to say, really," Ciccio shrugged. Then he went into a good fifteen minutes about himself.

He told me about his parents, Gregorio and Cecilia, who met each other in Arezzo and got married in 1625. Baby Francesco arrived a year later, and the family went to live in Florence, where his father began to practice medicine. He worked out of The Hospital of Santa Maria Nuova for many years before setting up an office in their house. You could tell Ciccio had great admiration for his father's work: he gushed about how Gregorio was an important contributor to the hospital's glowing reputation as an advanced research and treatment facility, and how successful he had become in private practice.

He told me about his mother, Cecilia, the rock of the family; a sensible woman who kept everyone grounded in faith and family. He spoke about his mom endearingly, with a reverence that I could appreciate.

He told me about growing up under the tutelage of the Jesuits, and how his instructors got him excited about science at an early age. Now that peaked my interest! He recalled spending the summer days of his childhood catching insects and studying their anatomy with his set of magnifying glasses – his favourite present ever! When it was time to go away for school, he chose to attend the University of Pisa. He had been there for many years, he said, and was glad that his official studies were over as of last month.

"Did you receive your degree?" I asked, placing my cutlery down on the empty plate.

"I did. Two of them."

"Oh! What did you get them in?"

"Philosophy," he said. Then after pausing to produce a cheeky smile, he added, "And medicine!"

"What? You are a medical doctor?" I exclaimed. The other *osteria* patrons tried not to take notice of the loud foreigner. I think it was the Chianti talking. "Well, that explains your interest in my treatment of the boy this morning. You were not surprised so much as..."

"Interested, *oui*," Ciccio interjected. He leaned toward me. "I am *very* interested in you, Natalia."

"That is, um...interesting, *oui*," I stumbled. "Well, well...two degrees! You are a man of many talents, Francesco!" Yes, let's talk about you again, okay?

"And many passions, Natalia," he said, looking into my eyes.

"Oh, you have hobbies, then? Please tell me about them!" Please, let's talk about something else!

"Let me see...I have an interest in wine," Ciccio replied, leaning back in his chair. "Are you enjoying the Chianti Rufino? I made sure to ask for the 1641 vintage. It was a particularly good grape season in the elevated regions that year."

"It is nice," I replied.

"This Chianti has a full-fruit nose, with a firm tannin grip in the middle palette, do you not think?" asked Ciccio as he finished his glass.

"Um, *oui*...it is, er...*very* nice. Very, ah...grippy."

"Oh yes, I almost forgot to tell you! I have an interest in poetry, as well!" he said, reaching into the pocket of his waistcoat.

"Oh?"

"*Oui*. I wrote a poem about meeting you!"

"You wrote a poem about me? This morning?"

"While I was waiting for you at the Palazzo Vecchio! I went inside, borrowed paper and quill, and put down my verse! Would you like to hear it?"

I didn't really know what to say, but what came out was, "Certainly!"

Ciccio cleared his throat.

In Tuscan lands, where Bacchus reigns,
A lady fair, Natalia by name,
Her smile, a burst of sunshine's rays
A flower in bloom, her beauty aflame.

Her voice, a song from distant shores,
Her laughter, melody of love,
In Tuscan lands, where Bacchus roars,
Natalia, a gift from heaven above!

"For you," he said, sliding the paper toward me across the table top.

I took the paper and gazed at the beautiful cursive writing. I was speechless.

"What is it?" Ciccio said with a look of alarm. "You do not like it?"

"Oh, non, it is not that!"

"I am sorry it is in French. *Non, non*…I mean it just sounds much better in *italiano*," he stammered. "Especially the part about your beauty on fire!"

"*Non, non*…it is lovely."

"Ah! Too much invoking of Bacchus! I knew it!" He took back the paper. "Curse my oenophilic sensibilities!"

"It is not that, Francesco," I cut in. "It is just, well, we have only just met, and…"

"And?…"

"And, perhaps we should not move things along so quickly in our friendship, having only recently become acquainted," I said quietly, trying to calm us both down.

"Not so quickly?" Ciccio responded thoughtfully. "*Oui*, Natalia, how very wise! Let us proceed at a more leisurely, considered pace." He nodded his head in agreement and gave me a smile.

Then he placed three silver coins on the table, rose up from his chair, and held out his hand.

"Come, I want you to meet my parents!"

Sigh. So much for taking it slowly.

Chapter 12

Our eight-minute walk to Francesco's parents' house took us northeast from the Duomo on the Via dei Servi to the Piazza della Santissima Annunziata. The houses along the route became progressively less well-to-do, and after we crossed the piazza they became downright dilapidated. We paused in front of a large, long four-story building with multiple arches along its frontage.

"This is the *Ospedale degli Innocenti*, the Hospital of the Innocents," said Ciccio, translating the Italian into French. "My father attends to many of the orphaned children that live here."

"I am sure this keeps him very busy," I said.

"It certainly does! And as you can tell by the district we have entered on our walk, his clientele also includes the indigent of Florence, as well. Come, our destination is just this way."

After another block, Ciccio stopped in front of a stately stone house on three levels, with big windows on every floor. The roof had rounded red tiles, which made the house stick out like a sore thumb amongst its neighbours. Probably on purpose, of course: Where's the doctor's office, you ask?...Why it's that tall building over there with the crimson roof. You can't miss it!

We walked up the pathway that led directly to a front door with no porch and we entered the house. The vestibule was quite large, with chairs running along the wall just like in a waiting room, which I'm sure it was. The chairs were currently empty. There were three rooms down the right side of the hallway, all with their doors closed. Examination rooms, I'd bet.

"I believe my father is busy with a patient at the moment. Let us go upstairs. Mamma will be in the kitchen, no doubt."

We climbed the staircase on the left which led to a large living room. The high ceiling in the room threw me off; this being the second floor, I didn't expect such spaciousness. The fresco on the left wall between two tall windows depicted a wine-country scene of rolling hills and orchards. The furniture was all wooden, of course, and very ornate, but the chairs and settee looked quite cozy. From the drapery to the carpets, from the tapestries to the throw pillows, the room exuded taste, but not at the expense of comfort.

A clanging sound followed by a cry of Italian exasperation emanated from a room down the hallway.

"That will be Mamma," Ciccio said with a smile as he led us to the back of the house. We entered a sunlit kitchen area where an elegant-looking lady in a bright floral dress with a lacey blouse was standing, arms crossed, over a set of copper baking tins. This woman was pretty much the opposite of the stereotypical Italian *nonna*-type.

"This is *ridicolo!*" the lady exclaimed, pointing at the tins with an open hand. "Where is my *padella di medie dimensioni!*" Piecing together her Italian in my English/French brain, I made out that she was looking for her medium-sized pan.

"I think Papà has it *nel suo ufficio*, Mamma," said Ciccio, pointing downstairs to the doctor's offices. "He was *acqua bollente qui*, this morning." He was boiling water in it, I think.

"Well, he should *ritorno* my *padella* if he wants to have a *dolce da mangiare* tonight!" Ciccio's mother uncrossed her arms when she finally noticed the stranger in her kitchen.

"*Ciao!* Who is this *signorina*, Ciccio?" she asked her son.

"Mamma, this is Natalia."

Ciccio's mom gave a slight bow, which I returned with a smile and a, "*Ciao, signora.*"

"*Dove vi siete conosciuti?*" she asked me. I was stumped. Ciccio noticed my hesitancy.

"*Oh, scusami* Mamma! Natalia *parle poco italiano. Lei è Francese!*"

"*Ah, vedo!*" she replied. She got it.

I wanted to attempt an answer, to tell her we met while walking down the street. So I tried this...

"*Io*, ah...*camminatore di strada...*"

Ciccio and his mom looked at me with mouths agape.

"Ah...you just told my mother you are a street walker," Ciccio said to me in French.

"Oh *non!*" I cried. "*Scusami! Io non sono...* I am not ..." I didn't know which language to use to explain myself.

The two of them burst out in laughter. Ciccio's mother produced a handkerchief from her sleeve to wipe away tears.

"Natalia, you made me *molto felice* today!" she chuckled. I was glad to make her happy. And relieved. "Please, sit while I *prendi la padella.*"

Ciccio and I sat down at the kitchen table while his mother went downstairs to fetch her baking tin.

"What is your first impression of my mother, Natalia?"

"She is a lovely woman," I replied in French. "Is she going somewhere special this afternoon? She seems to be dressed very fancily, and her hair and makeup are impeccable."

"*Non*, this is the way Mamma presents herself every day, even when she is engaged in housework. We used to have servants, but Mamma got rid of them because they could never do the chores to her satisfaction. 'Give me that broom and watch!' she would say, or, 'Step aside, and let me show you how to fold a napkin!'. Mamma prefers to do things herself, you see. If she was ever charged with assembling an army, I am afraid Mamma would end up the lone soldier on the hill."

"And she does all of this work in the house in her best clothes?"

"*Oui*. Inevitably, she will go out during the day. Mamma would never be caught looking like anything but the doctor's wife!"

Ciccio's mother came back up with the medium-sized baking tin. She stopped for 5 seconds at the top of the stairs to fix her hair. I stood up from the table.

"*Posso aiutare, signora?*" I said, asking if I could help.

"*Eh, ma no!* You are an *ospite* in our *casa*!" she said, indicating that I was their guest. "And please *mi chiamo* Cecilia!"

Cecilia went about collecting butter, eggs, milk, flour, and sugar while she asked me some questions through her interpreter, Ciccio.

"Natalia, *che ci fai a Firenze?*"

What was I doing in Florence? Hmm. "I am here to further my education. I hope to learn things that will help me in the future."

Ciccio told his mother that I was studying to become a doctor. She almost dropped the eggs on the floor.

"*Mi scusi? Un medico?*"

"*Sì*," Ciccio and I replied together.

"*Come può essere?*" She wondered how it could be! "*Sei una donna, non lo sei?*" Wasn't I a woman after all? I think she could see my discomfort with her question.

"In La-Nouvelle France, where I come from, women have equal opportunity to become whatever they choose," I said through Ciccio.

Cecilia paused, looked at Ciccio, and then smiled.

"*Questa giovane donna ha ambizioni di carriera! Mi piace!*" Even before Ciccio translated, I could tell she liked that I had career ambitions! She gave her son a wink.

Then she said through Ciccio that, yes, maybe I could give her a hand in the kitchen. I got up from the table and went to the counter where Cecilia had laid out all the measured ingredients. She then spoke to her son.

"Mamma asks that you combine the ingredients while she flours the baking pan," Ciccio translated.

"*Avec plaisir,*" I said, which got turned into *piacere mio* to indicate my pleasure in doing so.

I picked up the empty bowl in front of me and stirred together the flour, sugar, and what looked to be a teaspoon of baking soda with a large wooden spoon. I spied another empty bowl off to the side, picked it up, and cracked the eggs into it. After beating them with a fork, I mixed in the milk and the softened butter. Cecilia was busy with the pan, but I could feel her eyes on me the whole time.

As I carefully incorporated the wet mixture into a well I had made in the dry ingredients, she stopped my stirring hand, turned, and spoke pointedly to her son.

"*Dove hai scoperto questa donna?*" Was she asking where he found me?

"Mamma?" Ciccio asked.

"*Questa donna èdavvero incredibile!*" she exclaimed. Did she just say I was incredible? Tell me more!

And she did. Through Ciccio, she told me that only the cleverest of bakers would mix the dry and wet ingredients separately before adding them together. She had set up a test for me with the cake ingredients, and I had passed with *colori volanti*! She said I had learned my life-lessons well, and I was a credit to my mother and father. She also told me that the air of confidence I exuded was an outward display of my intelligence and personal dignity. And then she said something to Ciccio that he chose not to translate, and she followed up the statement with a winky face. It was hard not to catch that she thought I was *una bella cattura*.

"Francesco! *Potresti venire ad aiutarmi, per favore!*" a man's voice called out from the bottom of the stairs.

"It is my father," Ciccio said to me in French. "He requires my help. Excuse me, I shall only be a moment." He rose from the table and went downstairs, leaving the two of us women alone in the kitchen.

Cecilia moved the bowl of batter off to the side, dusted off her hands, and turned to me.

"*Caffè?*" she asked with a smile, tipping an imaginary cup toward her mouth.

"*Oh, sì, grazie!*" I replied with a confidently-aired, intelligent, and personally-dignified smile of my own.

While Ciccio was busy helping out his dad, Cecilia and I got acquainted over coffee. She spoke to me slowly out of kindness, and I replied slowly out of necessity. I continued to pick up Italian words and phrases, incorporating them into my growing vocabulary. This total immersion thing was working out well for me; sure I was struggling a bit in the *acque italiane*, but I was keeping my *testa* above the *superficie*!

Cecilia asked me about my studies. She asked how it felt to be a woman in the medical profession. She didn't know of even one female doctor in all of Florence! I didn't have to stretch things too far to answer that one, since women represented only one third of all doctors in my day. So I told her that while it felt strange at times to be in the minority, my professors did not show favour to anyone because of their gender. I used the French word *genre*, which Cecilia corrected to *genere* for me. She told me she was happy to hear this about my professors.

When Cecilia asked me where I was staying while in Florence, I was taken aback for a second. I hadn't prepared an answer for that one, and I felt dumb for not having thought that someone would ask me that! So I just did my best.

"I have room at Palazzo Medici."

"You are staying at the Palazzo Medici?" asked Cecilia. "How *eccellente*! Is it *bella*?"

"Oh, *bella, sì*," I replied. "My room nothing *speciale*, just a *tavolo* and two chairs. There is nice *pittura* on wall."

"What do you think of the Chapel of the Magi?"

"I no *visitato* the chapel."

"Oh my! You must!" Cecilia pointed to the ceiling. "It is *spettacolare!*"

"I must learn more of *Firenze*," I admitted.

"Then I will take you on a *giro*, soon!" she said. I was pretty sure that giro meant 'tour'. "It will allow me to *practica* my knowledge of post-Renaissance art with you!"

Well, that threw me off! I could have sworn we were in the Renaissance right now! I did have a lot to learn, all right.

We heard footsteps coming up the stairs and we both turned sideways in our chairs as Ciccio entered the kitchen.

"Father is attending to a very interesting case in his office," Ciccio said to his mother in Italian and then to me in French. "I was wondering if you would like to come down and meet him, Natalia, and also offer your opinion."

"I would be delighted to meet your father, Francesco, but I am certain that I could not offer anything of insight."

"That is not my opinion, after having seen you ply your trade this morning," he replied with a grin. "Come."

Ciccio took my hand and I rose from the table. Cecilia got up and went to the counter.

"I will finish the cake for our *festa* this evening," she said. "*Grazie* for the nice *chiacchierata*, Natalia."

"*Grazie mille!*" I blurted out.

"Ha! *Grazie mille*! Now that is *nuovo*!" Cecilia exclaimed. "I like that!" Then she whispered to her son.

"*Mi piace* her, too!"

Ciccio knocked on the door of the office, the first room on the right on the first floor.

"*Entrare, prego*," came a voice from inside. Ciccio opened the door, and I got my first look at a physician's office in Italy in 1647.

The room was small, not unlike most medical rooms in my day. There was a desk in the far-right corner along with two chairs - one for the desk, and one for the matronly older woman with a worried look on her face. There were two shelves above the desk that stored a small collection of books and jars of herbs. The simple examination table on the left side of the room was occupied by a young boy, lying with his shirt pulled up to expose his abdomen. A tall man in a black suit turned his attention to the two of us at the door. He had a full head of salt and pepper hair, a black moustache, and the kindest eyes I had yet seen in Florence.

"You must be Natalia," he said to me in French. "It is nice to meet you. I am Gregorio." He held out his hand and I extended mine, palm down. But instead of giving it a kiss, he clasped it, and gave it a regular-old handshake.

"You look surprised, Natalia," Ciccio said. "But Papà is the one who taught *me* how to speak French!"

"Ah, *oui*, I am surprised!" I replied, though it was the handshake that actually got me. "It is a pleasure to meet you, *dottóre*." I used the Italian honorific.

"My son tells me you are studying medicine in Scotland. Will you be completing your studies soon?"

"Oh, *non*, not for a few more years," I replied. A few more hundred years, to be precise.

"Well, this may be some good practice for you, Natalia," Dr. Gregorio said, turning to the patient. "This is Luca. He lives at the *Ospedale degli Innocenti*. And this is Maria, one of the nannies that look after the older children." Maria and I exchanged '*Ciao*'s. "Please examine the lad and give us your assessment."

I hesitated, but figured that I was under the supervision of two doctors, so I moved to the table.

"*Ciao*, Luca," I said to the boy in Italian. "My name is Natalia."

"*Ciao*," he replied sheepishly.

"Can you say to me where it, um…" I looked to Ciccio.

"*Fa male*," he said, helpfully.

"Can you say to me where it hurts, Luca?"

"Here, my *stomaco*," Luca replied, rubbing his tummy in a circle.

"I touch you there now. Is all right?" I asked. Luca nodded his head. I looked to the doctors in the room, and they nodded as well.

I placed my hands on Luca's abdomen and began to gently palpate. He was fine with the pressing until I got near his bellybutton, where he winced. I pressed again, this time a little lower and to the right, and quickly released the pressure. Another slight wince.

I brushed the hair from his forehead and took his temperature with my hand. Then I felt for the nodules in his neck and under his arms.

I turned to Maria and asked in Italian, "How Luca is eating?"

"Um…with a spoon?" she answered with a puzzled look. "Sometimes with a fork?"

And I was doing so well, too.

"Is he eating well?" Dr. Gregorio asked Maria, helping me out.

"*Sì, sì,*" Maria replied. "The boy eats *come un cavallo*!"

He was eating horse? Those poor orphanage kids! Ciccio took notice of me reining in my alarm.

"He doesn't eat the horse, Natalia…he only eats *like* one."

"Ah," I nodded with some embarrassment. I looked again to Maria, "No sickness? No, ah…" I turned my hand over three times in the air.

"*No,*" she answered. "He has not *vomito.*"

I turned to the doctors and gave my diagnosis in French. "His tender lower abdomen may indicate infection, but his temperature is normal, and his glands are not swollen. If he has been eating well up to this point in time, he may only have a stomach-ache, perhaps a slight blockage."

"And what would you prescribe, Natalia?" asked Dr. Gregorio.

Oh boy. How would I say 'an over-the-counter antacid' in the language of 1647? My mom used to give us ginger ale when we were small. No ginger ale here, I was sure of that, because my brother had a hand in inventing it over 125 years from now! I suggested the next best thing.

"Do you have any ginger root, doctor?" I asked.

"Indeed, I do." Dr. Gregorio reached for the shelf, picked up a jar, and produced a hunk of the root.

"*Bravo,* Natalia!" Ciccio exclaimed. "It is precisely what my father prescribed only minutes ago. See, Papà! Did I not tell you that she was wonderful!" Ciccio gave me a big smile. His dad did, too.

Dr. Gregorio handed the ginger root to Maria. "Make this into a strong tea and have the boy drink a large cup of it three times a day."

Maria rose up from her chair. Luca sat up on the table, pulled down his shirt, and jumped off like all was well again in his world. He led the way out of the office.

"If he gets any worse in the next few days, call on me at once," Dr. Gregorio said to Maria in a whispered tone, as he escorted the two to the front door. Ciccio and I followed a few steps behind.

"*Arrivederci!*" Dr. Gregorio called out as Maria and Luca made their way down the walkway.

"*Grazie, dottóre,*" Maria answered back.

"*Ciao, Dottóre Redi*!" Luca said with a wave as they turned onto the street.

"*Dottóre Redi?*" I exclaimed. Ciccio and Gregorio both turned around to look at one startled med student. "Your…your family name is *Redi*?"

"*Sì*," said the elder doctor. "I am Gregorio Redi."

"And you are?" I said to Ciccio in a shaky voice.

"Francesco Redi," he replied. Then he said, with a smile, "But I wish you would call me Ciccio!"

Suddenly, I saw a lot of dark, and I felt two arms catch hold of each of my own.

When I came to, Cecilia Redi was fanning my face with a kitchen towel and Dr. Gregorio Redi was cradling the back of my head in his hands. I was sitting one of the vestibule chairs, apparently waking up from a brief time-out with the rest of the world.

And there was Ciccio - Francesco Redi - caressing my hand.

"Natalia, are you all right?" he said in French. "You look to have seen a ghost!"

Not a ghost, Ciccio, no. I had seen a giant! A science giant! One the greatest scientists the world has ever known! And here he was, Francesco Redi, bent at the knee, showing concern, attending to my needs as any doctor would, and gazing at me adoringly with his big, blue puppy-dog eyes.

Uh oh.

"I…I am fine, Francesco, really. I was a little light-headed for a moment." I stood up, albeit groggily, and absently brushed myself off.

"Have you eaten today?" Cecilia asked me. "Maybe you need to eat something!"

"*No, no,* we have nice lunch," I answered back in Italian. "I must go now."

"Go?" Ciccio said with alarm, in French. "You must not go, Natalia! We have only…we have just…"

"And I am sure that we will see each other again soon," I said, shaking his hand. "But I must get back to Scot...er, the *scòtta* place..."

"You need to go to the *hot* place?" asked Ciccio, looking confused.

"Um, *oui*! My room at the Medici palace...it is so hot there! So very hot! Oh my! Phew!" I was stammering now, fanning myself with my hand.

"When can I see you again, Natalia?" Ciccio implored.

"Natalia, you must come with us to the birthday party tonight!" said the elder Dr. Redi. "Ciccio could escort you!"

"A party?" I asked.

"For our friend, Evangelista!" said Cecilia, not understanding the French, but getting the party-talk.

"For *your* friend, Evangelista, Mamma," said Ciccio. "I hardly know the man." He turned to me, looking desperate. "Natalia, please save me from this impending night of boredom!"

"There is a young woman that works for Evangelista who should be there this evening," said Dr. Redi. "She is a lovely person, and she even speaks French!"

"Oh yes, she is lovely," said Ciccio.

"You must come, Natalia!" said Cecilia.

I stood there looking at the three of them. They were just so nice. How could I say no, thank you. Or *non, merci*. Or *no, grazie*. So I just said...

"I will, *merci...grazie*," in both romance languages.

"Wonderful!" Ciccio exclaimed, "I will collect you at..."

"*Non, non*, it would be fine if I met you here!" I interrupted. "At what time?"

"Let us say 5 o'clock," said Dr. Redi. "That will give Ciccio just enough time to make himself presentable." He gave his son a slap on the back.

"Only two hours to make ready?" Ciccio said, looking at his dad. "I suppose you will be staying home, then, Papà!" He returned the slap.

"Eh! *Basta*, you two!" Cecilia announced, smacking both of her boys on the hands.

I made my way down the path and turned to say goodbye. We all said our *ciaos*, and I carried on down the street. When I looked back after half a block, there was Ciccio, waving a handkerchief and blowing kisses in the air.

Francesco Redi. No wonder he became so great in so many areas of life. This man was *appassionato*!

Chapter 13

After changing back into her regular clothes, Natalie was poised to leave the Byre Theatre from the main entrance when she felt a notification vibration in her jacket pocket. Stopping dead in her tracks, she quickly took the phone out and clicked on the video chat. Then Natalie got outside in a hurry; it was best if there were less people around to hear the dressing-down she had coming.

Her brother's image popped up on the screen.

"You can't do that! Completely unacceptable!" Connor's angry look made Natalie swallow hard.

"I know, I know. I'm sorry!" she replied, leaning back on the stone feature of the building.

"You know the rules! I was about to have a coronary!"

"Okay, okay, you don't have to shout. I get the message!"

"Well, let me hammer it home again, then. If you don't text back within 5 seconds after your last message, I'm thinking you're never coming back!"

"I know, I just…"

"You have to text back as soon as you come through The Portal!"

"I'll make sure I…"

"Did I ever do that to you after TTing? Huh?"

"No, you never…"

"Promise me that in the future, when you get back from the past, you'll let me know right away!"

"I promise, I promise!" Natalie cowered. "I've learned my lesson!"

"Good," Connor said with a sharp nod of his head. Then his facial features abruptly relaxed. "There. What'd you think?"

"That was a perfect impersonation of Mom," Natalie replied with some relief. "Thanks, bro. I needed that."

"Have you tried contacting our two bushwhacking parents lately?"

"All the time. Still nothing."

"Me, too. Nothing."

"I just can't believe there's no cell coverage anywhere in that forest, Connor. It's so not-this-century."

"Well, they warned us, didn't they. Anyway, if you really wanted to, you could wait a whole week before TTing again. Mom'll be back by then, and you can have the real-deal yell at you when you mess up."

"It's a thought, but I'm not sure I can resist the temptation to go back soon."

"Did you and Cheech have a nice lunch?"

"*Francesco* and I had a nice time, yes," Natalie answered curtly. "And his mom and dad are delightful. I'm going to tell you all about them tonight, because I've got to get to the Med School building now. I'm catching the bus to Victoria Hospital in Kirkcaldy!"

"Oh yeah, right. You're assisting in surgery. Are you nervous?"

"A bit. But I'm more excited. I think this is going to help me get my stress level down when I'm in the OR in the future."

"Well, that'll make one of us," Connor said with an accompanying yawn. "You have a good rest of your day. Mine hasn't started yet...I'm going back to sleep."

"Okay, you have a nice Friday at school. I'll see you tonight. And Connor?..."

"Yeah?"

"Next time, remember: Mom's head nod is a lot sharper. And she would have pointed at me, too."

"Good to know. But there won't be a next time, Nat!" Connor snapped his neck forward, poked his index finger at the camera, and signed off from Western Canada.

The hour and a quarter bus ride to Victoria Hospital was uneventful, save for the six-minute sheep-crossing delay at Cupar Muir. Natalie was a bit worried that she would be late in meeting Dr. Blanco, but her little-old lady seatmate said it was *mutton* to worry about. Natalie smiled and said she was glad this delay wasn't *un-ewe-sual*. After the little-old lady noted that Natalie had grinned *sheepishly*, the two women chatted the rest of the way like they had known each other for years. When the bus arrived at her stop, Natalie said goodbye to her travelling companion, wishing her a Fleece Navidad if she didn't see her again before Christmas. The little-old lady smirked and said to Natalie, 'Nice! I've never *herd* that one before.'

Natalie met Dr. Blanco in the surgeon's office down the hallway from the OR at ten minutes to one. The greeting was short and sweet; Dr. Blanco ushered his medical student to the surgical scrub area where they both began preparations for an emergency case that was brought to Victoria Hospital earlier that morning.

"Our patient is a fourteen-year-old girl," Dr. Blanco explained as the two of them began their hand and arm washing at adjoining scrub sinks. "She was complaining of a sore tummy for the past two days, and it wasn't getting any better. She began vomiting this morning, so her parents brought her to A&E. After taking an image, Dr. Siray found an enlarged appendix that appears to have burst. We're going to be doing an open appendectomy, because we're past the point of success with the laparoscope. Fingernails."

Natalie emulated her mentor, picking up the small scrub brush and getting to work on sterilizing her fingertips.

"What will I be doing to assist you, Dr. Blanco?" Natalie asked.

"As my student, you can be of service in retraction and suction. If you need assistance with any of the directions I give, the OR nurse will be right there to help you. Forearms now for three minutes." The surgeons lathered-up down to their elbows.

"Quite a few firsts today, Natalie," Dr. Blanco mused. "Your first surgery, and my first female appendectomy!"

"Really?"

"Yes. The incidence rate for appendicitis is 50% greater for males. And an appendectomy is three times less likely to be of the perforated kind in our patient's age group, too. So today's young lady is a bit of a *rara avis*."

"She's a rare bird, you say?" Natalie replied, looking over to Dr. Blanco.

"You passed the test, my student! How do you come by knowing this term?"

"I took Latin Studies in Grade 9. But I learned that one from my dad. He's a New York Times Crossword junky."

"More evidence that the Campbells are my people! Your father and I have similar passions. Don't tell me he's a doctor, too."

"He's an engineer for Dupont."

"Oh, well. You know what the old Meatloaf songs says?"

Natalie shrugged her shoulders as she used her elbows to turn off the sink taps.

"Two out of three ain't bad! Come on, Natalie! That's a classic!"

"I would never have thought the words meatloaf and classic could appear in the same sentence, sir."

"Well, let's hope you do better in the OR today!"

Natalie flushed and felt a rush of nerves at her mentor's comment. Dr. Blanco observed Natalie's reaction and quickly clarified his statement.

"No, no, Natalie, sorry! I meant, let's hope you do better with identifying the songs I've chosen for the surgery today!"

"Phew," Natalie sighed in relief. "I thought there must be some misunderstanding!"

"There Must be Some Misunderstanding!" the professor exclaimed. "Genesis! Nice one!"

Natalie gave the uneasy smile of someone not in the loop. Genesis? She was pretty sure she wasn't quoting scripture, there.

When they entered the operating room, gloved hands held up in the air, Dr. Blanco and Natalie were greeted by the nurse and anesthesiologist.

"This is Dr. Fyvie, Natalie. He'll be passing gas today."

"That's an oldie but a baddie, Dr. Blanco," Dr. Fyvie replied. He offered his hand in greeting to Natalie. She didn't take the bait.

"You wouldn't believe how many sterilized med students I trick with that one, Natalie," smiled Dr. Fyvie behind his surgical mask. "You've passed the first test!"

"I'm Camille, Natalie. Nice to meet you," said the nurse. "Is this your first surgery?"

"Yes, it is," Natalie replied, in what she thought was a calm voice.

"Well, just take a deep breath and know you're in good hands, despite Dr. Fyvie's presence," Camille said with a sly grin. "Now if you feel out of sorts at any point, there's the chair. I'll just step right in."

"Shall we proceed, then?" said Dr. Blanco, moving to the operating table. "Dr. Fyvie, you get to sit at the head of the table today."

"Thank you, doctor," the anesthesiologist said with a smile.

"And you must be Montana," Dr. Blanco said, turning to his patient. "That's a lovely name. Are you from America?"

"No," said Montana. "I was born in Aberdeen. My father loves western movies."

"Well, just be glad he wasn't into Star Trek, or you could have been named Rigel 7." Dr. Blanco gave his patient a wink.

"Ooh, I like that one, " Montana replied. "Rigel 7. I might change my name after this."

"You can't," replied her surgeon. "Everyone on Rigel 7 has green skin." He laid his hand on his patient. "Now, I want you to know that this surgery will go just fine. We've done this before. Aside from your lovely name, there's nothing special here."

"I'm here, though," said Camille.

"Yes, apart from Nurse Camille, nothing special," Dr. Blanco grinned. "Now, you're going to start feeling drowsy, Montana. I'd like you to start counting backwards from 100. Ready?" Dr. Blanco gave a nod. Dr. Fyvie started the IV. Nurse Camille pressed the start button on the remote. "Go."

As the song The Lion Sleeps Tonight quietly started on the overhead speaker, Montana began the countdown. She didn't make it past 93.

After the iodine-laden antiseptic was applied to the patient's abdomen, Dr. Blanco gave out his next order.

"Scalpel." Nurse Camille provided the instrument.

"Wait for it..." said Dr. Blanco. In three more seconds, the next song began on his personal playlist. "Rod Stewart, by way of Cat Stevens." Dr. Fyvie nodded his head in approval.

Dr. Blanco turned to Natalie, who was ready with the retractor. "I'm performing a Lanz incision, since her appendix is over here." The surgeon traced a shallow diagonal with his finger to the right of Montana's bellybutton. "It's a shifty little beast, the appendix. If it were over here I would do a Rutherford/Morison, and if it were here, I'd do a grid iron incision." Dr. Blanco traced out the different diagonals. Natalie nodded her head.

"Ready, all?" asked the lead surgeon. "Let's begin."

Dr. Blanco placed the scalpel down at the precise moment Rod began singing the chorus to The First Cut Is the Deepest.

After incision and retraction, the lead surgeon carefully teased a red, swollen, finger-length body from the large intestine to the song Come to Me, by Otis Redding. He then isolated the infected protuberance to the song All By Myself, by Eric Carmen. The base of the appendix was then tied off with a suture to prevent rupture, timed perfectly to the jaunty tune, Tie a Yellow Ribbon, by Tony Orlando and Dawn. With the appendix delicately supported, the surgeon snipped the angry-looking accessory to the song Scissor Man, by XTC, and tossed it into a nearby tray to Throw It Away, by Joe Jackson. A general inspection of the abdominal cavity was performed to the oldie Searchin', by the Coasters. Once the surgeon was satisfied that the area was clean, he began suturing the incision to the song Closing Time, by Leonard Cohen. Just a Song Before I Go, by Crosby, Stills, and Nash brought the surgery to a harmonious conclusion.

Throughout the entire hourlong procedure, Natalie looked every bit the part of an assistant surgeon: she was attentive to the lead surgeon's need for greater retraction when surveying the abdomen, and her suctioning of the surgical area was only once assisted by Nurse Camille, when she pointed to a tiny pocket of fluid that required attention. Natalie felt particularly good about being thanked by Dr. Blanco when she asked if he would like the overhead light adjusted, which he did.

After the patient was cleaned up and sent to Recovery, Dr. Fyvie gave Natalie a pat on the shoulder.

"Well, if that was your first time, it surely didn't show," he said. "Nice job."

"Thank you, doctor," she answered. "And thank you both for helping me feel comfortable today." Dr. Fyvie and Nurse Camille both gave her a smile and nod as they all exited the operating room.

In the scrub area, Dr. Blanco removed his cap, mask, and gloves, and disposed of them in a bin. Natalie followed suit. Then Dr. Blanco invited his student to have a seat on the bench across from him.

"Today's objectives," he said. "One: to alleviate young Montana's pain through the successful removal her appendix. Check. Two: to alleviate Natalie Campbell's discomfort in stressful surgical situations." Dr. Blanco made a finger swoosh in the air. "Check!"

"I did feel pretty good," Natalie answered. "I was sweating though."

"So was I! That nervous feeling doesn't go away over time; you just learn how to channel it to your advantage."

"How's that done?"

"By realizing that you can parlay that excitation to heightening your sense of awareness! I take the jittery feelings I get and direct them to an alert status, to help turn hesitancy to expectancy. I convert nerves into *nerve*. Get it?"

"I like that," said Natalie. "Convert nerves to nerve."

"But none of that is going to work unless you also know what you're doing beforehand, naturally. And here's what I noticed in the OR..." Dr. Blanco leaned forward. "You applied your knowledge and previous experience in the surgery today, and this afforded you the ability to stay one step ahead in your tasks. You proved to be a competent and effective assistant. Good show, Natalie."

Natalie leaned back against the wall and let out a sigh.

"Thank you, Dr. Blanco. Now, how about listing off areas for improvement?"

"Well, you can start by showing a bit more appreciation for the lead surgeon's appendectomy playlist. You could have at least hummed a few bars to amuse me."

"I didn't know one of those songs!"

"What? They're classics!"

"If you mean 'classic' as in 'old', then yes, those songs are as classic as dirt."

"Humph," Dr. Blanco protested. "Shall we see how our patient is fairing in the Recovery Room?"

"Only if I get to choose the music," Natalie replied as the two of them rose from their seats.

"Oh, no. I don't think I could handle all the atonal droning and thumping from your generation's idea of music!" Dr. Blanco opened the door to the hallway for Natalie.

"Actually, I was thinking we could play Getting Better, by The Beatles."

"Ms Campbell, there's hope for you yet!" Dr. Blanco said as the scrub area door closed behind them.

"And you didn't feel sick? Like you wanted to puke?" Connor asked his sister from the phone.

"Nope."

"If I was there, there would have been two unconscious people in the OR, because I would have fainted! Bam! Right on the floor!"

"That would make your prefrontal leukotomy easier to do, brother dear."

"What's that?" asked Connor, unaware of the medical term for lobotomy.

"Nothing for you to worry about, actually. There wouldn't be much to remove."

It was 9:30 pm that evening in St Andrews. Natalie had just finished a study session at the JF Allen Library and was preparing for her four-minute walk back to Agnes Blackadder Hall where the remains of a munchy box awaited in her dorm fridge. But she thought a quick convo with her brother was needed first, so she called him up. She caught Connor at the end of his school day - early-dismissal Friday - just before he was going to drive himself, Angus, Graeme, and Chris to the Fry Guy food truck in the mall parking lot to split two extra-large DIY poutines. Extra jalapeños.

"So, what have you found out about your new boyfriend?" Connor asked his sister.

Natalie gave her brother an air cuff on his screen head and proceeded to tell him all about her afternoon in Florence. Connor was pleased to hear that his sister had made some new friends in Dr. Gregorio and his wife, Cecilia. He shared her excitement in learning that Ciccio was, in fact, Francesco Redi: doctor, experimental biologist, parasitologist, and budding-poet extraordinaire. Connor was also sympathetic to Natalie's woozy reaction when she discovered their family identity: he had a couple of collapsy moments himself, in France, many years in the future. Or was it the past? These details can become sketchy to even the most experienced TTer.

Natalie then told Connor about being invited to a birthday party later that evening Florence-time, which she planned on attending tomorrow after a good night's sleep, Scotland-time.

"Who's the birthday boy or girl?" asked Connor.

"His name is Evangelista. Apparently, he's a friend to Gregorio and Cecilia. Francesco's not too keen on going, so he wants me to tag along."

"You mean he wants to show off his new girlfriend."

"Do you want another pixel smack? Anyway, I want to ask you for some advice."

"It's about *time*," Connor said with a smile, revelling in his punny-ness. Natalie gave a flinch.

"I'm curious about who Evangelista is," she explained. "I think I want to look up some info about him. And about Francesco Redi, too. But I remember how you were careful not to learn too much about the people of the past. You wanted to learn about them for yourself, to make your own impressions, and all that."

"You want to know if I'd do it that way again?" asked Connor.

"Yes."

"I would," her brother said matter of factly. "I toyed with the idea of doing an online search of everyone I met in France in 1771, but I'm glad I didn't. I honestly believe that my experience ended up being better off for not researching too much. It made the TT less scripted, if you know what I mean. I was free to make decisions and not worry about how those decisions would affect everyone else's future."

"Because of the *Butterfly Noneffect*?"

"The *Butterfly Noneffect*, right," said Connor. "It was a relief to learn that you'd have to do something really drastic to change the eventual outcome of any scenario in the past. Altering the future takes real effort! Mr. Mason-Ivy explained that the Noneffect was proved using computer models and qubits. I could explain it better with a diagram, if you'd like."

"I'll take your word for it," said Natalie, the *medical* science major. "So, you're saying when I go back to Florence, I shouldn't be afraid to improvise?"

"The more unrehearsed, the better, sis!" Then Connor's face became serious. "It took me quite a while to emotionally recover after I found out about Antoine's execution in my textbook. I tried not to let it bother me when I got back to Paris, but it was hard working side by side with him and knowing what was going to happen in his future. Believe me, Nat, you'd rather not know certain things, if you can help it."

"I get it," Natalie said soberly. "Thanks, Connor. That helps a lot."

"You're welcome," her brother replied. His face perked up as he said, "All right! Now, what are you going to wear to the party? Something fancy?"

"I was thinking I'd keep it simple, but accessorize."

"Chicky-O is going to go from feeling sick about this shindig to feeling sickly." Natalie stared blankly at the screen. "As in, sickly sweet." Still no sisterly response. "As in, 'Hey, everyone! Check out my arm candy tonight!'

Natalie answered her brother with a cold stare and a click of the power button.

When Natalie opened the door to her dorm room, she was startled to find Holly, Mark, and Marianna all sitting at the kitchen table, eyes fixed on a laptop screen.

"There you are!" Mark exclaimed in his orange aloha shirt covered in green palm trees and pink flamingos. "Another ten minutes and you were going to be in charge of music as well as bringing snacks!"

"Planning our Monday outing to Camusdarach Beach are you?" Natalie replied, closing the door behind her and dropping her book bag to the floor.

"*Sì*. But don't'-a worry, I'll make-a the playlist!" said Marianna.

"Just as long as it's light on the show tunes, girl," said Holly. "I'm not driving four hours with the Phantom of the Opera."

"Oh, is Filip going to wear his black cape again?" asked Natalie with a smirk.

"I saw that show years ago," Mark interjected. "Ugh. At the end of the first act, when the chandelier is supposed to crash, it came down at half speed and stopped a foot from the floor! As it's hovering there, you hear the pre-recorded sound of breaking glass, and then the curtain comes down. Ruined the whole show for me."

"A real *let down*, I take it?" Natalie smiled.

"Literally," Mark replied with a point of his finger.

"Okay, no Phantom, I-a promise," said Marianna. "Did-a Filip text-a you back?"

Holly checked her phone. "Yep. He says the hippy van is all gassed up and ready for Monday! He wants to know if Mark is going to bring his diving suit?"

"He is," replied Mark.

Holly sent the text reply. Seven seconds later she said, "Filip says he's going to bring his HPE, then."

"What's that?" asked Mark.

Holly texted the query. Then she read, "Hypothermia prevention equipment! He says you're nuts to swim on the west coast in October."

"Says the guy who frolicked in the North Sea in the dead of winter," Mark scoffed. "I'll be just fine, thank you. Tell him I'll spell him off as driver at the half-way mark, Holly."

"Okay, but I'm calling shotgun right now," she replied while texting.

"I am not-a very comfortable with this," said Marianna with concern in her voice. "What-a you going to shoot, Holly? I no like-a you bring a *pistola* on our trip!"

"What are we supposed to eat then?" Holly teased. "I was going to hunt down some fresh lamb burgers for us!"

Holly received a smack from Mark and Natalie, one on each shoulder.

"Calling shotgun means she wants the front seat," said Natalie to her roommate. Marianna took a turn smacking Holly. "Anyway, I think I should ride in the front with Filip. I'm going to bring the movie *Local Hero* for the three of you to watch. Filip and I have seen it, so we're in the front. You three sit in the back and watch it for the first half of the trip. Then we can enjoy Marianna's playlist for the second half of the journey!"

"Sounds like a well-thought-out proposal, Natalie," lauded Mark. "You'd make a fine holiday agent if it weren't for this distracting medical-school thing you're doing."

"Oh, all I ever need is a second to enact a travel plan," Natalie replied, amusing herself to no end.

Chapter 14

Ciccio stood at the door with his mouth hanging open. After five whole seconds of awkwardness, I started the conversation.

"Well, are you going to ask me in?"

He snapped out of his reverie, backed up two steps, and invited me to enter the Redi house with a sweeping arm gesture.

"I…I mean, you…" he stammered. Then he actually cuffed his face before saying, in French, "You look wonderful, Natalia!"

"Why, *merci*," I said sheepishly, trying unsuccessfully to suppress my blushing cheeks.

"And that dress! It is the epitome of sartorial splendour!" Ciccio kissed my hand. "It is so very complimentary to your striking beauty!"

"What, this old thing?" I said, in an embarrassing display of southern-belle coquettishness. "I just threw on the first thing I could find!"

…That would actually say 1647! I spent a good part of Saturday morning back home raking through the charity shop on Bell Street. Ava, my fashion consultant, dismissed any thought of accessorizing my previous purchase when I told her I was going to a party. She made me try on three outfits. They all looked very nice, but they didn't quite fit the ultra-premodern spirit. From my indecisiveness and declinations, Ava concluded that the dress I was looking for did not exist. But then she had a brainwave, and dug up a box from the backroom that contained costumes donated by the Byre Theatre. The very first thing she pulled out was a full-length pink dress with a black-accented corset fastened with six silver buttons. A lacey, ecru shawl was gathered in the middle with a big, black bow in the shape of a rose. It fit perfectly, and Ava gave out a sigh of relief.

After a brief curling-iron session to give me a few ringlets, and just the slightest bit of 17th century-type make-up, I was ready to go out on la *città*!

"And *you* look very nice as well, Francesco," I complimented. And he really did too, in his royal-blue suit and tan vest, with white knee socks and ascot. I was glad that Ava insisted on having me fancy it up a bit.

"Gregorio and Cecilia will be down momentarily," Ciccio said, motioning to the stairs. "The *vetturino* is coming for us in no time!"

I hadn't the slightest clue as to what a *vetturino* was, but I gave a head nod and eyebrow lift to show how impressed I was.

"Please come with me, Natalia. I would like to show you something!"

Ciccio took my hand and led me down the hallway, past the doctor's offices to the last room on the right. He stopped at the closed door.

"Now, what do you think is hiding in this room?" he asked.

"I really couldn't say," I replied.

"Well, guess!"

"*Non*, I really don't…"

"Of course you will never be right! But guess anyway!"

I decided to take a shot at it. "Could it be a room of specimens that you have collected since you were a child?"

Ciccio's face drooped in disappointment. He opened the door.

"Behold," he said unexcitedly, "my Room of Specimens."

The 4x4m room was encompassed by shelving that contained too many jars of various sizes to count. They were filled with all sorts of invertebrate creatures, all floating inanimately in their preserving solution – ethanol, by the smell of it. A small desk under the window was cluttered with papers, an open notebook at the ready. There were butterflies and beetles stuck on pins that were stuck in wooden blocks; there were dried out, dissected amphibians displaying their innards to the world; and there was a glass terrarium with a wooden lid at the very back that contained a rather large snake. It showed no concern over our presence in the room.

"That is Angelo the Asp," Ciccio pointed, noting my interest. And I was interested; it was a menagerie that rivalled Mr. Mason-Ivy's bio lab for its dedication to studying life. Well, dead life, anyway.

"Is Angelo poisonous?" I asked.

"Very. And he is also extremely uninterested in wine."

"Excuse me?"

"He will not drink Chianti, Barolo, or even try a three-year-old Barbaresco! He is a very unrefined reptile, do you not think?"

"Why would you give him wine to drink?" I asked with an appalled tone that Ciccio picked up on.

"To disprove the outrageous belief that vipers drink wine! Have you not heard this myth before?"

"I cannot say that I have. What is the basis of this belief?"

"I am not certain myself," Ciccio said, shaking his head. He walked over to the terrarium and gave Angelo a nose-scratch from this side of the glass. "It may be based in simple folklore. It may be that someone once saw a snake moving curiously near some spilled juice and made a sorry assumption. Perhaps a careless fellow saw the statue of the Greek god of wine, Dionysus, holding a serpent and put the two of them together as winebibbers!"

"Perhaps a slithering snake reminded someone of a drunkard swaying back and forth down the road?"

"Ha! I have never thought of that!" Ciccio exclaimed. "A brilliant deduction, Natalia! Snakes do not actually slither, they stagger from drunkenness!" Ciccio turned from the terrarium toward me. "In any case, it is a silly notion that must be dispelled if we are to become a more rational and enlightened society. Do you not think so?"

"I certainly do!" I replied, encouraging the emergence of the Age of Enlightenment.

"I hope to make my contribution to this growing scientific community, Natalia. I shall be registered at the *Collegio Medico* soon, and this may lead to a job as physician in the Medici Court. If that happens, I may be able to position myself as a researcher in the role of apothecary."

"Your dream is to do research?"

"*Oui*, that is my dream! To be free to investigate the secrets of the universe, to uncover the marvels of creation! And, of course, be paid handsomely for the pleasure of doing so!"

"One has to eat," I smiled. "I assume Angelo does, as well?"

"He had a mouse only yesterday, so he is quite content. He has not become so angered at his feeding schedule that he has shattered his glass enclosure and escaped." Ciccio pointed to the ceiling and exclaimed, "Another myth defeated!"

So, people in the 17th century think snakes drink wine and shatter glass, do they? Okie-dokie. Anything else, I wonder?

"I am currently studying the venom of this viper," Ciccio added. "I do not think it is poisonous if swallowed, but only if it is injected from the fangs."

"How will you test your hypothesis?" I said, not thinking.

"Hypothesis! Very good, Natalia!" Ciccio gave me an impressed look. "You are a disciple of Francis Bacon, I take it?"

"Bacon...*oui*," I stammered, getting ready to cook something up.

Just then a voice came from up the stairs, "Francesco? *Sei pronto per andare?*" It was Mrs. Redi, asking if we were ready to go. Thanks for saving my bacon, Cecilia!

"*Sì, mamma!*" Ciccio shouted in reply. "*Un momento!*"

Ciccio rolled up his sleeve and approached the terrarium.

"What are you doing?" I asked in a startled tone.

"Showing you how I will test my hypothesis," he answered, sliding off the wooden lid and raising his arm.

"Ciccio!" I shouted with panic.

"Ha! I knew it!" He withdrew his arm, replaced the lid, and laughed out loud. "I knew I could get you to call me Ciccio!"

"That was not funny!" I scolded.

"I am sorry, Natalia. Forgive me." He walked over and held out his bare arm to me. "Go ahead. I deserve it."

I gave him a good smack. Then we made our way to the front door.

Signor Esposito was the name of our *vetturino*. Our horse and buggy driver! He picked us up at the front door, helped me and Cecilia into the open-air carriage, and gave the men a curt bow before climbing into the driver's seat. With a 'click-click' we were off and riding in style down the surprisingly smooth cobblestone streets of Florence.

"You look lovely," Cecilia said as we turned onto the Via Roma, just past the Duomo.

"*Grazie, mamma!*" Ciccio answered with a smile, which got him a swat from his mother. He was balancing a cake tin on his lap that was covered with a cloth - Cecilia's contribution to the festivities this evening.

"*Grazie,*" I replied. Then, in Italian, I tried, "You look very lovely as well!" And she really did: her white dress with four white bows in the middle was stunning. Her white hat fanned out like an aura around her head, and was simply spectacular.

"Ahem," coughed Dr. Redi, resplendent in his red tailcoat and black vest.

"As do you, Dr. Redi," I added. Gregorio gave me a wink in return.

As we passed the Palazzo Vecchio, I took notice of the Medici coat of arms that was hanging over the door on one of the nearby buildings. My look of curiosity was observed by Dr. Redi.

"Do you wonder what the five red balls on the yellow shield represent, Natalia?" he asked in French.

"I was just about to ask," I replied.

"As all visitors do, eventually," Dr. Redi chuckled. "They are oranges! Two-hundred years ago, this fruit was exotic and very expensive. Not like today, where they are ubiquitous." Dr. Redi used the French word *omniprésente* for 'everywhere at once'.

"Why, they are so cheap today, you could prescribe them for *scorbuto!*" Ciccio said, giving me a wink. I gave him a wry smile in return.

"The Medici placed oranges on their coat of arms to signify their prosperity and influence," Dr. Redi explained.

"I suspect that five oranges told you how much *more* prosperous and influential they were than the average noble," I commented.

"Quite so!" replied Dr. Redi. "And today, our Grand Duke of Tuscany, Ferdinando the Second, could put ten oranges on the shield and it would not be an exaggeration!"

"They are filthy rich," Ciccio noted. "But to explain the oranges on the coat of arms, I prefer the old legend of Giovanni de Bicci de' Medici diving into the Arno to save a little boy from drowning. It is more romantic, do you not think, Natalia?" He said the word 'romantic' in a lovey-dovey sort of way.

"But that does not explain the oranges," I responded in a coolly-no-fooly sort of way.

"The boy's mamma gave Giovanni a bag of oranges as a reward!" Ciccio exclaimed.

"Giovanni was a champion of the people!" Cecilia said to me in Italian. "A great man! Not like Ferdinando today, who impoverished us with his *guerrafondaio*!" Ciccio translated *guerrafondaio* to warmongering for me.

"Oh, Cecilia, that is in the past!" said Dr. Redi to his wife.

"*Sì, mamma*. Ferdinando is a beloved ruler!"

"The two of you only like him because he is a man of science, like yourselves!" Cecilia said, irritated. She looked at me and said, "They all stick together, you know?"

I nodded. We really do stick together, us science types.

The hustle and bustle of the city from this afternoon was now replaced by an easy calm in the early evening hour. The sun was still high enough in the sky to provide warmth, but low enough to be blinding when looking off to the right. From my south-facing seat I could see we were approaching a bridge over a pretty wide river. Foot traffic was picking up again, and I could hear music in the offing.

"This is the Arno River," said Ciccio. "We are crossing it on the Ponte Vecchio."

The bridge – about as long as a football field - was busy with merchants selling their wares to people on their way home from work. There were some artists set up along the guardrail, painting the other bridges that were in view off to the west. A violinist and a flutist were serenading the passers-by with a spritely tune. The violinist looked a bit like my friend, Filip, if Filip wore a tricorne hat with feathers sticking out and up, completely at random. Good old Filip wouldn't be averse to sporting one of those at the pub next week, I'm sure! Dr. Redi tossed a coin to the musicians, and the flutist caught it with his right hand while still playing with his left. Cecilia gestured for me to turn around in my seat. When I did so, I got a beautiful view of the city skyline, with its church domes and roof spires. The Gothic-style architecture of the buildings - all pointed arches, stained glass, and stone carving – was a feast for the eyes. No cell towers, no streetlights, and no honking cars; just bell towers, sunlight, and the whinny of our carriage horse as it negotiated its way through the foot traffic of rush hour in Florence.

Once we crossed the bridge, we travelled a short distance before turning right onto the Via dello Sprone. In another block, our carriage stopped at a flat-roofed, two-story stone building, accented with a white plaster exterior. Signor Esposito assisted Cecilia and me from the carriage to the curb, since we were seated closest to the door. Dr. Redi paid the *vetturino* and arranged a return trip for later in the evening.

"*Grazie, signoro!*" I said to Signor Esposito, as he climbed back into the driver's seat.

"Call me, Tonio!" he replied. He clicked the horse into action, and called back as he carried on down the street, "It is my goal to serve you!"

The four of us made our way up the path and Ciccio knocked on the ornate wooden door at the entrance. After a second knock, the door was opened by a young man – mid-twenties, probably - dressed in a black suit with a white, collarless shirt. He had long, black hair that looked to be all his own.

"Well, well! The Redi's have *arrivato* at last!" he announced.

"Vincenzo! So good to see you, *mio ragazzo!*" Dr. Redi exclaimed to 'his boy'.

Then the kissing started in the vestibule. One on each cheek from Vincenzo for Gregorio and Cecilia. Ciccio got some of that, too, plus a hug that sandwiched the cake tin, and then a handshake.

"It is so good to see you, *amico mio!*" Vincenzo said in a raised tone. The party noise leaking from the adjoining room was approaching 'kitchen blender level' on the decibel scale. Vincenzo then turned to me.

"And who is this *creatura incantevole?*" he asked with surprise.

I was being called some kind of creature. I couldn't quite tell from his expression whether it was an enchanting or revolting one.

"*Mi scusi*," said Ciccio. "Master Mathematician Vincenzo Viviani, this is Natalia. Natalia, ah…" Ciccio was searching for a surname that I had never offered in Italy before.

"Campbell," I answered, shaking Vincenzo's hand. "Natalia Campbell."

"Natalia is from La-Nouvelle France!" Ciccio explained. "She speaks French, and is learning *italiano* better with each passing minute!"

Vincenzo turned the handshake into a hand-kiss, and didn't let go as he said, "*Campo Bella* would be your name in *italiano*, Natalia. It means 'beautiful land'. *Sì, sì*, you are certainly from a beautiful land, Natalia Campo Bella!" He kissed my hand again. Apparently Vincenzo was enchanted and not revolted. Ciccio, however, was not amused.

"Take that," Ciccio said, as he stuck the cake tin into Vincenzo's midsection, "to the kitchen, *amico mio*! So my mother's cake can be served to your guests. Guests that we should all go and meet this very instant."

Vincenzo Viviani took the tin with a smile and a bow, and excused himself. The four of us entered the spacious, exquisitely decorated, living room on the left. There must have been at least thirty people already present. The guests were all dressed beautifully, smiling broadly, and talking loudly. Servers in crisp, white shirts were making sure that the partygoers had food and drink to keep the spirits high.

"I am sorry about Vincenzo!" Ciccio said to me in a loud French whisper. "He can be so forward at times!"

Now that's the *pentola* calling the kettle *nero*.

Gregorio led the way to the centre of the room where a group of men were chatting. Cecilia made a beeline for a group of women conversing near the window. When we reached the men, Dr. Redi was exuberantly greeted by the one with stooped posture, black shoulder-length hair, and just about the coolest upturned moustache and pencil-thin goatee in all of 17th century Florence.

After their embrace, Gregorio turned to me and said, "Natalia, I would like to introduce you to a dear friend of mine. The man we are celebrating this evening!" The man turned and gave me a cordial smile.

"This is Evangelista," said Dr. Redi. "Evangelista Torricelli."

Chapter 15

Torricelli! The scientist who discovered pressure! Well, he didn't *discover* pressure, of course, but he did figure out how to describe and quantify it. And here he was, the man that Dr. Raven said was one of the greatest scientists of the 17th century, taking my hand and giving it a gentle squeeze. Like any Man of Pressure would, naturally.

"*Come va*, Natalia?" asked Mr. Torricelli.

"Please tell Signor Torricelli that I am truly honoured to meet him," I said to Ciccio in French. He conveyed the greeting to Torricelli. Two older men in the conversation circle looked rather impressed by my greeting.

"*Per favore*, call me Evangelista, eh?" he replied.

"Please excuse my *italiano*," I said in Italian. "I will do my best to be understood this evening."

"You have already made Torricelli's evening, Natalia," said the man on the right. "Evangelista is not *abituato* to being *lusingato*." I think he wasn't used to getting flattered. The man on the right held out his hand for me to shake. "I am Antonio Nardi." We shook.

"And this *bighellone* is Raffaello Magiotti," Antonio Nardi said with an elbow jut into the side of his friend, which caused both of them to lose some wine from their glasses. Raffaello – a ne'er-do-well, apparently - shook my hand as well.

"*Incantata* to meet, you Natalia," he said. "Are you visiting from France?"

"From La-Nouvelle France, *sì*," I replied.

"How *esotica*!" exclaimed Nardi, exotically. "What is life like in the land of ice and snow?"

"It is not so bad," I replied. "But sometimes…ah…*sona proprio frigida*!"

The men looked curiously at each other. Then Ciccio made a correction to *fredda*, and everyone seemed relieved by that.

"Antonio, Raffaello, Evangelista and I are all long-time friends," Dr. Gregorio Redi said to me. "We were all under the tutelage of Benedetto Castelli, may the Lord rest his soul."

"Such an *inspirato* mathematician!" Magiotti said inspiringly, with a finger pointed to the ceiling. "I owe him so much!"

"As do we all, Raffaello," Torricelli lamented.

"If it were not for him, the three of you would not have worked with The Great Man," said Dr. Redi.

"How true!" said Nardi. He looked at me and said, "*Mi scusi*, Natalia. The Great Man is…"

"Galileo?" I interjected. The men made that look again.

"You know of Galileo?" asked Nardi.

"*Sì*. I learned of him in *scuola*," I replied. "He studied the stars. And he dropped things from the top of the Leaning Tower of Pisa. To study their, ah…*movimento*?" I was showing off now.

"From the top of the Tower of Pisa?" said Magiotti. "Is that what we are calling the third floor of my house, now? Because that is where he performed those *esperimenti*."

"Where do these myths come from?" Nardi wondered out loud, just as Vincenzo Viviani returned from the kitchen. "Vincenzo, we have some more *informazione* for the book you are writing about Galileo, may the Lord rest his soul."

"Oh? And what might that be?" he asked.

"Our new friend from La-Nouvelle France has made us aware of a certain *pettegolezzo* that our beloved mentor performed his motion *esperimenti* from the Tower of Pisa!"

"You must be joking!" Viviani scoffed at the rumour. "How preposterous!" Then, after a 4 second lull, he said, "Yet, it does have its romantic side, does it not? Using the tower as a backdrop would certainly spice up that section of the book!" He turned to me and said, "Thank you for the inspiration, Natalia Campo Bella!" Then he kissed my hand again.

"Let me introduce you to some of the other guests that are here, Natalia," Ciccio interrupted as he took my arm. "We must not let these gentlemen *monopolizzare* your time!"

"Only if you promise to regale us with one of your poems a little later, Francesco," said Torricelli. "Your father tells me you are quite an accomplished *paroliere*!" Ciccio blushed at the compliment. I think he was being praised as a wordsmith.

"Well, I…*sì*…I would be delighted to recite some lines," Ciccio stumbled. "In honour of your birthday, Signor Torricelli."

"Evangelista, *per favore*."

Just then, music started up from the far-left side of the room. Ciccio led me to a group of people in the opposite corner. A young man with wavey, shoulder-length black hair spotted Ciccio and beckoned him over.

"Come, Ciccio…hide with us from the old people's music!" the young man exclaimed. "It is putting me to sleep!"

"I find it *soporifero*, myself!" Ciccio declared, giving his friend a pat on the back.

"Now, now, it is not so bad," said a middle-aged man standing next to an elegant-looking lady. "Do you realise that the one playing *Lagrime Mie* on the violin is Giacomo Carissimi?"

"*Sì*, but can you dance to it?" said the young man, shaking his wrist with fingers altogether. No one offered an answer.

"Natalia, I would like to *introdurre* you to my friend, Marcello Malpighi," Ciccio said by way of introduction. That surname sounded familiar to me. "Marcello, this is Natalia." He took my hand and gave it a kiss. I was going to get chapped wrist if this kept up.

"And this is Signor Giovanni Borelli and his wife, Claudia." I gave a slight bow to both of them. Ciccio added, "Natalia is from La-Nouvelle France." The couple looked impressed.

"Ciccio, Giovanni and I were having a discussion," said Marcello. "He says that I should consider medical studies when I finish my philosophy degree. Sound familiar?"

"See, Malpighi, I told you that medicine is in your future!" Ciccio declared. "Since I have known you, you have shown a keen interest in the anatomy and physiology of all creatures."

Malpighi. Why was that name familiar?

"And, besides, what will a philosophy degree do for you?" Signor Borelli added. "Except impoverish you for the rest of your life!"

"Now, Giovanni, behave," Claudia scolded. "Marcello is young, and has many years and adventures ahead of him! And not everyone in your circle must become a *dottóre*, you know?" Claudia turned her attention from her husband to me. "Now, what do you do, Natalia."

"I, ah…am studying to become a *dottóre*."

"I give up!" Signora Borelli announced, and left for the group of ladies that Cecilia Redi had found refuge with moments before.

"A woman *medico*?" Giovanni Borelli said to me. "This is highly unusual. You certainly do come from a different world, my dear."

Tell me about it, Giovanni.

"I have twice been a witness to Natalia's diagnostic skills, gentlemen," said Ciccio. "She would put the majority of us *medici* to shame with her *naturale* ability."

"Not to mention her *naturale* beauty," Marcello said with a mischievous smile, meaning to make me blush. Mission *compiuto*.

"*Bàsta*, you bad boy!" Ciccio blurted out. "I know your interests lie elsewhere." Ciccio motioned to the group of women in the other back corner of the room. We all turned to look.

"Eh, come on! Do not draw *attenzione*!" Marcello was reduced to school-boy panic as the group of women turned their heads toward us.

"Did she see me, Francesco?" asked Marcello, turning away nervously.

"Of course she sees you, Malpighi. You are not *invisibile*!"

"But is she staring at me?"

"I would not call it staring. More like looking."

"*Casualmente* looking or *intensamente* looking?"

"In between the two, I think. She seems to be curious about the crazy young man who is trying to hide in plain sight!"

   I glanced over to the women. It wasn't too hard to figure out who Marcello was all *eccitato* about, since there was only one young woman in the group.

"Is that her in the blue dress?" I asked.

"That young lady is the assistant to Signor Torricelli," said Giovanni Borelli. "Marcello met her at a dinner at my house last April, and he has been smitten ever since."

"Oh!" I exclaimed as I turned to Ciccio. I asked him in French, "Is this the French-speaking assistant I was to meet tonight?"

"The very same. Shall I introduce you?"

"*Per favore*," I answered.

We excused ourselves from Signor Borelli and Marcello Malpighi – Why did I know that name? – and made our way over to the group of women in the corner, stopping first to procure a cheesy canape and flute of wine from the servers. Ciccio analyzed the contents of his glass.

"Not exactly a full-fruit nose," he sniffed.

When we reached the women's group, Cecilia took my arm and began the introductions.

"Ladies, may I *introdurre* to you the young lady I have been telling you about. This is Natalia." I smiled and bowed my head to each of the five women sitting in a semicircle in front of the window. The last person to be introduced was the young woman who was standing off to the right.

"And this is the personal *assistente* to Evangelista Torricelli. Natalia, I would like you to meet Dianora Murelli."

Dianora Murelli smiled warmly, extended her hand, and we shook. It seemed the other women were taken aback by the greeting. Didn't women shake hands in 1647? Oh, well…they do now! Dianora was my height less two centimetres and most likely my age. Her hair was a dark shade of brown, just over shoulder length. Her hazel eyes discreetly examined me up and down.

"It is a pleasure to meet you, Dianora," I said in Italian. "I understand you speak French."

"*Si*, it is one of my languages," she said. "Are you from France, then?"

"I am from La-Nouvelle France," I replied.

"La-Nouvelle France!" Dianora exclaimed rather excitedly. "*Che meraviglia!*" I guess she thought that was wonderful.

"Come, let us have a conversation!" Dianora said in perfect French, taking me by the arm and leading me off to the quiet of the vestibule. I looked back to Ciccio and Cecilia with a shoulder shrug and sheepish grin. They smiled back and waved bye-bye.

"So tell me about yourself," said Dianora in French. "How have you come to Florence?"

"By the usual way," I said, not stretching the truth at all since I'd used The Portal a few times already. I went into my story about how I was currently visiting Florence by way of the Kingdom of Scotland, where I was studying medicine. Dianora was the first person not to bat an eye when I told them I was in university. She was very interested in La-Nouvelle France, wanting to know about my family and what life was like in such a vast, unspoiled country. I told Dianora about the four members of my family: my hard-working, dedicated parents and my hardly-working but dedicated brother. Then I told her all about Canada - not mentioning it by name, of course – relating the wilderness beauty and majestic scenery that was literally outside the door of our country home. I told her about the woodlands and the wildlife, the open skies and the rushing rivers. I told her about what the crisp October air felt like in your lungs. And I didn't have to imagine any of that scene from a 1647 perspective, either: I just told Dianora what it looked like outside our house almost 400 years from now. We both sighed at the conclusion of my heartfelt description.

Then I peppered Dianora with questions about her life. I learned that she too was here in Florence apart from her family. She had arrived here four years ago and found employment almost immediately as an assistant to Signor Torricelli, where she began translating documents and letters for him. Over time, he began to trust her with compiling and collating his notes, which led to the publishing of his first book, *Opera Geometrica*, a collection of mathematical and scientific works. Dianora then went into a semi-detailed explanation on cycloids, how Torricelli proved that the area under this rolling circle is three times the area of the generating circle, and how this vindicated the postulates of his mentor, Galileo Galilei. My head was spinning, but my genuine interest kept Dianora going, and I could tell she enjoyed relating her science story to a kindred spirit. I was about to ask her if she had been around for the invention of the barometer, but fortunately put the brakes on that dumb idea. What if it hadn't been invented yet? Yikes, Nat...cool your jets!

Dianora then told me that her current project was organizing Evangelista's notes for his next publication that would involve very complex mathematics. I'm glad she didn't go into details.

"There you are, you two!" said Dr. Redi in French as he entered the vestibule. "How are we getting along, then?"

"Famously, Gregorio!" Dianora exclaimed. "Natalia and I are fast becoming friends!"

"I am glad to hear it!" he responded. "May I request that you both return to the party now, as Francesco is about to honour Evangelista with a verse!"

"*Bien sûr!*" we both replied together and followed Dr. Redi into the living room, where the guests had assembled around a small stand at the far end. Francesco stepped up to the podium and cleared his throat.

"An Ode to Torricelli: Master of mathematics, physics, and all pressing matters in the air!"

That got a nice laugh, and pretty much answered my barometer question.

Francesco then recited a poem for the birthday boy, Evangelista:

In Tuscan hills where grapes abound
And Bacchus reigns with wine renowned
The brilliant mind of Torricelli
Unlocked secrets most compelling

With quicksilver in a tube sealed tight
A truth discovered to shed new light
Oh, how the air arounds us weighs
To fashion changes day by day!

Attend to him, ye poets and scholars
Be moved by his uncommon valor
Just as these verses do proclaim
The beauties of his wonderous game

> *Come, let us raise a glass and toast*
> *His honoured name, his noble post*
> *And pray his deeds may yet inspire*
> *Young minds to soar, their hearts to aspire*

"To Evangelista Torricelli!" Francesco announced, raising his glass in the air. His words were echoed by the guests, glasses clinked, and a hearty cheer went up. Francesco stepped off the riser and made his way over to me and Dianora.

"Did you like it?" he asked us.

"*Sì*, but more importantly," said Dianora, pointing to the guest of honour, "so did he!" Torricelli, receiving pats on the back from his friends, approached us.

"That was a lovely present, Francesco Redi," Evangelista said, wiping tears from his eyes. "*Grazie.*" He kissed Ciccio on both cheeks.

"It was my pleasure," Ciccio responded as the music started up again. "I hope the reference to Bacchus did not *distrarre* from the message."

"*Distrarre?*" Evangelista said, deflecting the comment. "It enhanced the poem, dear fellow! Aside from studying the secrets of the universe, there is nothing I love more in life than the flowing of good wine and fine verse!"

"It is the same with me!" Ciccio exclaimed in a manner that suggested another kindred-spirit moment was taking place.

"You and I should become *conosciuto* over a bottle and a book," Torricelli said, looking to become better acquainted. "Perhaps you could come by this week and assist me with a writing project with which I have been struggling."

"The play you have been working on?" Dianora asked. "The one about Dionysus in Tuscany?"

"*Sì*," nodded Torricelli. "But after Francesco's lovely ode this evening, perhaps I will move from Greece to Rome and replace Dionysus for Bacchus!"

"I am *incuriosito*!" said Ciccio. "We shall arrange a time for a visit!"

"As long as Dianora can put up with the two of us after a glass or two!" Evangelista winked at Dianora.

"I will occupy myself with important scientific matters while you boys giggle over rhyming *schema*," she smirked.

Dianora then took me by the arm, and we left Redi and Torricelli to hash out the details of their prospective partnership.

For the rest of the evening, we flitted from one gaggle of guests to another. We dropped in on a discussion between Viviani, Magiotti, and Nardi on the acceleration of free bodies along an inclined plane, as suggested by their mentor, Galileo. That conversation had me inclining to free-fall in plain sight. When the talk switched over to Magiotti's work on water and its resistance to compression, I had to resist the drowning feeling that was pressing on me. Then Nardi got excited and gave us a dissertation on the use of the 'method of indivisibles' to prove Archimedes' principles, which became the principal point of my divided attention. While Dianora enjoyed this physics gabfest, and even contributed some keen insights, she soon recognized my unease and excused us from the Math Club.

We got some treats at the snack table, and enjoyed a piece of Cecilia Redi's cake, which turned out to be a big hit. Light and fluffy, Dianora thought. I said, 'Why, thank you', and told her about my 'method of divisibles' in separating the wet ingredients from the dry before combining. She said she appreciated that dessert theorem, and we both had a good laugh. Then we noticed Giovanni Borelli waving to us from across the room. Marcello Malpighi quickly averted his gaze.

"I think Marcello likes you," I whispered to Dianora in French. Not that anyone else was listening or could understand, anyhow.

"He has been doing this shy-boy act for a year now," she whispered back. "He is nice enough, but far too young for me."

"He looks to be our age," I countered.

"He is an immature eighteen-year-old," said Dianora, "I am a mature woman of twenty."

"So am I!" I whisper-exclaimed. "I mean the twenty part, not the mature part." We both laughed again, and after Giovanni beckoned a second time, we went over to their klatch.

"Natalia, Dianora!" said Signor Borelli upon our arrival. "Settle an argument for us, will you? Malpighi, here, thinks the two of you are sisters, as do the ladies." He pointed to the group of women sitting next to the window while I contemplated that Malpighi name again. "I say, how can they be sisters when they look nothing alike?"

"*No*, we are not sisters," I said in Italian. "It is not possible."

"Yes, it is impossible," Dianora asserted. "We have only just met!"

"Long lost sisters, perhaps?" said Claudia Borelli. "You carry yourselves in the same confident manner."

"As women of substance would!" Marcello Malpighi chimed in as he looked at Dianora. His cheeks got really red, really fast.

"I thank you all for the *complimenti*," Dianora said. "But aside from both of us being twenty years old, we have little else in common."

"It can be easily settled, then," said Giovanni Borelli, "When were you born, Natalia?"

"Um…ah, my birthday was last week," I stammered. Last week hundreds of year from now, of course.

"And mine was two months before," Dianora added.

"So, not even twins, then," Giovanni concluded. "I am *revindicato*!" He looked vindicated, too, with that satisfied grin. Giovanni then looked over to Marcello who was recovering from embarrassment.

"Malpighi, *tutto bene*?" he asked.

Malpighi, tutto? Malpighi tut…Malpighian tubules! The excretory system found in insects! I knew his name sounded familiar! This is the guy who discovered how bugs go to the bathroom!

"*Sì*, I am just a little flushed at the *momento*," Marcello replied, which caused me to do a laughing spit-take with my wine when I put flush and excretory system together in the left side of my brain.

Signor Borelli offered me a handkerchief to wipe my chin. Marcello cleaned up the floor.

"There goes the woman of substance," Dianora said in French with a smirk.

The evening was winding down. The street was lined with lantern-lit carriages waiting to take the partygoers home. Tonio was waiting patiently in the best parking spot in front of the Viviani house. Dr. Redi and Cecilia were paying their respects to our host, Vincenzo, Ciccio and Evangelista were firming up plans for a mid-week social call, and I was saying good-bye to Dianora in the vestibule.

"We must make plans to see each other soon!" she said to me in French. "It has been a pleasure to get to know you!"

"*Oui*, it has been quite the evening!" I said in a bubbly tone. "It was so nice to meet you!"

"Where are you staying while here in Florence," asked Dianora.

"Well, there is a room at the Palazzo Medici waiting for me," I replied.

"The Palazzo Medici! So, you are not the guests of the Redi's, then?"

"*Non*. I only met them today."

"How were you planning on getting to the Palazzo Medici from the Redi house?"

"Well, I was going to walk…"

"You will do no such thing! It is not a safe area at this time of night. You must come and stay with me!"

"Oh, *non*. I really could not impose."

"It is not an imposition! I insist!"

In the next few seconds, I remembered one of my conversations with Connor. He said that the time would inevitably come when staying overnight somewhere would be an issue. If I went back to Scotland through The Portal tonight, I'd still have a problem when I returned to Florence: it would still be the middle of the night, and I would need a place to stay. I couldn't just wander around Tuscany like a…what did I say to Cecilia this afternoon?…a *camminatore di strada*? No, that wouldn't be appropriate at all! So, I made a decision right then and there.

"Well, if you insist!" I replied.

"Excellent!" Dianora chirped. "You shall ride with me and Evangelista. The carriage will drop him off at his house first, and then deliver us to the Casa D'ambrosio."

"Is D'ambrosio the name of your house?" I asked.

"*Non*, it is the name of the sisters to whom I pay room and board. My bedroom is large and has two comfortable beds, so there is plenty of space for us!"

"It is too good to be true!" I said, meaning every word.

"Then it is settled! I shall inform Evangelista of our plans."

Dianora left in search of Torricelli, and I went to tell the Redi's about my altered arrangements for transportation.

"What do you mean you are leaving with someone else?" said Ciccio with a discernable degree of panic in his voice. He continued with some more interrogatives. "Where are you going? How are you getting there? Why is this happening?..."

I paused a moment while he came up a final question.

"When will I see you again?"

"I will come by your house tomorrow morning for a visit, Francesco. Before I leave for..." I paused before saying 'the 21st century. "...the Palazzo Medici."

"Well, I suppose that will do," Ciccio said with the look of a wounded puppy. "I shall count the minutes until we next meet!"

"You will be asleep most of that time," I countered.

"Sleep? Signorina, you jest! My dormancy will be a fitful endeavour!" He kissed my hand and had trouble letting go.

"I am going to have to take that with me, Francesco," I said.

He reluctantly released his grip.

After saying my *ciaos* and *grazies*, I followed Dianora and Evangelista to their carriage. We clambered in and the carriage got going, Evangelista sitting across from the two of us women. Looking back, we could see Francesco and Marcello Malpighi in the lantern light. They were standing in the middle of the street, waving handkerchiefs and blowing kisses in our direction.

"They do that a lot here," said Dianora as our carriage turned the corner.

Chapter 16

The morning sun peeking through the thin curtains and landing on my eyelids woke me up from a deep sleep. I was dreaming that I was performing surgery on a med school dummy when its eyes suddenly opened, and it started to complain that I was not operating fast enough – he had a playoff game to get to! I said he could watch it on the operating room TV instead, but he got really agitated and said that he wasn't a spectator, he was the starting goalie! He told me his name was Bobby Nystrom and he was the only hope his team had to win the Cup. But I didn't buy it, and told him that Bobby Nystrom scored clutch goals in the playoffs, so he wasn't a goalie at all. Then the dummy called me a dummy and told me that he could play all the positions at once because of his magic skates! All he had to do was click his blades together three times to go from playing goal to right wing. When I asked where he got the magic skates, he pointed to the hockey net in the corner of the operating room. Francesco Redi and Mark Munroe were standing on either side of the net waving magic hockey-wands and saying, 'There's no place like home in the playoffs…there's no place like home in the playoffs…' When I looked between the goalposts the fuzzy light of The Portal appeared. Its illumination increasing in intensity until I opened my eyes to the morning sun peeking through the thin curtains.

The bed across the room from mine was already made, and a fresh set of clothes was draped over a chair at the foot of my bed. My party dress was hanging from a hook on the door.

The bedroom was pretty large, probably 5x5m square, decorated with paintings of Florentine cityscapes and Tuscan landscapes. There was a desk to the left piled with papers, a bookshelf next to it stuffed with references books, and an open wardrobe facing me that displayed an ample collection of dresses sorted by colour.

I sat up, stretched my arms with a yawn, and bounced a couple of times on the bed. It seemed to me that 17th-century bedding had gotten a bad rap because the mattress and pillow were both firm and soft. The bedsheets had a pleasant hint of lavender. The feather duvet kept me warm and comfortable all night.

I swung my legs and put my feet onto the floor. Ouch! A protruding floorboard nail almost caught me unawares but I sidestepped the obstacle. A pair of slippers had been set at my bedside. I slipped them on.

After getting dressed in the outfit left for me - which fit almost perfectly - I opened the bedroom door and made my way quietly down the sunlit, second-floor hallway. When Dianora and I arrived late last night the house was dark, and the half-moon directly overhead provided just enough light to visit the outdoor powder room and then climb the stairs to bed. Now I could now see that my overnight lodging was a very spacious home – a mini-mansion, if you will - that was ornately decorated, and so very tidy! All the pictures in the hall and going down the stairs were equally spaced and hanging dead straight. The furniture in the first-floor living room was arranged with exacting detail: end tables set at precise distances from sofas; sofas and chairs set at perfect right angles, equidistant from the walls; and the tapestries were draped to the same distance from the floor. The entire layout appealed to the OCD side of my personality to no end.

I could hear conversation coming from around the corner of the parlor, so I made my way to what I suspected was the kitchen to meet my hosts.

"I will make two *uova*, just in case."

"It is only *colazione*, Rita! It is too much!"

I stepped into the large kitchen with a massive stove at the far end. A woman in an apron, a brunette probably in her late twenties, was standing over the stove with three frying pans on the go. Another woman, a redhead probably in her mid-to-late twenties, was sewing a button on a blouse at the kitchen table. They both sensed my presence at the same time, looking toward the door. The woman with the apron scurried over to me like my hair was on fire and she was coming to the rescue.

"You must be Natalia!" she said, shaking my hand. "It is very nice to me you! I am Rita! I am making breakfast!"

"It is nice to meet you, Rita," I replied.

"I hope you are hungry! Sit, sit! Would you like a *caffè*? Or a glass of wine? What would you like?" I did my best to keep up with her rapid-fire *italiano*.

"Ah… *caffè* is *bene, grazie!*"

Rita took my hand and led me two more metres into the kitchen, stopping at the table.

"Natalia, I would like you to meet my sister, Nerina. Nerina, this is…"

"Natalia. I know," Nerina answered as she stood up, putting the blouse down on the table. "Welcome to our home, Natalia." She took a step toward me and kissed me on both cheeks. Rita turned and scampered over to the stove to grab the coffee pot.

"It is nice I meet you, Nerina," I said choppily, I'm sure. "Dianora tell you about me?" Obviously the case, but I was trying to make conversation.

"She did! And what a pleasant surprise for us!" Nerina gestured for me to sit, and we both took our places at the table. Rita was back in a flash with the coffee and poured some of the strong brew into the cup that was already set out for me. She added milk and sugar, stirred it up, and zipped back to the stove.

Nerina pursed her lips. "Maybe Natalia likes it black, Rita?"

"It would be too strong," Rita replied with her back to us, attending to the frying pans. "It is not good for the digestion to drink it that way."

"I like *like* this," I said to Nerina.

"You do not have to be polite, Natalia. My sister Rita is of the opinion that she always has the best opinion."

"Eh, when you know things, you show things," Rita responded with a shrug. Dianora entered the kitchen from the back door with a bundle of wood in her hands, which she laid in a basket by the stove.

"*Buongiorno!*" she said to me. "Did you sleep well?" Dianora opened the oven door and placed two logs inside.

"*Sì*, I very *comoda, grazie*," I answered.

"You see, Rita?" said Nerina, getting up to pour herself another cup. "I told you those beds were *va bene*! Just like Natalia's *italiano*!" She placed the dress she was mending on the floor next to her chair.

"The beds may be fine, but that will not stop me from restuffing them, my sister. I have my list of jobs to do, and they will all get done." Rita deftly carried four plates of food to the table and set them down. Then she moved the dress from the floor onto the hutch.

"*Tutti a tavola a mangiare!*" she announced. Everybody came to the table for breakfast.

"Whose turn to give thanks?" asked Rita.

"Nerina's, I think," said Dianora.

"Very well," Nerina responded. We all bowed our heads as Nerina thanked the Lord for a good sleep and good food, and asked for blessing for the day ahead. We all said 'Amen' and dug into the fried meat, eggs, and bread with butter.

"I hope you like them done this way," said Nerina as she cut into her eggs, allowing the yolk to run. "Because it is the only way Rita will ever serve them to you."

"It is the best way," said Rita as she cut her meat into same-sized pieces. "The *uova* must be cooked well, but not too much, and only with a pinch of rosemary." Rita looked across to me. "Do you want some juice?"

"Oh, *no*, I am fine," I answered.

"I will get you some juice!" She got up, dashed over to the counter, and poured orange juice for three. Nerina didn't receive a glass.

"I do not prefer warm juice," Nerina said to me as an aside.

"If it is too cold, it is not good for your stomach," Rita said matter of factly. I noticed a little smile emerge on Dianora's face.

"Well, Natalia, tell us all about yourself," said Nerina. "Do not worry about your *italiano*, we will help to fill in the *dettagli*."

I took a sip of juice, dabbed my lips with my napkin, and went into a broken-Italian description of my life. I told the women of my home and family in La-Nouvelle France, my medical school exploits in the Kingdom of Scotland, and I gave them a portal-less description of how I came to visit Florence. During my narration – which took the rest of breakfast to deliver - Rita interjected with questions that involved names, dates, places, and times. When Nerina interrupted, it was to ask me about impressions, feelings, emotions, and thoughts. When I was through with my story, the two sisters had extracted and formed a pretty decent picture of this girl from a faraway place.

Over another cup of coffee, it was their turn to story-tell. The two ladies took turns informing me about the two-hundred-year-old D'ambrosio family orchards in Tuscany: Rita recounting the details of the size and success of the family business, and Nerina recalling the beauty and splendour of the rolling hills. But neither sister desired to enter the family business – at least not right away, Rita clarified – so they asked their parents for some start-up money, bought this house, and went into business for themselves. Rita was a chef, who prepared food for Florence's best caterer. Nerina was a dressmaker who worked exclusively for the Medicis. Between the two of them, they were quite comfortable, Rita explained, and was about to go into the financial details when Nerina interrupted with, 'Let us just say we are blessed'.

Over one last cup of coffee, Dianora told the D'ambrosio girls all about last evening's party, sparing no *dettagli*. She updated them on how all the ladies were doing, related the latest news on what all the men were up to, and gave her opinion on the state of scientific advancements that may be in the offing.

"That is very interesting about the infinite surface area of Gabriel's Horn, Dianora," said Nerina, feigning interest. "But what I really want to know is…did Marcello Malpighi manage to say a complete sentence in your presence without fainting?"

We all burst into laughter. Then I added how I'd never seen someone turn so red in the face before. Dianora then pointed out that if you had ever seen a baby duckling following its mother around, you would have a clear picture of how Francesco Redi chased me around the party all night. Nerina laughed and slapped the table, which prompted Rita to tell us that her sister had the same problem with a certain puppy by the name of Giuseppe, who visited their house more than he visited the *gabinetto*! Nerina would have none of it, and said that if she was given a *sedicesimo* every time her sister's suitor, Lucio, dropped by, she could pay for the restoration of the Palazzo Pitti herself! I didn't get all the references or words, of course, but the general hilarity at the table got me laughing it up all the same.

Rita, deciding that the conversation was now over, got up from the table, collected the dishes, and darted over to the counter and wash basin. Dianora and I followed suit with the cups and cutlery, sans darting. Nerina picked up the dress lying on the hutch and resumed her work.

"Now, what is everyone up to, today?" Rita asked. "I have to prepare three-dozen *tartine* for a baptism."

"I must finish this dress for Vittoria della Rovere this morning and deliver it to her by midday," said Nerina.

"I shall be off to Evangelista's within the hour," replied Dianora. "I will be translating some correspondence for him today. To the Frenchman, Blaise Pascal."

Then the women all looked at me.

"Oh, I visit the Redi house," I said. "Then I go Palazzo Medici."

"Are they not doing construction there at the moment?" asked Rita.

"*Sì*, they are," I answered, picturing the 'they' as Andrea, Antonio, and Alfredo - my *amici* who liked my cake.

"You cannot stay at the Palazzo Medici, it is filthy!" Nerina protested. "Why not stay here with us?"

"Oh, I could not, ah…*imposer?*" I replied in French, looking to Dianora for help.

"*Imporre*," Dianora offered by way of translation.

"It is no imposition at all!" Rita announced. "You will stay with us while you are here in Florence. Bring your things from the Medici house this afternoon. We will have Dianora's room properly prepared for two!"

"I have not much clothes," I said, truthfully.

"We are a house full of clothes!" Nerina declared. "Every closet is packed! It will be nice to see someone wear all these dresses I have made!"

"I, ah…have not much money for you," I said, not as truthfully. I didn't have any money for them.

"Rita…Nerina," said Dianora. "I will double the amount of room and board I pay you for the entire length of Natalia's stay."

"Oh, I cannot accept…" I spluttered.

"*Per favore*," Dianora said with an upheld hand. "I have worked for Evangelista Torricelli for many years, he pays me very well, and I have spent next to nothing all this time."

"It is true, Dianora is a good saver," said Rita.

"It is true, Dianora needs to get out more," said Nerina. "But we do not need the extra money, my dear. You can keep it."

"The girl does make good *senso*, though," said Rita, pointing to the ceiling. "We will only take half again of your monthly rent."

"Then it is settled," said Dianora. All heads present nodded their approval.

"This is very *generosa, grazie mille*," I said. The girls all smiled. They liked that *grazie mille* line, I think. "*Per favore*, tell how I help in the house!"

"Well, there is one thing," said Rita with a smile, throwing a kitchen towel at me. "These dishes will not dry themselves, you know!"

"Of course they will," I heard Nerina whisper to Dianora as I went to the wash basin. "I have always let the dishes do that job for themselves!"

I did the sixteen-minute morning walk from the D'ambrosio house to the Redi house at a brisk pace. The nip in the air delivered a bounce to my step, and I was glad to be wearing the shawl that Nerina insisted I take along. She also offered to lend me a simpler dress to wear than my party outfit, but I declined, knowing that The Portal would only accept the clothing I came in with on my return trip to Scotland. TT rules are TT rules!

I knocked on the front door. After a short delay, Ciccio opened it.

"Natalia!" he beamed. Then he exclaimed in French, "You have returned to me!" He looked prepared to meet the day in his tan suit and freshly-powdered red wig.

"I only saw you a few hours ago, Francesco," I replied.

"A few hours had become a fortnight to me, *cara mia!*"

"I must agree that time is a relative thing," I said in a way that would make Einstein smile.

"Your dress is exquisite!"

"It is the same one I wore last night."

"And your hair…it is beautiful!"

"All I did was brush it."

"It looks different…"

"It is not washed."

"Well, your conventional presentation should be employed by all the overly-primped ladies of Tuscany!" Ciccio announced. "You have elevated the word 'plain' to new fashionable heights!"

"Francesco?"

"*Sì*, my sweet?"

"Are you going to invite me in?"

"Ah…ha, ha…*sì*."

Ciccio stepped aside and ushered me in with a sweep of the arm. As he closed the door behind us, I heard a moan come from the second office down the hall.

"It is the young boy from the *Ospedale degli Innocenti*," he said, noticing my concerned expression. "His abdominal pain has not subsided. My father has just finished a bloodletting, so we shall see if there will be improvement."

"A bloodletting?" I gasped.

"*Sì*, I know what you are thinking, Natalia. Why not a purging first?" Not exactly what I was thinking, actually. "But the boy has been vomiting all night, so that treatment step has been bypassed."

"May we go in and see the boy?" I asked.

"Of course!" said Ciccio.

We went down the hall. Ciccio rapped on the door twice and we entered the medical office. We were met by a repeat of yesterday's scene: the nanny, Maria, sitting on the chair; the young boy, Luca, lying on the table; the doctor, Gregorio Redi, standing over the lad, this time applying a compress to Luca's left arm. It was probably where he had performed the bloodletting.

"Natalia! Good to see you again," said Dr. Redi said in French. "Our patient has returned, unfortunately."

"*Oui*, I see this," I replied. Then, in *italiano*, I said, "I sorry you not better, Luca."

Luca returned a weak smile, then shut his eyes hard as a wave of pain overtook him.

"Francesco and I have both examined him, Natalia," said Dr. Redi. "We would appreciate a third opinion."

I stepped toward the table and asked Luca if I could examine him. He nodded. I pulled up his shirt and began to gently palpate his distended abdomen. When I pressed down at his bellybutton, yesterday's wince now elevated to a groan. When I palpated three centimetres out from his bellybutton, at roughly eight o'clock, the groan became a yowl. I turned to Maria.

"Luca, he eat yesterday?"

"He hardly ate a thing," said Maria. "He has lost his *appetito*."

I stood back from the patient. Luca had all the symptoms of appendicitis. Dr. Redi had Maria take over the holding of the compress and motioned for the three of us to step outside.

"What do you think, Francesco?" asked Dr. Redi in a hushed tone when we were in the hallway.

"I think it is as you say, father. The boy's imbalance of humors has caused abdominal pain and bloating. But I fear it is the black bile that is elevated, and not the yellow bile."

"*Oui*, it could be the yellow bile, I agree," Dr. Redi nodded. "What do you think, Natalia?"

Well, it certainly wasn't that! Imbalance of humors? Black and yellow bile? What were these doctors talking about? This wasn't 21st century med-school speak, that was for sure. But how would you say the word appendicitis in 1647 when, more than likely, the appendix hadn't been 'discovered' yet? So I just said…

"I am not quite sure, Dr. Redi."

"But you seem to be concerned over something," he remarked, my furrowed brow giving me away.

"I…I am concerned about the spreading of the malady," I said. Though I was really concerned about the possibility of Luca's appendix bursting and causing a life-threatening infection in his abdomen.

"*Oui*, I worry over a spreading of imbalance as well, which is why I took his blood," Dr. Redi explained. "I shall send him back to the orphanage with clear instructions on the application of the essential herbs, and we shall hope for the best." Dr. Redi then went back into the office.

"Is this all that can be done?" I asked Ciccio.

"This is the way this illness has been treated for centuries, Natalia. Some patients will make it through the next stage of fever and pain. The majority will not fare as well."

"Most people die from this?"

"They do. You have not seen this ailment much in your training, I take it?"

Oh, I've seen it up-close and personal, Francesco Redi. It's just something I can't talk about.

The office door opened. Maria came out with Luca, supporting him under his left arm. The two walked slowly to the front door. Before they left, Dr. Redi gave Maria a cloth bag that contained the herbal treatment. Maria thanked the doctor then looked at me and Ciccio. An expression suddenly came over her face, like she had forgotten something important.

"Oh, I almost *dimenticato!*" Maria said. She reached over to a waiting-room chair and picked up a piece of paper that was lying there. "This is for you, signorina. Luca was hoping he would see you again today, so he could give you this."

I received the paper from Maria. It was a charcoal sketch of a young woman in left profile, looking rather melancholy, with just the slightest upturn on the corner of her mouth.

"It is a picture of you, Natalia!" said Ciccio. "And it is beautiful!"

It *was* a picture of me. And it really was beautiful.

"Luca is very talented," said Maria. "At the orphanage, we call him *Luca fa presto*, because he can draw faster than most people can talk!"

I stepped toward the boy and took him by the hand.

"*Grazie*, Luca," I said.

The boy pulled me closer to him and craned his head to my ear. He whispered a reply.

"Signorina...help me," he said. "*Per favore*...help me."

I got to the Palazzo Medici a few hours later and entered by the main door. I could hear renovation work happening down the hall, but there was nobody in the courtyard area. I opened the first office door on my right and quietly closed it behind me. The fuzzy glow of The Portal was there to greet me.

I folded my shawl and placed it on the table top. It would be right here for me when I returned after my one-second departure. I walked around the desk with every intention of going straight home, but I pulled out the chair and sat down, with my elbows on my knees and my head in my hands. I was physically and emotionally drained.

I couldn't stop thinking about Luca. I was confident my diagnosis was correct: his appendix was inflamed, it could burst at any minute, and the subsequent infection could be fatal. *Would be* fatal. And here I was, in possession of the knowledge that could alleviate his suffering and potentially save his life. I had to act. No, I had to act *fast*.

But how could my intervention *not* change the future? What chain of events would be set off by my deliberate interference in past affairs? It could be catastrophic! No, I would be overstepping a time travelling boundary to get involved any further.

Or would I?

The internal conflict began to eat away at me. I could feel the pressure mounting.

But there was one great benefit I possessed in this circumstance: I could literally stop this scenario dead in its tracks while I left to sort out an answer.

I rose from the chair and turned to face The Portal. Then I left Florence for one second to go home and think.

The war veteran limped down Royal Hospital Road in Chelsea, his cane tapping on the cobblestone street. It had been over 37 years since he had last seen the Duke of Wellington, and he would not allow himself to miss the opportunity to see his commander one last time. In the distance, he could just make out Queen Victoria's entourage as it descended the steps from the hospital where the Iron Duke lay in state. The crowd that had gathered to pay their respects was growing larger by the minute.

There were other veterans dotting the assembled mourners on that Monday, identifiable in their double-breasted red coats with white facing. The war veteran took particular pleasure in the fact that his uniform still fit after almost four decades. Most of his comrades were presenting with open jacket this morning, not able to do up the either of the two rows of their chest buttons.

As the crowd moved slowly and orderly toward the door, the war veteran reminisced about that fateful day in 1815. He remembered the sound of the cannons, the smell of the gunpowder, the way the ground had shaken beneath his own trembling feet. He remembered the fervour he had felt, and the rush of excitement mixed with trepidation, as his outnumbered infantry charged the demoralized French troops from their position on the high ground. And he remembered the wounded, the dead, and the dying – something he had always tried to forget.

The moving crowd had now become a throng, with mourners being pressed for space. The war veteran steadied himself, applying added pressure onto his cane. When he reached up to his chest with his free hand, he felt something in his breast pocket. He extracted a piece of paper, unfolded it once, and smiled as he reread the message that had encouraged him on the battlefield at Waterloo all those years ago.

The war veteran had almost reached the hospital stairs when the jostling crowd became an unruly mob. Citizens began shouting, first in anger, and then in terror, as the crush of people moved unrelentingly toward the narrow doorway. As the veteran was putting the piece of paper back into his pocket, it slipped through his fingers and landed on the pavement. He bent to pick it *up, but it was no use; the mob had carried him away, lifting him up the stairs and into the hospital before he had a chance to even turn around.*

William Thomson waited patiently for his aunt and uncle as the last of the mourners were ushered out of the hospital later that day. He was in no hurry today, as the Royal Society meeting had been postponed until the following week. That was a good thing in the end; it had given him the opportunity to fine tune his presentation on electrical resistance and insulation, something he was hoping would drum up support for his ambitious project. He was about to light up a pipe of tobacco when he spotted a twice-folded piece of paper tumbling toward him on the cobblestone street. It was a curious phenomenon, considering the lack of any breeze.

Thomson bent down, picked up the paper, and unfolded it once. He read the brief message, which looked to have been written by a sure hand. Thomson smiled at the timely note of encouragement, and placed the paper in his jacket pocket.

He was convinced it was a message that was written just for him.

Chapter 17

Holly looked up from her laptop with an annoyed countenance. The study session at the JF Allen Library on Saturday afternoon was disrupted by a sudden blast of tinny-sounding music, emanating from Mark's direction.

"Give Marianna her phone back if you're going to insist on tweaking her road-trip playlist with that ancient dirge," Holly demanded. "We're living in the next century, you know?"

"Classic rock is *ancient*?" Mark queried. Holly responded with a perplexed look. "Okay, sure, I get it…it's in the name. But how is Bob Dylan's Positively 4th Street not a relevant song choice?"

"Because it's a song by Bob Dylan! Is he even still around?"

"Still around? He just released an album that's easily one of his greatest ever!"

"Is that really saying much, though?" Holly said with a snide grin, knowing exactly which buttons to push on Mark's yellow, banyan tree aloha shirt. "After going to one of his concerts a few years ago, my dad said that if you knew you had only six months to live, a Dylan show would be just the thing to see."

"Why's that?" Mark asked.

"Because a Dylan show takes an *eternity* to get through."

Natalie smiled in amusement from behind the enormous textbook she was reading.

"Har, har," Mark scoffed in reply to Holly's dig. "Look, if I don't inject some sanity into this playlist, it's going to end up being nothing but ABBA songs for the entire trip on Monday."

"Now *that* would-a be eternal bliss!" Marianna chimed in.

"Did you say eternal blister? Because that's how much it would irritate me!" Mark passed the phone back over to Marianna. Then he looked over to the pile of books that Natalie had accumulated over the past hour. He picked one up. "These are all on appendectomy. That surgery session at Victoria Hospital yesterday must have been a wee bit of fun, then?"

"I learned a lot," said Natalie, looking up from her reading. "Did you know there are four major incisions you can make, depending on where the appendix ends up in a person?"

"It moves?" Mark asked.

"It's a slippery little beast," Natalie quoted from Dr. Blanco. "We did a Lanz incision on the teenage girl yesterday, but I'm looking at a grid iron incision now."

"But?"

"What?"

"You said, 'But'," said Mark. "As if you were planning on doing another operation with a different incision."

Natalie gulped. That was exactly what she was planning.

"I, uh…I'm just thinking about what I'd do in another situation," she replied. "You know, like if someone was in desperate need, what would I do?"

"What do you mean? Like a 'bad accident' type of desperate need?"

"Uh huh."

"Where time is of the essence?"

"Right."

"And you have limited resources and surgical instruments?"

"Exactly."

"There's only one thing *to* do," Mark averred.

"And that would be?"

"Wake up from your dream and get some advice on how to handle stress better," Mark replied. "Natalie, you're getting worked up about things that haven't even happened yet!"

How wrong you are, Mark, thought Natalie. It's all happening right now, in the past!

"Mark is-a right, Natalie," Marianna cut in. "You are exhibiting all of the symptoms of some-a-one suffering from-a the CTP *sindrome*."

"The what?" queried Natalie.

"Chronic Time Pressure Syndrome," said Holly. "We've been reading about it."

"Did I miss a lecture on this? Why are you reading about…" Natalie stopped mid-sentence and stared at her two friends. "You were looking up CTP because of me, am I right?" Marianna and Holly sheepishly avoided eye contact. Natalie crossed her arms and pursed her lips.

"Well?..." she said in a tone that suggested both annoyance and acceptance. "What did you learn?"

The young women brightened right up, and Holly presented their findings.

"So, Marianna and I performed a 15-point inventory of your character traits, using parallel and exploratory factor analysis. Then, we took the data and did a convergent validity test, correlating the CTPI results with the PSS…"

"That's-a the Perceived Stress Scale," Marianna interjected.

"Right," Holly continued. "Once we were satisfied with the invariance testing and factor loading, we came up with a sound conclusion based on the data."

"Which is?" asked Natalie, with arms still crossed.

Holly took a deep breath and said, "You're in sad shape, sister."

"And how much do I owe you for that impressive diagnosis, doctors?" Natalie asked, a bit miffed.

"Natalie, CTP is a serious-o condition," said Marianna. "Don't-a you feel like you are always-a rushing around?"

"Well, yes, I suppose…"

"And there is-a no time to relax?"

"I guess so…" Natalie answered, absentmindedly picking up her phone.

"Always checking the time like you're going to be late for something?" Holly added. Natalie quickly put her phone on the table, screen-side down.

"They have a point, Natalie," said Mark. "It would be one thing if those traits were part of your personality, but we've all seen a wee bit of heightened anxiety from you lately. We're all just trying to help."

Natalie uncrossed her arms and place the palms of her hands on the tabletop. "All right then. You've covered the symptoms and the diagnosis. What are the treatments?"

Holly cleared here throat. "Well, none of us think your CTP issue is due to an inability to time-manage. You're a very organized person."

"Thank you," said the patient.

"And it is not-a due to poverty, famine, or disease," said Marianna. "So we think your CTP is-a conceptually based!"

"It's all in my head, then?" said Natalie.

"Exactly," said Holly, jumping in, "and studies have shown that increased self-awareness contributes to decreased stress, evidenced by the patient feeling less overwhelmed."

"Sure, but just acknowledging you've got a condition doesn't necessarily fix the problem," said Natalie. "What are the strategies for lessening time stress?"

"They say you should-a *stop time*," Marianna answered.

"Stop time?" Natalie replied, dumbstruck.

"It's a mental exercise," said Holly. "When you get a feeling of time slipping away, you close your eyes and picture a clock frozen in position. You don't consider the past, you forget about how it affects the future, everything gets centred in the 'now'."

"You must imagine there is nothing else but this-a particular moment in-a time," said Marianna.

Natalie took that next particular moment in quiet contemplation. She couldn't solely focus on the 'now' - on the contrary, the past was of the utmost importance to her. She couldn't forget about how the past would affect the future - on the contrary, that was something she had to respect. And, no, there *was* something else other than this moment in time – and she needed to prepare for it.

Natalie looked at Holly, Marianna, and Mark - at their concerned faces. They had only the best intentions in mind. She was so very thankful to have such good friends looking out for her.

"Thanks, guys," said Natalie with a smile. "I'll do my best to embrace the concept of stopping time, even though it sounds impossible."

"Good, *Bene*," said Holly and Marianna together.

"Great," said Mark, getting up from the study table. "Now let's all go for a walk to Jannettas for some gelato! My treat!"

Holly looked at Mark and then at her other friends in disbelief. "His treat? Well, I guess the impossible actually *is* possible."

"So, what was your memory verse for Sunday meeting today?" Connor asked his sister that morning, his time - that afternoon, her time.

"Two verses, actually. Philippians 4: 6 and 7."

"Be anxious for nothing, right?"

"Right. I've been thinking about verse 6 for the past week, so I added 7 today. Gotta guard the heart and mind with that peace, you know?"

"Oh, I know," Connor nodded. Then his image disappeared from the screen for eleven seconds.

"What are you doing?" Natalie asked her phone as she sat on her dorm room bed.

"Tying my laces. I'm going for a run after our chat."

"Yikes. Isn't it getting too cold to go outside now?"

"What are you talking about, Nat? It's a balmy 275K this morning!"

"Your Kelvins don't impress me, brother," Natalie scoffed. "It's 2 degrees Celsius there! I'd be running in my parka!"

"It's not even cold enough to run with gloves yet," Connor scoffed back. "You've gotten soft from all the nice Italian weather you've been getting in Scotland. Now, tell me...you haven't gone soft in the head too, right?" Connor propped up his phone on the kitchen table.

"If you mean what I think you mean, then yes, Connor. My intent is to go back to Florence and make sure Luca gets the proper treatment."

"An appendectomy?"

"Most likely."

"Natalie, this is just a bad idea!" Then, tapping the table top to make his point, Connor said, "This could really upset things in the future!"

"I'm aware of the risk, but…"

"The *Butterfly Noneffect* computer simulation shows an unaltered outcome for the future only when a qubit of information is *slightly* changed, not when a qubit is stomped on…"

"But I've been…"

"Stomped on, and then thrown at the wall…"

"I've been looking into…"

"Stomped on, thrown at the wall, and then run over by a bus full of bowling balls!"

"Okay, okay, I get it! Will you just hear me out for a second, please?" Connor and Natalie took a simultaneous deep breath. After a 9 second pause, Natalie spoke.

"You know how I told you the boy's name was Luca?" Natalie asked.

"Yes," Connor replied sedately.

"And how his nanny, Maria, told me his nickname was *Luca fa presto*?"

"Uh huh…"

"Well, I did a search for that name online."

"Oh, oh…"

"*Luca fa presto* is the nickname of Luca Giordano."

"Here we go…"

"This boy becomes famous, Connor! He goes on to paint *Venus and Mars*!"

"So he becomes an astronomer?"

"Not the planets! Venus and Mars from Roman mythology. He's going to be an artist that lives until he's 70!"

"Well, that's nice."

"What do you mean, that's nice? He can't become a famous artist if he dies from appendicitis, now can he?"

"You're assuming that he's going to die, Natalie," Connor said matter of factly. "Right now, history says he won't. History says he going to make it through this ordeal and live a long life, at least by 17th century standards. Your intervention may change all that."

"Unless I'm *supposed* to intervene to help create that history. Maybe this has been my job all along. Just like it was your job to save

Lavoisier's notebook from being burned up. Besides, as a doctor, I'll be taking the Hippocratic Oath!"

"What? You're going to pledge to be two-faced?"

Natalie rolled her eyes. "Not hypocritic, *Hippocratic*. Hippocrates was the Father of Medicine. In the oath, we vow to do no harm and to only do good. I think saving Luca Giordano's life qualifies as doing good."

Connor became pensive. Natalie could tell he had something to say but was looking for the right words.

"Look, I'll be careful," she said. "I won't act unless I'm sure an operation is what I'm supposed to do. You told me from the start that I had to find out what my mission was, what my job was going to be. I really think this is it."

Connor stayed quiet. Then he nodded.

"Look for a sign," he finally said.

"A sign?"

"Sure. Just keep an eye open for a clear direction. Like a Guiding Hand pointing right at that kid's bellybutton." Connor smiled at his sister.

"I will. I'll look for a Guiding Hand outlining a grid-iron incision! And I think I've already received Part I of that sign."

"What's that?" Connor asked.

"It was the way Luca said, 'Signorina...help me'. It was like he knew I was the one who *could* help him, Connor." Natalie choked back a lump in her throat.

"It was just like he *knew*."

Natalie walked quickly across Abbey Street in her Plain-Jane Florence outfit, her book bag bouncing on her shoulders. Before she entered the Byre Theatre, she stopped to read a plaque that was affixed to the stone wall. She had walked past it often, not paying too much attention, but the date on the plaque now caught her eye. Natalie paused to read the dedication to George Martine, the Scottish historian of St Andrews, who was born in 1635. He became the commissary clerk of the city and wrote a book called *The State of the Venerable See of St Andrews*, an important publication in understanding the conditions that were present in the Age of Enlightenment.

Natalie pictured George Martine in 1647, a lad of thirteen, frolicking at the beach near St Andrews Castle. He would be the same age as Luca Giordano that year. And in just a few minutes, Natalie thought, she would be contemporaries of George and Luca - no longer separated by the inconvenience of time.

Natalie walked up the stairs to the quiet room, past a poster advertising *The Wizard of Oz: Coming Soon This January!*

It was time to return to Italy. The Portal was waiting.

It was time to put her purpose into operation.

Chapter 18

It was early Tuesday afternoon in Florence when I popped back into the Palazzo Medici. I was going to head back to the Redi house right away, but I remembered that I'd only last seen them about fifteen minutes ago, 1647-time. So I killed two hours and a lot of nervous energy by taking a long walk along the Arno River – easier to keep my bearings by having the river alongside me - going east past the Piazza dei Giudici. On my walk back, I stopped across from the Basilica di Santa Croce and had a rest on the grass at the river bank.

I was feeling stronger in my conviction that Luca Giordano was in desperate need of surgery. He had all the signs and symptoms of appendicitis. I began to formulate a plan as to how I would broach the subject of an operation with Dr. Redi, or even Francesco if the situation presented itself. We would need the right instruments to operate. Did they have those? Where would the surgery take place? And what about anesthetic? What would we do for sterility? So many questions! But I did know one thing - sitting here and thinking about all of this wasn't going to get Luca anywhere.

I got up and made my way back to the Redi house, determined that the procedure I was constructing in my mind was the best course of action, and that all of my remaining questions would be answered in due time.

I arrived at the stone house with the red roof in mid-afternoon and knocked at the door. In almost no time at all, Cecilia Redi thrust the door open.

"There you are!" she exclaimed. "I was hoping you would be coming back soon!"

"Is there something wrong?" I asked in response to her flustered appearance.

"*Sì*. Gregorio has left for the orphanage to attend to the boy with the sore stomach. He told me to have Ciccio come to him with *la rapidità!*"

"Where is Francesco now?"

"He left for Evangelista Torricelli's house over an hour ago. They are spending the afternoon together immersed in *la arte poetica*. But Gregorio said something else..." Cecilia paused, took a breath, and looked into my eyes. "He said, 'If Natalia Campo Bella comes by first, send her to me *pronta*!'"

"I shall go at once," I said.

"Do you know the way?"

"*Sì*, I pass by the *Ospedale degli Innocenti* on the way to your house," I answered, pointing down the block to my left. "Before I go, may I make request, Signora Redi?"

"Cecilia. *Sì*."

"May I go into Gregorio's *ufficio* to collect things that will assist him?"

"He took no bag with him, so whatever you need to bring him can go into this *cartella*, here." She handed me a leather case with straps on the side. Cecilia moved aside and let me into the vestibule. Then she led me to the first office on the right and opened the door.

"Take whatever you need, Natalia. I shall be but a moment." Cecilia left me alone in the doctor's office while she went upstairs.

I walked over to the desk in the far-right corner and opened the drawers. No surgical instruments. I looked up on the shelf. Nothing. But when I turned around, I saw a compartment just underneath the examination table. Huh, guess I missed that before! I pulled out the drawer and an inventory of metal appliances lay open before me.

I resisted taking the whole lot, but instead went through a mental list of the instruments necessary for an appendectomy and selected the appropriate tools from the drawer. There were two small, sharp knives in the front that looked like scalpels to me. I took both and placed them into the leather bag. There were clumsy-looking rounded bands that could act as retractors. I put three in the bag. I took a pair of pincers that looked every bit like forceps, and a finely-crafted pair of scissors, too. I thought that there might be some use for probes, so I took three of the slender metal rods. I looked for something in which to wrap the spool of thread and needle I'd found, and I discovered a box of cloths cut into squares sitting on the shelf above the table. I took a handful of the cloths - good enough for surgical sponges - and placed them in the bag. But there was one thing missing, and I knew where to get it.

I brought the bag with me to the last room down the hallway. I opened the door, said hello to Angelo the asp, and made for the bottle of liquid on the counter. I removed the cork and had a sniff. Yep, it was ethanol, all right. Ciccio's invertebrate-specimen preservative would be an ideal sterilant for all the instruments I had collected. And for the surgeon's hands, too.

When I got to the vestibule with my satchel of surgical goodies, Cecilia opened the front door for me.

"You have a lot of things in that case!" she said with surprise. "Does the boy really need all that?"

"*Sì*, and Dr. Redi, too," I replied, walking down the path to the street. "He needs the best tools at his *disposizione*!"

The best tools *and* the best information that modern medicine can provide, too.

The façade at the front passageway into the *Ospedale degli Innocenti* was elegant yet simple, with a stylish walkway accented by terracotta decorations. Upon entering the main door, I was presented with a tidy, sparsely-decorated central courtyard with a chapel on one side and a dormitory on the other. Walking into the dormitory, I was met by a scene bustling with activity: toddlers playing with blocks, young children in small groups playing games with each other, older children in larger groups being instructed by teachers, nannies present everywhere keeping everything in order. The environment was friendly and well organized, reflecting the ideals of charity and compassion. I was instantly impressed.

I recognized Maria almost immediately. When she saw me at the entrance, she passed a toddler to one of her colleagues and rushed over to me.

"Signorina Natalia! It is so good to see you! You have answered my *preghiere*! You must come with me, *per favore*. Dr. Redi and Luca are this way."

Maria led me down a long hallway that terminated at the entrance to a large infirmary. The high-ceilinged room was crowded with beds arranged along opposite walls, half of which were occupied by sick and injured children. Caregivers were scurrying about, attending to their needs. At the far end of the room, Dr. Redi was standing over his patient. When he saw me and Maria, he waved us over to Luca's bedside.

"I am very pleased to see you," Dr. Redi said to me in French.

I nodded a reply, looking down at the young boy who looked more unconscious than asleep.

"After you had left the house, a lad arrived with a message sent by Maria saying that young Luca had taken a turn for the worse," Dr. Redi explained. "When I arrived, he was in terrible pain. In anguish. I felt it necessary to calm the boy, so I gave him a spoonful of the sweet syrup. It has rendered him unconscious and nonresponsive."

"What is in this syrup?" I asked, bending down to check on Luca's breathing, which was calm and steady.

"Honey mixed with *oppio*."

Oppio? Oppi…opium? Opium! No wonder the boy was unresponsive!

"I see you have my medical bag," said Dr. Redi. "What have you brought me?"

"I would like to talk to you about that," I replied. "Is there somewhere we can speak in private, doctor?"

"*Oui*. This way, *s'il vous plaît*." We left Maria with Luca and exited the infirmary.

Dr. Redi led me to a small office just down the hallway. He beckoned me to sit in the chair across from him after closing the door. I put the bag down on the floor.

"Dr. Redi…"

"Gregorio," he interrupted.

"Gregorio," I continued, "have you *esperienza* in *operativo* on a *paziente*?" I was peppering my French with *italiano* even more now, as my comfort level with the language was growing.

"Why, *sì*," Dr. Redi responded with a puzzled look. "I have performed many in an *emergenza*. I have amputated, blood let, and done a *trepanato* in the skull to remove pressure."

"Have you ever done a procedure where you opened the abdomen?"

"As in a *litotomia* to remove stones from the bladder?"

"*Sì*."

"No. Now, why do you ask these questions, Natalia?"

I took a deep breath.

"Gregorio, in my medical-training experience in Scotland, I recently assisted in a surgery that was performed on a young girl. The reason for the operation was to relieve pain - a pain that is identical to what Luca is suffering from right now. The pain was caused by an outgrowth on the, on the..." I made a twisting-tube motion with my hand, overtop my stomach.

"*Colon?*" he offered.

"*Sì*, the *colon*," I replied, making a quick mental note to trust my translational instincts in the future. "The outgrowth is an infected body that must be removed, or the patient may die."

"Did this girl survive the procedure?" he asked.

"*Sì*, she will make a full recovery," I said, then I gathered up the courage to add, "but we ensured there would be no *complicazioni* by cleaning all the instruments with this..." I pulled the bottle of ethanol out of the bag. "Cleaning everything, including hands, with alcohol, will prevent further infection." I opened the bag to show Gregorio the instruments I had brought.

Dr. Redi took the bottle and looked at it. He looked into the bag. He sat quietly for a moment, looking deep in thought. I was starting to shake, preparing myself for the derision I would face for posing such a preposterous 17th-century proposition. But Gregorio looked over and gave me a smile.

"My son and I have been discussing this very thing of late, Natalia. Through his research with parasites and toxins, and the studying of water samples with his multiple lenses that expose the tiniest of creatures, Francesco has proposed that there are even smaller living things in our world. He believes that these invisible creatures may carry a venom that cause disease and infection, and he thinks that they can be killed by the alcohol in his specimen-preserving solutions. I did not find myself in agreement with most of his ideas, but now you have come along to provide some *informazione* that I cannot dismiss. It makes me very curious." Dr. Redi paused again. Then he looked right into my eyes.

"I need to know one thing, Natalia…" he said. "Do you feel confident enough in your skills to lead me through this operation?"

"I do, doctor," I replied solemnly.

"Come then. Let us prepare the instruments."

I don't think Gregorio had any intention of washing his hands, but the smell of the ethanol on his fingers displeased him so he cleaned them off in a bucket of soapy water and gave them a good rinse. I did likewise. Then we took the sterilized instruments to a small, sunlit room next door to the office, and laid them out on a desk that sat to the right of the operating table. When Dr. Redi left to go get the patient, I took the opportunity to wipe down all the surfaces with an alcohol-laden cloth. When I was done, the room had a sanitized odor that smelled just right to me. The only thing missing from this OR scenario were the surgical gowns and masks.

In another minute, Gregorio appeared at the door with Luca in his arms. He laid the unconscious boy on the table and removed the boy's clothes. He then gave the outfit to Maria who was standing at the door. She had a curious look on her face, not exactly sure what was happening. Dr. Redi asked for us to be excused, then he shut the door on Maria's surprised expression. While he was doing all of this, I quickly cleaned off Luca's torso with another ethanol-laced cloth. When he returned to the patient, taking up his position on the left side of the table, everything was ready for Redi to get started.

Gregorio picked up the small sharp knife with a slight tremble hand, took a deep breath, and looked over at me. He was nervous. So was I. I gave him a reassuring nod.

Dr. Redi placed his finger three centimeters to the right of the patient's bellybutton, and traced a five-centimeter diagonal line from 11 o'clock down to 5 o'clock. He looked at me for approval. I nodded. He placed the blade of the knife down at the 11 and pressed firmly all the way down to the 5.

The operation was underway.

We made a good team, Dr. Redi and I. His surgical skills surprised me: he showed a firm, steady hand in making the incision, and he exhibited dexterity while using his probes to tease away the peritoneal tissue during the exploratory phase. I kept busy with the retractors and cloths, giving the surgeon an unobstructed, clean look into the abdominal cavity. When he found the large outgrowth on the cecum, at the anterior part of the large intestine, we both looked at each other wide-eyed; the appendix was about 7 centimeters long, bright red, looking angry and ready to burst.

After gently removing the mesoappendix tissue, I asked Dr. Redi to hold the retractor as I spooled off a length of thread and wiped it with an alcohol cloth. Then I showed him where he was going to ligate the appendix before removal. Gregorio took the thread and smartly knotted the distal section of the appendix as I held it in place with the forceps. When he was satisfied with the tie-job, I handed him the scissors. One snip later, and I was placing the vestigial organ on an empty plate on the desk.

Closing was performed without irrigation and suction, of course, but I made sure the intestinal area was clean and dry before suturing. My cloth count was consistent in and out; no foreign material was left in the patient. Dr. Redi's stitching technique was impressive: sutures evenly placed and in succession; the thread never needing to be tied or cut after each pass; tension evenly distributed along the suture line; and the knot that he made after the last pass was secured and snipped with elegance. Boy, did I ever learn a lot!

And I know Dr. Redi learned a lot, too.

And Luca? He didn't learn a thing. He slept soundly the entire time.

I stayed at Luca's bedside for close to an hour after we brought him back to the infirmary. Dr. Redi had just returned from the office when our patient began to stir. As his eyes opened after some rapid blinking, the young boy looked me squarely in the face.

"Signorina Natalia, is that you?"

"*Sì*, Luca. How are you feeling?" I asked, stroking his head with the back of my hand.

"I…I do not feel the pain in my belly," he answered, trying to sit up. "But…ow…there is a pain *on* my belly!" I eased Luca back down to the prone position.

"And you will feel some discomfort there for a few weeks to come, my boy," said Dr. Redi. "But the danger is now past, and you will be better soon." He squeezed the boy's toe underneath the blanket.

"I am very pleased to hear that young Luca has found relief, Dr. Redi," said a man's voice from behind Gregorio. As Gregorio turned aside, I made eye contact with a middle-aged man in a white jacket and blue pants, who stood only slightly taller than half of the doctor's height. He had a stern look about him. Maria was standing by his side.

"Ah, Bartolomeo, good to see you!" said Dr. Redi with a nod. The man nodded back.

"And who is this young woman?" Bartolomeo asked, still looking at me.

"Natalia Campo Bella, I would like you to meet Signor Bartolomeo di Antonio Canigiani. He is the *Priore dell'Arte della Seta* of the orphanage."

I stood up and offered my hand in greeting to the man in charge of the orphanage. The gesture was promptly ignored.

"I have been informed that a *procedura sperimentale* may have been used on the boy today," said Bartolomeo.

"Sì," replied Dr. Redi. "Something that was new to me, but not to Signorina Natalia, who assisted me in the *operazione*."

"*Operazione!*"

"We removed an inflamed outgrowth from the boy's *intestini*."

"You opened the boy's body to remove a growth?" Bartolomeo barked. "This is an irregular treatment!"

"I am feeling much better!" said Luca. I shushed him with a pat on the shoulder.

"Who approved this?" asked Bartolomeo with indignance.

"Well, it was not his parents since he is an orphan," replied Dr. Redi with a smirk. "Since I am the attending physician, I made the decision to operate."

"You needed to speak to me first, Gregorio!"

"For what possible medical reason, Bartolomeo?"

"I am feeling much better!" Luca reiterated.

"For the reason that you cannot perform experiments with the lives of others!" Bartolomeo pointed his finger at Dr. Redi. "You have not heard the last of this matter, Gregorio. I shall launch an *inquisizione* with the Italian government! Be prepared to face the *conseguenze!*" Then he looked at me again. "And that goes for you, as well, signorina!"

And with that, Signor Bartolomeo dilla della Whatevera stomped off, with Maria close behind.

"But I am feeling so much better," said Luca, encouragingly. I stroked his forehead again, then I stood up and walked to Gregorio.

"Are we in trouble, Dr. Redi?" I asked.

"Bah! *No!*" Gregorio scoffed. "Bartolomeo is full of hot air!" He placed his hand on my shoulder, reassuringly.

"Nobody expects an Italian *inquisizione!*"

"So, you really cut into the boy's abdomen? I did not think this type of thing was done in this day and age!"

Dianora and I were having a late-night snack in the D'ambrosio kitchen. The embers of the stove glowed softly, providing just enough light and heat on the cool October night. Rita and Nerina had gone off to bed an hour before, saying goodnight after we had all enjoyed a rousing evening of *briscola* in the living room. The card game was easy enough to learn, the trick being to use your trump cards wisely and assume a defensive position when you could. Nerina and I made a good team, with my guarded play complimented by her first-trick attack strategy. When I ended the final game by announcing '*Briscola!*' after playing my *bastoni*, Dianora called out '*Bravo!*' at the same time Rita said, '*La fortuna del principiante!*'. My improving *italiano* heard 'Beginner's luck!' being evoked.

"I did not think there was an issue with this type of surgery, but a certain Signor Bartolomeo seemed to think otherwise," I said.

"Do you think he was *consterné* that you did not ask his *autorizzazione?*" Dianora asked, mixing French together with Italian – something we were doing quite freely and frequently that whole evening.

"I believe he was mad, *oui*, though I am at a loss to understand why we would need his permission to operate. He is not a *medico*."

"*Non*, but he is the man in-charge of the facility. He is responsible to the *stato* and to the church for everything that happens at the orphanage."

"Do you think either would have a problem with a life-saving operation?" I asked with some indignance.

"The *stato* may object to the surgery on procedural grounds," Dianora said after taking a sip of tea. "The *chiesa* may see this type of surgery as a desecration of the human body."

I sat quietly for a moment and thought about what Dianora said. She had a point. Actually, two points.

"This is such a different time," I murmured aloud without thinking.

"I know what you mean," she replied, taking another sip of tea.

"Anyway, tomorrow is another day, and our landladies have something special planned for us," Dianora announced. "We are going for a ride in the country!"

"Well, that sounds exciting! Where are we off to?"

"We will be taking a carriage to a local winery for lunch. The details are being handled by Giuseppe and Lucio, in their latest attempt to gain favour with the D'ambrosio sisters."

"How are they doing?" I asked.

"In *briscola* terms, let us say their declarations are sometimes risky, they often play their trump cards too early, but they are encouraged to still be in the game."

The analogy made me smile. Then I asked, "You are taking the day off from work, then?"

"I am. Evangelista insisted. He says I have been working long hours lately and I need a break. Besides, he felt under the weather this afternoon with a cough starting and wants to take tomorrow to rest himself. It is a good idea. He has been pushing hard to finish a particular mathematical theorem that has plagued him for the past 18 months. Would you like me to explain it to you?"

"Oh, perhaps later," I replied. "When I have access to a better escape route." I could tell by her smirk that Dianora liked that one. Then I asked, "Did Signor Torricelli enjoy his visit with Ciccio today?"

"He certainly did," Dianora answered. "Those two have become fast-friends." Then she added, more somberly, "Francesco's visit today was a nice distraction from all the pressure Evangelista has been under."

By the tired look on her face, you could tell she meant, 'all the pressure *we* have been under.'

"Well then, we all need a relaxing day off tomorrow, so let's get a head start with a good night's sleep," I pronounced, rising from the table and putting our dishes in the wash basin.

The two of us went quietly up the stairs and prepared for bed.

I woke up in the middle of the night from a bad dream. I was back in the operating room. Luca was lying on the table in pain, and I was chained to a doorknob across the room. Maria was hovering in mid-air, shaking her head disapprovingly. Signor Bartolomeo was there, painting a red line on the floor between me and the boy. When

I called out in Italian for someone to help, no one came. Then I called out in French. Nothing. When I shouted in English, I woke myself up, my eyes staring at the moonlit ceiling of the bedroom.

I turned to see if I had awakened my roommate, but I hadn't. Her blankets were neatly pulled back on the bed, her nightgown draped over the footboard. Dianora was nowhere to be seen.

She had disappeared into the night.

Chapter 19

When I woke up in the morning and rolled over, Dianora was sitting on the edge of her bed, quietly getting dressed. I propped myself up, my elbow on the pillow.

"You were up late last night," I said.

"I was?"

"I woke up for a moment and you were gone."

"Oh, that..." Dianora said with a dismissive gesture. "That was just me being me. When I get restless and cannot sleep, I prefer to take a walk to clear my head."

"In the dark? In the middle of the night?"

"If I cannot sleep, that is usually the time it happens," Dianora said with a smirk.

She had a point there.

"Um, did you spill something on your arm?" I asked pointing, noticing a blotch on her skin just behind the right elbow. Dianora turned her arm over and looked.

"Oh, that..." she said again, just as offhandedly. "That is my birthmark. It is called a wine stain. Have you not seen one before?"

"No, I haven't," I admitted. "I know that sounds funny from someone studying medicine, but that is new to me."

Dianora got up and held out her arm in front of me to give me a closer look.

"Your blemish looks like the island of Japan," I said. Dianora turned her arm over again for another look.

"From your perspective, I can see what you mean!" she replied. "I feel very cosmopolitan today! Could you button me up, please?" Dianora sat down and I sat up to fasten the back of her dress. After I finished, she bounced up and slipped on her shoes.

"I will meet you downstairs for breakfast," she announced. "We have a busy morning before us! Come on!"

"How do you say, 'Stop nagging me, Mama!' in *italiano*?" I asked in French.

"*Smettila di tormentarmi!*" she replied. "But if I was your *mamma*, I would have done *this*, too!"

Dianora smacked me on the top of my head and dashed out of the room, giggling the whole way.

After I got back from freshening up in the outdoor facilities, the kitchen was alive with the sound of stomping feet, raised voices, and the clattering of pots. When I entered the room I saw Dianora, Nerina, and Rita, smiling and sitting at the kitchen table while two men argued over top of the stove.

"I will tell you for the last time, Lucio, so pay attention…the secret is all in the roasting!"

"Giuseppe, you can tell me a hundred more times and you will still be wrong. It is all in the grinding!"

When the two men spotted me, they left what they were doing and approached. Lucio, he with the shock of black hair and aquiline nose, took up my hand for a kiss.

"You must be Signorina Natalia! It is a pleasure to meet you! Lucio Desanto at your service!"

My other hand was taken up by Giuseppe, he with the receding hairline and protruding chin. He kissed my hand just a bit longer.

"Signorina, such a pleasure to finally meet you! Giuseppe Ledario, forever enslaved to your beauty and honour!"

"Forever is a long time, Seppe," Lucio scoffed. "But it is still not long enough for you to produce a sincere cup of *caffè*!"

Rita made a coughing sound and pointed to the stove with concern. "Ah, *gentinuomini?*"

The two men dashed back to the stove where their coffee beans were about to over-roast in the pan. I took a seat with the other women to watch the show.

"The beans are now braised to *perfezione!*" Giuseppe proclaimed, shaking the pan with clothed hand.

"If by *perfezione* you mean they need another two *minuti*, then *sì*, they are *perfetto*," Lucio observed over Giuseppe's shoulder.

Giuseppe let out an Italian 'harrumph', picked up the pan, and poured the beans into a large, ceramic container.

"I cook, you grind," said Giuseppe, handing Lucio the pestle and mortar.

"Now the women shall marvel at the exhibition of true skill!" Lucio declared as he commenced grinding the coffee beans in fancy circular motion. "I have been doing this since I was a boy!"

"Ha! I have you there, Lucio! I have been having coffee since I was in the womb!" Giuseppe boasted. "My mother drank so much *caffè*, I came out grinding my teeth!"

"That explains why you are always so bitter," Lucio said with a grin. He looked over to Giuseppe who was measuring out something from a white container. "What are you doing now?"

"I am getting ready to add some cinnamon into the grind."

"Sacrilege!" Lucio shouted.

"It will add a sweetness and depth that everyone here but you will enjoy thoroughly," Giuseppe countered.

"Do you know what belongs in *caffè*, my friend? *Caffè*! That is it! Anything else will ruin it!"

"Ugh! Do not be a stubborn donkey, Lucio! This only shows why your *caffè* will only be good, but never great."

"And your downfall, Seppe, will be your disregard for the purity that lies in this sacred seed! Now, you put this grind into the *caffettiera* while I get our treat for this morning!" Lucio turned around just before leaving the room. "And no funny business with the cinnamon!"

"*Va bene!*" Giuseppe called out to the departing Lucio. Then he gave us a wink and added a teaspoonful anyway, before putting the grounds into the coffee pot.

When the coffee was ready, Giuseppe brought it to the table and poured it into the six cups that Rita had put out. Lucio uncovered the breakfast treat he had brought, which drew a sigh of approval from everyone but me. I let out a gasp of recognition.

He had unveiled a white cake with a powdered-sugar *fleur-de-lys* stenciled on top!

"I know, Natalia! Isn't it lovely?" said Lucio. "I saw it in the baker's window and could not resist!" He cut into it and began placing pieces on plates. "It is a new recipe he has created. Apparently, his brother-in-law was given a cake very much like this one from a total stranger the other day. He loved it so much, that he asked the baker if he could reproduce it!" Everyone tried the cake.

"This is wonderful," Nerina gushed.

"I should say!" Rita proclaimed. "And it is so pretty, what with the symbol of Florence sweetly sprinkled on top!"

"The baker is calling it *Schiacciata Fiorentina*, in honour of the girl who brought his brother-in-law the cake. That is what she called it."

Actually, if I remember correctly, I had called it a *torta schiacciata*.

"Your *caffè* is very nice," Rita said to Lucio.

"*Ehm*?" said Giuseppe, clearing his throat.

"Your *caffè* is very nice, too," Nerina said to Giuseppe.

I was about to give out an *ehm*, myself. After all, wasn't I the one responsible for the breakfast cake?

Filippo the Coachman was in no particular hurry to get to Strada this morning. He must have been getting paid by the *ora*. I couldn't blame him for his tardiness, though: it was such a glorious October morning, with not a cloud in the sky and just a nip in the air to make it feel like mid-autumn. I didn't think it was too cold, and neither did Dianora who was sitting right across from me, but Giuseppe and Lucio sure did. They made sure Nerina and Rita were warm and comfortable, putting their arm around each lady and snuggling tightly. Uh huh. But the ladies didn't call them on it, so I suppose their boldness had been rewarded. We were all dressed in appropriate attire for an outing in the country: the men wore felt hats, white shirts, breeches and jackets; Nerina and Rita wore bonnets and embroidered linen dresses overtop their corsets; Dianora and I found floral-patterned cotton sun dresses in Nerina's closet, and put them on overtop our petticoats. We were encouraged to bring along sunscreen, so we grabbed our parasols before leaving the house.

As our carriage exited Florence via the city gate to the south, the beauty of the Tuscan countryside emerged. The surprisingly smooth road – with roadbed construction provided by the ancient Romans, Filippo explained – was lined with tall cypress trees, and fields of sunflowers and wheat and grapes. The small villages that we passed through along the way were marked by colourful dwellings made of stone and brick, their narrow streets leading to bustling marketplaces. The locals were going about their daily business - tending the garden, hanging the wash, chopping the wood. Little girls playing tag, little boys kicking a ball down the street like future Italian soccer stars. It was quite the idyllic scene - charmingly bucolic, Dad would have said, invoking his crossword-puzzle vocabulary.

When the carriage reached the Chianti region, the landscape changed abruptly. The hills became steeper, the road a bit more rugged. The horses mildly protested as they carried us up a particularly acute incline, but they were rewarded with a rest at the very top as we all took in the sight: the town of Strada, perched on a distant hill, its towers and stone walls standing majestically in the late-morning light.

Giuseppe explained that Strada was a small but prosperous town that was becoming well known for its olive oil production, in which he was becoming a principle player. Lucio explained that Strada had an impressive cathedral that displayed intricate carvings and colourful frescos on the ceiling, and how the renovation of said cathedral had been done by his own construction company. I was quite looking forward to exploring this sparkling settlement, but the carriage took a right off the main road when we reached the bottom of the next hill. When I asked about our destination, Giuseppe explained that we were heading to a little shack in the country for lunch. Then he gave me a wink.

In another ten minutes, we descended into a valley, turned a corner, and were confronted by a stunning vista: a plantation, stretching as far as the eye could see, with an orchard and vineyard rolling up, down, and around the Tuscan countryside. It was breathtaking.

"*Mamma mia!*" Nerina exclaimed on behalf of all of us.

As we trundled along, taking in the beauty of the fall colours, Dianora absently began humming a ditty. Lost in the moment, I suppose.

"La la-la la, la la-la la la…" she sang, the notes quietly rising and falling. Funny, but I recognized the tune.

"I think I know that *canzone*," I said to her in our jumbled French/Italian-speak.

"Ah, *mi scusi?*" she replied, a bit startled.

"That song you are humming. It sounds very familiar."

"It could not be," Dianora stated. "I mean, you are not from here, so you could not have heard it before."

"Sing it again, *per favore*," I asked her.

"Very well, if you *insistere*," she answered. She began humming a tune that had no discernible melody, like she was singing notes while being conducted by a baton-wielding monkey.

"No, no," I interjected. "Do that la la part again."

Dianora took a breath and quietly sang, "La la-la la, la la-la la la…"

"That's it!" I said pointing, but then I clammed up immediately. How could I say, 'That's the chorus to the song Mamma Mia, by ABBA!', when that oldie hadn't been released yet. I know ABBA's classic rock, but they're not *that* classic. Fortunately, Nerina jumped in just in time.

"I know that one, too!" she said. "It sounds like that song in the second act of the opera, *L'Ormindo!*"

"*Sì*, it does!" added Rita. "That one that is sung by…by?…"

"Osmano?" I cut in.

"*Sì*! Osmano!" Rita announced. "You have seen this opera, Natalia?"

"No," I replied. "But I have a friend, Marianna, who has." I looked at Dianora. "Maybe I heard *her* singing this tune, then."

"That makes sense," she answered.

"So you have learned this song from the opera, too, Dianora?" asked Nerina.

"I do not think so," Dianora responded. "I have never seen it."

Strange looks directed toward Dianora ensued, but were dispelled quickly as the carriage came to a stop.

"We have arrived!" Filippo announced.

Our carriage was parked on a smooth gravel driveway in front of a large water feature with a burbling fountain at its centre. To our left stood a stately, three-story grand villa, with balconies off every room. The façade was painted burnt sienna, and it blended in with its surroundings surprisingly well.

"Welcome to the shack in the country," Giuseppe smiled, as he and Lucio helped the ladies out of the carriage. And then, right on cue, the front door of the villa burst open, and a large man with salt-and-pepper hair strode onto the veranda with his arms outstretched in greeting.

"My friends, my friends! Welcome to my modest home!"

"Guido!" cried Giuseppe. "It is so good to see you again! I have missed you so!" He and Guido bearhugged it out on the driveway.

"Eh! Lucio!" cried Guido.

"Eh! Guido!" cried Lucio.

Another round of bearhugging broke out.

"And these two lovely ladies must be Rita and Nerina!" said Guido, kissing the correct hands, respectively.

"And may I introduce to you, Dianora Murelli and her friend, Natalia Campo Bella," said Lucio. "Ladies, this is Guido *Gentile*!" Lucio put emphasis on the *Gen-TEEL-eh* surname.

"It is my pleasure to meet you, Dianora!" Hand kiss. "And Natalia!" Hand kiss.

"Now, come, all of you!" waved Guido. "Freshen up in the house, before we go to the back garden to enjoy the feast I have prepared for us!"

Guido put his arms around the shoulders of the men and led us toward the villa, the three of them talking away a mile a *minuti*.

"It is so nice when old friends get together," I said to Dianora, as the trio of buddies were yucking it up.

"Old friends?" she replied. "Why, they only met for the first time last week."

The vineyard view from the back garden was impressive, as was the place setting for lunch. Could the Medici bank possibly have more silver than this? The seven of us were seated at a long table that had no available space once the *antipasti* was served and the wine started flowing. There were serving plates of prosciutto and salami, pickled vegetables, aged cheeses of all types and odours, two baskets of fresh bread, and a big bowl of what looked to be bruschetta that had enough garlic in it to flush your face with joy. Guido insisted we try a bit of everything, though he said we should avoid the candle wax in the centrepiece, as it had not been cured! Lucio liked that one, and after two glasses of Chianti he spread some wax drippings on his crostini, ate it in one go, and pronounced it perfectly seasoned, to the delight of the host.

I honestly thought that we were done when the servants removed the empty plates, but no, that was just the starter. Then came the *primi piatti*: Two giant platters of risotto accompanying a large bowl of pasta – *tagliatelle*, to be precise – that was served in a creamy, mushroom sauce. Was that saffron in the rice dish? I asked our host. Why, of course! he bellowed, pointing to the east and describing how the Dominican friars of Andalusia harvested this spice from the most vibrant of all crocuses. I wasn't sure if Andalusia was just over the hill or across the Mediterranean Sea, but not knowing this didn't spoil my enjoyment of the risotto.

"There is nothing like pasta is there?" Guido mused after taking a mouthful of the starchy goodness. "It is not just food, I tell you truthfully, it is a work of art unto itself, and a carrier of *gusto* and *struttura* that set one's tastes *accendi*!" A flavour and texture bomb, it certainly was!

"You would make me *affamato* if I were not eating already!" Giuseppe exclaimed, hungrily.

"Could you imagine a world without pasta?" Nerina posited.

"It is not *possibile*," Rita answered.

"*Perisca il pensiero*!" shouted Guido, perishing the thought. "No *testaroli* to dispel the pain? No *rigatoni* to pleasure the soul? No *ravioli* to lift the spirit? Why, life would not be worth living, would it friends?"

"No!" went the outcry, as Lucio lifted his glass.

"To our beloved pasta! May it be honoured with a national holiday!" We all heartily toasted to that!

"Not to change the *argomento*," said Dianora, changing the subject, "but have you heard that the nation of China makes claim to inventing pasta?"

Suddenly the table went completely quiet, save for the cutlery that clattered onto the floor from the stunned servants. The awkward silence continued for a good ten *secondi* during the *primi* until Guido stood up, his face red with anger, and declared…

"Lucio, assemble the chefs! Giuseppe, sharpen the forks! You women, inspect the *cannelloni*! This means war!" When Guido finally produced a big grin, everyone had a good laugh. The servants breathed a sigh of relief.

"China inventing pasta!" scoffed Rita. "Such a preposterous claim!"

"How rude," Nerina agreed.

Dianora gave me a mischievous wink from across the table. Oh, she's a *ragazza sfacciata*, that one!

The next course – the next course?! – was the *secondi piatta*, of course! A platter of lamb chops, a platter of grilled beef, a platter of fish with their heads still attached, a platter of roasted chicken…so many platters! The servants scattered *contorni* of seasoned vegetables, sautéed greens, braised artichokes, and more bread about the table. Those side dishes alone could have been a meal! At this point I was only picking at the platters, like everyone else, but that didn't stop us from polishing off the meat dishes in the end, and putting a good dent into the veggies.

After this, it was on to the *formaggi*, where we partook of an assortment of cheeses: a little Parmigiano, *un poco* Pecorino, *un po 'di più* Gorgonzola. The *dolci* consisted of fruit tarts of berries and apricots - topped with cream if you liked - and bowls of candied nuts. After the *caffè e disgetiva* which concluded with a shot or two of *limoncello*, we were all firmly established in a collective Tuscan food *coma*.

"Perhaps we could all use a good walk, *sì*?" said Guido, patting his tummy.

"*Oh, sì, per favore!*" was the general consensus.

"To walk off that meal, I need a hike to the *L'Oriente*," Dianora whispered to me with a sly, satisfied grin.

"You are feeling a bit cheeky today, are you not?" I asked Dianora as we walked leisurely between the rows of meticulously-cultivated grapevines that that were turning their fall colours of red and gold. Most of the grapes had been picked already this season, Guido explained, but there were still plenty left on the vines, in the hope of obtaining an extra-sweet late harvest this year. As the conversation turned to the Tuscan winemaking business during our stroll through the vineyard, Dianora and I steadily fell back from the pack, becoming immersed in our own dialogue, in French.

"*Oui*," she answered. "Please excuse my impertinence. It is just the fatigue coming out of me."

"I have noticed that you have been tired these past two days," I said. "Are there things weighing on your mind?"

"I have to admit that there are, Natalia," she said, kicking at a dirt clump. "There is so much work to finish for Evangelista at the moment that I can barely catch my breath. And what with him being sick and all…"

"I thought you said he was only under the weather, yesterday?"

"Well, I mean, if he *becomes* sicker, I will have to get his papers in order much more speedily, if you see what I mean."

I nodded, but I didn't really see at all.

"I am feeling out of sorts, Natalia. It is a funny sensation for me. At times I feel like *je est un autre*."

"You mean *je suis un autre*," I offered in correction.

"*Non*, I mean *I is another*, as opposed to *I am another*."

"I am not sure what that means, Dianora."

"A famous poet once said this. It is like...it is like I feel that sometimes there are two of me, Natalia. One of me is here, the other is looking at me from somewhere else, reflecting on what is happening in my life, helping to make sense of what I am doing here." She paused. "I am sorry, I know that is hard to comprehend."

"*Non, non,*" I replied. "I think I know what you mean. You feel like you are one person in two different places, trying to understand your place in both."

"That is exactly it," Dianora replied, pointing a finger straight ahead. "I am being pulled in different directions and I am searching for a *reason*, Natalia. And I know that reason is out there, somewhere." She stopped for a moment and looked up to the sky. A satisfied smile came to her lips. "But, you know, today has been a good day. And the future ahead will be bright, too. I just know it."

Yes, a bright future awaits, my friend. I know it, too.

It was a quiet coach ride back to Florence later that afternoon. We had pretty much used up all of our words for the day, and our energy reserves were being utilized for digestive purposes. Plus, the sun was beating down on us now, with the only relief being provided by the gentle breeze of the carriage moving forward. Slowly. Filippo was still in no hurry, as usual - time being money, and all.

The good-byes at Guido's estate took a while. There were hugs, kisses, and lots of tears. Then, after the tears, more hugs and a few more kisses. All of us women were getting a bit impatient with all this carrying-on while we sat in the carriage. After a final embrace, the boys all agreed to meet this coming weekend instead of waiting another whole seven days.

When we got back to Casa D'ambrosio on Via del Corso, Giuseppe paid our coachman with silver coins, and I made the mistake of calling him Tonio when I thanked him for the ride.

"It is a common mistake in our family business, signorina!" said Filippo, brushing it off. "Tonio is my brother!"

"You are very much alike, Signor Esposito," I said.

"We look the same, but could not be more different. Tonio is good at saving," Filippo said pocketing his coins, "but I centre my attentions on different goals in life." He tipped his cap to us as he rode off. "I was happy to assist you today! *Arrivederci!*"

An hour later, we were all having a cup of tea in the living room, resting ourselves after a long, hard day of relaxing. We had decided that dinner tonight would be out of the question, though Lucio suggested that maybe a late-evening snack would be in order before he and Giuseppe made their way home. You know, something light! he said. Rita suggested that *pane tostato e marmellata* would be a good little meal, but Nerina didn't want toast and jam; she requested something more *sostanziale - formaggio e pane*. Giuseppe liked the thought of 'more substantial' and added *prosciutto* to the cheese and bread suggestion. Lucio was in agreement with his friend, though the *prosciutto* would go much better with *uova e patate fritte*. Once the menu dust had settled, it was decided that a fry-up of ham, eggs, and potatoes would be in order, along with some cheese, olives, and pickled onions. Oh, and a little toast and jam for *dolce*, of course! So much for something light!

As we were reminiscing about Guido's vast cherry and apricot orchards, we were startled by a heavy knock on the front door. Rita sprang up to answer it, but Lucio was closer, so he opened the door and made way for a broad-shouldered man in a dark-coloured coat with an insignia on the breast pocket. He was carrying a baton in his right hand.

"Is this the D'ambrosio residence?" he asked in a husky voice.

"*Sì*, I am Rita D'ambrosio, and this is my sister Nerina. What can we do for you, *signoro*?"

"I am Signor Ciccarelli, the senior officer of the Bargello of Florence…"

I looked at Dianora, and she mouthed the word *police* to me, in French.

"…and I am looking for a Signorina Natalia. Is she here?"

I got all red in the cheeks and answered, "*Sì*, signoro...I am Natalia...er...Campo Bella." I stood up from the sofa.

"You are the young woman who assisted Dr. Gregorio Redi at the *Ospedale degli Innocenti* yesterday afternoon?"

"*Sì*, signoro," I answered as I started to tremble.

"Natalia Campo Bella, I have been ordered by the *Capitano del Popolo* of Florence to place you under arrest." Signor Ciccarelli stretched forward and handed me a piece of paper from his jacket pocket.

"This is preposterous!" Giuseppe cried out.

"What is the charge?" Lucio demanded.

I unfolded the paper, my hands shaking, but couldn't make out a word underneath the letterhead. Dianora stood next to me, held the paper steady and began reading it over my shoulder.

"It is all in the arrest paper, but I shall summarize," said the policeman. "This young woman is charged with unauthorized medical practice, practicing medicine without a license, violation of medical ethics, and violation of public health regulations."

"*Sì*, it is all there in the paper," said Dianora.

Everyone but Signor Ciccarelli and I had a stunned look on their face. Ciccarelli's look was quite sanguine. Mine was quite terrified.

The officer cleared his throat. "Signorina Natalia, you are to be confined to the *casa* of your choosing until *le udienza* with the *Podestà* can be arranged in the future. Do you *capisci questo*?"

My head was swirling, but I *did* understand what was happening. I had hoped that there wouldn't be any negative consequences from operating on Luca. But I was wrong.

"And Dr. Redi?" I asked the officer.

"He is under house arrest, as well. You shall both stand before the Chief Magistrate together."

Rita put her hand on my shoulder. "Natalia will complete her house arrest in *this* home, Signor Ciccarelli. And then she will be cleared of these ridiculous charges!"

"Very well, signora," the officer said as he marched to the door. "You have been assigned as her steward until the time of the hearing." And with that, Signor Ciccarelli exited Casa D'ambrosio.

When I woke up in the middle of the night, the moonlight was shining on the wall next to my roommate's bed. She was sound asleep. I quietly got up, changed into my street clothes – put a run in my silk stockings, argh! - and carefully made my way out of the room and down the stairs. In two minutes I had turned the corner from Via del Corso onto Via del Proconsolo, the quickest way to the Duomo.

The past day had held so much promise. It started out as a nice break from all the stress and strain, with food and fun and laughter and a nice conversation with my new friend. And then it all came crashing down.

Upon arriving at my destination, I was greeted by my fuzzy glowing hole in the wall. It was time to go home to Canada, to catch up with my other life, and to figure out my next steps.

I stood up straight, took a deep breath of the cool Tuscan air, and stepped into the Shimmering Light of The Gateway.

Chapter 20

The vinyl records room at CJSW had been downsized since the advent of the compact disc earlier in the decade. What was once an impressive library of music from every genre imaginable was now reduced to a collection no larger than what Hot Wax Records had on display just down the road - which was not very much. To most of the DJs at the campus radio station it was good riddance to that; CDs, the new audio kids on the block, didn't have ticks and pops and skips that old records did, and the ability to program tracks made the digital realm a convenience in which to work. Plus, vinyl could wear out from excess play on incorrectly-weighted cartridges, and it produced inner-groove distortion on poorly mastered pressings. Yes, the compact disc was the wave of the future in music reproduction, and those that clung to the tired ways of vinyl and magnetic tape were in danger of going down with the analogue ship.

There was only one radio show left on the programming schedule that even played records on the station's one remaining turntable, and that was Ken's Kuts – broadcasting five days a week from 3 to 4 pm off the CBC tower at 4000 Watts, on 106.9 FM. It sounded like a plum, drive-time slot, but most university students were still in class at that time of day, so listenership for Ken's Kuts was low. In fact, even the midnight to 3 am slot drew a bigger audience. But Ken was undaunted by the meagre fanbase; he played his platters, took a few requests - because few was all he ever got - and made sure that everyone knew they were listening to music that was made from the good vibrations of a cutting lathe, and not from the regimented arrangement of ones and zeroes by a computer chip.

There was only one key to the vinyl storage room, and that was in the possession of the volunteer who fetched albums for Ken during his program. No one else needed one. No one else ever went into that room. So there was never any worry that someone would pop in unawares and startle the record-retrieving volunteer, especially when she, herself, was popping into the room - through a fuzzily-lit hole in the wall that was connected to a large-domed cathedral in Italy.

After the volunteer changed back into her regular clothes – pleated tartan skirt, black canvas sneakers, and white sweater top - she fixed her hair into a side ponytail with a colourful scrunchie and picked up the three records from the table that she had left there a few seconds ago, or just over a day ago, depending on your frame of reference. She had learned to find the albums first before leaving on a trip, because if she postponed the job until she got back she could never remember the titles. It was a bit embarrassing to go back and ask Ken which albums he wanted again when she had just left the studio half a minute before, though one of those thirty-second excursions last week took her almost two months to complete! After locking the storage door behind her, the volunteer made her way down the hall, cut through the control room, and quietly entered the studio.

"You've been gone a long time, Michelle," said Ken, taking off his headset as *Music From Big Pink* by The Band played on the turntable. "Did you have trouble finding the Andwella album?"

"No, that one was easy," she replied, handing him the records. "It was the Delaney and Bonnie one that was difficult, because it was misplaced. Someone reshelved it under Eric Clapton, but I figured it out."

"Yeah, that can happen, especially when Clapton's name is featured on the cover," said Ken. He removed one of the lps from its sleeve and cleaned it with a record brush. "Ah, good old Mother Earth! I think I'm going to play I Need Your Love So Bad. What do you think?"

"It's a rad version," said Michelle, her French accent giving the 'r' of rad the raspy '*kkkk*' sound. "Tracy's voice is outta sight on that one!"

"Oh, it's groovy, all right," Ken agreed.

"Ken, no one says groovy anymore."

"They don't? What should I say, then?"

"You could say her voice is tubular!"

"Tubular?"

"*Oui*! It's very 'surf culture'."

"Yeah, I used to do a lot of surfing on the Bow River in my teens," Ken smirked.

"You did? You must have looked pretty pathetic."

"No duh. Hey, did I say that right? 'No duh'?"

"Your use of the modern lingo is becoming bodacious, *mon ami*." Ken smiled at that one and put his headphones back on. He faded the last two seconds of The Weight and flipped on the mic switch. He was back on the air.

"Hope you enjoyed that little slice of Canadiana by way of a drummer from Arkansas. Let's continue to take a load off Fanny this afternoon, and alleviate the burdens in your personal journey, with some more of that folky-country blues sound. This is live Delaney and Bonnie from 1969…Only You Know and I Know." Ken set the needle down perfectly in the lead-in groove and flipped off the mic switch.

"I've got it from here, if you want to get going, Michelle."

"I'll stick around until Gilliana gets…" the studio door opened right on cue, "…here."

"*Come state amici*?" said Gilliana. "Did you miss me?"

"I miss you even when you're here," Ken replied. Gilliana leaned over to the DJ, lifted one earphone, and let it snap back onto his head.

"He could have been on the air, Gilli!" Michelle scolded her friend.

"It's campus radio, Mich. No one's listening!" Gilliana pretended to lick her finger, touched it onto her hip, and made a sizzling sound to indicate that she had just burned Ken. Again.

"We're going to get a coffee in the Science B Building if you want to drop by after the program," Michelle said to Ken as she picked up her knapsack from the chair.

"I've only got another fifteen before I hand it off to Calvin's Funky Garage, so yeah, I can meet you there."

"Great!" said Gilliana. "Just look for the girls who are trying to appear invisible."

"*Appear* invisible?" queried Ken. "I don't get it."

"But Chase will," said Gilliana.

Ken let out a guffaw and gave Gilliana a high-five. Then Gilliana got five from Michelle as well, but it was a smack on the arm.

"You have to stop that, Gilli!"

"I know. Sorry," said Gilliana "But he brings it on himself, you know?"

"He's reaping the non-sequitur fruit of his just desserts," Ken said with a grin. "See what I did there?"

"I did, but Chase won't," Gilliana retorted.

"I'm leaving," huffed Michelle, exiting the studio.

"Wait up!" Gilliana shouted after her friend, and as she closed the studio door behind her, she said "Later, Ken."

"Much," he answered, preparing the next record for the airwaves.

"I like those leg warmers, Gilli. Are they new?"

"I got them yesterday. I think the hot pink goes nicely with the electric stirrup tights and my turquoise headband, don't you?"

Michelle and Gilliana left Mac Hall from the south exit and made their way around the building, heading north to Science B. The autumn air was cool on their faces, but not unpleasant since the sun was shining brightly behind them.

"By the way, did you know you've got a run in those stockings?" Gilliana said, pointing to Michelle's left leg.

"Yeah, I did that a few minutes ago when I got out of bed," Michelle answered. Then, in response to Gilliana's puzzled look, "I mean, when I got out of the…record room?" The correction didn't change her friend's baffled countenance.

"You've been acting strangely for the past few days, Michelle. Are you okay?"

"*Sì*. I'm just *un po' stanca*, lately," she answered wearily. "I need to get *più sono*."

"Maybe you *do* need some more sleep. You've been mixing your *italiano* and English together a lot. But I have to admit, I can't believe how good it's getting! I mean, you've only had that *Learn to Speak*

Italian book and my tutoring for two months, and you're already fluent!"

"I'm not *fluent*," Michelle said with a hint of false modesty. "But I have been practicing."

"I'll say you have! And your accent is perfect. A little old-fashioned sounding, maybe, but perfect. Say, why are you rubbing your shoulder all the time?"

"Oh, that," said Michelle, offhandedly. "I had to get a shot the other day at the campus clinic. I'm behind in my vaccination schedule. I was missing one from growing up in Quebec."

"Which one?"

"Typhoid."

"Typhoid? I don't think I've ever had a shot for that. Isn't it just for people with a high risk of exposure?"

"I don't know. I just needed it so they gave it to me, I guess."

"Eh...no harm, no foul," Gilliana shrugged.

The young women entered the building and turned right toward the small cafeteria and sitting area that was off in the distance.

"Do you see the guys?" Michelle asked, looking down the hallway.

"If you mean, 'Do I see the Hunkiest Man on Campus as reported by our Gauntlet newspaper?', then yes, he's sitting next to the window. You know, so everyone can see him."

"You promised to stop, Gilliana Rosa. Chase is a nice guy...when you get to know him."

"All right, Michelle Diane, I'll stop. But he makes it so *hard*. Anyway, it's probably just the jealousy coming out. Female undergrads fall all over him, and he pays them no attention. *You* pay him no attention and all he wants to do is impress you."

The women arrived at the window table and two men stood up to greet them. One of them was a tall, dark-haired young man with a nice smile. The other was an equally tall, blond, muscled young man who looked as if he had just parked his surf board at the door.

"Hey, Michelle!" said the chiselled one of the two. "You look nice. Even with the bags under your eyes."

"Hi, Chase," Michelle replied, taking a seat.

"Hi to you, too, Michelle's friend," said Chase to Gilliana.

"Always a pleasure," she responded to the slight slight. "Hello, Jay."

"Hi, Gilli," Jay responded. "I like your leg warmers."

"Yeah, they're really glowy, in a fluorescent sort of way," Chase agreed.

"Ah, thanks," Gilliana replied, gritting her teeth.

"Hi, Michelle," said Jay with a smile.

"Hey, Jay," she replied, returning the expression.

"Do you want something to eat?" Chase asked the women. "We were just splitting some fries. I don't know why I keep ordering these, the food here is terrible! And the portions are way too small!"

Gilliana suppressed a laugh after being kicked under the table by Michelle.

"I'll get some coffees for everyone," said Chase. "My treat." He pointed to Jay, "One cream, one sugar?" Jay nodded. "One cream, no sugar?" Michelle nodded. "And one black...like your heart?" Gilliana gave a smirk and Chase left for the ordering line.

"Oh, and one more black coffee for Ken!" Michelle called out to Chase. "He'll be here in a few minutes!"

"You got it!" Chase called back.

Michelle reached into her knapsack and pulled out an enormous reference book, which startled both of her friends when it slammed onto the table. She flipped to a bookmarked page and started to read.

"You electrical engineers win the biggest textbook competition, hands down," said Gilliana. "That one beats my vertebrate zoology tome by at least 500 pages."

"Some of my mechanical engineering texts are pretty big, but not like that," Jay remarked, pointing at Michelle's manual. "Actually, the CRC Handbook they made us buy in first year was about that size. I think I opened it once."

"Yeah, but it'll look great on your bookshelf in ten years," noted Gilliana. "Your dinner guests will be impressed, Jay."

"I can see it now. 'The vapour pressure of water at 298 Kelvins, you ask? Why I have that right here! Now, do you want that in kilopascals or millimetres of mercury?"

"Well, since I'm French, I'll take that in kilopascals, *s'il vous plaît*," Michelle interjected with a sly grin. "It's how we order all of our pressures." Jay's sideways glance gave away his pleasure over that one, just as Chase returned to the table, empty-handed.

"Stupid ATM machine wouldn't take my PIN number!" he complained as he dug into his suede leather jacket that was draped over his chair.

"It's just ATM, Chase," said Gilliana.

"I know, but it ticks me off!" Chase grumbled.

"No, I mean you don't call it an ATM machine, because the 'M' in ATM *is* the word machine. And you don't say PIN number either."

"You don't?" said Chase, perplexed.

"No, that's redundant, too," agreed Michelle.

"Redundant? *Redundant*?" Chase asked, looking at Jay.

"Afraid so, chum, afraid so." Jay answered with a grin.

"Hmm," Chase replied, thoughtfully. He found a twenty in his jacket pocket. "I'm going to have to change my mental mindset about those two anachronyms, then." Gilliana visibly cringed at the mangling of her native tongue as Chase left again for the ordering line.

"Do you see what I mean?" Gilliana said to Michelle. "The man is a walking tautology!"

"Lots of people make those mistakes, Gilli. You shouldn't be so hard on him."

"Michelle...he's a communications major! He wants to make a career out of using words!"

"I dunno. I think he talks pretty goodly," said Jay with a shrug. Gilli cuffed him with the back of her hand just as Ken arrived. He spun around a chair from the table next door and sat down.

"That's a big book for a little girl," he said to Michelle. "Hey, Jay."

"Hey, Ken. How was the show today?"

"As Uncle Neil said, 'My my, hey hey, rock and roll is here to stay!'"

"Yeah, but two albums ago he said, 'Take my advice, don't listen to me.'"

"I like that one," said Ken. "It reminds me of...oh hey, Chase!" Chase had just returned with a tray of coffees.

"Hi, Ken. Play any good CDs today?"

"Never, my boy. My program is strictly analogue."

"Too bad," Chase replied. "CDs are here to stay, pal." He passed out the coffees to a chorus of thanks and then took a seat. He looked over at Michelle.

"You could seriously hurt someone with that textbook," he said, then he rubbed his right arm, "Man, my tricep is killing me."

"Triceps, Chase," said Gilliana.

"No, it's just the one arm," Chase replied, oblivious to the correction. "I think I did too much in the gym this morning."

"I thought you had Linguistics this morning?" said Michelle.

"I did, but I didn't go," Chase said after a sip of brew. "Linguistics is so boring. It's really a below sub-par class."

"Yeah, what could you learn there, anyway?" Gilliana smirked.

"Exactly my thought, Michelle's friend. Now, are we all still on for the hockey game tomorrow? UofC versus UofA! Can't get any better than that on a Friday night!" Everyone reapproved the scheduled activity with a nod. "Great. I'll drive."

"Chase, your car is a Datsun 280Z," said Ken.

"Yes," Chase answered with a satisfied grin. "I know."

"It's a two-seater."

"Right. So I'm taking Michelle. How are you guys getting there?"

"Well, we can walk since the rink is only two blocks from Res," said Jay. "Why are you driving to the rink?"

"It's all about the presentation, Jay-Bird." Chase hair-flipped his blonde locks. "You gotta look the part."

After some idle chatter about profs and proofs and wonky bookcases, the group parted ways. Ken was off to the education building to have a chat with his Methods instructor, Jay had to prepare for a fluid mechanics lab, Chase was going back to his studio apartment in Varsity Estates to have a nap and fetch his toolbox for later, and the women left Science B together, on the way to their separate study spaces.

"Argh! Chase makes me crazy!" Gilliana complained. "He ego-trips all over himself for the past hour, mangling the English language at every turn, and then he goes and buys us all coffee and offers to fix my bookshelf! I can't stay mad at him!"

"I told you, Gilli, you have to give him a chance," said Michelle. "He's a nice guy. Try and be more like Jay. He's really patient with Chase."

"I really like Jay," said Gilliana. "He's more of the quiet, silent type."

"As opposed to the *noisy*, silent type?" Michelle quipped.

"Ack! You see what happens after hanging out with Chase? You come under the control of his vocabulary infection!"

"Controlled infection? That's actually an oxymoron, Gilli."

"No! No! Nooooo! I've got Chase Disease! " Gilli screamed, running away toward the Science A building with her hands flailing in the air.

Michelle unpacked the books from her knapsack into two stacks at her favourite quiet cubicle on the sixth floor of Calgary Hall. For her Canadian engineering studies there was Cheng's *Field and Wave Electromagnetics* and Malvino's *Electronic Principles*; for her Italian science studies there was Nicolini's *Torricelli and His World* and Giusti's *Torricelli e il suo tempo*. The Giusti book, written in Italian, was a slog to get through when Michelle bought it six weeks ago near the beginning of the current school year. But she had learned a lot of *italiano* since then: *Learn to Speak Italian* helped at the beginning; Gilliana's tutoring helped even more after that; but the four years she had spent in Florence had really helped her the most.

Four years!, Michelle thought to herself as she paged her way to the last chapter of the Giusti book. Had it really been that long? Well, not quite. She had arrived in Florence on Tuesday, November 17, 1643, and it was going to be Thursday, October 17, 1647, when she went back. So, one month shy of four years, actually. Not that anyone *else* was counting.

Michelle Morel began to reflect on her experience of the past two months at school, which included her 3-year, 11-month stint in Italy.

It was a crazy September day when she discovered the Shimmering Light in the vinyl room at CJSW. And here she thought her volunteer job at the radio station would be boring! When she stepped into the back wall of the vinyl room and out onto the alcove at the rear of the *Cattedrale di Santa Maria del Fiore* - the *Duomo* – she jumped back through the hole in a panic. It took her another two days to gather up the courage for a return visit, but by the end of that school week she had gone back to Florence over a dozen times.

Michelle was a quick learner. Once she found out where she was, and *when* she was, she started a crash course in all things *Firenze*. She read books and scoured the microfiche in the university library for any information that could help her assimilate into her new surroundings. She accessed Gilliana and Gilliana's Italian parents - on the phone from Kingston, Ontario - for cultural references and linguistic tips. The people at the Calgary Italian Club were really nice, giving her advice on where to go and what to see while in Tuscany. And she found a nice little shop downtown on 7th Avenue that specialized in simple clothing for her trips. *Faible couture* she would call it.

Michelle had figured out the properties of The Gateway – that's what she started to call the Shimmering Light - almost immediately: how time stood still on the opposite side once you'd left; how she could bring things with her into Florence, but not the other way around; and how her ailments didn't accompany her on any journey, which she first discovered when her seasonal-cold symptoms vanished going through The Gateway but instantly returned the moment she came back. Michelle discovered one more important thing as her time in Italy went from days to months and then years - she was getting older in Florence, but not at home. The process of aging was exclusive to the time frame in which you lived.

Rita and Nerina were now like family. Michelle had been with them almost the entire time in Florence, having met them on a Sunday morning outside the Duomo after services. They invited her to tea, they had a nice afternoon together, and now almost four years later they were all tighter than a cheese-filled *cannelloni*. Within a month of living in the D'ambrosio household and being employed by Rita as her assistant cook, Michelle was told that Evangelista Torricelli was looking for an assistant by a mutual acquaintance, Niccolò Cabeo, the philosopher from Ferrara. She was hesitant about taking on such an important role in the life of a famous scientist, cognizant of what could happen if she were to accidently cause a wrinkle in the fabric of time. She had read Bradbury, so she was aware of the *butterfly effect*. But upon returning to her university studies in Calgary, she felt all the signs were there to interview for the assistant's job: in Calculus class, Gabriel's Horn was brought up – something invented by Torricelli; in her Materials class, pressure tolerance was brought up – something measured in Torricellis; and then, in her Physics class, when her prof asked if anyone knew who first described the area and centre of gravity of a cycloid, Michelle raised her hand and offered the name, Evangelista Torricelli. The prof was impressed – his top student even knew the ancient scientist's first name! When Michelle returned to Florence, she applied for the Torricelli job and got it. Evangelista was ecstatic to have found such a capable, articulate assistant, even if her *italiano* was at times a little shaky.

    In the ensuing years in Florence, Michelle became fluent in the languages of Old Italian and Old Science. She started work with Torricelli at the tail end of his invention of the barometer, and she helped in translating his work into several languages for publication. She enjoyed that work very much, and hoped that she could utilize this skill in her career in the *future*. Then there was all the compiling and editing work for his book, *Opera Geometrica*, where Michelle learned more advanced mathematics than were offered in her degree program in Canada. She was with Evangelista throughout his work with melting glass for microscope lenses, his telescope-designing adventure, and, most significantly, she was there to help him through the fiasco known as the Great Cycloid Controversy. When Torricelli was accused of plagiarising the mathematics of its quadrature from the work of Gilles de Roberval, it knocked him into a depression that took over a year from which to emerge. Michelle thought that might be the very reason she had been 'sent' to the past, because Evangelista himself said he could not have survived the process of vindicating his name without her. But no, The Gateway was never closed to her after the controversy was settled, and until the Shimmering Light was extinguished, Michelle always felt there was more for her to do - that there was yet another reason she had to return to the past.

Michelle took a deep breath as she started to re-read the last chapter in Giusti's book on Torricelli, though she didn't need to. She knew the end. She had seen it coming, first-hand. The cough that had started only yesterday would worsen in the days ahead. Torricelli, the great physicist, inventor, and mathematician – Evangelista, her wonderful employer, confidant, and friend - would pass away from typhoid fever in one week's time.

Michelle closed the book and wiped away a tear. The time of her real work in 1647 Florence had finally arrived.

And it would be a difficult time, she was sure.

Chapter 21

"So, is our team any good this year?" Michelle asked Chase as they excuse-me'd down the row to their blueline seats at the Father David Bauer Arena.

"For sure!" Chase enthused. "They've won the majority of their games this season when they've outscored the opponent!"

Ken, Jay, and Gilliana stood up as their friends arrived, to facilitate the rearrangement of the assigned seating. Gilliana sat next to Michelle to have someone to talk to in case the game got boring, a scenario that usually unfolded two minutes after the opening face-off; Michelle sat next to Chase because Chase probably thought they were on a date, though that had never been officially discussed; Chase sat next to Jay because Chase knew he would have lots of keen observations to make during the game that Jay would appreciate; Jay sat next to Ken because he could talk about records and music as a break from all of the keen observations that he was appreciating.

"Thanks for getting us the great seats, Chase," said Ken.

"Glad you like them," Chase replied. "I like to sit in the Dinos offensive zone for the first and third periods."

"Hopefully, the ice'll be tilted in their favour tonight," Jay remarked.

"Yeah, that would make the uphill climb easier for them against the Golden Bears," said Chase, oblivious to the see-sawing similitude. "They've gotta come out tonight like they did against UBC. They were literally shot out of a cannon to start that game!"

Ken stood up and looked around the arena. He sat back down after doing a complete three-sixty.

"You'd think it'd be hiding in plain sight," Ken said with a mischievous smile. "I don't see it anywhere, Chase."

"What?"

"The cannon."

"The cannon?" said Chase. "There's no real cannon, Kenny."

"But you said *literally*, Chase. That means the Dinos were actually stuffed into, and shot from, a real cannon."

"It's a figure of speech, man," Chase explained. "They weren't literally shot from a cannon. They were just, you know, shot from a cannon in a literal-type of way. Jay, help me out here."

"Sorry, bud. Ken's right on this one. When you say literally in that context, you really mean metaphorically."

"So I should have said, 'They were metaphorically shot out of a cannon'? That sounds dumb."

"You could have just said, 'They were shot out of a cannon last night'," said Ken. "We all know it's a metaphor."

"That literally makes no sense to me," Chase answered.

Gilliana leaned forward, turned to the boys, and said, "In *that* context, the word 'literally' works just fine."

And in keeping with the evening's hockey context, Michelle gave Gilliana an elbow to the ribs for that remark.

After an uneventful first period with the teams deadlocked at zeroes, Chase announced that it was time for popcorn and licorice. He enlisted the services of Gilliana and Ken to help carry the loot back from the concession stand. Jay moved over one seat to engage in some engineering talk with Michelle.

"So, how's Electrical going, Mich? Midterms all good?"

"I had a tough Circuits exam last week. My prof gives these multiple-choice tests where you get possible answers for A,B, and C, but then D is 'two of the above are correct', E is 'all of the above are correct', and F is 'none of the above are correct'."

"Okay, that's literally torture," Jay said with a sly grin that made Michelle chuckle.

"But I did okay on it, so I really can't complain."

"Did you ace that one, too?"

"What do you mean, 'too'?" Michelle retorted. "I only got a hundred on one other midterm."

"So you *did* ace it."

"Okay, yes. But the other three were really tough."

"On which of those other three did you score less than ninety-five percent?"

"Um...well, none. But that doesn't mean they weren't hard, Jay."

"No, it just means that you're pretty awesome in engineering," Jay remarked. "And it looks like you picked the right major, too."

"Well, I think I did, but..."

"But?"

"I think I may switch over to Computer Engineering."

"Whoa! That's a pretty new program, Michelle. Could you move all your Electrical courses over for credit?"

"Every one of them," Michelle replied.

"So why the change?"

"It's all because of the Digital Logic Design class I'm taking. It's just so awesome, Jay!" Michelle turned in her seat toward her fellow engineering student. "At first, I thought it would be boring, you know. All the number systems stuff, binary this and octal that, the combinational circuit designing with all the multiplexers and encoders. But when we started doing Boolean algebra, with all that emphasis on logic expressions and truth tables and logic gates, something just clicked! I can't explain it! It was like, like..."

"You'd found your calling?"

"Yes! Like I'd found my calling! Like, this is what I was meant to do!" Michelle exclaimed. "I want to get into coding, Jay. I want to learn to write programs and...and..." Michelle stopped talking. Jay's expression had changed. "What is it?"

"I haven't seen you this excited in quite a while, Michelle."

"You haven't?"

"It's like you've had the weight of the world on your shoulders these past two months," Jay said with concern in his voice. "I guess I'm just relieved that you're really doing okay."

"You were worried about me, Jay?" asked Michelle.

"Well, sure...we *all* were," Jay emphasised. "Gilli says you've been distracted, but Ken thinks 'preoccupied' is the better word. Chase is a lot more optimistic, though: he says he's seen these *gradual* incremental improvements in your demeanour lately."

"As opposed to, say, an *appreciable* incremental improvement?" Michelle smiled.

"Exactly!" Jay declared, pointing to the arena roof. The two of them had a good laugh, with Michelle putting her hand on Jay's shoulder for support.

"See, I told you going out to a hockey game would do you good!" Chase declared, returning from the concession stand carrying four buckets of popcorn. Ken had all the drinks, while Gilliana carried one popcorn bucket and an arm full of licorice. Jay shuffled over a seat, and the treats were dispensed as the puck was dropped for the second period.

"Chase, this is enough food for entire section!" said Michelle. "I can't eat all this!"

"Don't worry, that's what I'm here for!" he replied, focusing his attention on the ice while shovelling popcorn into his mouth. "Did you see that, Michelle? How the D-man hit the centre with that pass vertically up the ice? That was beautiful!" Chase started a chant that had the whole arena going in no time.

"Way da go, Dinos, Way da go!" *Stomp, stomp*!

"I love it here, you know?" Chase said dreamily, looking up at the rafters. "How lucky was I to be born in my favourite hometown!"

It was crowded at Nick's Pizza after the game, but the five friends secured a table in the back courtesy of the owner's son, Tim, who had played football with Chase in high school. Once they were settled, the conversations continued from their short walk up from the arena on 24th Avenue. Ken and Chase were arguing over the result of the game. Ken believed that an extra, shortened period should have settled the tie. Chase scoffed at the idea of regular season overtime with the concluding statement, 'Never, not ever, in a million eternal years, will this happen, Kenny!' When Ken brought up the idea of an extra, shortened period with four-on-four play, Chase was done with the conversation and began to play cutlery drums to the Billy Joel song, Pressure, that was coming over a bit too loudly on the restaurant's overhead speakers. Ken then flipped to the other dinner conversation, already in progress.

"So, you're saying then that *The Wizard of Oz* is an allegory for self-enlightenment, and the yellow-brick road represents its pathway?" Gilliana said with the pursed lips of the unconvinced. "I don't buy it."

"You got a better explanation?" asked Jay.

"How about this," Gilliana offered. "*The Wizard of Oz* is a movie about feminism!"

"What? How do you arrive at that?"

"Okay, hear me out," said Gilliana. "Auntie Em is the matriarch that runs the show on the Kansas homestead, agreed?"

"She's got more lines than Uncle Henry, so sure," Jay conceded.

"And who's the sepia-toned antagonist?"

"That lady on the bike."

"Almira Gulch, right. Now, when you get to the technicolor part of the show, who's got all the power?"

"Not the Great and Powerful Oz?"

"In the end, we find out that he *has* no power!" Gilliana asserted. "It's the witches that have all the control! The *female* witches!"

"You're making sense, Gilli," Michelle interjected. "The Scarecrow, Tin Man, and Cowardly Lion are all men, and they're all lacking in something that renders them ineffectual!"

"Exactly!" Gilliana proclaimed.

"In my Children's Lit course, we learned something pretty cool," Ken chimed in. "L. Frank Baum's mother-in-law was a suffragist. That might not be a coincidence, Jay. The author was surrounded by feminists at the turn of this century when he wrote the book."

Jay nodded his head after a moment of reflection. "Well, when you put all of this together with the fact that the lead character in *The Wizard of Oz* is a woman, it's a pretty good argument." Then, to include his friend in the conversation, Jay said, "Whaddya think, Chase?"

Chase put down the cutlery and looked at the other four. "You gotta love Toto. That dog is the show."

Everyone went silent, looking for something to say but coming up empty.

"And maybe..." Chase continued after the pause, "the story is about how you *can* go home again, despite what Thomas Wolfe said back in the day. You just have to have the confidence and the faith to trust that in all circumstances, no matter how hopeless they seem, you can be brought back safe to the other side."

Everyone stayed silent, looking at each other in amazement.

"Um...that was really profound, Chase," said Michelle.

"Yeah, that was, ah...really perceptive," Gilliana agreed.

"Thanks," Chase replied with a smile. "I think I got that from Bill Murray in *Stripes*. Greatest movie *ever*! Hey, look, our pizzas are here! I think these rectangular ones taste better than the circles, don't you think?"

Michelle found it difficult to sleep that night. The late meal and late-evening socializing didn't help her in attaining somnolence, of course. But it was her thoughts that were keeping her up. Her mind was somewhere else, dwelling on the past. And trying to make sense of her role in it.

She decided she would go back to Florence in the morning and get a start on arranging her employer's affairs. There were documents to prepare and papers to collate. More importantly, there were comforts that would have to be set in place for Evangelista. Michelle went over her mental list of the people she would be contacting over the next week in Florence: the few remaining Torricelli family members; the more than a few friends and acquaintances; the considerable number of science colleagues and associates. Would it be appropriate to inform them before or after the fact? Was it even safe for them to visit Evangelista in his last hours? Michelle rubbed her sore arm, confident that she had taken the necessary measures to protect herself so she could be there for her ailing friend.

Michelle thought about her new friend in Florence, the young woman named Natalia. Aside from the twins Annamaria and Eleanora that she had befriended in 1644, there had really been no other close companions for Michelle. When the twins moved to

Salerno in 1646, she had made a conscious decision not to become too attached to any more people from the past. But this Natalia girl was different: she was a self-starter and a confident person, and she reminded Michelle of herself in many ways. This house-arrest ordeal had shaken Natalia, but the faith she had in a favourable resolution impressed Michelle to no end. She had a good feeling that Natalia was placed in her life for a reason, though she was unsure of what that reason was.

But she knew the Guiding Hand had a reason. And that was enough for Michelle.

William Thomson stared eastward from the bow of the HMS Challenger, water droplets glistening on his oversized oilskin, his uncovered head drenched from the ocean spray. When had he caught the maritime wanderlust?, he wondered to himself. He remembered that first cable-laying expedition on the Agamemnon sixteen years ago, in 1857, and how petrified he was on the choppy seas off the English coast. But his fear of the water on that adventure was soon superseded by bitter disappointment when the communication cable snapped less than 400 miles offshore. All that work and money laid to rest, useless on the ocean floor! It made Thomson all the more determined to see the project through to its completion. So there were many more voyages over the years, and his perspective on seafaring moved from loathing to tolerating to longing, and then, finally, to the purchasing of his own schooner, the Lalla Rookh.

Would this be his last cable-laying expedition?, Thomson pondered. His role onboard was strictly advisory now, his guidance appreciated but hardly necessary. His superiors were happy enough to permit him to sail on this extension of the communication cable off Brazilian waters, from Pará to Pernambuco, but Thomson knew that they were only throwing him a bone; the Eastern Telegraph Company had a tighter budget than the Atlantic Telegraph Company, so passengers that weren't involved with the physical aspects of the job were seen as extraneous. None of this bothered Thomson; he had done his job, and Europe was now connected to the Americas with high-speed transmission lines. Someone younger could finish the work in the Pacific.

Was it finally time to get back into the laboratory?, Thomson ruminated. There was so much left to discover, to uncover, in the fields of electricity and magnetism. Perhaps spending some time on the adjustable compass would be in order? Or fleshing out his idea on the vortex theory of the atom? Maybe he would find someone to assist him in setting up further experiments in atmospheric electricity? For that, he would require another kindred spirit along the lines of his old partner James Joule; they had made such a complimentary pair! Fellow scientists were calling their thermodynamic discovery the Joule-Thomson Effect now, which was quite the honour. Why, his dear friend Hugh Blackburn even suggested there would be a knighthood in it for Thomson; for the Effect and for the absolute temperature scale, of course. Thomson remembered joking to Blackburn about choosing the moniker Baron Kelvin in the unlikely event that knighthood ever happened - he was looking out on the River Kelvin flowing past his office window at the time. But the more he thought about it, the better that sobriquet sounded.

"Mr. Thomson! Mr. Thomson!" the first mate shouted from midship. "We've got trouble with the paying-out machinery, sir!"

William Thomson snapped out of his reverie and moved quickly to stern. He saw the issue immediately.

"There's not sufficient tension on the spool, gentlemen! We're getting cable drift and tangling!"

Thomson saw that the men were going to need help on the tensioner and brake. He removed his oilskin, tossed off his jacket, and set to work on fixing the problem. William Thomson had never recoiled from hard work, so going from chief engineer to cable boy in an instant caused him no distress.

But distress did come a few days later, however, when he realized that he had lost a treasure from his jacket pocket, most likely during the cable-drift correction. That message he had found years ago, written boldly by a sure hand and just for him, was nowhere to be found.

The twice-folded piece of paper was gone.

Chapter 22

I thought I was being extra quiet as I tiptoed back into the moonlit bedroom and slipped under the bedcovers, but the instant I placed my head on the pillow Natalia propped her head up on her bent arm.

"Well, that was a long walk tonight," she said in French. I raised up and mirrored her posture, preparing myself for a chat.

"How do you know I went for a walk?" I questioned.

"Because I couldn't sleep either, so I went outside for some fresh air. You were nowhere to be seen."

She had me there, but I employed my strategy of staying on the offensive so as to not draw attention to my activities.

"So you like to get up and go outside when you cannot sleep, as well? Where did you learn this tip for successful dormancy?"

"Where? Um…back home in Can…er, La-Nouvelle France," Natalia stumbled. I could have sworn she was going to say Canada, but that wasn't possible, of course; that name was still over two hundred years in the offing. "I suppose I picked up the habit from my mother. If she cannot sleep, she feels that doing something productive with the time is best. She is always doing things like baking cakes in the middle of the night."

"I can sympathize with this," I said, though it did seem her mother was more neurotic than I was. "Do you miss your parents?"

"I certainly do, Dianora! I have been at school in Scotland for a few years now, so I am accustomed to being away from home. But just because I am used to the distance between us, that does not make it any easier."

"We have a saying here…'Absence makes the heart grow fonder.'" I said this without worry; Natalia would never have known this little proverb from the future.

"*Oui*, I have heard this," she replied.

"You *have*?" I asked, with way too much startle in my voice.

"Well...I mean, we say it all the time...where I am from," Natalia stumbled again. "Why would you think it strange that I know this adage?"

"Um...well, I thought it might be exclusive to a certain time," I floundered.

"A certain *time*?" Natalia inquired, looking puzzled in the moonlight.

"Time? Did I say *time*? I meant, exclusive to a certain *place* in time, of course!" I was grasping now. "A place in time like Tuscany...which, at this particular point in time, is a place, you see."

"I see," she said with a skeptical look. She was a sharp one, this Natalia. I would have to be more careful with my choice of words around her. "I think we both better get some sleep, before we talk anymore gibberish, Dianora."

"A splendid idea, Natalia."

We both turned over, facing our respective walls. We were quiet for no more than 25 seconds.

"Dianora?"

"*Oui?*"

"How long do you think I will be under house arrest?"

"Not for very long I should think. The justice system works swiftly here in Florence."

"Swiftly as in swift to determine your innocence, or swift to...you know?..."

"What?" I asked.

"Swift to...er, *execute* judgement?"

"Oh, Natalia! There will be no executing of anything or anyone!"

"I am going to take your word for it."

We were quiet for another long while. At least 34 seconds this time.

"Dianora?"

"*Oui.*"

"Did you get to meet Galileo?"

"No, he passed away the year before I arrived in Florence. Signor Torricelli was with him until the end." Saying that made me think of the what was approaching for Evangelista, and me, in the coming week.

"Galileo was under house arrest for a long time, wasn't he?"

"For many years, *oui*. But that will not be your fate, Natalia." Then, with optimism in my voice, I said, "You will be fine, I just *know* it."

"I am happy that you can see the future so clearly, Dianora," Natalia said. "And I am thankful to have met such an encouraging, caring friend in my travels, as well."

"*Moi aussi, mon amie*," I said.

But as I drifted off to sleep, I did so with worried thoughts about my new friend.

"I think your stocking is broken," Natalia said to me at the breakfast table. Nerina smiled and craned her neck to assess the hole in my hose.

"Your *italiano* is the only thing broken around here, Natalia," I chided. "What you really mean is *strappata*, not *rotta*."

"Eh, I do not think Natalia is far off," said Nerina. "It looks *rotta* to me! Take it off and I will fix it, Dianora."

Rita, who had been cooking at the stove just seconds before, came darting into the kitchen from the dining-room entrance with Nerina's sewing kit. She plonked it onto the table while picking up my empty plate in one fluid motion before returning to the stove. Nerina got busy with my stocking, Natalia finished her *uova e pane*, and I started to clear the table and wash up.

"I have a thought about fixing your *strappata*, Natalia," said Rita. "While you are confined to the house, why not let me and Nerina give you lessons in *italiano*?"

"I would like very much this!" Natalia enthused. "I would enjoy being your *pupilla*."

"I think you would enjoy being in my class more than in my eyeball," Nerina said with a chortle. "This could be a lot of fun, Rita!"

"That is why I suggested it!" Rita laughed. "Nerina could instruct you in *dicorso*, and I could help you with your *scriturra*."

"But I wish to instruct in the *scriturra*, Rita!" Nerina protested.

"Two things about that, my sister," said Rita, sitting down at the table and pouring herself some *caffè*. "One: you are a gifted talker, Nerina, with a verbal flourish that is the envy of the finest orators in Tuscany. You are a natural fit for oral instruction." She sat back and took a sip of her brew.

"And Two?" asked her sister.

"You are the worst writer I have ever seen. To say that your *scriturra* is *illeggibile* is to provide you with the greatest of *complimenti*."

Nerina turned to Natalia and shrugged. "She is not wrong. You could learn to write from Rita, and I could teach you how to swear like a Venetian *gondoliere*!"

"Eh! *Basta*, Nerina!" Rita cried out, giving her sister a smack on the hand, which drove the darning needle into her thumb.

"Eh, yourself!" Nerina retorted, placing the injured digit into her mouth.

"*Bene*," said Rita, taking another sip. "And you can keep it there if you are going talk rudely!"

Natalia and I exchanged a smile over the bickering sisters. The brief conversational pause was soon interrupted by the sound of drums coming from down the street.

"There they are again," said Rita. "Should not those *ciompi* be thankful for small victories and be done with it?"

"Let them be, Rita," said Nerina, nearly finished her mending job. "It won't last forever."

"What is this about?" Natalia asked. I turned from the wash basin to give an explanation.

"The wool carders started a revolt a few months ago. They were protesting their working conditions."

"Which were *abissale*!" Nerina interjected.

"Abysmal, *sì*," I continued. "They began to march and play drums in the street to draw attention to their cause. The *ciompi* did well for themselves and received many concessions, though the Medici are still firmly in power."

"Good thing, too," Rita affirmed. "*Teppisti* is all they are!"

"*Teppisti*?" asked Natalia.

"A group of ne'er-do-wells," I chimed in. "Like a mob."

"Ah!" Natalie replied. "In Scotland, they would be called a bunch of hooligans!"

"*Hooligani*!" Nerina repeated, giving the word an Italian twist. "I like this very much!"

"Eh, you stop with the drums, you bunch of *hooligani*!" Rita shouted out the kitchen window, which cracked us all up.

I didn't add anything to the 'hooligan' conversation, though I was dying to. No one knew that I could speak English, too - along with the French and Italian - and I thought I'd continue to keep it that way. I just hummed a tune that I picked up from the drums outside and got back to work.

"I know that song, too!" Natalia exclaimed, pointing at me.

"What song?" I said. Argh! I was doing it again!

"That song you are humming. It is very familiar! Do that last part again!"

I began to hum a mangled version of the chorus of the song Fernando, by ABBA.

"I do not think this one is from *L'Ormindo*," said Rita. "I think it is more from Dianora's imagination."

"After a bad case of indigestion, I think," Nerina agreed.

"No, it is not the same song that I know," Natalia finally said with a shrug. "Actually, it could not be."

"I agree," I said. ABBA wouldn't be on anyone's mix tape for a few hundred more years, Natalia. Just saying. "Sorry about that!"

"It is not like you *fait éclater mon ballon*, Dianora," Natalia said in French. We shared a smile over that.

"Your stocking is finished, Dianora!" Nerina announced. "You may now go to work looking like a respectable assistant in whatever-it-is-you-do for Torricelli." I pulled up the good-as-new hosiery and made my way to the door.

"Enjoy your day of *italiano*, girls!" I called back. Then I added cheekily as I closed the front door, "I hope you *all* learn something today!"

As I turned right on Via Pandolfini on the way to Evangelista's, humming away to Fernando, a thought I had suddenly stopped me in my tracks. *Éclater mon ballon*, Natalia? Pop my balloon? There were balloons where Natalie was from? In 1647?

Huh. Go figure.

Evangelista Torricelli sat in his favourite chair in the living room with a blanket on his lap as I attempted to make sense of the piles of paper strewn about on the table and floor. He was feeling weak this morning he said to me when I had arrived an hour before; it had been a restless night as he alternated between feeling hot and cold. I tried to get him to eat the jam toast and tea I had prepared, but he had lost his appetite for the time being. When the doctor came by yesterday, he was not too concerned about the slight fever and rash that Evangelista had developed, prescribing only rest and herbs as a treatment. It was always rest and herbs in this day and age, which is why I was so impressed by Natalia's actions concerning the orphanage boy, Luca; what she did took real courage and insight. That girl was certainly ahead of her time.

"So, do you think there is sufficient material here to compile into a *lezioni accademiche* book, Dianora?"

"There are enough academic lessons here to make three books, Evangelista!" I replied. "You have a few choices here. Since you have dated all of your notes, you can arrange the lessons chronologically, if you like. Or you can keep the subjects distinct and not bother with the timeline."

"I think organizing by subject keeps things clear, don't you?"

"I do. And this is how I have separated the piles. This is the Mechanics section," I said pointing to the floor, "which contains the subsections Motion of Physical Objects, Dynamics, and Fluid Mechanics."

"Is buoyancy placed before hydrostatics in that last subsection?" he asked after taking a small bite of the toast.

"*Sì*, just as you presented it at the university."

"*Bene.*"

I then pointed to my left. "This large stack is the Physics Section. I placed Optics before Acoustics, and organized all the experiments by method, techniques, and instruments."

"I like this," said Torricelli. "Eyes first, then ears, then hands. Well done!"

"*Grazie*, I accept the *complimento*!" I replied. "Though I have no idea how I did that!" We had a nice laugh about it.

"All of this is the Mathematics section, then?" Torricelli queried, pointing to the table.

"It is. Here are the Numbers Theory lessons, followed by Mathematical Proofs and Geometry." I patted the largest pile. "This Geometry subsection is divided into proofs, constructions, properties of polygons, and properties of circles."

Torricelli shook his head. "Did I really teach all that, Dianora?"

"You certainly did, Evangelista. And so much more!"

"But will it be important to the future generations?"

"Your words carry much weight with me, *signoro*!" I said. "My back is still sore from pushing all this paper around!" Torricelli chuckled. "Honestly Evangelista, your work needs to be shared with everyone. It is indispensable to the advancement of science." I was speaking from experience there.

"Speaking of advancement, I have been meaning to show you something, my assistant! One moment!" Torricelli got up slowly from the chair and left for his study. He came back in two minutes with a thin folder of papers.

"See if you can make any sense of this," he said, handing it to me. "It is something I have been working on this past month."

I opened the folder and took two minutes to read over the first page. There were sketches of Gabriel's Horn – Torricelli's trumpet, actually, that he had used to explain infinite surface area versus finite volume years ago – but something was different this time: the calculation of the volume was not performed by using indivisibles and a series of concentric surface areas. The math was nothing I had seen previously in 1647. But I had seen it before, all right.

"You look puzzled, Dianora."

"*Sì*, I am," I replied. But I was actually stunned.

"I am not surprised. It is all a lot of gibberish at the moment, but I am hoping that I can sharpen this tool for greater utility." He bent down to point at a particular calculation. "What I have done here is to determine the accumulation of the quantity over a given interval. I call this part…"

"Integration," I said quietly.

"Why, *sì*…it is an *integrazione*. This notation here I have used to represent the volume as it approaches pi…"

"The limit."

"Um…the *limite*, *sì*. You are picking this up so very well! Now, I use this Latin notation to represent the *integrazione*…"

"The integral symbol," I murmured.

"If you like," said Torricelli. He then pointed to the bottom of the page. "The answer here could then be manipulated to derive…"

"The derivative."

"Ha! A *derivato*! I like this term!" Torricelli sat back down in his chair. "Well, what do you think about it, Dianora?"

"I think it is…I think it is wonderful, Evangelista."

Wonderful. Another name for the word *Calculus*.

I got back to Casa D'ambrosio in the late afternoon. It was an overcast, windy day and I was pleased that I took my overcoat with me when I left this morning, even though it was pleasant at the time. As I entered the house, I could hear laughter coming from the living room. It made me smile. I was leaving the gloomy day outside for an uplifting evening with my friends.

"I take it the *italiano* lessons are going well?" I asked as I entered from the vestibule. Nerina was wiping away tears with a napkin, Rita was holding her head in her hands, and Natalia had fallen over on the sofa from a giggling fit.

"Oh, they are going swimmingly!" Nerina replied, which made the girls crack up again.

"*Sì*, just peachy!" Natalia exclaimed, which made Rita lose it.

And when I said, "Something fishy is going on here!", the three of them just roared. When they finally calmed down, I got to the bottom of the jocularity.

"So, I had just finished saying that I felt really confident with all the *italiano* I had learned today," said Natalia, "and then Rita asked me if I wanted another piece of *crostata*. And I said, '*Sì, mi piace molto il pesce!*'" That made Nerina chuckle again.

"You really like fish?" I said, confused.

"The *lato sinistro* of my brain pictured a fish, when it should have pictured a peach!"

"Ah! That explains it!" I said. "You confused *pesce* with *pesche*!"

"But the look on Rita's face!" said Nerina with a chortle, pointing at her sister. "She was so insulted to hear that her peach pie tasted like tuna!"

That made us all titter. Then I asked Natalia about something she had just said, which I didn't catch right away.

"Natalia, why did you say, 'The *left side* of my brain'?" She looked at me like I had caught her with a hand in the *biscotti* jar. "You know, as opposed to just saying 'my brain'?"

"Did I say that?"

"You did."

"I, ah...well...I made a mistake there, too!"

"You did?"

"*Sì*! I confused *sinistro* with an English word. I meant to say something else!"

"Like the word 'sinister'?" I said, with the last word spoken in English.

"*Sì, sì*! That is it! I wanted to say I was thinking with the, ah...'sinister' part of my brain! Silly me!" Natalia sounded like she was trying to convince the both of us. Then, after a pause, she said, "Dianora, how do you come by knowing the word 'sinister'? I did not know you spoke English."

"I do not speak English!" I declared way too emphatically. "I, ah...I heard this word somewhere once."

"Somewhere?"

"*Sì*...um, in the street."

"The street?"

"*Sì, sì*! It was from a...a carriage driver!"

"An English-speaking carriage driver in Florence?"

"*Sì*. The horse was being bad that morning. Very bad. And the carriage driver was so upset he called the horse 'sinister'! But the horse was an Italian horse, so it heard *sinistro*, not 'sinister' and it turned left, running straight across the street into a market stand!"

"Goodness!" Rita exclaimed. "Was anyone hurt?"

"*No*, thankfully. But there were *pesche* and *pesce* everywhere!"

Rita and Nerina were relieved. Natalia looked at me quizzically with arms crossed. I returned the gesture.

Seven seconds later there was a knock on the door. I was up, so I answered it. When I opened the door, a frantic Francesco Redi burst into the vestibule.

"Where is she?" he shouted. "Where is Natalia?" He turned left into the living room. "There you are!"

Natalia's face betrayed alarm as she stood up from the sofa. Was it malice or distress in Francesco's eyes? I couldn't tell, and neither could Natalia. He charged up to her, his face stopping a foot from her own, and he stared right into her eyes for a good quarter minute, his countenance becoming redder by the second. He looked to be on the brink of erupting. I prepared myself for an intervention. Francesco reached out and grabbed Natalia by the arm. I took two steps forward, ready to jump in.

Then Francesco took Natalia by the hand, bent down, and kissed it repeatedly. He was on the brink of tears.

So, it was distress, then.

"Oh, my darling, Natalia! I have missed you so! *Come stai?*"

"Um...ah, *sì*, Francesco, I am fine," she answered sheepishly.

"You are distraught, I can tell!" he said.

"We were just laughing, in fact."

"Have they been feeding you?"

"I had some lovely peach *crostata* only a moment ago."

"It pains me to see you locked up in this prison!"

"Eh!" Rita and Nerina protested in unison.

"Francesco!" Natalia snapped. "I am under *house* arrest, not locked up in the dungeon of…of…?"

"*Il carcere delle Stinche*," I offered.

"The 'stinky' prison, right! I am not in any discomfort or dismay. Francesco, *per favore*, sit down and get a hold of yourself!" They both sat down on the sofa, Francesco sidling up close to Natalia. She hopped over and made a space between them.

"Call me Ciccio," he said, bouncing over toward Natalia to make up the distance. I sat down in the chair across from them. Rita cut a piece of *crostata* and passed the plate to Francesco. He nodded a *grazie*. Then Rita and Nerina left for the kitchen with the empty plates.

"How are your parents taking this?" Natalia asked. "Is your father going to be all right?"

"Oh, my father is just fine!" Francesco replied with a mouth full of pie. "He is still seeing patients at the house. I am taking up his rounds at the orphanage, so there has been no interruption in the providing of care."

"You saw the boy, Luca, today?" Natalia enquired.

"I did! And this only adds to my distress!"

Natalia visibly gulped and gave me a slightly panicked look.

"He…he is failing?" she asked.

"Oh, *no, no*…on the contrary, he is recovering remarkably well! He wishes to get out of bed and play *calcio* with his friends, but we told him no kicking balls for a month!"

Natalia exhaled in relief.

"The distress I have comes from my father and my *fidanzata* being imprisoned for no good reason!" Francesco declared. "I am incensed!"

"As we all are!" I agreed, wondering if Natalia knew that she was being called his borderline fiancée.

"I will be fine here with all of my *amiche*," Natalia said, putting stress on the word *friends*. She patted Francesco once on the knee. "Just *amiche*." Yep, she knew what *fidanzata* meant.

"Dianora, will I be able to visit with Evangelista tomorrow?" he asked me, putting down his plate. "Is he feeling any better?"

"He was feeling worse today," I said, truthfully.

"I will see him then. To raise his spirits!"

"Be mindful to distance yourself, though," I said, carelessly.

"What do you mean?" questioned Francesco.

What I wanted to say was, 'Well, he has a communicable bacterial infection and I don't want you to contract it!', but what I answered back was…

"Evangelista will engage you in all sorts of math talk if you are not careful!"

"Oh, that will not happen! We will be too busy writing poetry and drinking wine together!"

"Still, make sure you know whose glass belongs to whom!" Natalia insisted.

"Why would this be a worry?" he asked her.

"Well…er, to make sure you know how much wine you have drunk, I suppose."

"Um…all right," Francesco replied, a bit confused. He pointed at me and Natalia and said, "The two of you speak as if Evangelista possesses something that should be avoided."

"Oh, *no, no!*" "Not at all!" "*Non così!*" "Never!", the two of us rejoined.

"I find this interesting, because I have had thoughts about the transference of maladies lately," he said. "I believe there is something animate involved in many diseases!"

"You do?" Natalia and I said together. We gave each other a curious look.

"*Sì.* Many of my medical colleagues believe that disease comes from the polluting effects of dead material, but I am of the opinion that living things are the root cause of infection."

"So, you think that dead material does not *genera* living things?" Natalia asked.

"*Corretto!*" Redi exclaimed. "I do not believe that nonliving things give rise to life *spontaneamente!*"

So, Francesco Redi does not believe in the spontaneous generation of life? I think I learned something about that in biology class back in the day. Well, *ahead* in the day, actually.

"You must consider pursuing this through experimentation," said Natalia. "To disprove this idea of, ah…*spontaneo generazione*."

It sounded like Natalia and I took the same course! Not possible, of course.

"I shall do it, Natalia!" Redi pronounced, finger pointing to the ceiling. "Because of your untiring encouragement and undying belief in my abilities!"

Natalia gave an uncomfortable smile, and I could have sworn that she exhaled a barely inaudible 'Oookaaay'.

"Well, if you will excuse me, I have something I must attend to," I said, standing up from my chair. I figured I shouldn't wait any longer to go back home and get some things sorted out.

"Oh, *no*! *Per favore*, stay!" said Natalia.

"Oh, must you go so soon, Dianora?" Francesco chimed in. "*Ciao*, then!" You could tell by his tone that he was thinking *tre* was a crowd.

"You must not run off!" Natalia insisted.

"But if you must, by all means, run off," Francesco added, making a twiddling motion with his middle and index fingers.

"Dianora, you cannot leave me with…" I knew Natalia was about to say 'him', but she politely changed it to, "…this heartache over my house arrest!"

"Oh, I am sure you will be fine," I said, making my way to the door. "Rita and Nerina will come to your rescue in case of any *difficoltà*."

I left the house, with Natalia standing at the door and Francesco right behind her waving a good-riddance goodbye.

"When will you be back?" she called after me.

"Very soon!" I answered back. "In just a few *minuti*!"

But those minutes would be a few days, of course.

I had to get home to Canada and attend to some *introductory calculus review*.

Chapter 23

"I love that song!" Chase exclaimed. "What is it?"

"It's Mamma Mia, by ABBA!" Gilliana replied from the backseat.

"Ugh, I don't like ABBA," Chase declared. He pressed the fast forward button on the tape machine. Michelle let out an 'Aww', because she was enjoying the tune.

"Chase, you make about as much sense as a salmon trying to climb a palm tree using roller skates," Gilliana remarked.

"Salmons climb palm trees?" Chase whispered over to Jay who was riding shotgun. "Who knew?"

The tape stopped automatically at the next song break and began to play a guitar riff that sounded like the beginning of a TV cop show. Ken began to tap out the ensuing drum part on the back of Chase's headrest.

"Who's this, Kenny?" asked Chase.

"See if you can guess," he replied.

When the vocals started 14 seconds into the song, Chase let out a groan.

"What's wrong with this?" said Jay. "It's awesome!"

"Nothing, if you like music by has-beens," Chase answered. "Is he really still around?"

"Yes, Bob Dylan is still around," Ken said, annoyed. "He just put out a record that could be his best ever!"

"Whoa! You mean his latest record is only bad instead of horrible? Kenny, the guy sounds like a rusty lawnmower that rhymes!" Chase pointed at the glove box. "Jay-bird, let's play some timeless tunes for a change. See if you can find that Wang Chung tape, will ya."

The five friends were almost half way through their drive to Elbow Falls on their Saturday afternoon road trip. Chase insisted on driving, which was a good thing since no one else had a car. It was a bit of a tight fit for everyone in the turbocharged 1988 Mazda 323 GTX, but the stereo was great and the ride was smooth, so no one complained. Except for Chase, of course - Ken's mix tape selections were not his cup of meat, as Bob Dylan would say. But it still promised to be a fine excursion: the sun was out, the cooler was filled with pops and sandwiches, and no one named Michelle was allowed to bring a textbook along.

After the brief jaunt down Highway 66 from the right turn off of Highway 22, the university troupe popped out of the Mazda to the sound of roaring water that could be heard from the parking lot. The falls would not be raging like they do in late spring, but a snowy September in the Rockies meant a steady flow for the Elbow River in mid-autumn. It didn't really matter when you went to Kananaskis Country, though – it was always a treat of a retreat.

The friends unpacked the trunk and made the short walk to the falls. They stopped at the railing and took in the awe-inspiring sight of the cascading white water dashing over the rocky ledge. The towering Lodgepole Pine and White Spruce trees provided a lush, emerald contrast. With the snow-capped mountains standing out in sharp relief against the blue sky, it was an impressive and soothing display of nature's wonder.

The gang found a nice flat spot on the rocks five minutes upriver, spread out the blankets, and picnicked in the bright sunshine. During a lull in the conversation, Chase dug into his backpack and pulled out his new toy.

"Whoa, that is pretty sleek," Jay admired. "When did you get it?"

"A few days ago. Pretty small, eh?" Chase powered up his new, latest-model cellphone, that was now no larger than a milk carton. "I just want to see if I get reception way out here. It's supposed to have improved range." He pulled out the retractable antenna and pressed some buttons, seemingly at random. "Nothing. Must not be any towers nearby."

"That's not such a bad thing," said Michelle. "Who wants to see those things out here?"

"Well, me for one," Chase replied. "I just spent a whack of dough on this puppy. I'd like it to work everywhere…wait, I just got something!" He pressed some more buttons. "Argh! It keeps cutting out! Darn satellites!"

"Actually, it's not satellites at all," said Jay. "It's cables."

"Huh?" said Chase.

"Cellphones and World Wide Web transmission is pretty much all done through cables that were laid on the bottom of the ocean."

"No way," Chase said, shaking his head in disbelief. He shook his footlong cellphone at Jay. "This is digital high-tech, man! It's all wireless."

"Uh huh," Ken interjected. "Until you need wires, man…then it's analogue all the way, baby."

"Seriously?" said Chase.

"Seriously, bud," Jay responded. "After the signal hits the tower, it all runs through copper metal."

"So much for state-of-the-art, huh?" Gilliana smirked.

Chase looked at his phone, then tossed it back into the bag. "And here I thought we were on the verge of an idyllic utopia!"

Once everyone had their fill of lunch and enjoyed the treat provided by Michelle – a *fritole* dusted with powdered sugar that she had made in the middle of the night – Chase bounced up from his spot on the river's edge to announce it was time for a hike on the Elbow Valley Trail. Ken was in, Gilliana was reluctant though amenable to the idea, but Michelle said she would rather stay at the falls and just chill out. She couldn't tell anyone she had done a lot of walking around the past few days in the past, so she excused herself by explaining that she was too out of shape to enjoy a trek in the woods. No one thought Michelle was in any kind of poor condition - especially Chase, who was visibly disappointed in her decision. But it only took about 9 seconds for him to get over it. He re-tied his laces, grabbed his mini-pack, and enthusiastically led the way to the trailhead with Ken and Gilliana in tow. It was decided that Jay would remain to keep Michelle company, though she thought that was hardly necessary. But she was glad for the company all the same.

"You didn't have to stay here with me, you know," Michelle said to Jay, who was laying back on the flat rock with his hands behind his head, sunning himself. "I'm a big girl now."

"I know you're a big girl now, but I didn't really feel like going on a hike. By the way, that's a Bob Dylan song, you know?"

"You're a Big Girl Now. Side A on *Blood on the Tracks*," Michelle answered. Jay turned his head toward her with surprise on his face.

"Track 3. Okay, wow, I'm impressed you know that!"

"Ken played that song on the show a few weeks ago. I was kinda blown away by it! I borrowed the station copy of the album right then and I've been spinning it in my dorm room ever since."

"It's my favourite album of all time," said Jay, turning his face back toward the sun. "Bob was struggling with some heavy feelings during that recording. It comes out in the music."

"There's a lot of sadness in the lyrics. You really have to be in the right mood to get deeply into it."

"Melancholy is a word to describe that record. Well, except for Idiot Wind, that is!" Jay said this with a chuckle.

"Oh, for sure!" Michelle replied in kind. "Bob's just a tad angry on that one!"

"Can you imagine how uncomfortable it must have been for the backing band on that song? You're just hoping that Take One is a keeper!"

"'You know, Bob, we think this one would be better as a solo acoustic number!'" Michelle said, making Jay crack up. They sat quietly for over a minute before Jay broke the silence.

"So, are you saying you've been going through some tough times lately if you've been playing *Blood on the Tracks* non-stop?" Michelle took a moment to collect her thoughts, which prompted Jay to proceed with, "Sorry if I was prying, there, Michelle."

"No, no…it's okay. I was just thinking about how to express it," Michelle said carefully. "There's someone I know that's going through an ordeal right now…maybe not *right* now, at this very moment in time…"

"Is this person sick?" asked Jay, turning his body toward Michelle, propping himself up on his left arm.

"Yes. Very ill. I don't think this person has much time left. In fact, I know they don't. And it's just been difficult to accept."

"You're obviously close to this person. Are you separated by distance?"

"Yes, but I have the opportunity to be with them. I'm just...I'm just not sure what to do."

Jay sat up next to Michelle, the both of them looking out toward the river.

"I don't know if you knew, but I lost someone close to me just over a year and a half ago," he said. "It was my mom."

"Oh, I'm so sorry, Jay," said Michelle, placing a hand on his shoulder.

"Thanks, Michelle," he replied. "The reason I'm bringing it up is because the situation is the same, but different. My mom wasn't sick, she wasn't in an accident, she was just here one morning and then gone before the day was over. None of us got the opportunity to say goodbye."

"Oh, Jay, I'm sorry."

"Me, too. But that wasn't the way it was going to be, or even supposed to be. The Lord had a different plan, and I completely accept it. But if it *could* have happened differently, if there was an opportunity to be there with her before she left this world, I think I would have made sure to put everything else aside to enjoy those final hours together." Jay paused for a moment. "You get what I mean?"

"You mean that if I can be there to care for that person, nothing else really matters?"

"Right. I think that everything else just falls into place around those kind of moments."

At that moment, Chase, Gilliana, and Ken re-emerged from the trees.

"I forgot my phone!" Chase explained, reaching into his knapsack. "I wanted to get reception and call my uncle to tell him where we are! He loves this park!"

"Too bad you can't send him a picture," said Jay. "Maybe one day, your fancy phone will be able to do that, too!"

"Jay-Jay, you are a visionary dreamer, man!" Chase chuckled. "A cellphone that has a camera! What next?" He pulled out the antennae on his phone and jiggled it in the air. "Oh look, the compass in my phone is saying go this way!" Chase left for the trail laughing at his own joke.

"Come on you two, you're hiking with us!" said Gilliana. She pulled Michelle to her feet as Ken hoisted Jay up. "You'll be doing your part to keep us from getting lost."

"Okay, we're coming!" said Michelle. Then, with a wink to Jay, she said , "We don't want you to get Tangled Up In Blue spruce!"

"Okay, now don't start it until I give the signal," said Ken, about to lower the tonearm onto the record. Michelle's thumb was poised on the button, the remote control pointing at the VCR. When the stylus entered the groove and the first heartbeat could be heard from the stereo speakers, Ken gave the order, Michelle pressed PLAY, and the MGM lion growled on the screen.

"Enjoy," said Ken, sitting down on the floor next to the sofa where Michelle, Chase, Gilliana, and Jay started in on two big bowls of popcorn.

When the gang got back from their trip to Elbow Falls, it was decided that they would order pizza from Spiro's – two large pies; beef and mushroom, ham with fresh tomato – and make it a movie night. The stop at Blockbuster Video turned into more of a quest than Chase's cellphone reception foray in the bushes: no one could find a video that sparked their collective interest. *Die Hard*? Hard pass for Gilliana. *Broadcast News*? Old hat to Jay. *Big*? Little interest from Chase. *Fatal Attraction*? General repulsion. But when Michelle returned to her friends in the New Releases section with the 50th Anniversary Edition of *The Wizard of Oz*, Ken got as excited as a flying monkey and insisted on renting it. He had recently discovered something special that he wanted to share with them. What was it?, Chase wanted to know. Ah, that'll be a surprise!, answered Ken. Great, Chase replied with accompanying eye roll. Chase said he only liked surprises that were predictable.

At the 43-minute mark of the movie, Ken pressed PAUSE on the remote and turned to his friends.

"Well, what do you think?"

"Okay, that was pretty crazy!" Jay exclaimed. "How did you ever find out about this?"

"Totally by accident," Ken replied. "I had just started listening to *Dark Side of the Moon* on my headphones while my roommate was watching TV. He started channel surfing and stopped on *The Wizard of Oz*. So now I'm watching the movie and listening to Pink Floyd at the same time. Then I see the part where Dorothy finishes singing Somewhere Over the Rainbow and it cuts over to Almira Gulch on the bike, and it coincides *exactly* with the start of all the bells going off at the beginning of the song Time. I freaked out! Then Jody flips the channel again and I yell, 'No! Go back, go back!' I unplug the headphones and we watch the movie with *Dark Side* playing on the speakers."

"You must have gone nuts when Money started right when Dorothy opens the door and the world goes from sepia to colour," Gilliana remarked. "That was my favourite sync."

"I liked it when the farmhouse was spinning in the air to that song where the female singer is screeching away," said Michelle.

"That song is called The Great Gig in the Sky," said Ken.

"Oh, no way! That can't be a coincidence!" she declared.

"I can't picture Pink Floyd sitting in the studio, watching this movie, and writing songs to it," said Jay. "Ken just fluked into a synchronicity, I think."

"Now that's a good record," Chase interjected. "Back when Sting was cool." Nods of agreement ensued.

"I dunno, Jay. I think there's something going on here." Ken rewound the movie back fifteen seconds and played it over again to the last sounds on the album. "How do you explain that, huh? The Tin Man is telling Dorothy that he had no heart while the heartbeat sound is fading out on Side 2!"

"Pretty crazy, Ken," Gilliana agreed.

"And the song that was playing when we meet the Scarecrow? That was Brain Damage!"

"AH!" went the group on the sofa as Ken lifted the tonearm from the record.

"So, have I convinced you?" Ken asked.

Chase nodded as he got up and went to the kitchen. "I'm convinced I need more popcorn before I see how this ends." Everyone turned their heads toward him.

"You said you saw this movie when you were five," Gilliana rejoined.

"I can't remember anything about it except for Toto," Chase admitted. "I just can't stand musicals and all that harmonious racket. But I'll tough it out through this one and give you my unbiased opinion on how bad it was, later."

Ken brought the box of tissues from the kitchen which was passed down the sofa to a blubbering Chase.

"That was the best movie I've ever seen," he said, wiping the tears from his eyes. "It was so much more than a movie about a dog!"

"Oh, way more," Gilliana agreed, with a confused look.

"I mean, poor Dorothy. That was, like, the worst ordeal you could imagine." Chase blew his nose and continued. "She gets threatened by the Wicked Witch, almost gets killed by poisonous flowers, and then she's captured by flying monkeys! That girl was put through the wringer! And all she wanted to do was to go home!"

"She had to learn to appreciate how special 'home' really is," said Michelle, patting Chase on the knee.

"I guess so, but come on! I mean, couldn't that good witch have told her right from the beginning that those shoes were her ticket back to Kansas? That could have saved her a lot of grief!"

"And about an hour and a half of movie time," Jay nodded. "No, she may have always had the means to return home, but Dorothy needed to finish the job first. Whatever that was going to be."

On Sunday night, Michelle began the search for her travel sewing kit to repair another hole in her Italian outfit, this time one in her dress sleeve. She was going back to Florence tomorrow and wanted to make sure she looked presentable. She wouldn't have much time for little jobs like this when she got back to Italy.

As she rummaged through her closet, Michelle wondered if she was at all similar to Dorothy in *The Wizard of Oz*. True, they were both split between two different worlds, and they both looked really cute in a pinafore dress. But that's where the similarities ended for Michelle: Dorothy couldn't get home, but Michelle could go home anytime; Dorothy had the Yellow Brick Road to follow, but Michelle had no road map for her journey in Tuscany; Dorothy never had to deal with the passing of a loved one in that movie, but Michelle would have to face that challenge very soon. No, Dorothy's story wasn't like her own story at all, Michelle concluded. Though she was in favour of a happy ending, of course.

Now, where was that sewing kit? Michelle had looked everywhere, except underneath her enormous copy of the Concise Oxford English Dictionary. She lifted the tome. Of course it was there, where else could it have been! She sat on her bed, threaded a needle, and got to work.

Michelle's thoughts turned to the proto-calculus computations that Torricelli had shown her as she began the repair job. She thought about the unravelling of the complex mathematics of Gabriel's Horn as she considered the frayed hole. She thought about infinitesimal stitches closing arithmetical loopholes as the two sides of the fissure converged from the needlework. She thought about the knitting together of concepts that were destined to be joined when she tied the closing knot. And she thought about how this exciting and thought-provoking development in her Florentine life warranted more of her attention.

But not right now. Right now, it was going to be about attending to Evangelista's needs in his time of difficulty. Those other things, no matter how important, could definitely wait.

Michelle put the sewing kit back in the closet, but not underneath Mr. Oxford's book this time. She was about to close the door when something that had previously bothered her popped back into her mind. She picked up the dictionary and used the tab to start her search on the first page of H. She found the word she was looking for in 8 more seconds.

> hooligan *(pejorative): a person that causes trouble or violence: etymology – perhaps from Patrick Hooligan, hoodlum of Southwark, London, 1896.*

"1896?", Michelle asked herself out loud. "Natalia, you've got some explaining to do, *mia amica*."

Chapter 24

"What is that wonderful aroma coming from the kitchen?" Giuseppe called out as he and Lucio entered the front door of Casa D'ambrosio on Friday morning.

"We have chained Rita and Dianora to the stove today!" Nerina answered with raised voice. "Come and join me and Natalia for a *caffè*!"

Rita and I weren't exactly trapped at the cooktop, but we had all kinds of pots and fry pans on the go, and we were busy flipping, stirring, tossing, and correcting for seasoning. Rita had a catering event this evening – Vittoria della Rovere, the wife of Grand Duke Ferdinando, was throwing a big party – and she needed to start cooking in the morning to have it all ready for dinnertime. Natalia volunteered her services, but three was a crowd in Rita's cookery, so she sat at the table with Nerina to continue her *italiano* writing lessons with quill and ink.

Giuseppe and Lucio entered the kitchen and headed straight to the stove where I was stirring a big pot. I braced myself for the ensuing epicurean episode.

"May I?" Giuseppe asked, looking at the stirring spoon. I handed it to him and stepped aside. He dipped the spoon into the sauce, brought it to his lips, tasted it, and narrowed his eyes before speaking.

"Is this *pollo alla casalinga*, Dianora?"

"*Sì*," I replied.

"Is this Maestro Martino's recipe from his book, *Libro de Arte Coquinaria*?"

I looked at Rita, who answered in the affirmative. Giuseppe took another sample from the pot.

"It is almost perfect! But may I make a suggestion?"

"No," said Rita, but Giuseppe continued anyway.

"This chicken dish needs a *piccolissimo* of sweetness. Do you have any figs?"

"Figs? Are you insane, Seppe?" Lucio barked. "Let me have that!" Lucio grabbed the spoon, dipped it into the sauce, and had a slurp. I made a mental note to wash that spoon when they were done sampling.

"It needs a *piccolissimo* and a *granello* of sweetness, actually. I suggest dates instead of figs."

"By whose authority?" huffed Giuseppe.

"None other than Signora Latini of Napoli!" Lucio declared.

"Hmm…that is a fine authority," admitted Giuseppe.

"You two are *pazzi*!" said an annoyed Rita to the crazy twosome. She swiped the spoon from Lucio and tasted the sauce. Then she smacked her lips. Then she turned and said to me, "The dates are on the top shelf of the *dispensa*, Dianora."

"I shall *caccia* for them right away," I replied, leaving for the pantry.

"Dianora, what does the word *caccia* mean," Natalia called out to me in French."

"It means 'hunt'" I replied, returning with the dates.

"So you are the *chercheur*, then?" she asked.

"*Oui*," I said.

"And in *italiano*, you are?"

"*Il cacciatore*," I answered.

"I see," Natalia said with a smile.

"Eh, Lucio, what a fine name for this new recipe!" Giuseppe exclaimed. "*Pollo alla cacciatore*!

"Eh! Bravo, Giuseppe, bravo!" Lucio responded. "I like this name!"

Nerina laughed. Rita just shook her head. And Natalia went back to her writing with a smug look on her face. She was taking too much satisfaction in this accidental naming of 'chicken cacciatore' for my liking.

And another thing: her penmanship was the worst I'd ever seen! It's like she'd never used a quill before, splotching ink all over the page like a *novellina*! Chase would have called her a rookie newcomer!

Lucio poured a cup of coffee for himself and Giuseppe and the two sat down at the table.

"So, Natalia, how has captivity been for you?" asked Lucio. "Are you planning an escape?"

"My jailors have the door well-guarded," Natalia said with a wink at Nerina. "And the windows are shut tight!"

"What you need is a hole in the wall to get out of Florence!" Giuseppe kidded. Natalia gave out a nervous laugh at that one, much like I would have – but for a completely different reason, I'm sure.

"Ladies, may I have your attention," Lucio said after a lull in the conversation. Almost all of us stopped what we were doing. "Rita, you are a lady, too, you know?" Rita stopped her stirring with a sigh and turned to the table. "Giuseppe and I have a special announcement to make. Since our plan to take everyone out to dinner tomorrow night has been scuttled by Natalia's imprisonment, we have decided that we would bring the dinner to you!"

"Oh, how *bellissimo*!" "*Splendido*!" "That is so *magnifico*!" "*Che disastro*!" were the replies from the womenfolk.

"Do not worry, Rita!" said Lucio. "We shall do most of the cooking before we arrive. We are planning to make a feast!"

"I am calling it our *Grande Notte*!" Giuseppe declared with a raised finger.

"I think a Big Night would be just the thing," said Nerina, "though I am not sure what we are celebrating."

"Life, Nerina!" Giuseppe cried out. "We are celebrating life!"

"Perhaps we should consider a Big Night every day, then?" she countered.

"As long as you stay out of my kitchen," Rita said while adding more wood to the stove.

It was time for me to head off to Evangelista's house. I said my good-day's to everyone and made my way to the door. Natalia said she would see me out.

"Don't let her run away, Dianora!" Lucio called after us. "The Grand Duke might charge us with being *accessori* to a crime!" Laughter filled the kitchen.

As I put on my walking shoes in the vestibule, Natalia told me to hold still as she pulled off a loose thread from my dress sleeve.

"There, that's better," she said. "I see you have fixed the hole that was there last evening. Now when did you have time to do that?"

"I, ah...did it last night."

"Last night? I did not see you sewing last night."

"Well, you were asleep at the time."

"You were sewing in the middle of the night?"

"That is correct."

"You keep strange hours, Dianora," Natalia said curiously. "It is like time has a different meaning for you."

"Oh, you know how it is, Natalia," I said breezily as I dashed out the door.

"I certainly do!" Natalia said with a wave. Then she closed the door behind her.

"And then there was the time we took the coach to Monte Morello with Blaise Pascal! Do you remember how distraught he was that we would have to walk the rest of the way to the top?" Torricelli laughed at the thought, sitting in his favourite chair in the living room. His chuckling then turned into a brief coughing fit. He was having a good afternoon, but his symptoms were becoming more noticeable: a cough, headache, and general weakness became his ongoing complaints. But he was also in fine spirits as our talk went from work related issues to reminiscing about our past few years together.

"I remember how impressed he was once we got to the top and set up the barometer!" I replied. "He nearly tumbled down the cliff when he saw the mercury level drop in the column." I poured us both some more tea from the pot. "You convinced him that pressure in the air varied with elevation, Evangelista. That really made an impression on him, I think."

"I think so, too! He now agrees with me that we live in a 'sea of air' that exerts a force upon us all."

"And I believe that Pascal was just as captivated by the vacuum at the top of the column. He could not stop saying, 'Aristotle was wrong! Aristotle was wrong!' all the way back down the mountain."

"Well, Aristotle was not completely incorrect, as we know," Torricelli noted. "Saying that nature abhors a vacuum has merit, but now we know that nature does not disallow the existence of one." He wiped his brow with his handkerchief. "*Sì*, Dianora, that was such a lovely day at Monte Morello. And you were so wonderful, translating everything from French to Italian and back again so effortlessly. What would I do without you?"

"Oh, you would probably live in a 'sea of mismatched stockings', I suppose."

"Eh! I only wore them that way maybe twice!"

"A month!" I added. We both laughed. Evangelista coughed again and cleared his throat.

"As to the 'sea of air' postulate, I wonder if I should include an expansion of this idea in the *lezioni accademiche*."

"What did you have in mind?" I asked.

"My thoughts lately have centered on the air we breathe and its constituent parts. The force exerted by the atmosphere at different elevations may be due to the sum of all the vapours it contains at a given time."

"So, you are saying that all the different vapours in the air have their own pressures, and that they can be added together…"

"To get the total pressure, *sì!*"

"*Che figata*, Evangelista!" I marvelled, because I was pretty sure that the instituting of that gas law was over a hundred years away. "How did you come up with it?"

"I was afraid you would ask me this," Torricelli answered. "Oddly enough, I was thinking about all the stresses in one's life, the things that impinge upon us every day, and how they can accumulate over time. I picture these stresses – responsibility, expectations, deadlines – all adding together and expanding like a great bubble, until…until…"

"It bursts?"

"*Sì*, but this need not be the result if the bubble is made of strong stuff. Just like you, Dianora."

"Me?"

"I have seen how you handle all the strains in your life, my dear. You approach challenges with determination, optimism, and above all, with faith. You cope with the sum of all stresses very well."

"I have had the finest teachers," I said with a flushed face. "*Grazie*, Signor Torricelli."

"*No, grazie* to you, Dianora! Your modelling of resilience helped me to come up with a scientific principle on total pressure, you see! Well…a scientific postulate, let us say. It is yet to be proved."

"I am confident it will be," I said.

"Ah, there is the optimism that I cherish!" Torricelli said, wiping his brow again. He slowly rose to his feet. "Now if you will excuse me, I must go to my bed, Dianora. My illness is getting the better of me at this moment, I am afraid."

When I got back to Casa D'ambrosio later that afternoon, I took the long way around from the vestibule to the living room via the kitchen entrance. I didn't want to disturb the audience.

I stood quietly at the back as Francesco Redi concluded his recitation…

> *Within the vineyard's captive grasp she lies*
>   *Clusters of promise, bound 'neath the sky*
> *Sun's tender kiss, earth's embrace so pure,*
>   *Her essence captured, quietly secured.*
>
> *Through time and care, with art and patience, brewed*
>   *Her captivity transformed, liberation ensued.*
> *From thralldom's hold emerged liquid divine,*
>   *A heady elixir, a most cherished wine*
>
> *From cellar's chains, her sweet liberation pours,*
>   *Oh Prisoned Beauty! Joy's essence restored!*

Francesco dropped the paper to his side and took a deep bow. Rita and Nerina applauded with *'Bravo, bravo'*. Natalia, with a sheepish look on her face, was a bit more reserved in her clapping.

"Did you understand the poem?" Francesco asked the assemblage.

"*Sì*, it was about wine," said Rita.

"Again," added Natalia.

"Well, *sì*...but it had a dual meaning of course!" said Francesco. "Did you not see that the grape was a 'prisoner' in the vineyard, and the wine was 'captive' in the cellar, before it was finally released to the world in all its glory?"

"*No*," Nerina admitted. "But your poem did have nice rhymes."

"The 'she' of the last stanzas did not *remind* you of anyone in particular?" inquired Francesco.

"Is she sitting in this room right now with her arms crossed?" I asked from behind the women. Natalia turned to me with a disgruntled look on her face.

"Of course!" Francesco professed. He gazed at Natalia with puppy-dog eyes. "Did you like my description of beauty budding from confinement, Natalia?"

"I am still trying to figure out what my 'clusters of promise' are, Francesco," she answered curtly. "Care to *elaborare*?"

"I, ah...well..."

Just then, there was a knock at the door. Ciccio took advantage of the door-answering opportunity and bounded toward the vestibule. He returned in a moment with the Bargello of Florence in tow.

"Ah, Signor Ciccarelli, how can we help you," asked Rita.

"I am Signor Ciccarelli, the senior officer of the Bargello of Florence..." he said, removing a paper from his coat pocket.

"*Sì*, we know," said Nerina.

"...and I am looking for a Signorina Natalia. Is she here?"

"In the same place as last time," Nerina said, pointing at Natalia.

"Natalia Campo Bella, I have been ordered by the *Capitano del Popolo* of Florence to inform you that you will appear before the Chief Magistrate on the morning of Wednesday, October 23, at precisely 10 o'clock." Signor Ciccarelli stretched forward and handed Natalia the piece of paper. "Your house arrest will continue until this time, save for this Sunday morning, of course, when you may be accompanied to Mass by your designated steward."

Signor Ciccarelli gave a curt bow and left the house, closing the door behind him. Natalia stared at the paper, then looked up at the rest of us. She passed me the paper with trembling hand. I read the details.

"It seems that the Chief Magistrate is none other than Ferdinando the Second," I said with shock.

"Oh my, Natalia!" gasped Rita. "You have an audience with The Grand Duke of Tuscany himself!"

"Is that a *bene* thing or a *brutta* thing?" Natalia asked.

"I have heard that it depends on his mood," said Francesco with a gulp. "But I shall accompany you to your hearing, Natalia! I will offer the duke the finest bottle in my cellar! I will even write him a poem!"

"No!" the four of us women shouted together, perhaps a bit too forcefully.

"I am sure the wine will be quite enough," Rita said calmly.

It was a slog walking to the Duomo on Sunday morning after being up late the night before. Natalia suggested that we leave earlier and take a longer route to the church, to walk off some of the extra 'energy' we had stored from last night's dinner. No one protested.

Lucio and Giuseppe had put on a feast for the ages. The menu included *bruschetta* with fresh *pomodori* and *basilico*, *tortellini a brodo*, *arista di maiale* with *patate arrosto*, and for dessert, a *torta della nonna*. 'Included' was the operative word, because there were a host of side dishes floating around all night long, too. Giuseppe had proposed that the evening should be a joyous occasion, believing that Natalia's upcoming audience with the Grand Duke would result in a dismissal of all charges. Lucio seconded that emotion, and made sure our glasses were always full for every course. The evening ended up being a grand time for my Italian friends. Natalia's deportment was a bit more subdued, understandably, though she tried to hide her somberness for most of the party.

As we walked together down Via Calzaioli , a few paces behind Rita and Nerina and all dressed up in our Sunday Best, Natalia and I began to converse in French.

"I noticed you were a bit low during dinner last evening, Dianora. Is everything all right?"

Huh. I guess I couldn't hide somberness either.

"*Oui, oui*, everything is fine," I replied, but my expression betrayed me. Natalia pressed on.

"Is there something happening at your job, or with Signor Torricelli? You have been coming back to the house after your workday looking dejected. You have not been yourself lately."

Not myself lately? Dianora or Michelle?...University student or personal assistant? You couldn't have said it better, my friend.

"Evangelista is sick, Natalia," I admitted. "His illness has become worse these past few days. I am worried about him."

"I see," Natalia said thoughtfully. "Is there something I can help with?"

"There may be. But for the moment, I think I have everything under control…in terms of assisting Evangelista through this. You may not see much of me in the next week, Natalia."

"I understand, Dianora. Just remember, if things start piling up, I am here to help relieve some pressure." Natalia looked up the street and then pointed.

"Oh! Is that not the Palazzo Medici across the street up ahead?" she said in *italiano*. Her tone of voice suggested that she indeed knew this.

"*Sì*, your former residence!" said Nerina.

"Speaking of pressure relief," said Natalia, "I could use a brief stop before we get to the Duomo."

"We can go at the church," said Rita.

"I am not sure I can make it," Natalia replied.

"Of course you can! It is only another few hundred paces!" Rita insisted.

"But I really must," said Natalia. Then, under her breath, I heard her utter, "I really need to go now."

"Come now, Rita! The girl has to go!" Nerina chided her sister. "And see, the door is open."

"*Va bene*," said Rita. "But hurry up!"

We all crossed the street, and once we got to the entrance of the Medici house, Natalia dashed across the courtyard.

"I shall only be a moment!" Natalia shouted back to us as she entered the farthest door on the right.

Funny, but when she opened that door, it didn't look like a bathroom at all.

Chapter 25

Her brother said that it has something to do with superpositioning, whatever that meant. He explained that when a Transtemporal Trekker passes through the fuzzy-light portal, the wave function at the quantum level collapsed from multiple possible states to exactly one. Um...okay, Natalie had said to him. He made it simpler for his Med-Student sister: whenever someone passed through the fuzzy film, a tumbler mechanism for a time-travel door lock is created. Hmm...go on, said his sister. The result of making this tumbler is that when you return from the 'other side', since the position of every particle in that fuzzy light film is fixed, it can only accept an identical chiral confirmation of particles to allow re-entry. Chiral confirmation?, Natalie groaned. In layman's terms, it means there's a scientific reason for not being able to bring something back with you from the 'other side', Connor explained: it's just like trying to insert your house key in the car's ignition...it won't work!...because the TT tumbler can only recognize the pattern of the things that passed through the first time. All right, I think I get that, Natalie told him.

And all of this made sense to her from a purely practical standpoint, too. Natalie believed the TTer had been entrusted with a job to do, whatever that job might be. Bringing back souvenirs from the past to show off to your friends in the present wouldn't exactly be exhibiting a proclivity toward single-minded purposefulness, now would it? TTing is an adventure, yes. TTing is exciting, yes. But TTing is also a responsibility, and must be taken seriously. So, to promote the important nature of the work, The Portal was designed with a fail-safe; it would remove the temptation to bring back mementos by simply not allowing that to happen, thereby encouraging personal accountability in the TTer without removing the thrill of discovery. Yes, Natalie thought she understood the concept well.

But just because she had an understanding as to how and why The Portal acted the way it didn't mean Natalie appreciated its behavior to any greater degree upon her return from Florence. Because there she was, standing alone in the quiet room of the Byre Theatre, wearing nothing but her underwear and shoes.

Natalie smacked herself on the head. How could she not have remembered that she had been wearing a Sunday Best dress from Nerina's closet and not the outfit she came to Florence in? She blamed it on her excited state: Natalie only came up with the plan to make a break for home side as the women were walking to the Duomo that morning. She had proposed a longer stroll that would take them past Palazzo Medici, and then invented the story about having to make a pit stop. She thought she had been so clever!

Natalie toyed with the idea of returning to Florence right then and there, but decided against it. When would she get a chance to go home to Scotland again to get things sorted out? What if the hearing with the Grand Duke didn't go well on Wednesday, and she ended up not getting back to the Medici house again for a very long time? Or ever? No, this underwear issue was not a big deal in comparison. She could only smile at her dumb decision to wear her Florence outfit to the Byre Theatre, and not bring it along as a change of clothing like she always did. She now had no street clothes to change into! She didn't even bring along a jacket for a cover-up! Rotten nice-weather day in Scotland!

Natalie peeked her head out of the door and looked down the hallway. No one around. She dashed across the hall to a door that was slightly ajar, gave a quick knock, and entered the darkened room. She fumbled for the light switch, found it, and flicked it on. Natalie had discovered the second-floor utility room that was stocked with an assortment of buckets, brooms, and cleansers. A hardhat sat on the back shelf. She passed up on taking it with her, believing that if anyone was to see her wearing that head gear with only underwear on, she would have way too much *more* explaining to do.

Natalie's next dash across the hall proved more successful. When she turned on the light, she was staring right at a costume rack in the middle of the room. She couldn't believe her luck! She gave a fist pump and began to rifle through the hangers, looking for anything in her size. But there was nothing. There were only little britches and little shirts and little dresses and little blouses! It was a costume rack for munchkins! But Natalie persevered and found something at the very end of the rack that would fit her to a tee. She gulped, sighed, put it on, and went back to the quiet room to collect her things.

The patrons of the BrewCo on the main floor stopped in mid-sip as Glinda, the Good Witch of the North, descended the staircase. Natalie graciously accepted their hoots and applause with a curtsey and made a quick exit from the Byre Theatre.

"I am in love with-a that beach!" Marianna shouted out from the backseat of the van as the movie credits began to roll on the laptop screen. "I can't-a wait! When will-a we get to the beach? I'm-a so hot!"

"I'm still hoping before 10:30, barring any more engine issues, that is," Filip replied from the driver's seat. He glanced in his rear-view mirror at Mark, who was sitting between Marianna and Holly. "That was some pretty impressive problem-solving you did there, mate."

"My uncle had an air-cooled '79 VW Transporter with the same overheating issue," said Mark. "We cleaned out the cooling fins and the temperature gauge went right back to normal!"

"Was your uncle's Transporter a vibrant tangerine like Filip's Westfalia and your aloha shirt?" Holly asked.

"No, it was baby blue, like Filip's seat cover and my magnetic irises." Mark batted his eyelashes at Holly. She flipped down the lid of the laptop that was balanced on Mark's knees.

"But do we really need to run the heater full blast all the way to Camusdarach?" Natalie asked from the passenger seat. "My legs are on fire up here!"

"Just a heat-draining precautionary measure," said Filip. "We'll all survive."

"It's-a no better back here, Natalie," Marianna complained. "Plus, sitting next to Mark is-a too hot!"

"Why thank you," Mark replied cheekily, drawing his shoulder into his neck.

"Not that-a kind of hot, *imbecille*!" said Marianna, smacking Mark on the arm. "But you are kind of-a cute."

"So, what did you think of the movie?" Natalie asked her friends on the rear bench seat.

"I loved it!" Marianna responded enthusiastically. "But who was-a the *Local Hero*?"

"I think that was Mac," said Holly. "He was going to make all the townspeople rich with the oil company purchase of Ferness. I love it that the executive guy…what was his name?…"

"Happer," Natalie responded.

"Right…I like how Mr. Happer flips the script in the end and turns the place into an oceanographic research facility."

"Maybe in the end it's Happer that becomes the local hero," Mark offered.

"I like that," said Filip, moving the van over slightly to let a lorry pass before reaching the bridge over the River Tummel. "And I liked the bunny, too."

"'We have an injured rabbit also'," Mark recited from the movie.

"Poor little *coniglietto*!" said Marianna with a pouty face. "At least he was-a tasty."

"Ack!" her travel mates shouted together.

"Marianna, it's time to pass me your phone. We need some tunes," Marianna handed Natalie her phone over the headrest.

"Okay, Filip, how do we do this again?" asked Natalie, lifting up a tangle of cords and adapters from the floor of the passenger seat.

"All right, one more time," said Filip. "You attach the Lighting-to-3.5-millimetre adapter into the phone first. Then you connect the female-to-female auxiliary cable to the headphone jack…"

"Like this?" asked Natalie, holding up the wires.

"Like that," Filip nodded after glancing over at Natalie. "Now, connect the cassette adapter to the other end of that cord. Yes, that's right. Now, carefully insert the cassette body into the 8-track adapter. No, no…turn the cassette the other way around. Yes, that's…no, now flip it over and line it up with the holes in the 8-track…it should snap into place." The assemblage went click. "Perfect!"

"It would have been a lot easier just to hire a band and strap them to the top of the van," Holly smirked.

"Ooh, a rooftop concert!" Mark said excitedly. "Think they'll play Get Back?"

"To where?" Marianna asked.

"Okay, now insert the 8-track into the stereo," said Filip, pointing to the console. Natalie clicked the large piece of plastic into place. "Ready everyone? Press play, Natalie!"

Natalie touched the playlist called *Musica Per Studenti di Medicina* on Marianna's phone. In 4 seconds, the van was filled with a distinctive keyboard riff that grabbed everyone's attention.

"Mamma mia, it's Mamma Mia!" cried Natalie. When ABBA's Agnetha Fältskog began singing the first verse, she was immediately accompanied by all five singers in the Westfalian tour group, MFNHM, featuring Mark Munroe toggling between lead air guitar and headrest drums.

After providing rousing accompaniment to a host of classic rock tunes for the past 55 minutes, coupled with some fine disco van-dancing, Filip pulled into a petrol station in Fort William. Holly pumped gas, Marianna bought cold drinks for the picnic at lunchtime, Natalie cleaned the windscreen, Filip stretched his legs, and Mark checked his phone map for directions.

"The Prince's Cairn is right off the A830 on the way to Camusdarach Beach," Mark said to Filip, showing him the map. "We should be there in 45 minutes."

"Let's call that an hour after a quick detour down the High Street. I'd like to get everyone a mid-morning treat."

"Did you say treat as in, 'You're treating'?" asked Holly, returning the nozzle to the pump and printing off the receipt.

"I did," Filip replied. "But it's going to be a particular kind of treat. A Mystery Treat!"

"Ooh! I love Mystery Treats!" said Natalie, all excited.

"What is a Mystery Treat?" Marianna asked.

"Well, it wouldn't be a mystery if I told you, would it?" smiled Filip.

"I'm not-a sure I like-a the mystery of the Mystery Treat," Marianna frowned. "But I will not-a be the pooper of-a the party."

"Great!" said Filip. "So, let's do like the last song said and 'Fly Robin Fly!'"

Everyone re-piled into the 1977 Westfalia and the friends boogied on down to the High Street, where they easily found parking.

Filip cut the engine and turned to his friends. "We're looking for a sweet shop."

"There's one right over there," said Holly, pointing across the road about five stores down.

"Perfect!" said Filip. "Stop number one! Let's go!"

The Mystery Treat troupe followed their leader into the sweet shop, where Filip called out to the shopkeeper, "Good sir! We have come to purchase Mars Bars! Do you have any in stock!"

The shopkeeper behind the counter chuckled and replied, "Why, I have the finest Mars Bars in all of Scotland, laddy! How many would you like?"

"There are five of us, so let's make it six!"

Filip paid for the candy and the troupe exited the shop and gathered in a circle on the sidewalk.

"Now, before I pass these out, you have to make a promise," said Filip earnestly. "You must promise to eat these."

Holly looked perplexed. "Why wouldn't we eat them, Filip? They're Mars Bars."

"I've eaten them before, bud," said Mark. "Not exactly a mystery, here."

"We even have-a these in Italia," Marianna chimed in. "Nothing *speciale*."

"Promise?" said Filip, placing a hand on his heart.

"Promise..." replied his four friends, with hands on heart and a complete lack of enthusiasm.

"Good. I'll hand them out to you once they're ready."

"Once they're ready?" Natalie wondered aloud as Filip scanned the High Street.

"Ah! There we go! This way, gang!" Filip led them across the street and down the block until he turned into the last shop on the corner.

Bert's Hippy Chippy.

"No, no, no, no…" Mark protested as they entered the take-away fish and chip shop. "That's not going to happen!"

"It is!" said Filip. "You made a hand-to-heart promise!" Marianna and Holly looked horrified. Natalie smiled and just shook her head. Good ol' Filip.

"You must be Bert!" Filip said to the man standing in front of the fryer.

"I is!" Bert answered with a gravelly voice. "What can I do you for, boy?"

"How much would you charge to prepare these delectables for us this morning?" Filip placed the six bars on the countertop. Bert let out a guffaw.

"Haven't done one of these in a few years. Battered and deep fried, of course?"

"Of course!" Filip replied.

"I'll do the lot for two pounds."

"Deal!"

Bert took the candy bars and began unwrapping.

"I didn't see it coming, but I should have," said Mark, shaking his head. "Deep-fried Mars Bars."

"They're actually called Battered Mars Bars, right Bert?" said Filip.

"I calls them disgusting, lad. But you only live once, I suppose."

"And that-a one life is flashing before-a my eyes," said Marianna.

Bert dunked each of the bars into some thick batter and plopped them into the fryer. "You're lucky that the oil is fresh this morning. I would have to charge you extra if this were halibut flavoured!"

When the coating was fried to a crispy brown, Bert drained the candy logs. He wrapped them in newsprint and wished the young fools well as they left the shop. On the sidewalk, Filip doled out the 'treats' on paper napkins.

"Behold the Battered Mars Bar!" Filip proclaimed, raising his greasy confection in admiration. "A chocolatey core of goodness encased in a crunchy fortress! A delicacy that evokes a tear from both dentist and nutritionist! A sight that would make Willie Wonka himself pause in astonishment!"

"I'm astonished by the oil spill on my serviette," said Mark with unveiled alarm. "This could be labelled an environmental disaster!"

"Just the smell of it is giving me atherosclerosis," Holly added.

"It is time to tantalize the tongue, my friends!" Filip announced. "*Slàinte Mhath!*"

"Slanj-a-va" the friends replied without enthusiasm. They all took a first bite in their gastronomic adventure.

As the chewing progressed from opening phase to closing phase to occlusion, four out of five sets of eyebrows raised up in amazement.

"Um...this is really good," said Natalie. "It's like a guilty pleasure, squared."

"It defies all culinary norms," Filip agreed with his mouth full of indulgence. "The initial wave of sweetness from the nougat and caramel is quickly followed by the harmonious marriage of chocolate and oil!"

"Like a rebellious romance between confectionary and frying pan!" Mark gleefully added.

"It is-a making me question my life choices!" Marianna declared. "Why did I-a not try this sooner? I might have-a become a ski jumper instead of a doctor!"

Filip looked over to Holly, whose face was showing anything but pleasure. "Not a carnival ride for your taste buds, I take it?"

"The only rollercoaster here is in my stomach," Holly retorted. "I'm feeling equal parts queasiness and shame." She passed the half-eaten remains of circus-fare over to Mark, who gratefully accepted the offering.

"We need to set off for The Prince's Cairn," said Filip, looking at the time on his phone. "It's time to visit the graveyard!"

"Where I'll be burying all of you once the Mars Bar plaque hits your coronary arteries," Holly said without a hint of sarcasm.

The winding road from The Prince's Cairn to Camusdarach Beach invoked plenty of oohs and ahs from the Westfalia passengers. The picturesque beauty of the Scottish countryside was on full display that morning: the rolling hills dressed in autumnal bronze and crimson; the verdant glens shrouded in mist and mystery; the grazing sheep casting the occasional indifferent glance, like they were posing for their umpteenth postcard picture. The sunbeams played peek-a-boo through the foliage, creating a dappled dance of light on the asphalt as the van negotiated the tight highway turns. Through the occasional breaks in tree cover, a glimpse of Loch Ailort could be had; its serene surface rippling ever-so gently, mirroring the sky above. Then, at last, Camusdarach Beach appeared before them, the pristine golden sands stretching out endlessly from south to north, the shoreline being kissed by the ocean from the west.

"It's just like in the movie," Natalie gushed. "Only so much better!"

"That's because it's now in 3-D," said Mark, equally impressed.

Filip parked the van, and the group made their way to the sand with picnic supplies in tow. Natalie led the way as they walked south to a sheltered spot where the beach met a jagged rock face. The lapping of the water on the shore was the only sound that greeted their arrival.

"This is it," she said excitedly, turning to her friends. "This is Ben's Beach! And this is the exact spot where his beach hut stood in the movie!"

"It's completely unchanged," Holly marveled. "All these years later, and this place looks exactly the same! Well, except for no beach hut, of course."

They spread a blanket on the sand and unpacked the cooler. Egg salad sandwiches, cut-up veggies, and a big bag of crisps were placed in the middle and the five sat down to eat. Sea gulls appeared overhead out of nowhere, in anticipation of any leftovers.

"Oh, here are the drinks!" Marianna said, reaching into the cooler. "I bought a six-a-pack at the petrol station store!"

Mark pulled a can from the plastic holder, read the label, and held it up for Marianna to see. He said, "You know that this is *ginger* beer, right?"

"Oh my! I hope it's-a not too strong!" she replied. Her friends all smiled.

"No, no, Marianna," said Natalie. "It's just perfect!"

Filip made a toast to fine dining and fine friends and the Westfalia gang had a fine lunch together on Ben's Beach. After the last of the carrot sticks were meted out, Natalie stood up, reached into the cooler, and produced a rectangular pan under wraps.

"Ta da!" she exclaimed, conjuring up dessert. As she removed the pan from the bag, Marianna let out a squeal of excitement.

"Oh, how wonderfulla, Natalie! You made another *Schiacciata Fiorentina*! I love how you make-a the flower on the..."

"Excuse me?" Natalie interrupted. "What did you call my cake?"

"*Schiacciata Fiorentina*," Marianna repeated. "Just like I did last-a time we had it."

"But last time we had this, you said you'd never seen a cake like this before," Natalie insisted. "You said, 'I never-a seen anything like-a this before!'"

"Um...somebody help-a me out here," said Marianna, turning to Holly and Mark.

"She's right, Natalie," said Holly. "Last time we had this cake was in the seminar room. Marianna said it was great that you made a skatchia-whatchmacallit. You said, no, you'd made a cake with a Quebec flag on it."

"Then you gave her a wink, and I made a transverse incision across the patient's *fleur*, that Marianna corrected to *fiore*," Mark added. "Then we ate the cake."

"But...but that's not how it happened!" Natalie asserted.

"Natalie, this type of-a cake was first made in Florence hundreds of years ago," Marianna calmly explained. "It even-a has a legend attached to it."

"It does?" Natalie asked nervously.

"*Sì*. A *mysteriosa* girl walked into the Palazzo Medici on Grand Duke Ferdinando's birthday, laid this cake at-a his feet, and disappeared into the thin air!"

"Disappeared!" Mark exclaimed. "Like, poof, she was gone?"

"*Sì*, like-a the poof!" Marianna replied.

"Well, why not?" said Filip with a smile. "People were popping in and out of existence all the time in Ferdinando's day, you know?"

Natalie became unsteady on her feet and were it not for Mark's quick response in helping her down to the blanket, she would have collapsed on the sand.

"You don't look so good," said Holly to her friend. "You need to lie down in the recovery position."

"No, no…I'll be okay," Natalie protested. "Maybe I just stood up too quickly, that's all.

"You're all white in the face, like you'd just seen a ghost," said Filip. "Or that mysterious cake-delivery girl!"

"No!" Natalie cried out. "No one's seen her! She's not popping in and out or poofing around or anything like that!"

Holly took a napkin and dabbed the beads of perspiration off Natalie's forehead. Marianna looked worried.

"I knew-a that ginger beer was-a too strong!"

The two female med students came to an agreement over the treatment of their patient. Once the recovery position suggestion was rejected, it was determined that said patient would remain on the blanket in a half-lotus position for at least one full hour, under the supervision of a caregiver. Fluids were to be administered regularly, pulse rate monitored on the quarter hour, temperature taken with the back of the hand whenever the thought arose. Once they were satisfied with their prescription, Marianna and Holly got up and went for a walk down the length of the beach. Filip said he would be heard from shortly and went in the opposite direction. That left Mark as the attending physician to their patient, who once again protested that the whole thing was just a silly misunderstanding. Probably just a momentary flash of benign paroxysmal positional vertigo, she maintained. Mark disagreed with the BPPV diagnosis and stretched out on the blanket to enjoy the afternoon sun.

"You don't have to stay, you know," Natalie said meekly. "Don't you want to get your scuba gear ready?"

"I didn't bring it," Mark replied.

"What? I thought you were looking forward to a dive in the bay."

"I was, but you should always dive with a buddy, and when Filip showed up this morning without his stuff, I figured it wasn't meant to be. So now I get to spend the afternoon with my other buddy." Mark gave Natalie a wink and turned his head back toward the sun.

The pair were quiet for over a minute before Natalie broke the silence.

"Thanks for staying."

"My pleasure." Mark rose up onto his elbows and looked over at Natalie. "Want *my* diagnosis?"

"Sure, I guess."

"I think you've been under some kind of additional pressure lately that none of your friends are aware of. You've been trying to hide it, but it gets the best of you at times."

Natalie looked off into the distance. Then she said, "There *has* been something pressing on me, Mark. I've been dealing with some things from the past and they're reaching a critical mass at the moment."

"Do you want to talk about it?"

"I kinda do, but I can't really. It's something I have to figure out on my own. For now."

"Okay. But if you need someone to talk to, I want you to know that I'm here for you, Natalie."

"Thanks, Mark," Natalie sighed, patting his hand twice. The third pat was held a bit longer. The fourth didn't lift back up. Mark closed his hand around Natalie's. Then he looked into her eyes.

"Just promise me that if this thing you're dealing with gets any deeper, you'll remember that it's best to have a buddy go along with you."

"I promise," Natalie replied with a squeeze of her hand and a smile.

At that moment, a buzzing sound filled the air above their heads. The sustained resonance was soon joined by an overlapping melody that soared above the drone. A simultaneously majestic and melancholy strain cut through the surrounding soundscape, perfectly complimenting the scenery, demanding attention from all listeners. Mark and Natalie turned their heads and looked up to their left. Standing at the top of the craggy cliff facing the ocean was Filip, filling the air of Camusdarach Beach with the sound of the bagpipes.

"He's playing the theme from the movie," said Natalie. "It's so beautiful. And so perfect."

"You got to hand it to Filip," said Mark. "He picked the right instrument for the setting. He's definitely *our* local hero."

Mark returned Natalie's hand squeeze as they looked out over the ocean together.

The van ride back to St Andrews later that afternoon was a mostly quiet affair. Everyone was tired from the sun and the far-too-competitive game of ultimate frisbee. With endzones etched in sand, and the out-of-bounds area marked by the ocean on one side and the primary successional grasses on the other, there was a lot of running throwing, catching, and 'accidental' bumping going on for a solid hour and a half. Mark took advantage of the soft sand, laying out for every catch even when it wasn't necessary. Holly proved she had the best arm, consistently hitting her teammates with pin-point passes. Filip and Natalie were reliable, if not spectacular, receivers. Marianna intercepted the most passes, mostly because the term *interferenza* was not in her English vocabulary.

"Hey, I love this song," said Mark, looking up from his phone. Everyone in the van but Filip was looking at a screen at that moment. "What made you pick that one for the playlist?"

"I knew you liked Bob Dylan, so I swipe-a through his music and stop at a random spot," said Marianna. "It all sound-a the same anyway."

"Well, regardless, it was a good swipe," said Mark. "*I and I* is a great song."

"Is that an, 'Aye, aye, captain', Aye and Aye, or 'An eye for an eye' Eye and Eye?" asked Holly.

"Neither," answered Mark. "It's 'I' as in 'Me, Myself and…'"

"That makes no sense," Holly rejected.

"Hang on, it's all in the last line of the chorus, here." Mark sang along with the refrain, emphasizing the last line. "Hear that? '*No man sees my face and lives*'. That's what God said to Moses when Moses asked to see His glory near the end of the book of Exodus."

"Where does the 'I' come in?" asked Holly.

"Near the beginning of Exodus, Moses asks God what His name is, so that he could tell the children of Israel. And God says out of the burning bush, '*I am that I am*'!"

"Nice," said Holly. "The song title makes sense now. Well, kind of."

"I know it's a bit cryptic, but that's our Bob."

"I like that analysis, Mark," said Filip, moving the van over slightly to let an AMC Pacer pass before reaching the bridge over the River Tummel. "And knowing Mr. Dylan, he could also be referring to Rimbaud's *Je est un Autre*."

"What was that?" asked Natalie, catching the last snippet of the conversation.

"I is Another," Filip repeated in English. "It's the concept of self-reflection and the exploration of identity. Like you're looking at yourself from a distance and trying to make sense of it all."

"I think I've heard this before," said Natalie. "Is this Rimbaud a famous poet?"

"He is," Filip replied. "He lived in the late 1800s."

"The late 1800s!" Natalie shouted, startling Marianna into dropping her phone.

Natalie crossed her arms and looked out the backseat window.

So, the famous poet you quoted lived in the late 1800s, eh?, Natalie thought to herself. Dianora, you've got some explaining to do, *mia amica.*

Chapter 26

On Tuesday morning, Natalie entered the quiet room of the Byre Theatre with a cup of hot tea and steely-eyed determination. She had spent the past evening doing research on the best way to represent oneself in a court proceeding. The overwhelming response to that online query was, 'Don't. Just hire a lawyer!' When Natalie altered the search to include the year 1647, the search engine response was, 'Did you mean the year 1947?'. The hits included a court of appeals proceeding in Oregon, opinion number 1947, where the defendant was chided by the judge not to offer him money to settle the case. Natalie made note of this and would remind Ciccio to keep his 'bribery wine' at home on the day of her hearing.

Finding the internet not exactly helpful with advice for her particular situation, Natalie took out pencil and paper and prepared a declaration of innocence that would show deference to the magistrate yet assertiveness in explaining her position. She wouldn't bring this paper back to Florence with her, but it was good to get some thoughts down before she left, she thought. When she was done, Natalie looked over her legal defense and was quite pleased; she was now almost looking forward to presenting her case…*Law and Order: Florence*, starring Natalia Campo Bella as DA Jackie McCoy! She committed the jottings to memory and placed the paper in her bookbag.

Natalie then made a video chat call to bring her brother up to speed with her latest exploits and got the earful she had been expecting. What do you mean you've been under house arrest?, he said. What do you mean you've got a court date?, he cried. What do you mean you've eaten a deep-fried Mars Bar?, he shouted with alarm. Natalie calmed her brother down and explained that, by all accounts, the surgery on Luca had been a success and she was hoping that this would help resolve her case favourably. Connor said he hoped so, too. And he was also very impressed by his sister's bathroom-break escape to The Portal, and her dogged determination to finish that entire Battered Mars Bar.

When she tried to call Mom and Dad, Natalie got nothing. She checked the calendar: it would only be a couple more days until they were out of their deep-woods isolation and Natalie could get her mother's help with this challenging circumstance. She really missed her mom and was hoping to see her again soon.

Natalie took a last sip of tea and placed it on the table next to her bookbag. She didn't finish the cup, because she knew the tea would still be hot when she got back. When she turned around to leave through The Portal, she noticed the protruding little leather book on the bookshelf. She smiled and tucked it back in line with the others. Then she quickly stripped down to her undergarments, took a deep breath, and walked into the fuzzy light.

Amazing. I mean, Wow! I step through The Portal, and my Florence outfit simply reappears on my body! Now that's the way to get dressed for the day! As Marianna would say, 'Just-a like-a the poof!'

I was brushing myself off – I don't exactly know why – when the door to the office suddenly opened. It took me by complete surprise: I didn't think that Dianora was so close behind me when I left for Scotland just a few seconds ago. I straightened out my dress and gave a sheepish smile.

"Well, I guess this isn't the bathroom after all!" I said in French.

"And you couldn't tell that the moment you sprinted in here?" asked Dianora with a puzzled look. "You had to walk around that desk at the far end of the room just to make sure?"

"Ha, ha. Exactly," I replied, making my way to the door. "Just to make sure. Ha, ha…"

"Uh huh," was Dianora's only response to that lame attempt at an explanation. Before I stepped past her into the courtyard, I turned to look back into the office. The Portal was gone.

"Did you forget something?" Dianora asked, looking at the blank back wall of the office.

"*Non, non*…it's just, ah…a nice room, you know?"

"Just a nice room? Er...okay..." Dianora then closed the door behind us and we left to rejoin Rita and Nerina on the walk to the Duomo.

"Just a moment!" I said. Then I turned around and raced the ten paces back to the office and opened the door. The Portal on the back wall glowed brightly upon my return. I gave it a 'good-bye-for-now' wave and headed back to Dianora.

"It really *is* the nicest room," I professed.

"Two chairs, a desk, and a picture on the wall," said Dianora shaking her head. "I thought you were a La-Nouvelle Francophone, not a Spartan."

"Call me anything you like, Dianora! Just do not call me late for dinner!" I said, taking Rita and Nerina both by the arm.

"Where did you get your awful sense of humor?" I heard Dianora mumble as we traipsed down the cobblestone street.

I spent the following three house-arrest days re-preparing for my hearing with the magistrate, recalling the things I'd written down in the quiet room back in Scotland. I wrote so many notes that Rita had to go out and get some more paper and ink. She insisted that I use paper, and not the cheaper-to-buy parchment that was sold in the market; it would make a better impression on the Grand Duke, she said. My quilling was getting better by the page, and I grew to appreciate the fine tip of a swan feather over goose, even though goose gives you another sentence and a half before you have to dip. Nerina checked my spelling and grammar after every page and offered some tips on how to deliver my testimony before the judge. I wasn't to say *insisto* since that would be too direct. *Mi permetta di insistere* added the necessary politeness to the insistence, but *le prego di accettare la mia insistenza* could come across as a bit too 'wishy-washy' for a court proceeding. At least that's what I thought Nerina meant when she said, '*Ooh, suona troppo annacquato!*'

I was planning to bring all of my notes with me to court, but only use them in case of emergency. I was going to present my case from memory, with the intention of exuding confidence and poise. I practiced my defense in front of the mirror in my room, turning potential frowns to relaxed expressions, and pointy hand gestures to open-palmed requests. I wanted to appear assertive - *assertiva*, but not pushy - *invadente*; deferential – *defernte*, but not indignant – *indignata*.

The evidence I would present consisted of the two visits Luca had made to the doctor's office where his condition was diagnosed and treated (unsuccessfully), and the opinions of Dr. Gregorio Redi and Dr. Francesco Redi that indicated Luca's prospects of recovery looked grim (permanently unsuccessful). The witnesses for the prosecution - Maria the nanny, and Bartolomeo di Antonio What's-His-Name the *priore* of the orphanage - couldn't exactly be discredited. But they weren't doctors, they lacked medical training, and they were not even present during the operation. Hardly in a position to criticize the medical procedure employed, Your Honour! In my summation, I would ask the court to consider the suffering of a young boy as superseding an antiquated ordinance that stifled the progress of medical science. If by some terrible miscarriage of justice I was found guilty, I would ask the court for a single favour: to say my goodbyes to everyone at the Palazzo Medici. Then after they escorted me there I'd say, 'I have to go to the bathroom!', and make a mad dash to The Portal.

Ciccio came over every afternoon with the intention of helping me prepare for the hearing, but invariably ended up getting upset over the whole matter, threatening to file a lawsuit against the Grand Duchy of Tuscany for defamation of character, slander, and general obnoxious behaviour. It was either that or challenge the magistrate to *archibugi* at twenty paces. When I asked Ciccio what that meant, he closed one eye and shaped his thumb and forefinger into a gun. There were firearms in 1647? That blew me away, so to speak.

After his visit with me, Ciccio would then spend some time with Evangelista Torricelli. He was worried about his friend. It seemed that Torricelli was not getting any better, despite all the rest, care, and medicines he was receiving. Ciccio had seen this before and he feared the worst: *febbre putrida* was a difficult illness to treat, and many people succumbed to the high fever and debilitation. And he was concerned about Dianora, too. She was looking tired and drawn from attending to Evangelista every day and night. He was hopeful that all would be well soon, but his face betrayed a growing doubt about a positive outcome.

I hadn't seen Dianora for two days now. She had warned me on Sunday night that this might be the case, explaining how she would be attending to Evangelista's needs until the end of his sickness. It was the way she said, 'end of his sickness' that struck me; way more fatalistic sounding than optimistic, if you ask me. It was like she *knew* what was going to happen somehow. I tried to encourage her, and she appreciated my efforts I could tell, but there was a cloud over her head that wouldn't pass. I told her that if all went well on Wednesday with the hearing, I could be more help to her in caring for Signor Torricelli. She said she would appreciate that and gave me a hug; a tight, 'thanks for being my friend' kind of hug. We both said we'd pray for each other this week.

I miss her a lot.

"You look very nice, Natalia. I like what you did with your hair!"

Cecilia Redi could tell I was nervous. We were riding in a carriage on the way to the Palazzo Vecchio, where the hearing with the Grand Duke would take place at 10 am. I was sitting next to Francesco, who kept patting my hand reassuringly. Cecilia and Dr. Gregorio were sitting across from us and appeared relatively subdued, like they were only going to the market to get some *pane* for dinner.

"*Grazie, signora,*" I replied. "But I must give credit to Signorina D'ambrosio for creating all the ringlets." Nerina used hot tongs for a curling iron and beeswax for styling cream to give me a 17th century coiffe.

"She did a wonderful job!" said Ciccio. "You look *incantevole!*"

"*Grazie*, Francesco," I replied. "Yet, I am hoping that the magistrate will look more favourably upon my confident stature and compelling arguments than my outward appearance."

"I hope so, too, for this is only proper!" Cecilia decreed. "Now, hold still a *minuta* while I put a little *rosetta* on your cheekbones." She reached across and dabbed some crushed-flower powder on my face.

"What do you think?" Cecilia asked, passing me a pearl-handled pocket mirror from her purse. I took a look and passed the mirror back with thanks.

"I look almost as good as Signora Redi today," I replied. Cecilia put her hand to her chest and smiled.

"Why, how lovely of you to say so! Ciccio, this girl is winning me over!"

"She has been triumphant in victory over my heart as well, Mamma!" Ciccio crowed.

"And one more victory this morning would make the day even better," I said solemnly, joining Dr. Gregorio in a contemplative look out over the Arno River.

We entered the Palazzo Vecchio through the main doors next to the Statue of David and presented ourselves to the chamberlain that was sitting at the administrative desk. After referring to his reception book, the chamberlain checked us in and passed us off to a court secretary, who was holding a collection papers in his hand that was almost as large as mine. He escorted us to an impressively large room that must have been half a football field long and half again as wide. There were frescos on all the walls featuring battle scenes, political events, and figures representing the virtues that every court of law should extol. The ceiling had an ornate design of decorated wooden beams that added to the grandeur of the space. There must have been seating for at least five hundred; rows of hard-backed benches separated by a centre aisle occupied the majority of the space. The room was as cold as its marble floor. The court secretary led the way to the front of the hall.

"Have you been in the Sala dei Cinquecento before?" he asked the group, turning backward as he walked forward. We all shook our heads no. The Hall of Five Hundred, was it? I called *that* one. "It is not a room that is used very often for court proceedings. We usually entertain those in the Cappella dei Priori, or the Stanzino del Guardaroba. But since Grand Duke Ferdinando himself will be presiding today, we are using the Great Room!"

We were led all the way to the front of the room where two short benches, one on either side of the aisle, faced an elaborately decorated chair. It looked more like a throne than a judge's seat. The court secretary had Dr. Redi and me sit on the bench to the right. Francesco and Cecilia sat behind us in the front row of seats, a good 3 meters behind. There were two people sitting in the other short bench across the aisle, looking straight ahead, stone-faced: Maria the nanny and Bartolomeo di Antonio Whatcha-Ma-Call-Him, the *priore* of the orphanage. Witnesses for the prosecution, I assumed.

"All rise," said the secretary, as the door to our right opened. An entourage of courtiers entered the room, followed by the magistrate himself, Ferdinando II de' Medici, Grand Duke of Tuscany. He was dressed in a blue suit coat with a white-lace shoulder piece, puffy blue trousers, and white knee socks. A t-shaped red ribbon hung over his left breast. His close-set eyes, upturned black moustache, and triangle goatee gave him an austere appearance. I was instantly struck with a feeling of dread; you could tell this man meant business, and his business was putting criminals in prison. I gulped.

The Grand Duke ascended the two steps up to the judge's seat, turned sharply, and sat down. The courtiers stood at ease on either side of the riser. The Grand Duke removed a handkerchief slowly from his sleeve and flicked it twice in the air in a ceremonial fashion.

Then Ferdinando II de' Medici brought the cloth to his face and blew his nose.

"Would someone close the windows in this blasted place! I am freezing up here!" he shouted. Courtiers dashed about in a frenzy, shutting windows up and down the hall. "I mean, really! It is the last week of October, after all! Fresh air is important, but so is comfort! Am I right?"

We all nodded in agreement. Stunned agreement.

"And why, pray tell, are we using this cavern today for a hearing, Martino?" asked Ferdinando II de' Medici glaring at his secretary.

"The smaller rooms are being used for civil cases today, *signoro*. And it was felt that this proceeding has an importance that warrants utilizing the most august of rooms."

The Grand Duke did an eyeroll as the courtiers all stumbled back into place. "Martino, how many people do you see here before you today?"

Martino counted out loud, pointing with his index finger. "*Uno, due, tre, quattro, cinque, sei*…there are six, *signoro*."

"That is correct, Martino. Well done. Six. Six people! Do you know how much it costs to light all these lanterns with *spermaceti* oil?" An awkward, 8 second pause ensued. Martino finally responded.

"A lot, *signoro*?"

"*Sì*, Martino. That is exactly how much it costs, down to the last *quattrino*! A lot!" The Grand Duke of Tuscany sighed and blew his nose again. "All right, what have we got here today? Who are all these people?"

Martino lifted up a piece of paper and began reading. "Signor Bartolomeo di Antonio Canigiani has brought forth a dual charge of unlawful surgical intervention and creating bodily harm against the defendants, Dr. Gregorio Redi of Florence and his assistant, Natalia Campo Bella of…er…of no fixed residence."

"Where are you from, young lady?" the Grand Duke asked me. I stood up to show respect.

"From Scotland, *signoro*. But I am originally from La-Nouvelle France."

"Yet you speak such fine *italiano*! Do you speak French *and* English as well, Natalia Campo Bella?"

"*Oui* and Yes," I replied, which delighted the Duke to no end.

"Natalia, say, '*La tua parrucca è troppo stretta sulla tua testa*!' in English for me."

I hesitated, only because I wasn't sure if I had heard him correctly.

"Your wig is too tight on your head?" I finally managed to answer.

"Your-a weeg is-a too tite on your-a haid! Ha, ha!" The Grand Duke clapped his hands with glee. "I now have a perfect response for King Charles the next time I see him! He says the silliest things, you know? Tell me, Natalia, what do you think of my shirt?" The Grand Duke unbutton his jacket to display an orange shirt, decorated with violins and cellos. I was stunned into silence at the sight; it looked like Ferdinando II had gone through Mark Munroe's closet this morning and picked out one of his aloha shirts!

"You do not like it?" he asked me.

"*No, no,*" I stumbled. "It is not that. It is just…well…"

"I knew it!" the Grand Duke exclaimed, not hiding his disappointment. "I told Vittoria when she picked it out for me that this fashion statement would be too *stravagante*!" He turned to the secretary. "Make a note, Martino…no more wild shirts!" Martino put quill to parchment and scribbled down the edict.

Duke Ferdinando gave me the lowering-hand gesture. I sat back down, hoping I hadn't been found guilty of insulting a magistrate's wardrobe. The Duke turned his attention to the prosecution side of the room.

"Now, Signor Bartolomeo di Antonio And-So-On, what is your complaint against these two medical practitioners?" Bartolomeo stood up.

"I am accusing them of unlawful surgical intervention and…"

"*Sì, sì,* I know all *that*. Just tell me what they have *done*."

"They operated on a boy in the orphanage without consent."

"Operated? They cut open his body?"

"*Sì, signoro.* Into his belly."

"For what reason?"

"The boy had a stomach complaint."

"A stomach complaint?" said Duke Ferdinando. He then pointed to Maria the nanny "You there, the lady who looks like she bit into a bad plum…how sick was this boy?"

Maria stood up. "Well, he was ill for a few days…"

"Getting better each day that passed?"

"*No, signoro,* but…"

"Getting worse?"

"Well, perhaps…"

"Perhaps? Was the boy feverish?"

"*Sì, signoro.*"

"Did he ever lose consciousness from the pain?"

"*Sì.*"

The Grand Duke of Tuscany crossed his arms. "Do either of you have medical training?" They both shook their heads.

"You two sit down," said the Duke. Then he turned to Dr. Redi and me. "Dr. Gregorio Redi, did you operate on this boy."

Dr. Redi stood up. "I did, *signoro.*"

"Because the boy was ill?"

"*Sì, signoro.*"

"On the verge of death, even?"

"We believed so, *signoro.*"

"The 'we' being you and who else?"

"My son, Dr. Francesco Redi," Gregorio said, turning and pointing at Ciccio. "And my surgical assistant, Natalia."

"Do you have medical training as well, young lady?"

I stood up. "*Sì, signoro.* In Scotland." I held out my prepared notes and began my defense. "Honourable Grand Duke of Tuscany, on the morning of October the…"

"*Grazie*, Natalia," Ferdinando II interrupted. "The two of you may be seated."

We sat back down. So much for presenting my own defense. I guess I should have called Saul.

"One last question," said the Grand Duke turning his head. "Where is the boy now, Lady of the Plum?"

"At the orphanage," Maria answered.

"And what is he doing right now?"

"Right now?" she answered with a question.

"*Sì.* Right now. As in right this very moment."

"Most likely playing *calcio* with his friends, I should think."

Ferdinando II de' Medici, Grand Duke of Tuscany, leaned back in his chair and pointed to the prosecution. "Rise, *per favore.*" Bartolomeo and Maria stood up. "Now…shoo!" The two of them looked at each other, bewildered. "You heard me…shoo! Go on! *Avante!*" The Grand Duke flicked his hand in a repeated motion. "Shoo, shoo!" Bartolomeo and Maria made their way quickly down the aisle. "*Più veloce*! *Più veloce*!" The two of them picked up the pace and skedaddled out of the Sala dei Cinquecento.

When the door closed at the far end of the hall, Ferdinando II beckoned to the courtiers on his left. "A table! Bring me a table!" In 22 seconds, the courtiers returned and placed a table in front of the judge's seat.

"Dr. Redi, Natalia, *per favore*," said the Grand Duke, motioning for us to approach. Ferdinando got up from his chair, bounded down the steps, jumped onto the table, and laid down before us.

"Now, tell me everything you did to fix the boy!" He rolled up his shirt and exposed his stomach. A big grin came over his face.

"This type of thing fascinates me to no end!"

It took longer for Dr. Gregorio and me to explain an appendectomy than to do one. The Grand Duke asked so many questions! Why was the incision done at that specific angle?, he asked us. How did you find the infected bit of intestine? How did you clamp and remove the tissue? Where did you perform the surgery? Was there enough light? How many stitches did you need to close the incision? When are you going to do another, because I want to be there!

After the Grand Duke – 'Call me Ferdinando, friends!' – slid off the table, he had the courtiers set it for tea. We all enjoyed *biscotti* and *torta* and a conversation about all things science. Who knew that the Grand Duke…er, Ferdinando…was a technology junkie! He had a room full of hygrometers, barometers, and telescopes at the Palazzo Pitti that he played with every spare moment. He was very excited to tell us of an instrument that he was working on himself…a liquid-filled thermometer!

"It is in the *prototipo* stage at the moment," Ferdinando said after a sip of tea. "But I am confident that I shall have an operational one in no time."

"What is the liquid you will use in the glass column?" Francesco asked.

"I have tried *mercurio*, just like in Torricelli's barometer, but I have been experimenting with coloured spirit of wine in the past month. I have made 360 gradations on the glass, like the degrees in a circle, but I am feeling this is *eccessivo*." Ferdinando then blew his nose again. "Blast it all! I have picked up a cold from this drafty cavern!"

"Perhaps you could use your thermometer to see if you are feverish," I said, making a contribution to the conversation. The Grand Duke froze in mid-sip and everyone turned to me with interested looks.

"And how would one do this, young lady?" Ferdinando asked.

Uh oh. What did I just do? I mentally sighed and decided to plow ahead.

"Well, if one was feeling hot, perhaps a thermometer might record a change from normal," I offered.

"I see!" the Grand Duke said with excitement. "And where would you stick the thermometer to record a reliable temperature in the body?"

"I suppose you could put it in your mouth, or another *orifizio*," Ciccio winked.

"I feared that this conversation would not *end* well," said Cecilia. That made the Duke of Tuscany laugh so hard that he wiped his eye on a courtier's sleeve.

We all enjoyed another cup of tea, a few more biscotti, and an extended science conversation sprinkled with the occasional backside pun. I had become, needless to say, the *butt* of many jokes.

After the secretary informed the Grand Duke that he had to meet Signora Vittoria for a luncheon date, Ferdinando escorted us to the door.

"It was such a pleasure to have met all of you today!" he said while taking a deep bow. "You do not know what a delight it is for me to converse with like-minded *scienziati*. I wish I could do it more often!" We returned the bow and made our way down the steps toward our carriage.

"Oh, Natalia!" cried out Ferdinando II de' Medici, "Best of luck in your studies in Scotland! Try not to get *behind* in your studies!"

The Grand Duke of Tuscany let out a belly laugh and slapped a courtier so hard on the back that the man tumbled down the steps of the Palazzo Vecchio.

I asked the Redis if they wouldn't mind dropping me off at a different address on their way back home. Ciccio was disappointed that I wasn't returning to their house for the afternoon, but he understood once he heard the address I gave to Tonio the carriage driver.

When the carriage stopped to let me off, Dr. Redi opened the door and escorted me down.

"It turned out to be a fine morning, did it not?" he said. Then he kissed my hand. "Well done, Natalia."

"I did not do much," I replied.

"You have done so much, my dear. So very much." Dr. Gregorio got back in the carriage, Tonio click-clicked the horses, and the Redis were off.

"Try not to miss me too much!" Ciccio called out, waving his handkerchief all the way down the street until they were out of sight.

I walked up to the front door and knocked twice. A bleary-eyed, mussy-haired young woman opened the door.

"Natalia! What are you doing here?" Dianora exclaimed.

"I've come to lend a hand," I said. "And to keep company with my good friend."

At my insistence, I kept watch over Evangelista while Dianora took a well-deserved nap, at my insistence. She only protested a little before lying down on the sofa and zonking out for a solid two hours. I got to tidying up in the kitchen and even made a snack for Signor Torricelli, who woke up an hour after I arrived. He was surprised to see me, but even in his slight delirium he knew who I was! My turn to be surprised! He said that he remembered me from the party, and that Francesco had been keeping him abreast of my house-arrest situation. When I told him the result of the hearing with the Grand Duke this morning, Evangelista smiled and took a bite of prosciutto. Then he went back to sleep.

When Dianora woke up, we had a good chat about our past few days. She told me about all the paper sorting and organizing she was doing for Signor Torricelli: she was putting the finishing touches on a compilation of Torricelli's notes that he was calling *Lezioni Accademiche*, and, sadly - as requested by Evangelista only yesterday - she was also helping him arrange his *Testamento*. Dianora found that to be an emotionally difficult job, though Evangelista saw it as a dutiful undertaking whose time had come. He was not getting better, she told me solemnly. The doctors that came by, Francesco included, were not holding out much hope for a recovery. Evangelista Torricelli wasn't either.

Dianora asked me about the hearing, and I spared no detail in the telling of the story. She enjoyed the part where our accusers were shooed out of the Sala dei Cinquecento, and was pleased that the Grand Duke was finally in the finishing stages of developing his 'spirit-filled thermometer', since he had been working on it for a long time. How did you know about his thermometer?, I asked. I was taken aback to learn that Dianora had known Ferdinando II de' Medici for over three years! Apparently, the Grand Duke and Torricelli had met each other through Galileo years ago, and always kept in touch regarding their experiments that used glass-constructed measuring devices. When I asked her why she didn't tell me that she knew the Grand Duke, Dianora said that she didn't want to say anything to me that would unduly crush or raise my hopes for the hearing. But she had a good feeling that Ferdinando, being a man of science, would rule favourably for a procedure based in that discipline. I told her I was very glad about that!

As nightfall encroached on our umpteenth game of *briscola*, Dianora announced that it was time for bed. We had already arranged that I would spell her off at 2 am from attending to Evangelista, who would be in and out of consciousness and require a cool compress every half hour or so. The sofa made a comfortable-enough bed, so I covered myself with a wool blanket and then said goodnight to Dianora as she closed Torricelli's bedroom door behind her.

I slept soundly for about an hour and then quietly got up from the sofa. I crept to the vestibule, slipped on my shoes, and opened the front door. I stepped outside ever-so-silently, and then let out a cry of fright when I discovered someone on the landing standing next to me.

"Going somewhere?" Dianora asked, arms crossed.

"I could ask the same of you!" I answered with the same gesture. "What are you doing out here?"

"I just needed some air," Dianora said, defensively.

"Well, I did, too!"

We both stood there for half a minute, taking turns inhaling deep breaths of cool night air.

"You put on your shoes?" I said.

"You did as well. Are you going for a walk?"

"Well, I was thinking about it," I replied. "And I may do just that right now."

"I think I will, too, but only for a few minutes," said Dianora.

"Fine. Which way are you going?"

"I will go that way," said Dianora, pointing down the street to the right.

"Oh, that was the way I was going," I said with some concern. I didn't know another way to the Palazzo Medici and The Portal.

"Well, then," said Dianora. She pointed in the opposite direction. "I will go this way so we do not end up tripping over each other in the middle of the night."

"Good idea!" I answered with relief.

We walked down the pathway, turned in opposite directions, and strolled down the street. I picked up my pace which increased from saunter to jog to full-out 100m dash by the time I reached Via Calzaioli. When I looked back, I could just make out Dianora in the distance.

That was odd. She looked like she was sprinting, too.

"So I told King Edward that getting to Fiji is quite simple, really. You go to America, cross the continent to San Francisco, hop on a boat and take the second turn to the left!"

The hearty laugh shared by the two men was momentarily interrupted by a rough patch of sea that had them both reach for the railing. Once steadied, they continued their walk along the deck.

"I liked that one, Sir John. I hope you won't mind me borrowing that line for my lecture in New Zealand."

"I won't at all. And I told you to drop the 'Sir', Samuel."

"Ah, I see what you did there, Mr. Thurston. Very well. I shall dispense with the Sir if you promise to hold the Mark!"

John Thurston smiled at his scraggily-haired, mustachioed new friend. They had become inseparable since setting sail from the Sandwich Islands only the week before, finding that their common loves of cigar smoking, billiards, and river boat piloting kept the conversation flowing and the boredom at bay. It would be another week before they docked in Suva Harbour and Sir John resumed his duties as Governor of Fiji. But the two men had a sufficient supply of stories and myths to exchange for the remainder of the trip.

"Did you do much writing last evening?" John asked Mark.

"I did! I'm now thinking that this 1895 speaking tour around the world might inspire my next book. What do you think of the title, 'Following the Equator'?

"Succinct. I like it. Though I enjoyed that mouthful-of-a-title your book had a few years ago, too."

"'A Connecticut Yankee in King Arthur's Court'?"

"Yes, that's the one. Where the engineer travels back in time. That was a fun read! Did you know that a countryman of mine has just put out a book about time travelling to the future in a machine? I think his name is Wells. It looks like you've started a new literary genre, Mr. Twain."

"I certainly hope not! This time-travel stuff became a tired idea to me before my pen wrote the words Chapter Two!" Mark Twain then stopped and pointed to his right. "Did you drop something, John?"

John Thurston bent down to pick up a twice-folded piece of paper that blew toward him and stopped at his boot. He unfolded the paper once and read the message.

"What do you make of it, Mark?"

"Written by a sure hand, certainly. It seems to have been written just for you, old boy."

John Thurston smiled, folded the paper back up, and placed it in his pocket.

"I'll be off to my quarters now," said Mark Twain, veering off to the companionway at midship. "Time for an afternoon siesta!"

"A continuation of your morning siesta," Mr. Thurston said with a smile. "I'll see you at dinner, Mark. Would you like to borrow that Japanese-print shirt I wore the other night? The one that all the Hawaiian men are now wearing?"

"I would not be caught dead in that multi-coloured abomination," Mr. Twain exclaimed before heading below deck. "This Mark says, 'Aloha to that apparel', good Sir!"

Chapter 27

"But it *did* happen, Connor. I lived it!"

"I know, Nat. But none of your friends experienced that conversation in the seminar room the way *you* did. You introduced that cake to the world in 1647 and changed the timeline, simple as that. You're the one that gave *skatchatorri florentine* to future generations, sis!"

"*Schiacciata Fiorentina*, brother dear. *Schiacciata Fiorentina*."

"Whatever. The point is, the past got altered a little bit and it seems to have only changed a friendly conversation in the future. No harm, no foul. Besides, have you thought that maybe you actually *are* the person that's supposed to introduce *skatchmatcha firetina* to the world?"

"Ahhh! My brain hurts!"

Natalie and her brother were deep into a Tuesday evening video chat via laptop, Scotland time. Back in Canada, Connor was devoting a lunch-spare time block to his sister before his Period 5 chemistry class. He told her he couldn't be late for that one, as Mr. Dyson was going to blow up some ethanol in a swoosh bottle! Whatever that was.

Natalie spared no details when describing the court proceedings to Connor. He found the whole story rather amusing, and twice had to be shushed by the school librarian after erupting into laughter. He found a lot of similarities between Ferdinando II de' Medici and Inspector Gadbois, the police constable that chased him around Paris in 1771: they may give the initial impression that you were talking to a fool, but holding onto that perception would be at your peril! Connor was visibly relieved to learn that Natalie was cleared of all charges, and that she could now move freely about Florence again. And that was good, he reminded her, because, since The Portal was still operational, there was apparently still a job for her to do.

"Let's change the subject," said Connor. "What's left to do in Italy?"

"Well, I think I need to visit Luca one more time. I want to see how he's doing." Natalie picked up her phone and started a search. "There's something that's been bugging me, though."

"Care to share?"

"It's about Luca Giordano's early life. All I can ever find online is that he was born in Naples in 1634 and then he becomes an apprentice to the painter Jusepe de Ribera in 1650. There's nothing mentioned in between! His life story goes dark for 16 years. What's all that about?"

"You'd think that being an orphan would qualify as interesting personal history."

"Exactly! Why wouldn't his time at the *Ospedale degli Innocenti* be of interest to history? It's not like it's embarrassing to be an orphan."

Connor was quiet for a moment. Then he said to his sister, "Unless he wasn't an orphan."

"Um, he lives in an orphanage, Connor," Natalie said with an eye roll. "That's where Dr. Redi and I did the operation, remember?"

"Sure. But what if his parents were still alive?"

"Okay, wait, whoa, hang on! Are you saying that Luca's not an orphan?"

"Maybe he ran away from home, Natalie."

Natalie took her own quiet moment. Then she said to her brother, "Sixteen blank years in Luca Giordano's history. Nothing written about his childhood by historians or relatives. Maybe because it's embarrassing that the family history…"

"Includes the story of a runaway," Connor interjected. "It's totally possible, Nat. Luca may not be an orphan after all. He may still have parents in 1647."

"Maybe even parents that care for him and are grief-stricken over their lost little boy!" Natalie's narrowed eyes looked right at Connor. "Maybe that's the job, bro. Maybe that scenario has to be fixed."

"Agreed," said Connor. "Whether that's the reason The Portal is still open for you or not, that's a job that's got to get done."

"Yep. But it's going to have to wait for a few days after I return to Florence because I'm going to help Dianora look after Evangelista Torricelli."

"He's not going to make it, is he?" Connor asked with concern.

"When I go back it'll be the start of Thursday, October 24, 1647. Torricelli passes away on October 25th."

"Whoa. That's going to be a rough couple of days, Nat. I'm sorry."

"Me, too. Evangelista is a lovely man. Dianora is very fond of him."

"How is she holding up?"

"She's tired, you can tell. But she's determined to make Torricelli comfortable in his last few days." Natalie paused a moment. "It's funny, but it's almost like she can see the outcome of the whole ordeal, Connor. She's a pretty special person. And she kinda reminds me of you."

"She does?"

"Yeah, she likes math and she's super sassy."

"But can she throw a javelin?" said Connor with a smirk. He held up his phone to the laptop screen. "I just found her in a search, Nat. It says here that Dianora, Torricelli's servant, will inherit a sum of money after his passing."

"I read up on that a while ago," Natalie replied. "She deserves it. And Dianora isn't his servant, you know. She's his assistant."

"That's a way more dignified title. Do you know a guy named Ceccotto?"

"No, I don't," Natalie answered.

"He's the chimney sweep. He's going to inherit Torricelli's old shoes and socks! Have you met his brothers, Carlo and Francesco? They're going to get most of his estate."

"No, but maybe I'll meet them tomorrow," said Natalie. "Who else is mentioned in the will?"

"Just the executor. A guy named Serenai."

"I don't know him."

"He was friends with someone named Viviani."

"Oh, I know Vincenzo Viviani. He's the one that hosted Evangelista's birthday party. He gave me the surname, Campo Bella."

"Right. Well, the two of them are going to be in charge of sorting through all of Torricelli's notes."

"That's not exactly right," corrected Natalie. "That's what Dianora's been doing. She's organized everything into a book, too!"

"A woman not getting her props? Not exactly unheard of in 1647, Nat."

"And for a few hundred years after that, too, bro," Natalie replied. "Have you heard from Mom and Dad?"

"Nothing. And I've been trying to call. You?"

"Nothing. I wouldn't be surprised if Dad's phone was dead, but Mom would be keeping hers charged. They must still be pretty deep undercover."

"Probably deep, deep, deep, *deep* undercover, like Axel Foley in *Beverly Hills Cop*."

"Yeah, just like that, Connor," Natalie replied, shaking her head. "Because our Mom is a spy."

"No, but she's a TTer, and so are her children. So maybe not *Beverly Hills Cop*, then. More like the family in *Spy Kids*!"

"Now you're talking," Natalie smiled. "Okay, bro, I gotta go. You have to get to chemistry class, and I have to prepare for a visit with Dr. Blanco tomorrow."

"More appendix talk with your prof, eh? You going to show him how you did the *redicut* on that Luca kid?"

"Not very likely!" Natalie laughed. "And I like that incision name you invented there."

"What did I invent?"

"Redicut! I get it. Dr. Redi with the word cut."

"Yeah, well that's what you called it before you did the surgery on Luca…the redicut."

"I did no such thing," Natalie said, looking annoyed.

"We were talking about you looking for a clear direction. You said, 'I'll look for a Guiding Hand outlining a redicut incision!'"

"I said grid-iron incision, Connor. There's no such thing as a redicut incision."

"Well, there *is*, because you told me you were going to do one," Connor maintained. "Then I said, 'Hey, do you think it's called redicut because it's named after Dr. Redi?', and you said, 'Hey, I never thought of that!' And then we both laughed. Don't you remember?"

"Connor, that's not what happened." Natalie was starting to feel funny again, like she did the day before on the beach.

"Oh wow! This is the coolest thing, Nat!" Connor was shushed by the librarian again. He lowered his voice and continued. "We had a previous conversation about a grid-iron incision, then you went back in time and actually invented it, but the incision got renamed after Dr. Redi! You changed the timeline around something the two of us had been discussing! That is so cool!"

"That is *not* cool, Connor! That is not cool at all!"

"Like I said before, Nat - no harm no foul! At least, there doesn't *appear* to be any foul…"

"What do you mean by that?"

"Nothing. Nothing at all."

"Why would there be a foul. Who did I foul?"

"No foul, sis. There's no foul! Remember the *Butterfly Noneffect*! Embrace the *Noneffect*!"

Natalie took a deep breath. "I'll try, Connor. But I seem to have a knack for changing the future!"

"That name change is just a little thing, Nat. It'll be all right, you'll see. Nothing else is going to change!"

"Are you sure?"

"Well, no actually," Connor admitted. "How can I be? To everybody else, the way things *are* right now is the way things have always been. You're the only one who will ever experience any change in the timeline, Natalie."

"That's no comfort, little brother."

"That's transtemporal trekking, sis!" Connor blew a kiss from Canada, and Natalie's video window went dark.

Ten minutes later, there was a knock on the door. Marianna called out for Natalie to answer it, as she was up to her elbows in semolina flour making tagliatelle. Natalie hurried from her bedroom and got to the door in the middle of the second round of knocks.

"I've just discovered something and I need to show you!" Mark exclaimed, rushing past Natalie and depositing himself on a kitchen chair.

"You're-a soaking wet and-a getting water all over my clean floor!" Marianna protested.

"It'll evaporate, I promise!" Mark took out an empty soda pop bottle from his jacket pocket and plonked it on the table.

"You've discovered that they still make pop bottles out of glass?" said Natalie.

"That, and something else," Mark replied, pointing to the bottle. "I figured out where the halfway mark is."

"What do you mean?" Natalie queried with a puzzled look.

"I mean, I figured out a way to determine the precise location where half of the liquid remains in that bottle, or in any bottle." Mark crossed his arms and presented a look of satisfaction.

"How hard is-a that?" said Marianna, cleaning off her hands in the sink. "Just-a use one of these." She held up a measuring cup.

"Without using a measuring device of any kind, though," Mark responded. Natalie picked up the bottle and examined it.

"It looks like it could be right here," she said, putting her finger on a spot near the middle.

"But the glass is all curvy and it's got a long neck," noted Mark. "Are you sure?"

"Well, I'm not sure. I'm estimating."

"But what's the *precise* location of the fluid midpoint?" Mark asked.

"You could-a pour out what you think is-a half into a cup," Marianna offered. "And then-a pour out the other half into a similar cup and weigh-a them in your hands!"

"That's a good idea, but it's still estimating," said Mark. Natalie turned the bottle ninety degrees in her hand. Mark's eyes widened. "Getting warmer!" Natalie turned the bottle another ninety. "That's got it!"

"Got-a what?" said a confused Marianna.

Mark rose from the chair, took the bottle from Natalie, and filled it up to the top with water from the sink. He placed it on the table beside two empty Portmeirion tea mugs. "Now ladies, watch and learn."

Mark poured out an amount of water from the bottle into a mug. He stopped, checked the volume level, poured out a little more, and checked again. He poured and rechecked two more times until he was satisfied. The water level in the bottle was just below the start of second curvy section down from the top. He placed the bottle back down on the table.

"There. The halfway point, as previously determined."

The two women looked at each other with unconvinced frowns.

"Prove it," said Natalie.

"Got a felt pen?" Mark asked. Marianna passed him one from the counter.

Mark made a mark at the waterline. Then he picked up the bottle and placed his palm on the top, sealing the lip. He tipped the bottle over 180 degrees. The fluid level returned to the same mark on the bottle.

"And there it is!" Mark glowed. "That's exactly half of the liquid in the bottle!"

"I'm not-a convinced," said Marianna, hands on hips.

Mark poured out the rest of the bottle contents into the other mug. The women both looked down into the two tea cups. The liquid levels were identical.

"Okay, now I'm-a convinced," said Marianna, nodding her head.

"That's pretty impressive, Mark," said Natalie.

"I know! If the liquid level returns to the same mark when you tip a container upside down, you've found exactly half the volume! It works the same for any bottle of any shape!"

"Well, not-a every bottle, of course," Marianna insisted. "I have-a to go make a call now." She went down the short hallway and closed the bedroom door behind her.

"What do you mean not-a every bottle?" Mark shouted.

"You have-a to be able to see through it!" Marianna shouted back from behind the door.

"She's got you there," said Natalie.

"Indeed," Mark admitted, as Natalie sat across from him at the kitchen table. They were quiet for 13 awkward seconds.

"So, you came over to talk pop bottles, did you?" asked Natalie, absently picking up one of the mugs.

"Well, not exactly," Mark said shyly. "I came over to see you."

"You wanted to check up on me after that little glitch at the beach yesterday? I'm fine, really."

"No, it's not that."

"You want to go over some Immunology notes?"

"No, not exactly…"

"Because if you want to talk parasites…"

"Natalie!" Mark interrupted. Then he said, calmly, "I just came over because I, ah…wanted to be with you. That's all."

"Oh! I see. So the whole pop bottle thing?…"

"A ruse, of course. All of us smitten males do that sort of thing, you know?"

"Bring an empty pop bottle over to a young lady's house?"

"Well, yes. That and, we always invent ridiculously elaborate scenarios just so we can spend some quality time with the person that makes us happy."

"Always?"

"Always."

Natalie smiled demurely. "Would you care to stay for a cup of tea?"

"That would make me happy, too," Mark replied.

Natalie picked up the mugs and went to the counter. Mark made himself comfortable and took off his jacket.

"Hey, where's your aloha shirt?" she asked.

"My what?"

"I've never seen you not wear an aloha shirt before."

"I'm not sure what that is, Natalie, but I look forward to your explanation."

Natalie hid her frazzlement well, save for the clunking down of the tea mugs. She turned the tap to fill the kettle, and in her mind she hoped that this newest timeline alteration would be a no harm, no-foul one as well.

"Oh, ha, ha…never mind, Mark! I'll save that explanation for another *time*."

Early next morning, Natalie stood at the entrance to The Portal and took a deep breath. She wasn't exactly sure what the rest of her job in Florence entailed, but she was confident that she would be given the necessary resources to get it done.

And she was thankful that Dianora would be there to help.

Chapter 28

Michelle Morel was buried behind a stack of reference materials in her favourite sixth floor cubicle at Calgary Hall. Most of the books were for her engineering course work, but a few were specific to the history of calculus. It was the calculus books that occupied the majority of her time on Monday morning, with one of them attracting the most attention: a dusty tome that contained the English translation of a pamphlet titled *Nova Methodus Pro Maximis et Minimis* by the German mathematician Gottfried Leibniz. Michelle liked that the book contained photos of Leibniz' 1684 hand-written notes in Latin, because they spruced up the dry presentation of the text with their crazy symbols and diagrams. It reminded her of the scattershot notation that dominated Torricelli's scientific speculations in his own notes. And those Torricelli notes reminded her of her dear friend that she had momentarily left peacefully sleeping back in 1647. Michelle was suddenly overtaken with a wave of guilt, feeling as if she had abandoned Evangelista in his hour of need. But that wasn't the case, of course; Dianora would only be gone for a few minutes, Florence time. She would return to his side after spending some time in study and reflection back home.

As Michelle finished reading Leibniz' notes on tangents - the Latin not fazing her for a moment since she was now conversant in the classical language – she marvelled at his introduction of the term *calculi* to describe the computations involved with fractional quantities. And his use of the differentiation terms dx and dy, which were still in use to this day to describe the derivative of the function f, was equally interesting to her. But Leibniz' use of the symbol $\int$ to describe integration had Michelle confused, so she opened another book from her stack. *The History of Mathematics* made it clear: Leibniz was the one who invented dx, dy and the symbol $\int$ to describe specific calculus operations. That made Michelle curious: she could have sworn Evangelista had used the symbol $\int$ to describe *integrazione* in the notes he had recently shown her. Hmm, she thought. This would require some further investigating when she got back to Florence, as Torricelli may have beaten Leibniz to the invention of $\int$ by almost 40 years!

Before taking a break, Michelle took another book off the cubicle shelf. She parsed the early chapters of *The Personalities of Science* and found the section that described the life and work of Francesco Redi. He was described as the 'founder of experimental biology', 'the father of modern parasitology', and through his vital work in disproving spontaneous generation, he became 'the designer of the scientific method'. Michelle nodded, with raised eyebrows. Now that was impressive!, she thought. A two-page description of his abiogenesis experiment followed, complete with an artist rendering of jars, flies, maggots, rotting meat, and cheesecloth. The section on Redi concluded with a mention of his literary career: he became a famous poet, having written the much-loved and revered *Bacchus in Tuscany*. Michelle furrowed her brow and shook her head. Now that was hard to believe!, she thought. But Michelle then shrugged her shoulders and acknowledged that, for a twenty-something, Ciccio Redi's verse wasn't really half bad, and could only get better. And we can all get better over time, can't we?

What Michelle didn't find in *The Personalities of Science* – or any other science history book she had inspected, for that matter - was any mention of Francesco's dad, Dr. Gregorio Redi, or a certain assistant he may have had that helped him perform a controversial operation on a young boy in 1647. So, her friend Natalia had no history, then? Hmm. Michelle found that hard to believe and unfortunate at the same time.

She got up from her seat, had a good stretch, and grabbed her knapsack. It was time for a study break!

"Hey, what's shakin'!" greeted Ken, as he swivelled in his studio chair and removed his headphones. He had just placed the needle down on She Blinded Me With Science, by Thomas Dolby. "I was expecting you!"

"But it's not my volunteer day today," Michelle replied, plopping her knapsack on the floor and taking a seat next to the deejay.

"Yeah, but you usually come to the studio around this time every other day."

"No I don't."

"Sure you do. Like clockwork. You're a little neurotic, Michelle, but in a good way. Hear the song I'm playing? That's cuz I knew you were coming!"

"Nice try," Michelle said with a smirk. She picked up an album from the console. "*Night Beat*, by Sam Cooke. Now this one reminds me of my dad."

"Your dad has good taste, that's a great record. The mono version of it is rad. Which song do you want to hear?"

"How about Nobody Knows the Trouble I've Seen?" Michelle replied, passing Ken the record.

"Whoa. Feeling the weight of the world on your shoulders, pal?"

"Maybe a little. But this song reminds me that someone somewhere is having a tougher day than I am. So, I need to count my blessings, right?"

"Sounds right to me!" said Ken, cuing up the first track on *Night Beat* on the second turntable. "You just reminded me that I need to call *my* dad tonight and see how he's doing. You talk to your parents lately?"

"Not as much as I should," Michelle admitted. "But I did call them a few days ago. My mom asked if I was eating properly, and my dad wanted to know if I was up to any adventures lately. I told him that aside from a trip to Elbow Falls, it was business as usual…lots of studying, lots of sorting through notes."

"And not enough sleep, of course."

"Which my dad reminded me was necessary. He's worried about me burning the candle at both ends."

Ken nodded. "That's a great saying isn't it? Burning the candle at both ends. It's like you're living this dual life, you're trying to accomplish the work of two people, and time isn't on your side."

"Tell me about it!" said Michelle.

Just then the studio door burst open and a flustered and breathless Chase stood before them, waving a VHS tape in his hand.

"Phew! I knew I'd find you here, Michelle."

"Am I really that predictable?" she asked, palms facing upward.

"You're a creature of habit that likes routine," Chase replied. "Anyway, I need you to come with me, Michelle. I need your help!" Chase couldn't stand still. He was bouncing excitedly on the balls of his feet.

"What is it?" asked Michelle in a worried tone, because this was Chase, after all.

"Yeah, what's with all the hopping around?" asked Ken, not really worried since this was Chase, after all.

"It's Danny Gallivan!" Chase shouted. "Guys! I'm going to meet Danny Gallivan in one hour!"

"You're what?" asked a stunned Ken. "Are you kidding?"

"Who's Danny Gallivan?" asked Michelle.

"Whaddya mean, 'Who's Danny Gallivan?'," Chase barked. "Danny Gallivan! The voice of the Montreal Canadiens! The greatest sportscaster in the history of sportscaster-ing!"

"He did the play-by-play on *Hockey Night in Canada* for over 30 years," Ken added.

"I didn't watch *Hockey Night in Canada* growing up," Michelle responded.

"You didn't watch HNIC? I mean, how's that possible? You're a Canadian!" Chase was dumbfounded.

"I'm from Quebec, remember?" said Michelle. "We watched *Le Soiree du hockey* on Saturday nights."

"Okay, *irregardless* of that, Danny Gallivan is here!"

Ken gave his standard shiver to Chase's nonstandard English usage. Then he asked, "Where is here?"

"Take a deep breath and explain it to us, Chase," Michelle suggested.

Chase took a deep breath and began his story. "My Media and Society prof, Dr. Dutton, is friends with Danny Gallivan. Danny is in town to help the Canadian Sports Hall of Fame find a new venue. He's dropping by the university to visit his old friend this afternoon and speak to the Com students for half an hour in the theatre!"

"So, *everyone* is going to meet Danny Gallivan, then, and not just you?" asked Ken.

"No, no…I'm going to have a 20-minute session with Danny in the Communications Lab at 2:30! I arranged it with Dr. Dutton!"

"That's outta sight!" Michelle enthused. "How did you manage to arrange that?"

"By utilizing my persistent persuasiveness and charming charmfulness, of course."

Ken gave Chase a suspicious look. "So, you shamelessly begged at Dr. Dutton's feet, then?"

"Like a seagull for French fries at Peter's Drive-In," said Chase.

"What's with the video tape?" inquired Michelle.

"This is Game 6 of the Flames Stanley Cup win over Montreal this spring. Danny Gallivan is going to listen to me do 10 minutes of play-by-play!"

"And then you'll be critiqued by a broadcast legend!" Michelle declared.

"Critiqued?" asked a perplexed Chase.

"And then you'll be extolled by a broadcast legend!" corrected Ken.

"There we go!" Chase exclaimed. He checked his watch. "Michelle, you've got to come with me!"

"What do you need me for?"

"I want you there for the session! You're my moral support! I need your calming influence! C'mon, let's go!"

Chase bolted out of the studio. Michelle got up from the chair and grabbed her knapsack.

"What he needs you for is an audience," said Ken as he started up the Sam Cooke record.

Michelle gave Ken a wink and closed the studio door behind her.

"Mr. Gallivan, sir, let me initially say first what an honour and privilege it is to meet you, sir!"

Chase's eyes were wide with admiration as he shook the hand of his boyhood idol. Danny Gallivan returned the greeting warmly, even though the handshake had gone awkwardly into double overtime.

"It's very nice to meet you, Chase. And who is this young lady?"

"Oh, that...I mean her...um, this is Michelle." Chase gave a sweeping open-palm gesture. "Michelle, may I introduce to you, Sir Gallivan...er, Mr. Gallivan. Mr. Danny Sir Gallivan...er..."

"It's nice to meet you, Mr. Gallivan," Michelle interjected, shaking his hand.

"Please, call me Danny, Michelle," he replied.

"Won't you please be seated, Danny Michelle...er, Mr. Danny, sir," Chase said, inviting everyone to take a seat. The three of them sat down facing the main TV monitor in the Com Lab.

"So, you want to be a broadcaster, do you, Chase?" Danny asked.

"In the worst way, sir."

"Call me Danny, Cha..." Mr. Gallivan abruptly stopped, suddenly aware that finishing the sentence could result in him next being called Danny Chase. "Just call me Danny. In your mind, what are your strongest assets, Chase?"

"Well, I have a love for the love of sports, and I think I have the mental mindset to do play-by-play at the highest level!"

"The *mental* mindset?"

"Yes, Danny, sir."

"As opposed to the *physical* mindset?"

"Exactly," said Chase, pointing at Danny.

"Well, then," said Danny Gallivan, blinking twice in rapid succession. "Shall we begin?"

"Yes, sir!" said Chase, popping in the game tape. "Let me just say, Danny, that I've been waiting a long time in perpetuity to do something like this with someone like you." Chase put on a headset and positioned himself in front of the screen.

"Michelle, could you please pass me that pad of paper and pen?" Danny Gallivan said, pointing to her right. "I think I'll need to take some notes."

After 10 minutes of second period action, Danny Gallivan reached over to the VCR and pressed PAUSE, stopping Chase's play-by-play in mid-slapshot.

"I think that's enough for today, Chase."

"Did that give you a good picture of my abilities, Danny?" Chase took off his headset and placed it on the console.

"Oh, it most certainly did, son. Let's go over a few things."

Danny Gallivan shifted slightly in his seat and flipped back two pages on the legal pad. He looked over at Chase, who was smiling from ear to ear.

"Let's start with the positives, shall we? You have a vocal tone that is easy to listen to, Chase. Your delivery is very smooth."

"Thank you, Mr. Gallivan. I get that smoothness from my mom."

"I see," said Danny, looking up at Chase above his reading glasses. He returned to his notes. "You enunciate clearly, you engage the listener…"

"I get that from my dad."

"And your enthusiasm is infectious."

"I get *that* from my dog."

"Okaaay…" Danny flipped the page. "Now, let's talk about what you need to work on."

The smile dropped from Chase's face. He looked over to Michelle and gulped.

"Chase, to effectively communicate in the broadcast industry, you need to be on good speaking terms with the English language, along with having the desire to constantly improve in your knowledge of it."

"So, you're saying that those two things should be in concert together, then?"

"See, that's it right there, Chase. You're being redundant. The words 'in concert' actually mean 'together'. When you say, 'in concert together', you're actually saying, 'together together'. You did this two other times during your call of the game."

"I did?"

"Yes, you did." Danny flipped to the next page. "You described the Canadiens' troubles on the powerplay as being on a vicious 'carousel cycle'. By definition, a carousel *is* a cycle. Then you said, 'The parity in the NHL is very even right now'. Parity *means* evenness, Chase. You ended up saying, 'The evenness in the NHL is very even right now."

"So, what you're saying is that I've been reiterating myself repeatedly, then?" Chase asked. Danny Gallivan's eyes widened in disbelief. Michelle's eyes closed tightly from a wince.

"In a way, yes, that's what I'm saying, Chase. So try to cut down on repeating yourself in the same sentence. Like when you said, 'MacInnis shoots the puck vertically down the ice!' or 'Mullen made a great solo effort there, all on his own!'"

"Thanks, Mr. Gallivan," said Chase. "I'll certainly give that a 110% effort."

"Now, about that word you used," Danny said, flipping to the last page of notes. "Frazzlement, was it?"

"That's not a word, is it?" said Chase, sheepishly.

"It's not."

"I won't use it again, sir. I promise."

"No, no! That's not what I'm saying. I loved your use of that very much!"

"You did?"

"Son, I invented words myself!" Danny said with noticeable pleasure. "My broadcasting career wouldn't have been anything special without sayings like, 'The Savardian *Spinarama*'!

"Whoa, you actually invented the word spinarama, Danny?" Chase marvelled.

"I did! I once got a scathing letter from a university professor who was affronted when I said, 'Robinson unleashed a *cannonading* drive!'.

He told me there was no such word as cannonading. So I wrote him back a nice letter."

"What did you say?" Michelle asked.

"I said to him, 'There's no such word as *cannonading*? Well, my friend, there is now!'"

The three of us laughed together.

"So, Chase, my advice is to have respect for the language, but don't be afraid to contribute to the lexicon."

"I will, sir. And I won't, sir!"

"Good!" said Danny, rising up from his chair. "It's been a pleasure to meet you!" He said both of their names as he shook their hands. Then he put his hand on Chase's shoulder and said, "I'm sorry if I was a little hard on you with all the corrections, Chase. But I want to tell you something…you have real talent, my boy. I see a bright future for you in this profession." Danny patted Chase twice one the shoulder, handed him the notepad, and turned to leave.

"Now put your best *right* foot forward and work hard at your craft, son!" Danny said with a wink as he left the Com Lab. Chase and Michelle stood silently for moment as they watched Mr. Gallivan walk down the hallway. A misty-eyed Chase broke the silence.

"Danny Gallivan. A legendary legend if there ever was one."

Gilliana and Michelle were having a chin-wag in the common area of the dormitory that evening when Jay arrived and plonked himself down on the sofa across from the women.

"You're looking all excited," Gilliana said to him. "Care to share?"

"I just found the solution to a problem I've been working on, so I'm pretty stoked."

"You balanced a tough chemistry equation?" asked Michelle.

"You finally found balance in your life?" asked Gilliana.

"*No* to the first question, and *I wish* to the second," Jay responded. "It's an engineering problem. Wanna hear it?"

"Absolutely!" Michelle enthused.

"...not!" Gilliana exclaimed, getting up from her chair. "I'm going to go watch *Quantum Leap* and then I'm off to bed."

"*Quantum Leap*?" questioned Jay. "Is that the new time-travel show everyone's talking about?"

"It's really good," Gilliana replied. "It's got a cool premise, the writing is top-notch…"

"And Dr. Sam Beckett is a dreamboat," Michelle interjected.

"Ah, the truth emerges!" Jay pronounced.

"Well, cute never hurts a storyline," Gilliana responded with a wink. "Later, dudes."

"See you tomorrow, Gilli," said Michelle with a lift-up hand wave. She turned to Jay. "So, what's the problem?"

"With *Quantum Leap*? Nothing, really. I just find time travel stuff a bit old, you know."

"No, I meant, so what's this engineering problem?"

"Oh, right! Well, it has to do with the mathematics of laying a pipeline, the use of extraneous materials, and the concept of over-engineering. You still want to hear it?"

"You had me at mathematics, Jay. Go ahead."

Jay leaned forward on the sofa. "Okay, so, let's say there's a rich industrialist who wants to lay a pipeline all the way around the world, so everyone can have access to the oil he's taking from the ground."

"Not exactly possible," noted Michelle.

"Right. There are mountains, there are oceans. But let's just say that it's possible to lay the pipeline flat around the world, for argument's sake."

"Okay, for argument's sake."

"Great. Now, the rich industrialist is there at the ceremony where the two ends of the pipe are going to be joined. The crane lowers the last piece in, the pipeline is joined, the job is done and everyone cheers. But the rich industrialist sees a 10-metre section of extra pipe lying off to the side. He looks at his chief engineer and says, 'I didn't become a rich man by wasting materials! Open up the line and insert that extra 10 metres of pipe, Wally!"

"Wally?"

"Wally's the chief engineer. So, Wally tells his boss that it's not a good idea, because the extra 10 metres will create a gap between the bottom of the pipe and the ground. The rich industrialist scoffs at the idea that adding 10 metres to a pipe that goes around the entire planet will make a noticeable difference."

"So the question is, how big is the gap?" said Michelle.

"Would you need a microscope to see the gap? Could you slip a piece of paper under the gap? Could you walk under the gap?" Jay leaned back on the sofa. "The question is, what's the height of the actual gap, from the ground to the underside of the pipeline?"

Michelle reached into her knapsack and produced a sheet of paper and a pen. She quickly scribbled down a formula.

$$c = 2\pi r$$

She showed it to Jay, who said, "Good start."

Michelle did some more scribbling and added a bit of head scratching to the operation. She turned the paper to Jay after 4 minutes, pointing to a circled section.

$$r_1 = c/2\pi \qquad r_2 = c + 10/2\pi$$

"Radius One is from the centre of the earth to the top of the earth," Michelle explained. "Radius Two is from the centre of the earth to the bottom of the pipeline. The only difference in the two formulas is the extra 10 metres added to the circumference of the earth. The difference between the two radii is the gap."

"So what's the gap?" asked Jay.

"Well, all I need is the circumference of the earth, and…"

"No you don't," Jay interrupted.

"I don't?" said Michelle, looking down at the paper. She stared at it for 22 seconds. "Oh, duh! The circumference is constant to both equations! I could substitute any number in for 'c'!"

"Even zero!" Jay inserted.

"Even zero," Michelle nodded and smiled. "So, for the first equation, putting zero in for c gives your radius equals zero. And putting zero into the second equation leaves you with ten over two pi, which is five over pi, which is five over 3.14, which is…"

"1.59 metres, to three significant digits," said Jay. "So, the difference between zero and 1.59 is…tada!…1.59!"

Michelle leaned back in her chair with an impressed look on her face. "That's pretty awesome, Jay. It's hard to believe, but the math doesn't lie. You could bend over and walk underneath the gap that's created!"

"And that gap is all around the entire earth, too! Although there are some pipeline-suspended-in-mid-air problems attached to that!"

Jay and Michelle had an engineer's chuckle over that one.

"Well, thanks for coming over with an evening brain-teaser, Jay," said Michelle.

"I knew you'd like that one," Jay said. "Well, I mean, you *and* Gilli. I came to see *both* of you, of course."

"Of course! Because you *knew* Gilli the zoology major would love that pipeline problem." Michelle said with a slight smile. "You sure you didn't drop by for another reason?"

"Okay, whoa, Michelle. Do you think the pipeline problem was some sort of ruse I concocted?"

"Don't all you smitten males do that sort of thing?"

"Smitten male? That's not me, girlfriend…I mean, *friend*! Besides, you and Chase…"

"Are *just* friends," Michelle interjected. "That's all."

"That's all?" said Jay, leaning forward again on the sofa.

"Totally."

"Yeah, but does Chase know that?"

"Now *that's* a different question," Michelle answered. "But until I find out the answer to that, you and I could still go to Mac Hall for an evening cup of tea, couldn't we?"

Jay smiled. "We certainly could."

The two of them collected their things and walked together to the dormitory exit. Jay held the door open for Michelle.

"We males always invent ridiculously elaborate scenarios just so we can spend some quality time with the person that makes us happy, you know?"

"Always?" asked Michelle.

"Always," smiled Jay.

In the CJSW record room on Tuesday morning, Michelle stood at the entrance to The Gateway and took a deep breath. She knew what the rest of her job in Florence would entail now, and she was confident that she possessed the necessary resources to do it well.

And she was thankful that Natalia would be there to help.

Chapter 29

I got back to Torricelli's house in record time. I stood at the top of the walkway to catch my breath before making my way to the door. I looked up at the quarter moon hanging in the cloudless sky, thankful that it had given just enough light for my evening sojourn to and from the Palazzo Medici. As I turned down the path to the house, I saw Dianora at the landing. She was trying to look composed, standing there under the awning with a smile on her face. But I could tell by her deep breaths that she had been running, too.

"Well, that was a quick *walk*," she said in a half whisper as I climbed the steps to the entrance.

"I felt like I needed to pick up the pace a bit tonight, to get the blood flowing," I replied in French. "And you look like you just finished a *maraton*."

"A *maraton*?" Dianora replied. "What do you mean by that?"

Oh, no. There was no way they were running marathons in 1647! I tried to think fast.

"Did I say *maraton*? Ha, ha…what does that mean, anyway? I meant to say *marron*. You look like you just finished a *marron*."

"I look like I just finished a *chestnut*?"

"*Oui*! A chestnut!" I whisper-exclaimed. "You have the satisfied look of someone who just ate a chestnut! It's an old La-Nouvelle France expression. Have you not heard that one before?"

"*Non*, I have not," Dianora replied suspiciously.

"Well, you now have a new saying to add to your repertoire! Ha, ha!"

"I shall spare future generations the torture of this idiom by striking it from my memory," Dianora smirked. She opened the front door and we kicked off our shoes in the candle-lit vestibule.

"Well, if I was going to run in a race I would want to wear your shoes," I said to Dianora, looking down at her flats. "They look very comfortable." They actually looked a little too comfortable. A very

21st-century comfortable, just like my own footwear! But that wasn't possible, of course.

"Ah, well that is the latest style from the fashion houses this fall," Dianora replied. "I think they call it, ah…*eleganza sensiblile*!" She looked satisfied with her answer.

"And which designer made your shoes?" I asked. I was genuinely curious, because I didn't think they had fashion houses in the 17th century.

"Oh, these are from the, ah, Guccarmani collection. They are very forward-thinking in their designs, are they not?"

"Very *post-moderne, oui*," I agreed.

I sat down on the living room sofa while Dianora went to check on Evangelista. She came back in two minutes and sat down on the chair facing me.

"He is still sleeping soundly," Dianora said. "I cooled his forehead with the cloth. I am afraid the fever has not broken."

I nodded my head. I wondered if it ever would.

"You can go back to sleep, Natalia. I will stay up and attend to Evangelista until the morning."

"I won't sleep again tonight," I said. "I can look after Evangelista if you would like to get some rest."

"*Non, merci.* I am up now, too." Dianora looked at the cards on the table. "*Briscola*, anyone?"

"I could play a hand or five," I replied. I got up to light another candle.

"I will shuffle the deck!" said Dianora.

"You always do," I answered. "You are a creature of habit, Dianora. Did you know that?"

"So I have heard," she replied with a smile.

"*Sì*, a little more, *per favore*," said Torricelli, weakly. He took another sip of broth from the spoon I was holding. Dianora wiped his mouth with a napkin.

"That is almost the whole bowl, Evangelista!" I praised. "You have done very well!"

"*Grazie*, Natalia. *Grazie*, Dianora. I feel a little better this morning."

"You look better, too!" Dianora said, encouragingly. "Why, you will be up and experimenting again in no time!"

"That would be nice," Evangelista replied with a weak smile, "but it is all in His hands, of course."

"Of course," Dianora and I said together, somberly.

"Now, if you will excuse me, young ladies, I will take a morning nap. I must gain energy for the day ahead."

Dianora and I stood up. She fluffed Torricelli's pillow and I tucked in his blankets. Then we left the bedroom, closing the door quietly behind us.

"I think he looks much better this morning, don't you?" Dianora said in a hushed tone, looking as confused as she was relieved.

"I do!" I replied, with the same look.

We went to the kitchen and sat down at the table. I poured us some *caffè*.

"I really hope he has a good day, today," Dianora said after a sip. "What is the date, Natalia?"

"Thursday, October 24," I replied.

"And that makes tomorrow the 25th, then."

"That is usually how it happens." I took a sip and continued. "If you like, I will go out this morning to the market."

"*Oui, merci*, that is a fine idea. If Evangelista has as many visitors today as he did yesterday, we will need quite a bit of food. I will give you the money."

"Oh, no, that is perfectly fine. I will…" I stopped in mid-sentence, looked to the ceiling, and shook my head.

"You have no money, remember?" Dianora chuckled.

"A minor detail," I suggested. "But before the market, I will first make a stop at the *Ospedale degli Innocenti*."

"To see the young orphan boy, Luca?"

"To see the young boy Luca, *oui*," I said, taking another sip of *caffè* and not using the word orphan.

Because that was yet to be determined.

I walked into the courtyard of the *Ospedale degli Innocenti* and went straight into the dormitory. The little children were once again busy in small group activities, playing and sorting and painting. I walked over and stood a short distance behind a group of older children who were sitting on the floor facing their instructor. The teacher was quizzing them with a map of Europe that was propped up on an easel. She would point to a country, all the children would respond with the name. Then she would point to one of her pupils and they had to provide the name of the specific province being pointed at, and the name of the capital city! I did all right with the countries – they had hardly changed over all these centuries – but the provinces and capitals had me stumped. Who knew that the capital of the Duchy of Savoy in Italy was Turin? I didn't, but Luca sure did. He got an *ottimo lavoro!* from his teacher. I could tell he was beaming from ear to ear even with his back turned to me.

Maria the Nanny spotted me from across the room and came rushing over. I turned and walked toward her, wondering how things would be between now that the trial was over. I was hoping she could let bygones be bygones.

Maria came to a stop two feet in front of me. She grabbed my hand. Then she bent over and kissed it repeatedly.

So, I guess we were good, then.

"Oh, Signorina Natalia! I am so *incantata* to see you again!" She kept hold of my hand.

"As am I to see you, Maria."

"Please forgive me for all that you were put through!"

"That is all *dimenticato*, Maria!" I said. "It is all in the past!"

"Oh, you are *troppo gentile,* signorina, *troppo gentile*!" She kissed my hand one last time and returned it to me. "You have come to see Luca, no doubt! I shall fetch him for you."

Maria went over to the geography class and tapped Luca on the shoulder. She whispered to him and then pointed over to me. I smiled and waved.

Luca didn't wave back. He got up from the floor, dashed over to me like his pants were on fire, and threw his arms around my waist.

"Natalia! Natalia! Natalia!"

"*Sì, sì.* That is my name, Luca! How are you?"

"I am *meraviglioso!*" he announced. "Look, look. I am cured!" Luca pulled up his shirt to reveal his scar. The 'redicut' incision looked to be healing up very nicely.

"Do you still have my picture of you, Natalia?"

"*Sì*, Luca. It is sitting on my night table right now."

"I have drawn many more since I last saw you!"

"*Luca fa presto* has been a very busy artist, signorina," said Maria as she approached. She mussed his hair and said, "Would you like to see his latest drawings?"

"I would like to very much. But I wonder if I may first have a private word with Luca, if that would be suitable."

"Of course!" Maria exclaimed. "Would you care to use the chapel for your *conversazione*?"

"That would be fine. Would that be fine with you, Luca?"

"*Sì*, Natalia!"

Luca took me by the hand and lead me down the hall. We walked under the roundel of the main entrance into the softly lit interior of the *Cappella degli Innocenti*. I left the door open and we sat down together in the back pew.

"The *Ospedale degli Innocenti* is a lovely place, Luca."

"I like it here at the orphanage. I have many friends."

"How long have you lived here at the orphanage?"

"Not too long," he replied.

"And how did you come to live here?"

"I was wandering in the streets of Florence when a *bargellino* found me and brought me to this place."

"I see. May I ask what happened to your parents?"

"My parents, they are not here." Luca looked up at the ceiling of the chapel.

"And the rest of your family?"

"The same. They are not here." He looked up to heaven again.

"Are you sure that they are *there*," I said, pointing up. "And not, over *there*?" I pointed to the south wall.

"*Che cosa?*" said Luca, with a look that displayed more nervousness than perplexity.

"Perhaps your mother and father are still in Napoli and not in *paradiso* yet?"

"Napoli? I...I am an orphan," Luca mildly protested. "I no longer have parents."

"What did you tell the *bargellino* and Signor Bartolomeo at the orphanage when they asked you for your last name."

"I told them I was a *scugnizzo* and did not have one."

I was pretty sure he was calling himself a 'street urchin'. I was also pretty sure he was a big-time fibber.

"So, your surname is not Giordano, then?" I asked.

Luca's face went ashen. He stared at me, glassy-eyed.

"Luca Giordano of Napoli," I said to him. "Your father is Antonio Giordano, the painter. And your mother is?..."

"Claudia," he answered with his head down. "Claudia Fulco." Then he looked up at me. "How did you know?"

There was no way I could tell him that, of course. I settled for, "Perhaps while you were *inconscio* during the time of your surgery, you may have said something." I gave him a shrug.

"In my mind, I must have wanted to tell someone, Natalia. I have for a long time, but I lacked the courage."

Luca began to unload his burden right there and then. He told me how he had become upset with his parents over his strict upbringing, how he never got his way in anything at any time. One day he became so frustrated he hid himself on a caravan that was leaving Naples. When hunger got the best of him, and before the travelling entourage discovered the stowaway, he jumped out of the wagon right in the middle of downtown Florence. Luca made fast friends with some street-savvy youths and learned to fend for himself by begging and 'borrowing'. This newfound way of life lasted until autumn, when the streets and the weather both became less friendly.

The police found him, dirty and cold, in the apse of the *Santa Maria del Fiore* and took him directly to the orphanage. He maintained to all interrogators that his parents had recently died, and that he had no other family to be returned to. Signor Bartolomeo - after investigating Luca's story throughout Tuscany and finding no relatives of the boy - welcomed him to the *Ospedale degli Innocenti* with open arms.

"But your parents, Luca. They must be very sad over their missing boy."

"God was sad too," he said, wiping away a tear. "And angry with me. I thought that I was being punished when I had the stomach sickness, and that I would die because of my lie."

"God is not angry with you, Luca. He loves you."

"*Sì*, I know this! Because He answered my prayer and brought you to help me! And now I am better!"

I took Luca by the hand and looked into his eyes. "And it is time to make everything right, Luca. You need to go home now."

"*Sì*, Natalia. I need to go home. Right away. Will you help me speak with Signor Bartolomeo?"

"I will help you right now," I said, with an arm on the boy's shoulder. "Let us go and talk with Signor Bartolomeo di Anto...della...di..."

"Ha, ha! I do not know how to say his name, either!"

Luca and I both laughed as we stood up and left the chapel. He put his hand back into mine.

"Will you come and see my drawings, too? You can pick out one to keep! So you can remember me!"

"That would be nice," I said. "I am sorry that I have nothing to give you in return."

"Signorina Natalia!" Luca exclaimed. "You gave me this!" Luca pulled up his shirt again to reveal his scar. Then he stopped and looked up at me with a big grin.

"I will always have this to remind me of you, Natalia."

Francesco Redi came out of the bedroom and closed the door gently behind him. I poured a cup of tea and handed it to him. He sat down on the sofa across from me, letting out a sigh after taking a sip.

"Did you have a nice visit?" I asked.

"We did, Dianora. We picked up where we had left off in our writing of some comedic verse together and amused ourselves to no end. Evangelista is quite alert and attentive today. He is resting now."

"What do you think, Francesco?"

"It is as you say. He is doing much better than yesterday. Much better." Francesco took another sip of tea. "But I must disagree with Dr. Buonaiuti's assessment from earlier this morning. I do not think he is on the other side of this illness."

"He still has a fever," I noted.

"*Sì*, and until it breaks, I would caution becoming too hopeful, as I have seen this before with this particular sickness, Dianora," said Francesco, placing his cup and saucer on the table. "One day, the patient is delirious and at death's door. The next day, the patient is rational and looks to have defeated the illness."

"And then?"

Francesco leaned forward on the sofa, hands clasped and resting his elbows on his lap. "And then, with spirit and energy drained, the patient succumbs and departs the very next day."

I tried to hold back my tears, but it was no use. I picked up the handkerchief on the table and dabbed at my eyes. Even though I knew what would happen tomorrow, on October 25, I still had difficulty resigning myself to Evangelista's passing. It was all becoming too real.

"It may not happen, Dianora," Francesco said softly. "He may get better. But plans should be in place, just in case."

I collected myself, folding my hands on my lap. "Evangelista has asked his brothers to come by this afternoon. Then he wants to see Lodovico Serenai and Vincenzo Viviani afterwards, to go over his will. Lodovico is the executor."

"Evangelista senses that his time is short," said Francesco. "He is tying up the loose ends."

I nodded and warmed Francesco's tea.

"Lodovico is a capable man, but at times he confuses expediency with haste," said Francesco. "Watch him carefully, Dianora. It would be most unfortunate if he were to mismanage the legacy of Evangelista Torricelli."

Just then, Natalia came through the front door with two sacks of groceries in her hands. She placed them on the floor and entered the sitting room. Ciccio Redi stood up to greet her.

"Dear Natalia! How wonderful to see you!" He stepped forward, took her hand, and gave it a kiss. Natalia gave Francesco a 'nice-to-see-you-too' pat on the shoulder and sat down next to him on the sofa.

"How is Signor Torricelli?" she asked.

"Resting now," I replied. "He had a nice morning with Ciccio." I poured Natalia a cup of tea, which she gratefully accepted.

"Dianora told me you went to the orphanage, my darling," said Francesco. "How is the boy doing?"

"Luca Giordano is perfectly well and will be on his way to Napoli tomorrow morning."

"Napoli?" Francesco and I said together.

"Sì. To be reunited with his father and mother!"

"*Suo padre?*" "*Sa mère?*" Francesco and I both asked with surprise.

Natalia then told us the story of her morning at the orphanage. She explained how she and Luca had a frank talk in the chapel, where he confessed to her that he had run away from home. Natalia convinced him it was time to go home, and they went to see Signor Bartolomeo, the chief administrator. Bartolomeo graciously offered to arrange the boy's trip to Naples the very next day.

"My father will be delighted when I tell him this story, Natalia!" Francesco exclaimed, but not too loudly so as to wake Evangelista. "You have changed this boy's life, not once but twice!"

"It was all in aid of setting him back on his proper path," Natalia said, matter of factly. "It just had to be done, you know?" She said that last part like she really *did* know about Luca's proper path.

"Speaking of a proper path, I have had my own revelation," said Francesco, slapping his hands on his knees with excitement. "My morning with Torricelli has convinced me that my true calling is not medicine! I will be changing my career to pursue my passion for the written word! I shall become a poet!"

"*Que dis-tu?*" "*Che cosa?*" Natalia and I both asked with shock.

"I knew you would approve!" Francesco enthused, misreading the room.

"You...you cannot abandon your medical practice, Francesco!" Natalia protested.

"You cannot leave your research behind!" I insisted.

"Oh, they can always become my hobbies," Francesco maintained. "My dream is now to give performances of my verse to appreciative crowds! I could write *libretti* for the opera! I can hear the stage calling me right now!"

"That is not the stage calling, Francesco, that is the *spazzino* outside calling for today's garbage!" Natalia declared, shaking her fingers-collected hand in the air. She was becoming a real Italian, all right. "Think of all your future patients that will need care and attention!"

"Think of all the experiments yet to be done in the name of science!" I added.

"Think of the *future*!" we both said together.

"Ladies, ladies! *Basta*!" Francesco rose up from the sofa. "I told you this because I was counting on your support! I can see that my hope in attaining your encouragement was misplaced!"

"Francesco, *per favore*, think about it first, before you make a rash decision!" Natalia implored.

"I have *made* my decision, Natalia! It breaks my heart that you choose not to encourage me in it!"

And with that, Francesco left the house in a huff. But at least he closed the front door quietly.

Evangelista did his best with the soup and bread at lunchtime. He wasn't particularly hungry, but he said that he needed to gain sufficient energy to entertain his important visitors that afternoon. Natalia and I sat with him, ate with him, and had a fine conversation with him about the marvels of creation and all the wonderments that were left to uncover in the universe. Natalia told us how she was looking forward to the day when you could take a tablet of medicine to cure a disease! That made me bold enough to predict that perhaps one day we would be able to measure pressure and temperature and even one's heart beats all on the same device! Evangelista appreciated our speculating, saying that all of these things are possible simply because we can imagine them! Natalia and I enthusiastically agreed with that! Interestingly, she seemed as confident as I was about the discoveries yet to be made in the future.

The conversation turned from marvels and wonders to problems and puzzles. After both of us were repeatedly stumped by Evangelista's offerings, Natalia picked up a green-tinted bottle of medicine from the nightstand and asked us where the mark should be placed to indicate half the volume. I had no clue, but Evangelista took the bottle, looked at it, poured out some liquid twice into a glass, capped the lip of the bottle in his hand, and turned the bottle upside down. The liquid level returned to the same spot both times. He passed the bottle back to Natalia, who looked stunned.

"It is simple, really," said Evangelista. "If the fluid level returns to the same mark in both the upright and inverted positions, you have half the volume of the bottle!"

"Correct!" Natalia exclaimed, impressed.

"Oh! I have one!" I announced, and I went on to describe the pipeline-around-the-world scenario I learned from Jay, only I turned the oil pipe into a water pipe, and the unit of length from metres to cubits. Evangelista thought for a moment - no more than 21 seconds - and then made a raised-finger proclamation.

"You could easily crawl under the gap made between the water pipe and the earth, since the space created is one and three-fifths cubits tall!"

I did the math in my head: one and three fifths is one point six. And 1.6 was close enough to 1.59 for me to declare...

"That is amazing, Evangelista! How did you do that?"

"With what little of this remains functional," he said with a smile, pointing to his head.

Then Evangelista told us a funny story about the time that Galileo - being blind for the last three years of his life - almost fell out of the third story window of his house. Torricelli caught him at the last moment, the only victim of the stumble being Galileo's teacup.

"I said to him, 'Ah, Galileo! Your cup has succumbed to your theory on falling bodies!' He turned to me with a smile and replied, 'I know that had the teacup and I both fallen out of the window together, we would have hurtled to the ground at the same rate, Evangelista...but I am so glad not to have tested that particular hypothesis today!"

We all had a good laugh over that one, just as a knock came from the front door.

"That will be my brothers," Torricelli said after a brief coughing spell. "Would you welcome them and then direct them to my room, please."

Natalia and I got up and fulfilled the request. The three men spent the better part of two hours together, talking behind the closed door of Torricelli's bedroom. When the visit was over the two brothers left the house arm in arm, dabbing tears from their eyes.

It was the same result after Serenai and Viviani had their visit an hour later.

"Oh, Lodovico, poor Evangelista!" Vincenzo Viviani exclaimed in a hushed tone in the sitting room after their visit. "He seems to be in better health today, yet his farewell to us was so very final!"

"*Sì*, Vincenzo, *sì*! It is like he knows his time is short!"

Natalia rose from her seat next to me on the sofa. "I am going to attend to Signor Torricelli," she said, leaving for the kitchen.

"Why else would he instruct us as to the distribution of his books and notes?" asked Vincenzo. "He wishes to set everything in order."

"Dianora, can you show us what we will be up against when it comes to Torricelli's library?" Serenai asked me.

"Come with me and I will show you," I replied. I took the two men down the hallway, and we spent no more than ten minutes examining the collection in Torricelli's study before returning to the sitting room.

"This will be a very big job, Vincenzo," Serenai sighed, plopping into the armchair. "There is a wagonload of classic literature in that room!"

"Not to mention the *copioso* number of folios of his very own scientific observations!" added Viviani. "It will take years to sort through it all."

"Well, not really," I said. "You see, we have been…"

"*Sì*, I agree…years to sort through it all," Serenai replied, ignoring my interjection. "Can you imagine the work it will take to compile his notes into book form?"

"Well, actually, the *lezioni accademiche* is essentially *preparato* for…"

"It will be a momentous task," Vincenzo answered his friend. "Perhaps more than one man could perform."

"*I* have almost completed the…"

"Dianora?" Serenai asked. "Could you run along and get us some more *biscotti, per favore*?"

I got up from the sofa, my clenched teeth covered by my pursed lips. I didn't exactly storm out of the room, but there were grey clouds forming above my head. When I got to the kitchen, Natalia was in the process of leaving for Evangelista's bedroom with a tray of food and some fever-damping cloths.

"Is everything all right?" she asked. "You look angry enough to chew through a leather patch!"

"That is still attached to the *toro*!" I exclaimed. Natalia shushed me to a lower volume. "Those men are planning to box up Evangelista's work and stow it who-knows-where, Natalia! It is not right!"

Natalia put the tray down on the kitchen table and placed her hands on my shoulders. "Dianora, it may be very hard for you to understand now, but this may all be for the best. You must allow Viviani and Serenai to perform this task in the way they are meant to do it."

It was the way Natalia said *meant to do it* that snapped me back to my 20th-century senses. It was like she knew that the stowing away of Torricelli's notes was destined to happen.

"All right, Natalia," I said. "I will try to let things proceed without too much interference."

"That is just as important for *me* to remember," said Natalia, as she left for the bedroom with the tray.

I returned to the sitting room with a plate of *biscotti* and a better attitude.

"So, it is settled, Vincenzo. If dear Evangelista succumbs to his illness, we shall divide his classic literature collection amongst his friends and package up his writings for another day." Serenai took a cookie from the plate. "*Grazie*, Dianora."

I sat down and nodded my head with a strained smile.

"It is a fine *strategia*, Lodovico, said Viviani. "*Saluti!*" The two men toasted their plan with teacups raised.

"Dianora? *Un momento, per favore?*" It was Natalia, peeking around the bedroom door for my attention. I rose from my chair and went to her.

"Before he rests his eyes, Evangelista says he would like to see you. Alone."

Natalia opened the door wider to let me pass. Then she left, closing the door quietly behind her. I sat down on the chair next to the bed.

"You have had a very busy day," I said. "You must be tired."

"I am depleted, Dianora," said Evangelista weakly. "I have given my brothers and my friends their instructions, and said my goodbyes. There is not much left to do now."

"Now, now," I said, taking him by the hand. Then, as convincingly as I could, I said, "You may recover from this, yet, Signor Torricelli."

"Oh, Dianora, you know as well as I that the end is near." Evangelista tried to sit up a little straighter. I propped up his pillows for him. "I have one more thing to do. Please open the wardrobe, will you?"

I stood up, walked to over to the clothes cupboard, and opened both of the doors.

"The metal strongbox behind the shoes. Could you bring that to me, *per favore*."

I bent down to retrieve the box. It was heavy enough that I needed two hands to lift it. I brought the box to Evangelista, placing it on the bed next to him.

"Open it," he said.

I undid the latch and lifted the lid. The strongbox was filled with gold coins.

"That is for you, Dianora."

"Evangelista! I cannot…"

"You will, my dear."

"But there is so much…too much…"

"It is hardly enough to leave to my trusted assistant," he said, taking my trembling hand into his own. "To my dear, dear friend."

"I do not know what to say, Evangelista."

"Just say that you will think of me from *time to time*," he said with a smile. "There is one more thing. The folder on top of the bureau, *per favore*." I retrieved the thin folder of papers and placed it next to the box. I had seen this folder before.

"These are the notes for the mathematics we were looking at previously, remember?" I certainly did. It was the folder that contained mankind's first-ever foray into calculus. "I have added a few more pages since then. And taken a few out, too. I would like you to keep this."

I was stunned. "But why? Should this not be combined with your other notes?"

He patted the folder of papers. "It could be, but something tells me that this would be better off in *your* care, Dianora."

I opened the folder and looked at the first page. The writing was in Latin. The terms dx, dy and f, were scattered about the page; a string of five dx's were encompassed by five symbols that each looked like a square-root sign. But that symbol wasn't a square-root sign. It was the symbol to describe a certain calculus operation. It was the symbol, $\int$. The symbol that was supposedly invented by Leibniz.

Almost 40 years from now.

When I left the bedroom, I asked Viviani and Serenai if they had seen Natalia. They told me she had gone out to get some fresh air. I asked if they would stay for a few more minutes and mind Evangelista while I joined her. *Nessun problema*, Vincenzo answered. I darted out the front door with the folder in my hand. When I reached the street, I saw Natalia dashing off in the distance to my right.

I dashed left.

Chapter 30

I was out of breath when I reached the alcove at the rear of the *Cattedrale di Santa Maria del Fiore*. I felt out of shape. That run should never have taken fifteen minutes! My lungs were on fire! Note to self, Michelle: start a proper exercise program in Italy as soon as possible. But first things first - right now I had some mathematical fact-checking to do.

I laid the folder down on the cobblestone of the alcove one metre from the wall that was to the left of the doorway, right in front of The Gateway that was glowing fuzzily behind me. Two elderly ladies dressed head-to-toe in black passed by on the road as I was arranging papers from the folder onto the walkway. The *signora* nearest to me smiled and waved. I waved back from my kneeling position, returning an awkward grin. I glanced back at The Gateway. As expected, it had disappeared from view.

After I spread the papers out in order, I stood up and quickly walked down the path to the roadway. The ladies were far up the street now, and no one else was within two hundred metres. I went back to the alcove and opened the back door of the church. No one coming down the hall, and no one coming down the stairway on the right. Perfect.

I stood in front of the rematerialized Gateway, the papers behind me on the ground. I took a deep breath and stepped into the Shimmering Light.

In the vinyl records room at the CJSW radio station, Michelle quickly changed from the white blouse, shawl, and full-length dress of her late 1640s outfit back into the oversized sweater, leggings, and leg warmers of her late 1980s outfit. She mussed up her hair to give it that Julia-Roberts-Mystic-Pizza look, checked herself in the mirror, and exited the room. As she passed through the studio, the DJ chair was still spinning from an apparent quick exit. Michelle decided not to wait around for Ken; she'd see him upon her return in the next hour or so. As she closed the door behind her, Michelle couldn't help but notice the piles of CDs on the console. What were *they* doing there? Being prepared for the bonfire, she assumed.

It took little time for Michelle to get from Mac Hall to the library building with the additional adrenalin coursing through her body. She moved with purpose to the fifth floor and through the stacks that stored the oldest science and math volumes, coming to a dead stop at the moldiest section of books on the shelf. After a brief scan of the titles, she found the text she was looking for. Dropping into the lotus position, Michelle opened the book titled *The History of Mathematics* and leafed through the pages until she came to the article, *Nova Methodus Pro Maximis et Minimis*, Gottfried Leibniz' seminal work in calculus. There they were on the first page: dx and dy, the unique calculus terms that he coined in 1684 to describe his mathematical operations. The same terms that Evangelista Torricelli used in his personal notes. In 1647.

But Michelle was more interested in another page in the book. Now where was it? She flipped around until she found what she was looking for in Appendix II: the samples of Leibniz' hand-written notes. Michelle looked intently at the page containing all the crazy symbols and diagrams. Her heart began to race. She leapt to her feet and bolted from the fifth-floor stacks. In her excitement, she almost exited the library without stopping at the desk to check out her book. The queue was long, but a kindly clerk took notice of the young lady bouncing up and down at the back of the line and motioned for her to approach, taking pity on the student who looked in desperate need of a bathroom. Michelle checked out the book, thanked the clerk, and sped off for Mac Hall.

The DJ chair had stopped spinning, but still no Ken behind the console when she arrived back at the studio. A CD was playing in the machine, its case lying open on the desk. *The Raw and the Cooked*, by the Fine Young Cannonballs? Huh, thought Michelle. And all this time, she thought they were Cannibals! Go figure.

After closing the vinyl-room door behind her, Michelle changed back into her Florence togs. She opened the book to Appendix II, placed it on the floor, and knelt beside it. She stared at the first three lines of the 'crazy symbols and diagrams' page, written in Latin, taking note of the crossed out first two lines and the mathematical equation $y = \int y dx\, dx$ on the third. Then she pivoted in her kneeling position and crawled through the Shimmering Light.

I scanned the papers that I had left on the cobblestone path only a second before and picked up the last page to my right. The first two lines were crossed out. The third line contained the mathematical equation $y = \int y dx\, dx$. I started breathing hard.
I turned around and crawled back through The Gateway.

Michelle examined the seventh line of the same page in the book, counting five of the $\int$ symbols that were lined up in a row in the next mathematical equation, $y(s) = \int \int \int \int \int dx\, dx\, dx\, dx\, dx$. There was a strange-looking diagram off to the right that appeared to be an inverted line graph with the axis in the top left corner. It was crossed out.
Michelle spun back around and went through the hole in the wall.

Line seven. Five of the $\int$ symbols lined up in a row. The equation $y(s) = \int \int \int \int \int dx\, dx\, dx\, dx\, dx$ staring me in the face. The crossed-out line graph with the axis on the top left, right there off to the right.
Shouldn't I just bring the book to Florence and compare these two pages side-by-side, instead of the all this dashing back and forth? No, girl, come on! If I got caught here in Italy with a book from the future, there's no telling what hereafter events could be altered by my carelessness. Nope, this was the best way…

Michelle crawled out of the hole in the vinyl-room wall, looked at the book, and noted the cross-outs from lines 14 to 17 and a t-shaped diagram on the left side of the page that was labelled with the letters H, E, E, B. There was no doubt about what she would see when she went back to the cobblestones at the *Duomo*…

…three cross-outs from lines 14 to 17, and a t-shaped diagram that gave me the HEEBie jeebies. Suspicions confirmed. This page lying in front of me from Torricelli's notes wasn't *similar* to the Leibniz note in Appendix II of the book…

"It's the exact same page!" Michelle exclaimed out loud to herself as she stared at the book on the vinyl-room floor. Down to every jot and tittle, as her mother would say.

Michelle closed the book and placed it on her lap as she sat on the floor, thinking. Evangelista Torricelli had entrusted her with a folder of notes - a folder that contained the beginnings of what would *become* calculus. If she turned the folder over to Lodovico Serenai for safe keeping after Torricelli's passing, it would end up with all of Torricelli's other notes and essays - unopened, unread, and unpublished. But Gottfried Leibniz would have to be in possession of the entrusted folder before 1684, so he could use them to *invent* calculus! Michelle arrived at the inescapable conclusion with the conflicting feelings of added pressure and blessed relief. She was now convinced of her time-travelling purpose in Italy. It had never been clearer.

Michelle stood up, and leaving the book on the floor she dusted herself off and stepped into the Shimmering Light.

Natalie arrived at her usual study table at the JF Allen Library and shook off the water-proof rain jacket she borrowed from Marianna before sitting down. It was coming down hard in St Andrews on Wednesday morning, but Natalie decided to brave the elements and find a quiet space on campus to get some work done before her first class of the day. A toasted English muffin with Scottish Marmalade and a cup of Irish tea had started her off well this morning. The slices of Welsh *bara brith* she produced from her jacket pocket would complete Natalie's UK breakfast in fine fashion.

As she read over her Immunology notes, the section on penicillin reminded her of the conversation she and her friends had had with Dr. Silver on making your own antibiotics. Natalie amused herself by doing a quick online search of the term 'making penicillin' and the typical slew of unstudied, quack therapeutics studded the search results. Sticking to the articles from medical sites, Natalie found that Dr. Silver had her history down pat: the ancient Egyptians did use moldy-bread and moldy-fruit poultices to treat infection, and even added honey to the bandage to stave off further infection. Huh, thought Natalie – those ancient Egyptian doctors certainly weren't aware that the hypertonic sugar solution of the honey would kill bacteria, but look at what a little trial-and-error experimenting could produce! In the *European Journal of Medicinal Chemistry*, Natalie read that the piperine-based sulfonamides found in black pepper also had promising antimicrobial properties. So, spice up your moldy bread with some pepper and honey at breakfast-time and, Bam!, you're in for a non-bacterial day! Natalie smirked at that thought as she took a bite of her *bara brith*.

After highlighting some text in the Respiratory System chapter of her anatomy textbook, with underlined emphasis on the words larynx and pharynx - which were not pronounced lar*nyx* and phar*nyx*...Yikes! - Natalie did another search. This time on the selected works of Evangelista Torricelli. She discovered that Torricelli wrote only one book in his lifetime, *Opera Geometrica*, the book on geometry that Dianora helped him organize. Three other books were released posthumously – *Trattato del moto*, *Lezioni accademiche* and *Esperienza dell'argento vivo* – the latter two remaining unpublished in

Torricelli's lifetime, and in his contemporary's lifetimes, too. Natalie grimaced at that. She and Evangelista had overheard the sitting-room discussion of Serenai and Viviani from the bedroom; they heard how the two men were planning to stow away Torricelli's notes for a future day. Apparently, the world wouldn't end up seeing those notes well into the future, Natalie thought. She recalled how Evangelista was somewhat distraught over their plans, and it was with some urgency that he asked her to call Dianora to the bedroom. Natalie wondered about that private conversation, and would be sure to ask Dianora about it ever so discreetly when she returned to Italy. She had ducked out of Florence pretty quickly that afternoon, feeling the need to return home and collect her thoughts.

After spending the next half hour doing some advanced reading for her Blood and Gastrointestinal class – the acronym GERD for gastroesophageal reflux disease striking her as rather onomatopoetic – Natalie did a search on Francesco Redi. She had to correct the name before pressing enter on the keyboard because she had written Ciccio instead of Francesco. The first hit to come up wasn't what she had expected; the link was not highlighted to indicate she had visited the site previously. Natalie checked the spelling of the name. No, all good there. She clicked on the new URL and within two seconds a different portrait of Redi than she was used to appeared on the screen. Instead of the man with the cascading brown ringlets of hair and inquisitive expression staring at her from the past, a man with jet-black curls and furrowed eyebrows was looking off to the left, avoiding eye contact.

Natalie scrolled down the page. There was poem about the Tuscan countryside, followed by a poem about Bacchus and his visit to a vineyard. She scrolled further. Another poem about Bacchus. Then another. Where was the information on his science career? I must be on a page dedicated to his poetry, Natalie thought.

She returned to the search page and clicked on another link. Francesco Redi…Tuscan poet…Bacchus…wine…more wine! Natalie kept searching, typing in the qualifiers 'toxicology', 'parasitology', and 'experimental biology' if front of the name Redi. Nothing came up. Nothing but poems. Poems about wine and Bacchus and lost love. Lost love? Natalie began to tremble.

"He was serious!" she said out loud to no one else.

Natalie couldn't believe it. Ciccio Redi had made good on his threat – he had left his medical practice and a life of science behind to pursue his passion for poetry! Natalie stared at the screen in disbelief. And then her eyes widened. And then she began typing furiously. And when her searches came up blank she typed and retyped and re-retyped, the computer keys going from being tapped to being clacked to being twacked. Nothing. The two words in her search never came up together. It was like the concept had never existed. There was no association of the term with Redi, or Tyndall, or Virchow. She couldn't find a picture of Pasteur's swan-neck flask anywhere. What had happened to the scientific discovery that life only arises from life?

What had happened to the disproving of *spontaneous generation*?

Natalie closed the lid of her laptop and pushed herself away from the study table, her face becoming ashen.

"What type of world have I come back to?" she said in a faint whisper.

In an instant, Natalie made the decision not to find out. She gathered her things and tore out of the library. She raced back to her dorm room at Agnes Blackadder Hall in two minutes, stuffed her Florence clothes into her bag, and took off for the Byre Theatre where The Portal awaited.

As she ran down the wet streets of St Andrews, Natalie arrived at an inescapable conclusion with a feeling of panic and dread. She was now convinced of her time-travelling purpose in Italy, down to every jot and tittle as her grandmother would say. It had never been clearer.

Natalie sprinted up the steps to the quiet room on the second floor and changed into her Florence outfit. She dusted herself off, took a deep breath, and stepped into the fuzzy light.

Chapter 31

I got back to Torricelli's house later than I was planning to. I had to wait an extra five minutes to escape from the portal room at the Palazzo Medici because of all the construction work that Andrea, Antonio, and Alfredo were performing in the courtyard. But when the Duomo bells sounded at 3 o'clock and Antonio let out a, "*Ci prendiamo un caffè!*", it only took a *secondo* for the boys to clear out on their coffee break. I followed suit and high-tailed it back down the Via dei Calzaiuoli.

Before I turned down Evangelista's walkway, I spied a lone figure tearing around the corner of the next block. When she saw me, Dianora braked and began to stroll down the street in an easygoing fashion. She whistled her way toward me with both hands behind her back in a far-too-obvious attempt to appear nonchalant. She looked every bit the *gatto* that swallowed the *uccello*.

"Where have you been?" I queried in French.

"I was about to ask you the same thing," she replied.

"You seem to be out of breath, Dianora."

"I decided to stretch my legs a bit, get the blood flowing." She did a few on-the-spot leg lifts to accentuate her point.

"I see. What are you holding behind your back?"

"*Quoi?*" she responded, disingenuously. "Oh, this? This is just some papers, you see." Dianora brought the folder into view, but kept it tight to her chest with both hands.

"I do see," I replied. "May I ask what they are?"

"Of course you may," she answered. Then she just stood there for 7 silent seconds.

"So, what are those papers you are holding, Dianora?" I asked with raised eyebrows.

"Oh, they are just…just…" Dianora was having a tough time coming up with something. The discomfort was growing on her face by the second. "Oh, Natalia! I need to confide in you. Can you keep a secret?"

"Most certainly, Dianora!" Can I keep a secret? You bet your sweet 21st-century bippy I can!

Dianora opened the folder and held out one of the papers for me to look at.

"These are some of Evangelista's notes on mathematics," she said. "I do not expect you to understand anything that is written there, Natalia. I am only showing this to you to underscore how very important I believe these papers are."

I scanned the document. There were a lot of crossed-out lines, a couple of diagrams, and something that looked like a line graph, only inverted. But when I saw $y = \int y dx\, dx$ and the accompanying equation $y(s) = \int\int\int\int\int dx\, dx\, dx\, dx\, dx$, I had to hide my surprise. This was calculus notation! The same symbols and script that I used in that math course back home! How was this even possible? Calculus hadn't been invented yet in 1647! And then I remembered the Anatomy Lab chat with Dr. Raven in Scotland last week, when we were talking about measuring blood pressure in millimetres of mercury. In torrs! What was it he said?... that Torricelli pretty much invented calculus, and even Leibniz gave him credit!

Oh, wow! I was holding the beginnings of calculus right here in my hands!

"This...this looks very, ah...significant, Dianora," I managed to say, supressing my astonishment.

"*Oui*, Natalia. I really think this is important," she replied. Important? Girl, if you only knew!

"Did Evangelista give this to you?" I asked.

"*Oui*, for safe keeping," she replied. "He does not wish this to be included with his other notes. The ones that will be entrusted to Lodovico Serenai."

I stared at the equations for another moment. No, these papers couldn't be left to languish with Torricelli's other notes - the ones that would be released posthumously, too many years from now. These papers needed to find their way into the hands of a calculus caretaker!

"I understand completely," I said to Dianora as I handed back the page. "Evangelista needs you to protect this information. I will help you do this any way I can."

"*Merci*, Natalia. It is so good to have a friend like you." Dianora took my hand and gave it a squeeze. "Especially now, during this time with Evangelista. I have never undergone this type of thing before…being at the bedside of one who is…who is…" Dianora was glassy-eyed as she searched for words.

"And I will be here for you through all of this," I told her, returning a hand squeeze. "And for Signor Torricelli."

"*Sì*. For Evangelista."

We kept holding hands as we walked up the pathway to the front door.

As we entered the front door and stepped into the vestibule, Viviani and Serenai rose from the sofa in the sitting room to greet us.

"Ah, there you are you two!" said Lodovico Serenai. "We were wondering when you would return! Vincenzo and I must leave right away for an engagement!"

And here I thought they were going to greet us. Silly me.

"Please excuse us for keeping you, *signori*," Natalia answered back politely. "Dianora and I had to attend to some future business."

She wasn't kidding about that. At least for me, that is.

"I see you have a folder of papers, there, Dianora," Vincenzo said, pointing at me. "Is this something to add to the material in the other room?"

"Ah, *no*," I said. "It is not anything you need to be bothered about."

"Oh?" inquired Lodovico. "What is it then?"

"It is…ah…well…" I was searching for an answer and coming up blank. Then Natalia came to my rescue.

"It is a collection of recipes!" she chimed in.

"Recipes?" said Vincenzo Viviani. "Like for cooking food?"

"Of course!" Natalia replied.

"*Sì,*" I affirmed. "Some of the very best cooking has food in it, you know?"

"*Sì, sì,*" Natalia added. "When cooking includes food, it becomes very eatable, would you not say?"

"Oh...*molto* eatable, *sì. Molto.*" I was grasping now.

"*Interessante,*" said Lodovico. "May I have a look?"

Out of instinct, I pressed the folder to my chest. My defensive posture drew disturbed looks from the two men. Natalia was quick on the draw once again.

"Certainly, you may have a look, Signor Serenai! Only be forewarned that the symbols used to *differenziare* the quantities can be difficult to *comprendere.*"

Differentiate? Nice one, Natalia. Using calculus terminology in this circumstance was flukily appropriate!

She kept going.

"And the descriptions on the *integrazione* of the ingredients are a bit challenging, to be sure..."

Integration? Okay, hang on...

"...but being such intelligent men, you would *derivare la funzione* of the terms immediately, of course!"

Derive the function? What the...?

"Lodovico, we have no time for this," Vincenzo Viviani interrupted, ushering his friend to the door. "We are late enough as it is! We will see you again tomorrow, *signorine!*"

The two men tipped their hats to us and were off. I turned to Natalia and gave her a suspicious look.

"*Che cosa?*" she responded. "I told you I would be here for you, Dianora." She gave me a cheeky wink.

"And you were, *grazie,*" I replied. "You employed a fine strategy in tiring them out, I must say."

"*Sì.* I thought they might give up if I pushed them to their *limiti!*"

Natalia chuckled and turned toward the sitting room. I had reached my limit too! I was just about to confront her over her use of all the calculus jargon when the front door banged open.

"Ciccio, *come stai?*" I said, as a dishevelled Francesco Redi brushed himself off in the vestibule.

"*Bene*, Dianora, *bene*," he answered. "And how is Evangelista this afternoon?"

"I am just going in to find out," said Natalia, who had turned from the sitting room to enter Evangelista's bedroom. She closed the door quietly behind her.

"Do you think Natalia is angry with me?" Ciccio asked in a whisper.

"Why would she be angry with you, Francesco?" I whispered back. "*You* are the one that left in a rage this morning."

"It was more of a huff than a rage, Dianora. But, *sì*, I was distraught that Natalia could not come to terms with my change of vocation."

"About that," I replied, taking Ciccio by the hand and sitting him down on the sofa in the next room. "The two of us are only worried that you are making a rash decision, Francesco."

"As was previously stated."

"Then allow me to say it this way: you are making a poor decision."

"How can you be so sure?"

I paused to collect my thoughts. I felt like this was my chance to help steer the future of experimental science back on course.

"Your reputation of being an insightful young man precedes you, Francesco. Everyone admires your attention to detail, your bursts of inspiration, your…"

"Cleverly crafted verse?"

"Well, *sì*…this goes without saying," I said, not wanting to say any more about that. "But it is the quality of perseverance that has distinguished you from amongst your peers, Ciccio."

"Who says this about me?"

"Well, Natalia has mentioned this."

"She has?"

"Most certainly!" I replied. Well, Natalia had mentioned a time or two that Ciccio was a rather *persistent* young man. "Natalia admires your *resoluteness*, Ciccio." Though she may have used the word stubbornness, come to think of it. "And oh, how she does esteem your passion and curiosity!" Or did she say Francesco was curiously passionate? No matter. I was reeling him in now.

"Natalia has said all this about me?" he asked, with fingers placed on chest.

"In almost those words," I replied. "Her praise for your personal character all stem from the abilities you have honed in science, Ciccio. From *science*."

Francesco Redi was quiet for a moment. He was about to say something in response when the bedroom door opened and Natalia stepped out half way.

"Francesco," she said quietly. "Evangelista would like to see you."

The two of us made our way into the bedroom. Natalia sat on the chair next to the window and I sat at the foot of the bed. Francesco sat in the chair next to the bed, having been beckoned there by Evangelista's weak gesture. It was the frailest I had ever seen him.

"Is it well with you, Ciccio?" he asked his friend.

"I am fine, Evangelista. May I take your pulse, *per favore*."

Torricelli held out his hand. Dr. Redi placed his right index finger on the patient's wrist. With his left hand he held Evangelista's right hand and didn't let go after finishing his inspection.

"Well? Could you find it?" asked Torricelli.

"It is present but very weak." Dr. Redi placed his right hand on the patient's forehead. "And you are still with a fever."

"I am dying, Francesco."

"Now, now," Dr. Redi chided, squeezing the patient's hand. "Do not say this, Evangelista. You may recover to full health. I have seen it before."

"I am sure you have, my friend," said Torricelli. Then he pointed at Natalia. "But Signorina Natalia tells me that you may not be making many more house calls."

Francesco looked over to Natalia, who shrugged sheepishly.

"I have been mulling over the idea of changing professions, *sì*," Francesco Redi admitted. "Writing verse has been a passion and life-long dream of mine. I feel the pull of the poetry muse, Evangelista."

"Ah, Calliope has a strong influence, does she not?" Evangelista paused to cough. "But perhaps you should turn your attention back to Urania, for she has guided you well thus far, Ciccio."

"Urania? The muse of the heavenly places?"

"*Sì*. She has been a faithful companion to people like you and me, Ciccio. We must not disappoint her."

"I have not looked to the stars like you and Galileo have, Evangelista. My gaze has been directed downward."

"Oh, but I disagree," said Torricelli, patting Ciccio's hand. "What you have learned about life on earth, the things you are investigating in your laboratory at home, the knowledge you have accumulated in your medical studies – all of this has furthered your understanding of the mind of God! Do you not agree?"

"I certainly do," Francesco nodded.

"God told our first parents to subdue the earth. He means for us to investigate the things in His creation and put them into our understanding. There are secrets of the universe yet to uncover, and we who have been blessed with the spade of science are compelled to dig, Ciccio!"

Francesco gave Evangelista a smile and a squeeze of the hand.

"I have enjoyed our time together these past few days, Francesco," Torricelli continued. "They have lifted my spirits immeasurably. Your writing talents are notable and impressive. Calliope will always smile upon you, for she always has your welfare in mind. But it is Urania that calls you with outstretched arms, Ciccio, for she has the welfare of the whole scientific world in mind."

We all sat in silence for a good while as Evangelista drifted off to sleep. The three of us stood up and made our exit. Francesco quietly closed the bedroom door behind us, and we took up our regular spots in the sitting room.

We all sat in silence for another good while before Francesco cleared his throat.

"Perhaps I have been too rash in my thinking," he said, with eyes affixed to the floor. "Perhaps I have been listening to the wrong muse. Perhaps I need to continue to…to…"

"Dig?" Natalia offered.

Francesco Redi looked at her with a smile, and said, "*Sì*, Natalia, *sì*. I have been entrusted with a spade. I must continue to dig."

"You look to have made a sound decision, Ciccio," I said to him. "And you have the appearance of a satisfied man."

"I do?"

"*Sì*. You look like you have just eaten a chestnut."

"A chestnut?" he asked with a confused look. "Who coined that ridiculous saying?"

I pointed over to Natalia. She looked back at me sternly with arms crossed.

Like she'd eaten a bad chestnut, or something.

"I am sorry…that I could not…eat anything tonight, Dianora."

"It is fine," I replied, patting his forehead with a cold compress. "Just fine."

It had been a difficult afternoon and evening for Evangelista. When he was awake, he was in discomfort and his sleep was fitful. After Dr. Redi stepped up the dosage of the prescribed tincture, it seemed to help a great deal; Evangelista's breathing became more regular and he could sleep a bit longer before the next cycle of pain started. No doubt the opium in the medical mixture was having a calming effect.

The hallway clock chimed. It had just turned twelve. Friday, October 25 had arrived.

"You are looking…tired, my dear," Evangelista said to me. "Why not get…some sleep."

"No, I am fine. Would you like some more *acqua*?" I dabbed a fresh compress on his cheeks. His fever was still very high.

"Any more water…and I shall be swimming…to Heaven's gates." He managed a small chuckle. "Are your friends…still here?"

"*Sì*. Natalia and Francesco are in the sitting room."

"Natalia is a *buon amica*, is she not?"

"She is. She has been a great help to me. To all of us."

"I think she has been like a sister to you, *no*?"

"We are becoming close," I said. "She is a kind and thoughtful person."

"And a very clever one…just like you, Dianora."

I smiled in response, patting his neck with the towel.

"Something tells me…the two of you…are related, somehow. You certainly…look like sisters."

"We do?" I said as I wrang out the towel in the basin. "I do not see it, myself. Anyway, it is quite impossible, Evangelista."

"Highly improbable…perhaps. But not…impossible, my dear. Nothing is impossible for the Hand that guides all things."

Of course the tincture was talking now, but I nodded my head in agreement as I folded the towel and placed it on the nightstand.

Evangelista reached out and took my hand in his.

"Dianora…I want to tell you…that you have been like a sister to me, as well. You have been more…than an *assistente*. You have been…a *compagna*. And such…a *buon amica* to me." He held my hand tightly.

"And you have been more than my *padrone*, Evangelista," I replied, unsuccessfully keeping my emotions in check. "You have been my *mentore* and my *buon amico*. I could not have had a finer *grande fratello*."

We smiled at each other with tears in our eyes, holding hands until he drifted off to sleep.

"You have been very quiet this past hour," I said to Francesco. We were seated across from each other in the sitting room, absently reading the books on our laps. "You have not turned a page in 20 *minuti*."

"I have been deep in thought, Natalia."

"About what, may I ask?"

Francesco closed his book and put his fingers to his chin. "I have been thinking about disease and infection. I have been considering all the theories we currently have regarding their spread, and how unsatisfying I find all of them."

"Unsatisfying? In what way?"

"Well, take the idea of disease being caused by an imbalance in the four humors. While I can appreciate certain aspects of the theory – especially the discrepancy in the black and yellow bile content of an infected creature – it hardly explains how a perfectly healthy person and a sickly individual can both contract the same disease, express identical symptoms, and become equally as ill."

"I understand," I said. Except for the black and yellow bile thing.

"The miasma theory also has its good points, but people that live in an area of noxious fumes do not become infected with disease any more often than people who breathe the fresh country air, in my experience."

"I see," I said. Except for that miasma thing.

"And the theory of astrological influence as the cause of disease I dismiss out of hand."

"As do I," I said. No exception there.

"So that leaves us with contagion theory as the most likely culprit for spreading disease."

"Person-to-person *trasmissione*, then?"

"*Sì*," Francesco replied. "But the question is, what is it that is being transmitted during close contact with an infected individual? Some believe it is a type of humor. Others believe it is an essence. I am not so certain it is either."

"What could it be, then?" I asked, earnestly.

"Well, what if infections were caused by the tiniest of living creatures? Creatures that evade our powers of visual discernment."

"That sounds intriguing, Francesco," I said, leaning forward. "*Per favore*, continue." I was getting excited by what I was hearing.

"In my studies of worms and insects - like the ones in my Room of Specimens – I have marvelled at how many varieties of creatures are *parassiti*, living exclusively off of their hosts. As they grow, they can become very harmful and even cause death. This makes me wonder: what if, when we are sick with a disease, we are spreading *invisibile parassiti* to one another?"

"This sounds amazing!" I said, not exaggerating in the least. "So, you believe that living creatures cause disease?"

"Sì. This would explain so much, Natalia!" Francesco leaned forward in his chair. "It is difficult to understand how identical symptoms arise *spontaneamente* in sick people if they are infected by a nonliving source, because the degree of illness should vary. But if people are infected by identical *living things*, then their matching symptoms would make perfect sense!"

"So, you are saying that in any given disease, the cause of it may be an infection from a living creature?"

"Precisely! And these creatures are all *generato* by reproducing after their kind, and not produced from nonliving material, either."

"No *spontaneamente generato*, then?"

"*No*. No *spontaneamente generato* of life from the nonliving." Francesco Redi leaned back in his chair with a mildly-satisfied look on his face. "What do you think of these ideas, Natalia?"

"I think your theories are wonderful, Ciccio."

"Ciccio! You called me Ciccio!" Francesco's look went from mildly satisfied to super happy. "I have found a way to please you at last!"

I woke up on the sofa just before the chime on the hallway clock struck two. Francesco was fast asleep in the chair, his head resting on his shoulder.

I got up and walked toward Signor Torricelli's bedroom. I could hear a faint sniffle from the other side of the door. I went in.

Dianora was sitting on the chair next to Evangelista. She was holding his hand. She turned her head toward me.

"It is over, Natalia," Dianora said. "Dear Evangelista is gone."

It had been a difficult morning for Rahoul. The sugarcane train had been late in arriving at its plantation stop – the train on which Rahoul and his daughter had secured transportation to the coast. Then, at the halfway point of the trip to Lautoka, the rail line had to be cleared of downed trees from the previous night's rainstorm. When they arrived at the port city – coined Sugar City by the locals – the streets were too muddy for the carriage to take them from the sugar mill to the harbour. So, Rahoul strapped his daughter's clothes trunk to his back and the two of them trudged through town, arriving at the ship with only an hour to spare.

Rahoul was used delays like this, having endured twenty-eight rainy seasons since landing in Fiji as an indentured servant in 1888. The monsoons in his native India had been just as bad, he remembered, but not as continuously dreary. And the cyclones that hit Fiji! How they tore through Viti Levu every year without fail! They made his life miserable in those first years of working at the plantation. He would always be thankful that his plantation master discovered he had abilities other than physical; that he had an aptitude for numbers and problem-solving. His work at the plantation eventually became clerical, he gained status amongst his peers and superiors, and soon he found himself in the employment of the constitutional monarchy, working for the High Commissioner for the Western Pacific, Governor of Fiji. It was satisfying work. He married, they had children; life in the capital city of Suva was good. When Rahoul was reassigned to the country to run the sugarcane plantation, he accepted the job with trepidation, believing it was a demotion of sorts. But he soon learned that nothing was further from the truth: the new position came with a fair amount of responsibility, a welcome increase in salary, and a great deal of prestige. As time progressed, Rahoul's only concern was for his children; all four had displayed academic promise in their schooling, but there was no university in Fiji to advance their studies. A difficult decision was soon made – when the children were of age, they would continue their education in India, at the University of Calcutta.

So it was a difficult morning for Rahoul, and not because of the late train or the fallen trees or the muddy streets. It was because the family repatriation to their homeland would start this very day with his daughter. Rahoul was saying goodbye to his Paramita today. His heart was much heavier than the trunk on his back.

"Well, baba, this is it," said Paramita to her father as they stood to the side of the ship's gangway. "I must be off!"

"Before you go, bitiya, I want you to have this." Rahoul produced a twice-folded piece of paper and handed it to his daughter. "This was given to me by Sir John Thurston, twenty years ago in 1895, when I left Suva to run the plantation. He found it on the deck of a ship! Its message encouraged him very much, and he thought it might do the same for me. It did. And now I would like you to have it."

Paramita unfolded the paper once and read the message, which looked to be written by a sure hand. She felt like it was written just for her.

"Oh, baba…this is of great encouragement! I shall treasure it forever!"

"Well, at least until you pass it along to the next person who…"

"…is moving ahead yet looking back toward home?"

"Yes, bitiya. Yes."

Rahoul embraced his daughter. He watched her ascend the gangway, and they waved goodbye to each other when she reached the top. Rahoul kept waving as the ship began its slow departure from the harbour. He moved to the very end of the dock and kept waving.

He was still waving when the ship was but a dot on the horizon.

Chapter 32

"You want me to look up what?" Connor asked.

Natalie stared with incredulousness at the computer screen and said, "Do you seriously not know about Pasteur's swan-neck flask experiment?"

"I'm not taking biology, remember. I'm a physics and chem guy!"

"You should have learned about Pasteur in general science in Grade 10!"

"I must have been away that day," Connor said through his laptop.

"You must have been asleep that day," Natalie replied.

"Can't exclude that possibility, Nat. That may have been taught to me in my pre-SLANT period."

"SLANT? What's that?"

"Something you *lean on* to stay awake in class," Connor answered with a grin. He began to type on his keyboard. "Swan-neck flask? Yep, there's a ton of hits. It's linked with the terms 'spontaneous generation' and 'Pasteur's experiment'. And there's a whole Wikipedia page on it, too."

Natalie breathed a big sigh of relief that was noticeable from across the Atlantic Ocean.

"Don't tell me, let me guess," said Connor. "You were too afraid to type it in yourself in case it didn't come up, and it confirmed that you'd changed the future."

"Uh huh. And now I'm feeling a lot better because Francesco Redi is going to remain a science guy."

"It says here under 'spontaneous generation' that Francesco Redi is the scientist that disproved the theory of life arising from nonliving material with his maggots-and-rotting meat experiment. Yich! You've got some interesting friends in Florence!" Connor then looked directly at Natalie. "I just want to say again that I'm sorry about your friend, Evangelista, sis."

"Thanks, Connor. He was a lovely man, and I'm glad I got to know him. The funeral is in two days, so I'll be going to that."

"I take it you checked to see that The Portal was still up before you left the theatre."

"I did, and yes, it's still open for business," Natalie replied. "So that means there's something left for me to do for someone in Italy, I suspect."

"That's what it usually means, all right," her brother answered back. "Though Mom would say there could also be something waiting there just for you, too."

"Speaking of Mom, have you heard from our parents?" Natalie asked.

"Nothing so far. But I'm expecting that'll change in the next day or so. Their blackout period is coming to an end."

"Good. My plan is to go back for the funeral tomorrow…"

"Tomorrow?" Connor interrupted. "I thought the funeral was in two days?"

"In two days, Florence time. I'll go back to Italy *tomorrow*, Scotland time. Haven't you TT'd before, brother dear?"

"Sorry, Nat. You'd think I'd know better."

"Right? Anyway, I'll go to the funeral, then repatriate to Scotland and have a chat with Mom, and then go back to Italy the next day if The Portal is still open."

"Do you think it could close after the funeral?" asked Connor.

"It's possible. I might be going back only to help my friend Dianora get through the next couple of days. She's taken on a lot of responsibility for Torricelli's affairs and it's weighing on her. She hasn't been herself lately, and I'm worried about her health."

"So, Dr. Campbell is still on-call in Florence, then?"

"Maybe," Natalie chuckled. "But at least the pressure's off, for now. Luca Giordano is going back home to do some painting, Francesco Redi is going back to his Room of Specimens to do some science-ing. I feel like things are winding down in 1647."

"Good. But just be careful, okay."

"I promise," said Natalie, crossing her heart. "But the pressure is picking up here at school. I've got a big assignment tomorrow morning that I've got to prepare for, before I leave for the continent."

"I won't keep you, then," said Connor. "Good luck with both of those, Nat. I'm sure everything will be great. Just like you've swallowed a chestnut!"

"Uh…what?" Natalie asked.

"A chestnut. You know, as in the old saying…"

"The *old saying*?" Natalie interjected. "Oh, man! I can't believe it!"

"Don't tell me, let me guess," said Connor. "That old chestnut about a chestnut is something my sister came up with a long, long time ago, isn't it?"

Natalie gave Connor one of her sheepish shrugs.

"You nailed it, Natalie. Simple as that."

"Mark's right for once, Natalie. You killed that Anatomy Lab!"

"She did-a not kill it, Holly! That-a cadaver was-a dead already."

Sitting at their regular table next to the 'church-pew' bench at Jannettas Gelateria the following afternoon, Natalie and her med school friends celebrated the completion of their Rotating-Station Anatomy Lab assignment with gelatos all around, Marianna's treat. Mark was wearing a polo shirt, not an aloha shirt, which was bugging Natalie more than she let on.

"Well, I *do* feel pretty good about how it went," said Natalie, unable to hide a smile.

"Pretty good doesn't cover it!" Mark exclaimed. "Natalie, when I rotated to that station and saw all those thoracic flag pins sticking in places I didn't recognize, I nearly had a coronary myself!"

"That was a brutal 5 minutes of Q and A," Holly agreed.

"*Brutto*, Holly," Natalie corrected. "It was a *male* chest cavity." She gave a sly wink to Marianna, who winked back in Italian.

"Everyone in the lab room let out a sigh when they hit that station, Natalie," Mark continued, after a bite of Pistachio and Coffee. "When

I looked back to see your expression after we rotated, and I saw you not bat an eye, I was really impressed. But when I glanced back after 2 minutes and saw that you were done, my jaw hit the floor."

"Literally, since he was at the mandible station at the time," Holly remarked before crunching into the cone of her Hazelnut and Chocolate. "You were clutch, girl…Bobby Nystrom clutch."

"More like-a Bobby Osmano clutch, like in *L'Ormindo*!" Marianna offered by way of a hockey-opera mashup.

"It was hard, I'm not going to lie," Natalie said after a lick of Sicilian Lemon and Vanilla. "But I took all of your advice about pressure situations: I prepared myself as best I could; I visualized the possible situation beforehand; and I made sure to breathe and relax. And it didn't hurt that I snuck into the lab and hour beforehand and wrote down all the questions!"

"You did-a what?!" Marianna exclaimed, licking the scoop of Vanilla and Tayberry from her cone right onto the table.

"I'm kidding, Marianna!" said Natalie with a laugh. Marianna glowered at her *amica* as she re-coned her gelato. "Anyway, we all have to Bobby Osmano-it tomorrow on that Immunology exam." Her friends all nodded in agreement.

Just then, a gust of wind blew into the shoppe. A lone figure sporting a leather bomber hat, aviator jacket, and orange guitar case made his entrance.

"Filip!" the cheers rang out from the Jannettas Gelateria patrons.

"Hello, all!" Filip replied with a smile and a wave. He made his way over to his table of friends, plonking himself down on the 'church pew' next to their table.

"Who texted you that we were here?" asked Holly, looking around.

"No one," Filip responded. "I just had a feeling, you know? A feeling that said, 'It's time for ice cream.'"

"When isn't it?" asked Mark.

"When it's time for deep-fried Mars Bars, mate!" Filip replied with a chuckle and backslap for his bro.

"Filip, how's it *gaun*!" said the manager of the shoppe, coming out from behind the counter. "Naw, don't get up! Can I get you your regular then?"

"Please, Callum! I see you have my stool set up today." Filip pointed over to the riser at the back wall.

"It's always set up for, *you*, lad! Now, one Spiced Apple and Caramel with Toasted Almonds, coming up!" Callum left for the gelato counter.

"That's not even on the menu," Holly smirked. "How do you do it, Filip?"

"Clean livin', Holly-dear. That, and my disarming charm."

"We were talking about disarming before you came in," said Mark. "We just finished an Anatomy Lab where we rotated through stations with cadavers."

"Sounds dead awful," said Filip, flashing a smile. "Aren't you glad I'm here to change the subject?" He changed the subject. "On the drive over, I was thinking about Dorothy Gale and…"

"The *figura* skater?" Marianna interjected.

"That's Dorothy Hamill," Holly chimed in. "He's talking about the famous writer and poet."

"No, that's Dorothy Parker," Mark corrected. "Filip's talking about the American singer and actress from the 1950s."

"Isn't that Dorothy Dandridge?" Natalie interrupted. "Filip's Dorothy was a civil rights activist back in the day, at the…"

"Height?" Filip interjected.

"Yes, at the height of the…"

"No, not Dorothy Height, either," said Filip, putting an end to the confusion. "Dorothy Gale is Dorothy from *The Wizard of Oz*!"

"That's her name?" said Holly, surprised. "Dorothy *Gale*?"

"Gale?" asked an equally surprised Mark. "As in, 'Say, it's windy outside!' As in, 'Hey, isn't that a tornado?'"

"Blew your minds, didn't I?" said Filip without apology. Callum returned with a double scoop of the secret house-specialty, which was accepted with thanks. "Anyway, I was thinking about Dorothy and her friends falling asleep in that field of poisonous poppies. Now, aside from the obvious analogy one could draw from this particular scene and the rising sentiment of anti-imperialism in the early 20th century..."

"Anti-imperialism?" Holly inquired.

"As seen in the soporific lion, of course."

"Ah, I see," said Mark without seeing, eager to move the conversation along.

"Aside from that, I was wondering what would have happened if Dorothy didn't wake up?"

"Well, the scarecrow could inject her with point 3 milligrams of adrenalin from an EpiPen," said Natalie.

"Canine EpiPen for Toto, though" added Holly. "A pretty low dosage one, to be safe."

"Maybe justo wave a doggie treat under his-a nose," Marianna offered.

"I think the answer is kind of obvious, don't you think?" said Mark, finishing off his cone. "No Dorothy, no movie. Roll credits."

"Sure, but what happens to the Scarecrow, the Tin Man, and the Cowardly Lion?" Filip countered. "Without Dorothy around, their lives go unfulfilled! Not to mention the devastating affect her disappearance would have on Auntie Em and her Uncle What's-His-Name."

"Henry," Natalie proffered.

"What are you getting at with your question, Filip?" Mark wanted to know.

Filip cleared his throat. "Dorothy Gale, through some miraculous occurrence, ends up in a foreign place. She makes new friends and is involved in their lives to such an extent that she is becomes the catalyst to them finding their hidden potential. Only then is she allowed to return home – when her job is done."

"So, Dorothy represents who, then?" asked Holly.

"Dorothy is the Ideal Everyman!" Filip pronounced, with a finger pointing to the ceiling. "Or Everyperson, if you will. Her selfless actions, her unflagging energy devoted to caring for others, Dorothy's grace under pressure – all of this make her the model to which everyone should aspire!"

"So, Dorothy isn't a lost little girl," said Holly. "She's a woman on a mission! I like it."

"Yes, on a mission! And..." Filip drew a circle in the air to encompass his friends. "what we need to understand is that we are *all* Dorothys, charged with the responsibility to help our friends fulfill their dreams and aspirations."

"And the reward-a will be there, in-a the end," said Marianna. "It was all in-a the shoes!"

"And that reward, of course, was always with her, she just didn't know it." Filip handed the rest of his gelato cone to Mark and picked up his guitar case. He rose from the pew and went to the podium. The delicate strains of Somewhere Over the Rainbow soon wafted over the hushed patrons of Jannettas Gelateria.

Natalie was silent for a good while after the song ended. She was thinking about the responsibilities one takes on when they're a Dorothy.

Later that afternoon, Mark insisted on walking with Natalie to the Byre Theatre, since it was on the way to the Neuroscience Building, after all. Natalie pointed out that going to the NS Building this way would necessitate crossing oceans and continents to get there, since he was walking in the complete opposite direction. Mark just shrugged and said he needed to work off the cone and a half of gelato. Natalie took Mark's hand when crossing at the roundabout before heading south. They maintained that handhold all the way to the theatre entrance. Their awkward goodbye at the door made them laugh. Their parting hand squeeze made Natalie's heart skip.

Natalie walked into the Byre Theatre lobby. It was quiet at the BrewCo on the first floor, the only customers being a couple at the far table next to the window with their hoodies up and sunglasses on. Indoors. On a cloudy day. Natalie gave a 'to-each-their-own' shrug and made her way up the steps, the sound of The Maytal's song, Pressure Drop playing off in the distance.

After changing into her Florence clothes in the second-floor bathroom, Natalie entered the quiet room and shut the door behind her. She didn't need to turn on the light because The Portal was glowing in anticipation of her arrival. Natalie placed her belongings on the table and was about to make her exit through the fuzzy light when she noticed the little leather book sticking out of place again on the bookcase. She smiled, thinking how insistent this little fella was! Instead of pushing it back in flush with the other books for what seemed like the tenth time, Natalie picked up the little leather book from the shelf to have a look at it. There was just enough light in the room to read the embossed lettering on the cover: New Testament. Huh, how nice, Natalie thought…a pocket New Testament right here on the shelf! That'll come in handy if I need a verse when I'm studying here at the…

It was just then that Natalie heard a loud thump in the hallway. She could hear the shuffling of feet close by. In a panic, Natalie stuffed the little leather book into the front pocket of her dress.

Then she dove headlong into the fuzzy light.

Michelle took a deep breath of the cool air outside of her dorm and started off for the Science B building. She was feeling good this morning; much better than she did yesterday before she left Florence through The Gateway. She had been getting run-down in Italy from lack of sleep, and she knew that she'd feel that way again when she went back – that was the way The Gateway worked – but the *mental* rest she was getting from being home was helping a lot. She could deal with the physical-fatigue part when she returned to Florence by getting a good sleep at Rita and Nerina's house.

As she cut across University Way, Michelle's thoughts turned to that busy and sad Friday morning at Torricelli's house after his passing. She had done her best to keep it together by keeping herself occupied. She tidied up Evangelista in his bed, preparing for the viewing by family members and friends who would be coming at daybreak. Natalia and Francesco had been a big help, preparing food and coffee in the kitchen. When Torricelli's brothers arrived, the mourning began in earnest. By noon, it felt as if all of Evangelista's friends and relatives – and a good portion of the general population - had come to pay their respects to the noted scientist. Natalia and Francesco had made two trips to the market for assorted dainties and fruits, while Michelle – Dianora to her Italian friends – cleaned plates and cups for the constant rotation of visitors to the house. When the crowd thinned out by mid-afternoon, the local parish priest and Torricelli's brothers removed Evangelista's body in preparation for the funeral service to be held in two days' time. The brothers entrusted Dianora with the closing up of the house, and this she did after straightening, organizing, cleaning, and rearranging. Before leaving for the D'ambrosio residence with Natalia, Michelle took the folder of calculus papers and the strongbox of coins from the bedroom closet, placed them in a sack, and left Torricelli's house, locking the front door on the way out.

As Michelle walked by Mac Hall, her thoughts then skipped to the phone call she had just had with her parents in Trois-Rivières. Her *Maman chou* was concerned that she had not been eating, but Michelle assured her that she was eating quite well, and a variety of cuisines, too. Her *Papa adorè* didn't bring up her burning the candle at both ends this time, but he did say something that made Michelle take notice; he advised her to allow the trusted people in her life to make decisions on her behalf, to have confidence in their expertise, and let them carry on with the work, if need be. Where that came from Michelle had no idea, but since Papa was one of her trusted people, she thanked him for his counsel.

When she entered the Science B building, Michelle was waved over to a cafeteria table by her three friends. The song Under Pressure was playing faintly through the PA speaker, courtesy of CJSW.

"Thank goodness you're here!" Gilliana announced. "Please, save me from their inanity!"

"Um…I think the word is *insanity*?" Chase incorrectly corrected.

"That, too!" Gilliana cried.

"Here, let me get that," Jay said, rising to help Michelle remove her knapsack, the strap of which was caught on the epaulet of her jacket. His hand on her arm caused Michelle's heart to skip a beat.

"These two lunkheads are trying to convince me that the Wizard in *The Wizard of Oz* is a football coach in disguise!"

Jay chimed in, "Well, not..."

"Exactly!" Chase interjected. "There's no other way to interpret his character!"

"And what's your evidence for this?" asked Michelle.

"Just wait," Gilliana scoffed.

Chase cleared his throat. "I explained that the Wizard is a symbol of authority. Right? He holds power and influence over people. So, he's just like a football coach! Then I made a striking comparison between the Wizard and Bill Walsh, coach of the Forty-Niners."

"Which I changed to Knute Rockne, since he at least pre-dates the film," Jay added.

"Right," said Chase. "But Gilli was unconvinced."

"Because I say that the Wizard character in the movie represents illusion, deception, and the power of belief," Gilliana stated with arms crossed.

"Which only supports my thesis!" Chase countered. "The illusion of Joe Montana's deep ball that turns into a check-down pass, the deception of play-action with Roger Craig, the power of belief exemplified in the 'The Catch' by Dwight Clark in the dying seconds of the 1981 NFC championship game against the Cowboys! It's like the Wizard invented the West Coast Offense!"

"And you agree with this, Jay?" asked a stupefied Michelle.

"Not at first. But when I substituted Sid Luckman for Joe Montana and put in Bronco Nagurski for Roger Craig, Chase's theory started to make sense to me."

"We had trouble with subbing out Dwight Clark, though," Chase admitted.

"I don't even think they had wide receivers before 1939," Jay shrugged.

"Anyway, I think I made a pretty good argument," said Chase, leaning back in his chair with a satisfied grin. "The Wizard was modelled after a football coach, namely, that Noot guy."

"My head is spinning," said Michelle.

"See?" said Gilli, thrusting an upturned palm. "Inane *and* insane!"

"One last thought on that," said Jay. "For all his planning and arranging and scheming, it wasn't Coach Wizard that finished the job in the end. It was Dorothy that had to carry the ball over the goal line herself."

"Dorothy punched it in!" Chase exclaimed. "Take *that*, Team Wicked Witch!"

"Dorothy hits Kansas paydirt!" Jay followed up. "Take *that*, flying monkeys!"

"Dorothy knocks it out of the park!" Michelle contributed with raised voice and air punch. "Take that you…you bad other peoples in…that movie…" The table went quiet.

"That's baseball, Michelle," said Jay, shaking his head.

"Not even close," said a disappointed Chase.

"And with that, Gilli left for her bio lab," said Gilliana as she stood up and flung her knapsack over her shoulder. "Later dudes and dudette. Oh, and Chase…"

"Yeah?"

"I may not agree with your theory, but at least it wasn't peppered with spoonerisms and mondegreens." Gilli patted him on the shoulder and headed off.

"Mondegreen?" said a perplexed Chase, looking over to Jay. "I would never have said that. Mondegreen played for the Packers, didn't he? I don't like the Packers."

Chase and Michelle walked out of Science B together on their way to Mac Hall. After a minute, Chase asked Michelle if she would sit with him on the bench off the pathway so they could have a talk. Michelle had an idea about what was coming.

"Michelle," said Chase, taking her hand. "I think it's time for us to break up."

"Break up?"

"Yes."

"Were we ever going out together in the first place?"

"I know this is going to be tough for you," Chase said tenderly. "We've been so close."

"This is the first time you've held my hand."

"It's no use for either of us to get upset, Michelle..."

"I'm fine, Chase."

"If you need someone to blame, then go ahead, blame me!"

"For what? You've never done anything. Like, really."

"I've been distracted, Michelle. The truth is, I'm interested in someone else."

"That's good."

"But I didn't know how to tell you. I didn't want to crush you."

"Do I look crushed?"

"Oh, I'll just come out and say it, then! Michelle...I'm interested in Gilliana!"

"Gilliana!" Michelle exclaimed.

"I knew you'd be upset! But I can't help it, I'm attracted to her, Michelle. And I know Gilli's interested in me."

"Oh, boy, Chase, I don't think..."

"The way she always looks at me with that lovestruck expression..."

"That's a furrow in her brow..."

"Her cheeks getting all red from embarrassment..."

"From anger, usually..."

"That particular tone in her voice when we talk..."

"That's called a natter."

"Oh, I'm so sorry, Michelle. Can you ever forgive me?"

"I'll do my best," said Michelle. "Oh, look Chase! There she is now, heading into the Science A building!" Chase turned his head, his face flushed. "Go to her, Chase! Go to her now! Run!"

Chase leapt up off the bench and slung his knapsack over his shoulder. He held out his hand to Michelle and they shook.

"No hard feelings? After all, we're still friends, right Michelle?"

"Always!" she answered.

"Great! See ya later, elevator!"

And with that, Chase was off to find Gilliana.

Two minutes later, Michelle turned the corner to the CJSW studio only to find Jay leaning on the wall near the door.

"How are you doing?" he asked.

"I take it Chase mentioned to you that he was breaking up with me?"

"He did. I didn't know how you were going to take it, though."'

"Well, after he left to hunt down Gilli, I had a pretty rough 30 seconds, there."

"Did you go through the stages of grief and anger?"

"Uh huh. Then for the next whole minute I went through bargaining and depression."

"A whole minute?

"I know, a bit indulgent of me. But after going through acceptance for the past 30 seconds, I've come to a conclusion."

"And what's that, Michelle?"

"After I finish my adventure in the record room, you're taking me out to Piazza's on a proper date, Jay."

"I was thinking Spiro's? Their Beef and Mushroom pizza is a personal fave."

"If they do halves, I'll make my side Ham and Fresh Tomato."

Jay took Michelle's hands into his. They stared at each other for a whole quarter minute. Not one awkward second elapsed.

Michelle returned Jay's hand squeeze, turned around, and entered the studio.

"Hey, girl! Nice of you to show up!" said Ken, as he swivelled in his chair.

"Um…hi," said Michelle, staring at Ken's face. "How did you grow that so fast?"

"My goatee?" he answered, stroking the beard. "The one I've had ever since I've known you?"

"Uh…never mind. Have you got some records for me to shelve?"

"Vinyl? Never! Get with the times, girl!" Ken handed Michelle a stack of CDs. "Digital is the future!"

Michelle blinked twice, took the stack, and made her way to the back room.

She wasn't sure if getting the calculus papers to Leibniz would bring back Analogue Ken, but she was more determined than ever to finish her adventure and find out.

Chapter 33

The white-robed clergy members lead the way down Via de' Pucci to the Basilica di San Lorenzo. One priest carried a tall crucifix above his head, the other waved a censer that dangled from a gold chain. Torricelli's funeral coach drawn by two white horses followed closely behind. The pallbearers walked beside the coach: Vincenzo Viviani, Lodovico Serenai, Antonio Nardi, Raffaello Magiotti, Giovanni Borelli, and Dr. Gregorio Redi. The family members, including Evangelista's brothers, walked slowly behind the coach. After them came the close friends, where Dianora and I took our place. We were escorted on either side by Francesco Redi and Marcello Malpighi. An impressive number of mourners had collected behind us, growing larger as we got closer to the church. Everyone from the coach on down was dressed in black mourning attire, with the majority of ladies wearing black veils as well. Many of the mourners carried candles and crosses. Some people on the side of the street held up banners. One of them read, *En Virescit Galileus Alter*. Dianora smiled, glanced over to me and whispered, "Here blossoms another Galileo." I smiled in return.

The church bell tolled as the procession arrived at the front steps. The pallbearers removed the casket and followed the clergy through the main entrance. I was awed by the beauty of the cathedral: rounded arches held up by ornate columns lined the aisle on either side; the bright ceiling of white and gold squares reflected light off the diamond-patterned tile on the floor; the balcony over the altar on the west wall was elegantly designed. Dianora noted my interest in the balcony as we took our spot in the fifth pew. She leaned over and whispered, "Designed by Michelangelo."

The funeral mass began with two hymns, *Dies Irae* and *Miserere Mei, Deus*, which were beautifully sung by a choir. The priests then led the mourners in prayers and scripture readings which took up the majority of the service. The homily was appropriately long, given Torricelli's accomplishments. The priest seemed to know a lot about

Evangelista's work, citing particular principles and theories, and discussing them in more detail than you would normally expect a man of the cloth to know about the departed. You could tell he was a lifelong admirer.

Following the homily, which also served as the eulogy, there was more praying, kneeling, and standing before the recessional hymn, *Lacrimosa*. I thought that the funeral service was taking an emotional toll on Dianora, seeing as how she lifted a handkerchief to her face numerous times. But I soon saw the toll wasn't emotional but physical; she was dabbing her brow, not her eyes. It wasn't warm at all in the basilica – it was rather cool, in fact – so her perspiring was odd, to say the least. I whispered an 'Are you all right?'. She assured me that she was with a nod but no smile. But I had my doubts, and decided that I would follow up with a doctorly check-up after the service.

A blessing concluded the service and the mourners were dismissed from the cathedral. Dianora and I stopped at the bottom of the stairs and joined the assembled crowd.

"I suppose we would be off to the cemetery now?" Marcello Malpighi asked no one in particular.

"Did you not hear, Marcello?" said Francesco Redi. "Evangelista will be entombed in the basilica."

"Such an honour!" said Cecilia Redi.

"And so very appropriate," Dr. Gregorio Redi added. "Torricelli deserves to be immortalized for his outstanding body of work, does he not?"

We all nodded our agreement. Vincenzo Viviani and Lodovico Serenai then approached the group.

"A lovely funeral service, would you not say?" said Viviani.

"A bit long, of course," said Serenai. "The priest could not stop talking! But is it not always this way?"

"The service could have been twice as long and never have fully covered Evangelista's accomplishments," Dianora replied with noticeable irritation.

"Well, of course," Serenai answered defensively. "I was only saying that…"

"Evangelista Torricelli was a great man, worthy of our admiration," Dianora continued. "At least future generations will afford him the respect that is due! Now, if you will excuse me..." Dianora walked quickly back up the stairs and entered the cathedral.

"What did I say?" Serenai asked.

"Too much and not enough, all at the same time," said Francesco Redi. "Lodovico, if you handle Torricelli's estate the way you handle yourself in conversation, Evangelista's legacy is in the most wretched of hands!"

Serenai gasped, took a step backward, then turned around and left. Vincenzo Viviani gave us all an awkward smile and followed after his *amico*.

Dr. Gregorio put his hand on his son's shoulder. "Ah, Ciccio! That was highly rude and completely necessary, all at the same time!"

That drew as much of a chuckle from the group as could be expected right after a funeral.

"I am going to see about Dianora," I said to Francesco.

"I will wait here for you," he replied.

"As shall I, for I wish to speak to Dianora," said Marcello.

I climbed the stairs, entered the basilica, and quietly made my way to the front where Torricelli's casket lay open. Dianora was standing next to it, her hand resting on Evangelista's.

"I learned so much from him, Natalia," she said. "About science. About mathematics. About life."

"I know how hard this is for you, Dianora. You have lost someone that was more than a mentor. You have lost a dear friend."

"*Sì*, a dear friend." She wiped a tear away.

"What will you do now?" I asked her. I had been wondering this for the past few days.

"I will be leaving Italia very soon, Natalia."

"Leaving Italia? Where are you going?"

"I have a job to complete. Before I come back to return home."

"Come back to return home? Return to where? Dianora, I do not understand..."

"I have said too much already," she interjected. "It is time for me to complete my purpose here, Natalia."

Dianora bent down and gave Evangelista Torricelli a kiss on the cheek. Then she lowered the lid of the casket. As she turned toward me, a glazed look came over her eyes and she staggered into my arms.

"Dianora, are you all right?"

"I...I just need a drink of water, Natalia. I have been feeling dizzy today."

"It is understandable, *amica*. Come, let us go home to the D'ambrosio house where you can rest."

Dianora and I left the cathedral together hand-in-hand. Francesco and Marcello were there to greet us at the bottom of the stairs.

"Did you say goodbye to Evangelista one last time?" Francesco asked.

"*Sì*," Dianora replied.

"Dianora, may I speak with you?" said Marcello Malpighi. "*In privato?*"

Dianora looked over at me and Francesco and gave an embarrassed shrug. She and Marcello stepped off to the side of the church stairway. Marcello spoke to Dianora in an animated whisper, with a lot of hand gesturing toward himself.

"What do you think he is saying?" Francesco asked.

"It is hard to say," I replied.

"Do you think he is asking for her hand in marriage?"

"Proposing right after a funeral? That would be an odd thing to do, would you not say?"

"*Sì*. But if I only had his courage, I would…" Francesco's sentence was interrupted by the return of Dianora. Minus Marcello.

"So, is he going to get the ring?" asked Francesco.

"Actually, Marcello broke-up with me," Dianora said.

"I did not think you were seeing him," I said.

"Neither did I," she replied. Then she murmured, "Huh…that is twice this has happened in the past two days."

Twice?, I thought to myself. Was she saying she was dumped by Torricelli because he died? That was kinda strange talk.

"*Ehi! Venite tutti quanti!*" It was Dr. Gregorio Redi calling for the three of us to high-tail it over to the horse-drawn carriage where he and Cecilia were waiting. We climbed in - Dianora being helped into the carriage by Francesco – Tonio the coachman clicked it into gear, and we were off.

Or was it Filippo? It was hard to tell those Espositos apart.

"But this is so *improvvisa*!" Rita exclaimed. "I am completely *impreparata* for this!"

"Come, come now," said Nerina, passing her sister a handkerchief. "*Rilassati, sorella!*"

"How can I take it easy when our beloved Dianora says she is leaving us!"

Rita was practically inconsolable at the kitchen table after Dianora dropped the *bomba* on us that she would be leaving Florence very soon, most likely for good.

"We always knew this day would come, Rita," her sister explained. "It is time that our fledgling left the nest. Now that Torricelli is gone, she must seek employment elsewhere." Nerina turned to Dianora. "Where do you plan on going?"

"There is a trip to Leipzig in my future, I believe," Dianora answered. "But before that, in my, ah…*immediate* future, I shall return home."

"Natalia, what do you think of all this?" Rita asked me.

"Well, I, ah…I am not sure how to tell you this, but…"

"You are leaving as well?" asked Nerina, her bottom lip aquiver.

"I shall be returning home very soon, *sì*."

Nerina snatched the handkerchief from her sister and dabbed at her eyes. "Now this is too much sorrow! *Troppo dolore!*" She rose from the table and exited for the sitting room, with Rita sobbing behind her.

"Perhaps you could have waited until *my* news had sunk in a bit," Dianora said to me with a 'what-were-you-thinking' look.

"*Ehi*! I am not the one that started the tears tonight! You are the one that opened the door!"

"*Sì*! And you broke it off its hinges!"

We both sat there with crossed arms, avoiding eye contact until we had both calmed down. I broke the silence.

"So, where is Leipzig?"

"It is in Ger…it is in Saxony," Dianora responded with a hiccup. Was she about to say Germany? Did that country even exist yet?

"And what awaits in Leipzig?"

"The completion of a task I have been given, Natalia."

"By Evangelista?"

"In a way," she answered cryptically. "The undertaking I was given four years ago has reached its culmination. The finish line is in sight." Dianora looked right into my eyes. "And what about you? Why are you leaving now?"

"Because…because my work here is done, as well. At least, I think it is."

"You *think* it is? That is a strange way to talk, Natalia."

"You should talk, *sorella*! You have been speaking in *enigmi* ever since I met you!"

"*Enigmi*? Me? I am not the one who dropped the mathematical terms *integrazione* and *derivare la funzione* into an everyday conversation! And where, pray tell, did you get the word *hooligan* from?" Dianora crossed her arms again.

"Probably from the same place you read *Je est un Autre*!" I countered, letting my emotions get the best of me. "What century produced *that* little *bon mot*, hmm?"

"It is not a *bon mot*!" Dianora said with anger as she rose from the table. "It is an expression that describes multiplicity of self! Something that you have failed miserably to hide, Natalia!"

"I would say the same about you, Dianora! If Dianora is your real name, that is!"

"My real…?" shouted Dianora, all flustered and red in the face. "Who *are* you, anyway, *Natalia* Campo Bella…?"

Dianora staggered backward and rocked on her heels.

Then she collapsed onto the kitchen floor.

"Dianora!" I cried, jumping up from the chair. I quickly bent down and placed her in a recovery position as Rita and Nerina dashed into the kitchen.

"Help me get her to bed," I said to them. I touched Dianora's forehead. My worst fears were now being realized.

"She is burning up!"

Chapter 34

After struggling to get Dianora up the stairs to bed, the three of us set to work preparing a sick room. Rita positioned an extra table next to the bed, placing on it a wash basin of cool water. Nerina cut up a heavy cotton sheet into squares, each measuring twenty-by-twenty centimeters, to be used as face cloths. I changed Dianora into her nightgown and prepared the bedding. I draped only one sheet over her after easing her down on the mattress. Dianora was barely conscious the entire time, but she said *merci* to me after I had tucked her in. I pulled up a chair and sat down next to her.

"I will make some *zuppa di pollo* for Dianora's dinner," said Rita, standing at the foot of the bed. "She will need to eat something to give her strength."

"I will help Rita in the kitchen," said Nerina. "Are you going to stay here with Dianora, then?"

"*Sì*," I confirmed.

"*Bene*. If you need something and wish to alert us, use this." Nerina passed me a little ceramic bell that tinkled as I placed it on the table. The sisters left the room, closing the door quietly behind them.

Dianora was lying on her back, half asleep. I reached over and touched her forehead with the back of my hand. She was hot to the touch. I dampened a face cloth and patted her brow and cheeks, eliciting a moan of gratitude from the patient. I repeated this procedure every five minutes or so as Dianora drifted in and out of consciousness. Time marched slowly as the afternoon became late afternoon and passed into evening. Rita quietly entered the room, carrying a hot bowl of soup.

"Do you think she can eat something?" she said softly, placing the bowl on the table.

"I do not think she is able to yet, Rita."

"She is sleeping now, I see."

"*Sì*. Less fitfully in the past half hour."

"Here, take this for yourself then," Rita said, passing me the soup. "When Dianora wakes up, ring the bell and I will bring up another bowl."

"*Grazie*," I replied.

Rita pulled down the window leaving it open just a crack, and then quietly slipped out of the room.

I took a sip of the chicken soup from the silver spoon. "You don't know what you're missing, Dianora," I said to her in French. "This *zuppa* is *merveilleux*." I reached over and stroked her cheek, which drew a faint smile to her lips.

I ate the soup and contemplated while Dianora slept. It was clear that she was displaying the same symptoms as Torricelli. She had spent so much time with him over the past week of his illness - how could she not become infected with the typhoid bacterium? There were so many times where I wanted to pull her back from close proximity with Evangelista and say, 'Here, let me do that'. *I* was even nervous to be around a person with typhoid fever, and I had been immunized against it back in Scotland, thanks to Dr. Silver and company. Dianora wasn't immunized against typhoid, of course, so I probably should have done more to protect her from getting it. But what was I supposed to say, since people in the 17th century didn't understand how infections were transmitted? I wasn't going to risk another court appearance with Ferdinando II de' Medici because I insisted on attending to the sick wearing a mask and gown! He'd have thrown the *libro* at me for sure! No, I had to play it straight. But in doing so I think I found out why The Portal was still open for me: I was supposed to be here for this moment - right here, right now. I needed to be here for Dianora. For my new good friend.

My best friend in Florence.

Nerina came into the room with a lantern that was turned down low. She placed it quietly on the table.

"It is getting dark now, Natalia. You must be tired. Would you like to lie down and rest while I watch over Dianora?" She motioned over to my bed on the opposite side of the room.

"I will stay up with her a bit longer," I replied.

"Are you *affamata*?"

"*No*, I am fine. The soup was very nice. And filling."

Nerina picked up the empty bowl from the table and made her way to the door. "I shall come back soon to relieve you." Nerina closed the door behind her.

I reached over and put my hand on Dianora's forehead. No change. Still hot. Too hot for my liking. And she was sweating now. I applied a cold compress and said a prayer.

"She took a little soup, but not much," said Nerina as she stood up from the bedside chair. "She continues to slip in and out of *coscienza*."

I had just returned to the sick room after spending some time resting on the sofa downstairs. It was well past midnight now and the streets were quiet and dark, as was the house.

"Are you sure you have rested enough, Natalia? I could stay with Dianora awhile longer."

"*No*, I am fine, Nerina, *grazie*."

I sat down on the chair and dampened a fresh cloth. Nerina put her hand on my shoulder and gave it a gentle squeeze before she left the room.

"*Salut*, Dianora, *come stai*?" I said to the unconscious patient, mixing my French and Italian. "I want to tell you that you're putting up a good fight." I touched her forehead and found it to be as hot as before. Still no change, no sign of improvement. "You are going to beat this thing, I just know it." I towelled off her cheeks and neck with the cool compress. "You are one of the strongest people I know, Dianora." I patted the top of her head with the cloth and then combed her hair out with my fingers. "There. You look a little more presentable now, *sorella*." I rearranged the bedsheet and folded the top of it just below her neckline. I sat back and placed my hands in my lap.

"So, *mia amica*. How would you like to hear about where I am from? Would you like me to tell you about *ma famille*?"

Dianora was sleeping peacefully now.

"Great!" I said in English. "Now, where should I begin? How about at the beginning? Would that be all right?" I didn't wait too long for a response. "Great! Okay. Well, I grew up in a small hamlet in Alberta, Canada, on an acreage just outside of the big city where I was born…"

Over the next hour – though it could have been longer – I told Dianora all about growing up in Canada. I reminisced about my childhood: the days spent playing soccer in the yard with my brother, Connor; our elaborate and futile attempts at catching the neighbour's cat with a box, a stick, and a long string; the bike rides down the hamlet road to the school playground where the weekly monkey bar competition took place, which continued until my brother got old enough to finally win; the ice cream sandwiches at the general store; my first day of Kindergarten, where I refused to be left behind by my mom, clutching the doorframe of the classroom with my little fingers while being pulled into class by that stranger Mom called, 'Your New Teacher'.

I segued into talking about my parents. I told Dianora all about my dad, John Campbell: his job at Dupont in the big city; his daily dominance over the New York Times Crossword; his love of all things analogue, which included clocks with sweep hands and music played on a turntable from vinyl records; his morning runs that kept him in shape and supplied him with a ridiculously large collection of bungee cords that he would find scattered about his highway route. And I told her that I knew no one who was more clever, more funny, or more dedicated to family than Dad. But that's what Dad actually says about his wife.

Then I told Dianora all about my mom: her outstanding work as a translator for app designers; her amazing culinary skills that kept our family well fed and constantly on our gustatory toes; her amazingly analytical mind that could switch with surprising ease from a complex math equation to a discussion of European history as she helped her children at the homework table; the lovingkindness, thoughtfulness, and faith that she exemplified every day, and how I hoped that even a portion of my Mom would be seen in me as I got older.

"You would like her, Dianora," I said, applying a compress to her forehead. "You both have a lot in common."

Just then, Dianora began to mumble, her head turning from side to side. It looked like she was having a bad dream. Her eyes began to flutter and she began to speak in low tones.

"There, there," I said, dabbing at her cheeks with the cloth. "It's all right."

"*Evangelista...il lavoro...*" she muttered in Italian. "*...deve essere fatto...*"

"*Sì*, Dianora...the work must be done," I replied, patting her forehead. "When you are better."

"*Non, papa...quand j'aurai fini le travail...*"

"Your father will see you soon, *oui*," I said in French. "You will finish the work..."

"*Alors je reviendrai... à Trois-Rivières.*"

"Trois-Rivières?" I exclaimed, sitting back. "What do you mean you'll go back to Trois-Rivières?" Was there even a Trois-Rivières in France in 1647? Did I mention my mother being born in Trois-Rivières when I was telling her about myself. No...I know I didn't! What the...?

"I'm coming back, Jay...wait for me...I'm coming back..."

I sat there with my mouth open. That was English. Dianora was speaking English!

"*The Gateway...I must get to...The* Gateway!" Dianora's eyes suddenly opened. She stared at me with a glazed look, like she was still in the bad dream. "You must get me to The Gateway!" She grabbed my hand. "Please! The Gateway!...The Gate..."

Dianora let go of my hand, her eyes closing as she slipped back into unconsciousness.

I sat there looking at her. Staring at her. And then I began to tremble.

I jumped up from the chair, opened the wardrobe, and rifled through the dresses and outfits that were folded on the shelves.

"Where are they? Where are they? Okay, got 'em!"

I took out the blouse, dress, and shoes that Dianora wore the most and placed them on my bed that was next to hers. The blouse, dress, and shoes that she always wore when she disappeared at night.

I unfolded the blouse and held it up to the dim lantern light. I examined the collar.

"Oh, my. Oh…"

I put down the blouse and picked up the dress. I turned it inside out and ran my fingers down the seam.

"Oh, no, no…"

I picked up the shoes and examined the heel and sole. Nothing. I turned back the flap on the leather upper. Nothing. I licked my finger and rubbed the inside edge of the shoe. I rubbed hard. Black ink began to collect on my finger, exposing the hidden print.

I sat down on the bed with the shoe in my hand, and stared at Dianora. The blouse had the remnant of its laundry tag still stitched into the collar. The dress had the remains of a clothes' label stitched into the seam. And the shoe. Oh, the shoe…

"Arnold Churgin," I read out loud. "Size 7.5. Made in Canada."

My heart was racing. I sat down in the chair and leaned over toward Dianora. I moved her hair back over her ears. I looked hard at her face and saw my brother, Connor. I reached over and felt her left earlobe. It was pinched at the very top. I reached up to my left earlobe, to the identical spot that was pinched in the very same way.

I stroked her cheek that was flushed red from the fever.

"Dianora? Dianora?"

I waited a moment, then stroked her cheek again. I held her hand.

"Michelle. *Michelle, peux-tu m'entendre*? Can you hear me, Michelle?"

Michelle opened her eyes slightly and looked at me. A smile came over her face. We looked at each other for only a brief moment, but it felt as if our eyes had locked over centuries of time.

Then her eyelids closed again and she returned to unconsciousness.

"No. No! NO!" I exclaimed as I squeezed her hand. "You have to come back! Mom! MOM!"

Suddenly, the door burst open. Rita and Nerina rushed in.

"*Che cosa sta accadendo?*" Rita shouted. "Natalia! Is Dianora all right?" She dashed over to the bed and placed her hand on Michelle's forehead. She turned to Nerina. "She is hot, but she is breathing."

"Natalia?" Nerina said with concern, her hand on my shoulder "Are *you* all right?"

"Um…ah…" I stammered. I was searching for words. My mind was racing, like my heart. I stood up from the chair.

"I have to go!"

Rita gave me a perplexed look. "Go? Go where? The sun is barely rising, *ragazza pazza!*"

"No, I need to leave now! Please sit with her, Rita. I need to get something to help Dianora!"

"There is nowhere to go at this hour, Natalia!" Nerina called out as I quickly left the room. "Be *sensata*, dear girl!"

But I was already running down the stairs on my way to the Palazzo Medici.

On my way to The Portal.

I tore down Via Calzaioli, my mind racing to formulate a plan. First, I would enter The Portal and get back to Scotland. Then I would quickly go over to the Med School pharmacy and get some antibiotics. No…I wouldn't have to go *quickly* because time would stop here until I got back. Right. I wouldn't have to rush when I was back home…only here! Okay. How am I going to get antibiotics at the pharmacy, since I can't write a prescription yet? Would Dr. Blanco write me one? I could tell him I have a sore throat and I need some penicillin. Is Mom allergic to penicillin? Maybe tetracycline then. Or cipro. I would have to look up the best treatment for typhoid and get that! It wouldn't be a problem to bring the pills back with me through The Portal. I would take them out of the plastic jar, wrap them up in a cloth, and bring them back here to Florence. I'd make sure no one was in the room when I administered the drugs to Mom, of course.

Mom! So this was your transtemporal trek, the one you were going to tell me and Connor all about when I came home from med school at Christmastime! Mom! MOM! What is going on?!

I sprinted across Via de' Cerratani, where I had to dodge a horse cart - the only other moving thing I encountered on the street. Okay, so I'll get to The Portal, get back to Scotland, and call Connor. He could help me with...Wait! No, no! Don't call Connor! And don't try to call Mom and Dad, even if they're no longer incommunicado! Because something might be changed at home because of all of this - something that I just couldn't handle: what if my family weren't there? What if Michelle doesn't, doesn't...and what would happen to Dad? Were they married yet in her future? Dianora said she was a 'mature woman of twenty' when we met at Torricelli's birthday party. Mom would have been twenty in the late 1980s. So, there wouldn't be a John Campbell in the picture yet, at that time. If something happens here, something bad, there would *never* be a John Campbell in the picture. And that means no Mom or Dad or Connor in *my* picture!

And not even a *me* in my own picture!

I ran faster.

The door of the grand archway was closed when I got to the Palazzo Medici. I dashed down the block to the garden entrance. It was open. I ran down the hallway, dodging ladders and buckets and all kinds of construction materials. When I got to the courtyard, I slipped on the tiles and almost fell. There was dirt and dust all over the floor. I regained my balance and walked across to the other side, toward the office. But when I got there, the door to the office was gone. So was the desk, the three chairs, and the picture on the wall. Gone.

The faint morning light that was coming through the window illuminated the back wall. I walked over and placed my hands on the wooden planks that covered a hole to the outside. The stone wall was gone. The office was gone.

The Portal was gone.

Chapter 35

I sat down on the front steps of the Palazzo Medici under the grand archway, with the family coat of arms above my head. I was breathing heavily. I had spent the last 15 minutes racing through the palace in a panic, opening every door I could as I searched for the fuzzy light. I looked everywhere: under tables, behind wall-hangings, around furniture, underneath carpets. I ran around the garden, looking behind the bushes and under the hedge. I sprinted around the outside of the building, desperately groping at the stone blocks on the ground floor, hoping that my hand might slip through the masonry. Nothing, nothing, nothing...NOTHING! There was no portal to be found anywhere.

The warmth of the early morning sun was having no effect on me. I was trembling. Was this really happening? How could this have happened? Why had this happened? What had I done? Or not done. How was I going to get home? I was now stranded in Florence. Trapped in 1647. A prisoner of time.

"*Cosa sta succedendo, signorina?*" asked an approaching voice. I raised my head and recognized the tall man with the toolbox. It was Antonio.

"It is our French-speaking cake girl," said Andrea, the short man carrying the ladder.

"But look...our cake girl has been crying!" said Alfredo, the man in the straw hat. "*Signorina*, what has happened to you?"

"I...I have lost something," I answered, wiping away the tears from my cheeks. "And I do not know if I will ever find it again."

Antonio put down his toolbox and sat on my right. Andrea put down the ladder and sat to my left. Alfredo sat a step below me and took off his straw hat.

"What is your name, *cara ragazza*?" Alfredo asked.

"My name is Natalie," I answered.

"Natalie, you seem to be lost," said Antonio. "Are you lost?"

"I am. And I do not know what to do."

The four of us sat silently for half a minute. Andrea was the first to speak.

"It was a difficult thing for me to climb that, at the very beginning," he said, pointing to the ladder on the base of the steps. "I was afraid of the height. Was I not, Alfredo?"

"*Pietrificato!*" Alfredo replied.

"But every day, I summoned the courage to climb up a little farther. Every day, one more step up. Little steps."

"*Bambino passi!*" Antonio added.

"*Sì, sì...bambino passi,*" Andrea agreed. "Every day, I took a deep breath and summoned the courage to go on. And soon, I was able to reach the ceiling of the courtyard!" Andrea smiled at me.

"I was very anxious, too, when I began the job of restoration here at the Palazzo Medici," said Antonio. "It is a delicate matter to work around these objects of art with my crude tools." He pointed at his toolbox sitting next to the ladder. "But I was chosen for this job by the Grand Duke himself because of the care I display when restoring."

"Antonio has a true heart for preserving antiquity," Andrea nodded.

"*Grazie, amico,*" Antonio said with a smile. "I have a passion for putting things right. For making things better for everyone. But the work we accomplish together here at the palace is *niente* without Alfredo."

"*Sì, sì...*nothing without Alfredo!" Andrea added.

"What do you do?" I asked the man with the straw hat.

"Alfredo is the brains behind the *operazione!*" Antonio exclaimed with his finger pointing to the heavens. "He sees things others cannot!"

"You are too kind," Alfredo said, embarrassed.

"It is true!" said Andrea. "He has the *visione*, you see!"

"It is nothing like that," Alfredo said dismissively. "By His grace, I have been given a gift, it is true. But it is more about honing your ability to retrieve *informazione*." Alfredo tapped his head twice and put his straw hat back on. "*Capisci?*"

I looked at Andrea, Antonio, and Alfredo. The three of them gave me a collective, knowing smile. I stood up and descended the stairs to the street.

"*Grazie, amici,*" I said. "You have helped to remind me that I possess the answer to my problem here, here, and here," I said, pointing to my abdomen, my heart, and my head.

"It appears our French-speaking cake girl is ready to grapple with destiny!" Andrea announced. "Should you need any more *consiglio*, come back to Palazzo Medici anytime!"

"If a problem is too difficult for us, we will call upon the services of the Grand Duke himself!" said Antonio.

"*Sì, sì,*" Alfredo enthused. "Ferdinando de' Medici is a *mago* when it comes to solving problems!"

"A true wizard, *sì!*" Andrea and Antonio said together.

"*Arrivederci!*" I said to them. "And if I do not see you in the future…*grazie, ancora.*"

"*Arrivederci!*" the three of them shouted as I hurried down the street. I turned when I heard Alfredo call out. He was waving his straw hat in the air.

"I know you will miss me most of all, Natalie!" he cried.

Alfredo was given a backhanded smack on each shoulder by Antonio and Andrea.

I began my sprint back to the D'ambrosio house with coherent thoughts running through my head. I had been sent to the past with a job: to help fix the paths of Francesco Redi and Luca Giordano - the continued appearance of The Portal in Scotland had made obvious to me. And now I was not being allowed to bring back medicine for my mother from the future - the disappearance of The Portal in Florence had made *that* obvious to me. But the message that I had been sent via the workmen was crystal clear: I was to gather up courage from all the baby steps I had made to get to this point in time; I was to take heart, because I had been specially chosen for this work; and I was to apply my accumulated knowledge to solve any problems that lay ahead.

As I turned the corner onto Via Calzaioli, I thought about my young mother lying sick in bed and I felt the stress rise up again. How was I able to help her without modern medicine at my disposal? What could I do to help her combat the infection? Where would I find the resources? What *were* the resources? Who could get them for me? Why was this all happening to her? Why Mom? Why?

I stopped to catch my breath and a flood of thoughts rose from my subconscious...

Under pressure...Visualization...the parasympathetic system can be controlled...Pressure...deep breaths, visualize...CTP, it's all in my head...self-awareness will decrease the stress...less overwhelmed...Be prepared!...That's why we practice our practise!...Visualize all the possibilities...breathe and relax...Dorothy, the Ideal Everyperson...her selfless actions...unflagging energy...grace under pressure...grace under pressure!...Pressure Drop...Pressure Drop...Stop the clock...Freeze the clock!

Then I heard my Mom's voice...

One way to handle high-pressure situations is to commit the outcome to someone other than yourself...wherever, and even whenever, you are.

I looked up. The dome of the *Cattedrale di Santa Maria del Fiore* stood high above me. The golden ball at the top of the spire was glinting in the sunlight, with the cross at its apex projecting straight into the heavens above. I closed my eyes and said a prayer.

I felt the pressure - the total pressure - lift off my shoulders like a storm cloud breaking up and leaving behind a brighter sky.

I ran quickly up the street to the D'ambrosio house.

"Natalia! You have returned! Come quickly, *per favore!*"

Nerina appeared frantic as she flung open the front door upon my arrival, concern etched on her face. I followed her as she bounded up the stairs to the sick room. Lucio and Giuseppe had arrived; they were waiting in the hallway looking worried and distressed.

"What is it?" I asked. "What is wrong?" My heart rate elevated.

"Dianora has had an *incidente*," Lucio said, trying to act calm.

"She has fallen and hurt herself," Giuseppe added.

I rushed into the room ahead of Nerina. Rita was sitting on the bed next to my unconscious mother, holding a wad of the compress cloths on Mom's right arm, just under her shoulder. It was soaked in blood. There was blood all over the bedsheet. There was blood all over the floor. Rita turned toward me.

"It is all my fault!" she said with exasperation. "I left her for one moment! She must have awoken and tried to get up. She fell and her arm was scraped by a nail on the floor!"

That protruding nail that I found on my first morning here.

"Let me see the wound, Rita, *per favore*."

I sat down in the bedside chair and replaced Rita's hand on the wound with mine. I lifted the cloths. The gash was over three centimetres long and quite deep. The nail had penetrated the epidermis and the dermis, and looked to have cut into the subcutaneous tissue layer, as well.

"Will the wound need to be closed?" Lucio asked.

"*Sì*," I answered. "I will have need for your sewing kit, Nerina."

"*Sì, sì*, right away!" She dashed out of the room.

"Should we call the doctor?" asked Giuseppe.

"Natalia *is* a doctor, Giuseppe!" Rita answered curtly. "She is more than capable of handling the *situazione*!" Giuseppe nodded.

"Rita, we will need more cloths," I said. "Could you…" But before I could finish the sentence, Rita was out the door.

"And I will fetch some clean bedsheets too!" she shouted from the hallway.

"I will help Nerina!" said Giuseppe.

"And I will help Rita!" said Lucio. "And get a bucket of water to clean the floor!"

The men bolted from the room. The sound of scampering feet and cupboard doors being slammed began to fill the house.

I lifted the cloths and had another look. The oozing had slowed. The staunching of the blood flow was working, but the cut would need to be closed. With my free hand, I felt Mom's forehead. She was still burning up. I reached out for a clean cloth, soaked it, and dabbed her cheeks and neck with the cool compress.

A feeling of dread suddenly came over me. Mom was succumbing to the typhoid fever. Her temperature was too high; it would soon have an effect on the functioning of her organs. The cut on her arm could become infected, and probably *was* infected by the entry of the nail; the tetanus bacterium could cause spasms and difficulty in breathing.

Dianora…Michelle…Mom was slipping away. And here I was, with all the information but none of the medications that could save her life.

But before the pressure got to me I closed my eyes, took a deep breath, and started to think. Images came to my mind: of hospital beds in the ICU; of respirators and ECGs; of oxygen masks and IVs; of IVs filled with aminoglycosides and fluoroquinolones; of antibiotics pressed into pill form; of penicillin being administered in liquid form to children; of mold growing on bacterial plates with uncontaminated rings; of bread mold and poultices and ancient Egyptian physicians…

"Rita! Nerina! *Tutti quanti…venite qui adesso!*" I shouted. Everyone piled into the sick room at once.

"There is very little time to do a very important procedure," I told them. "This will sound *pazza* to you, but I need you to trust me. Will you do that?"

"*Sì, sì*, whatever you say, Natalia!" said Rita. The others replied with fervent nods.

"Who knows where we can find old, stale bread? Bread that will have the blue and green on it."

"*Muffa?*" asked Nerina, making a face that indicated something spoiled.

"*Sì…muffa* on the bread."

"Ah! She means *stampo per il pane!*" Lucio interjected.

"Ah!" went the other three Italians. There was a collective moment of contemplation before Giuseppe finally spoke.

"Raniero is the baker at the market! And his shop is on Via Condotta just down the road! He never sells everything he bakes!"

"*Bene*! You and Lucio must go there immediately and bring back as much *stampo per il pane* as you can carry! And if there is more than you can carry, find more arms!"

"Right away!" they said together as they tore out of the room. I looked at Rita.

"Is there honey in the pantry?"

"*Sì.*"

"And *pepe nero*?"

"*Sì?...*" she answered again, this time with a curious look.

"I need you to grind the black pepper as finely as you can with a *mortaio e pestello*. And Nerina, do you have strong, clear *alcolica* in the house?"

"*No*, but I can buy some *grappa* down the street. It is very strong and clear."

"*Perfetta*! Have all of this on the kitchen table, along with the bread, when the men return, *per favore*. And more cloths!"

The women hurried out of the room to their appointed tasks. I rinsed a compress in the water basin and patted Mom's cheeks.

"I know, Michelle…it looks like we're pulling the goalie, now," I said to my mother as she lay unconscious on the bed. "But I can assure you the science is solid. Just the way you like it."

There was a great commotion downstairs three quarters of an hour later. Nerina entered the sick room with the news.

"The boys are back, and they have brought so much *stampo per il pane* you could start a poor man's bakery!"

Nerina spelled me off and kept pressure on Mom's wound as I left for the kitchen. When I got there, I was greeted by three smiling faces and two huge crates of old bread.

"It was supposed to be fed to the pigs, but the farmer did not come for two days, so Raniero let has have it all!" exclaimed Lucio, presenting the bread with a sweep of his hand.

"Is it stale enough for you?" asked Giuseppe.

I turned over the loaves in the first crate. The mold dust puffed into the air.

"They are all perfectly bad," I answered.

"Truly awful in a wonderful way!" Rita exclaimed.

Lucio gave Giuseppe a pleased-as-punch punch on the arm.

"Now, we must hurry," I said, beginning my instructions. Rita jumped into action before the word *hurry*. "The three of you need to scrape the *blu-verde* powder off of the bread into a big bowl." Rita placed a large bowl on the table before I said the word *bowl*. "I will need the *grappa*, Ri…" She handed me the alcohol and a stack of cloths before I could say her name. "I will be back in *un momento*!"

I dashed upstairs and took over from Nerina, who left to join the bread-mold scrapers. I uncorked the alcohol and had a sniff. Except for the strong smell of ethanol, I couldn't detect any aromatics in the *grappa*. *Perfetta*! I removed the latest bandage from Mom's arm. The blood flow from the wound was decreasing. I dampened two cloths with *grappa*, keeping the bottle in my left hand.

"I'm sorry about this, Michelle, but it has to be done."

I wiped the wound with the alcohol cloths. Mom moaned softly. Then I irrigated the wound with alcohol straight from the bottle. Mom's eyes popped open, she exhaled sharply, and then she eased back into unconsciousness. I strapped some fresh, *grappa*-laced cloths to her arm with a scarf from the closet and called for Nerina to spell me off again.

When I got downstairs to the kitchen with the grappa in hand, the wooden bowl on the table was a third of the way full with blue-green dust and scrapings of bread.

"This will do nicely to start," I said.

Rita, Lucio, and Giuseppe watched as I carefully cleaned a spoon and another bowl with the *grappa*, and wiped them dry. I transferred all of the mold into the clean bowl and added warm water, a tablespoon at a time, to create a thick slurry. I added some black pepper from the mortar and stirred the mixture well. I dampened a cloth with warm water, wrung it out, and applied a good portion of the slurry to it. I picked up the honey jar from the table.

"*Venite tutti con me, per favore,*" I said to the group, and they followed me up the stairs. When we got to the sick room, Nerina stood up from the chair. I sat down and turned to my four medical assistants, the cloth with the bread-mold paste in my hand. I began my explanation.

"A very long time ago, doctors in Egypt discovered that infections could be treated with a poultice that contained bread mold and black pepper. Dianora's fever is caused by an *organismo* that has infected her body. This *organismo* is coursing through her body right now, creating, ah...*chaos*..." I used the English word.

"*Sì...caos,*" said Lucio. "The *organismo* creates a mess!"

"*Sì*, and this mess can be fixed by the substances in the *stampo per il pane* and the *pepe nero,*" I said. "They will kill off the *organismo intruso*, and any others that entered through the nail wound."

I untied the scarf, removed the bandage from Michelle's arm, and applied the bread-mold poultice directly onto the wound. She didn't stir. I placed another cloth on top and spread a thin layer of honey on it.

"The honey will prevent any further infections that come from *organismi* in the air," I explained.

"In the air?" Rita said with some alarm.

"You need not worry about them unless you have an open wound," I reassured her. I covered the honey cloth with a plain cloth and tied the poultice snuggly to my mother's arm. I sat back in the chair.

"And now?" asked Nerina.

"And now, we wait for the medicine to work its way through Mich...my moth...er, Dianora's bloodstream." I got some strange looks for that *passo falso*.

"Is there anything else we can do?" Giuseppe asked me.

"*Sì*. We need to continue to make bread-mold paste so we can change the poultice every hour, on the hour."

"I watched you carefully, Natalia," said Rita. "I can make the paste!"

"I will wash this floor and cut more cloths!" said Nerina.

"I will scrape more *muffa* from the bread!" said Lucio.

"And I will scour the rest of Florence for *stampo per il pane*!" said Giuseppe.

The four medical assistants left the room to attend to their responsibilities. I felt Michelle's forehead. There was no change. I dampened a cloth with cool water and patted her cheeks and neck and chest.

"Doesn't that feel better, Michelle?" She didn't respond. I put my hand on her arm. "Just remember: you're a strong woman Michelle… you can do this. You can get better. I'll be right here. I won't leave you."

I fixed her hair, stroked her cheeks with the back of my hand, and sat back in the chair. As I absently brushed off my dress, I felt a bulge in the side pocket. I reached in and pulled out the pocket New Testament that I had placed there in a panic back in Scotland. It brought a smile to my face.

"Let's do a study, shall we?"

I flipped through the pages and stopped at the gospel of John.

"Why don't we start here? Chapter 6, verse 35. It seems rather appropriate, don't you think?" I held Michelle's hand.

"It's going to be all right, Mom. I just know it."

Chapter 36

I woke up with the sunlight on my eyelids. I found it too difficult to open them. My head felt weightless, as if it was going to float away, but my arms and legs were too heavy to lift. A groggy sensation overcame me. I tried to open my mouth, but my lips were shut tight. I felt the touch of a hand stroking my forehead and cheek, and heard myself moan. When I finally did get my eyes open, I could barely make out the smiling face hovering over me.

"*Bon matin*, young lady," said a woman's voice in French. "It is good to see you alive and well." She brought a wet cloth to my lips to unstop my mouth.

"Where…am I?" I managed to ask.

"You are in your bedroom at the D'ambrosio house. Do you remember the names of your hosts?"

"Ah…Rita…and Nerina," I answered.

"*Très bien*. And who am I?"

"You are…Natalia."

"*Exactement*! And what is *your* name?"

"I am Mi…Dianora," I said, hazily.

"Well, Midianora is certainly an interesting name! It sounds very biblical. Like you are from the land of Midian, or something. One last question…What city are you in, presently."

"This…this is Florence."

"*Sì*, this is Florence," said Natalia, switching over to Italian. "But you were not born here, is that right?"

"No, I was not," I replied in Italian. "I was born in…in…"

"In a place somewhere other than here," Natalia answered for me, as she wiped my face with warm water. "Do not worry. Your memory will come back as you *recuperare*."

"Recover? Recover from what?"

"You have been very sick, Dianora."

"Sick? What do you mean…?"

"You have been sick with typhoid fever. I am almost certain of that. But you have pulled through admirably. Do you remember fainting at the kitchen table?"

"I…I think so…"

"Well that was three days ago."

"Three days ago!" I exclaimed weakly. I tried to sit up, raising myself with my elbows. A sharp pain from my arm caused me to wince and drop back down onto the bed.

"You had a little accident on a protruding floor nail on the first day," Natalia said, pointing at the bandage on my arm. "It was quite the gash, but it is stitched up quite nicely now. Nerina liked my needlework. She says I would make a fine seamstress."

"I do not recall any of this."

"I am a bit surprised by that since you put up quite the fuss! But after Francesco upped the dosage of topical laudanum, you hardly felt a thing!"

"Francesco Redi was here?"

"That was yesterday. He was a great help. And so were Rita and Nerina, of course. Lucio and Giuseppe will probably sleep the whole day today after running through the streets of Florence for 48 hours looking for old bread."

"Old…bread?" I asked. I couldn't have heard her correctly.

"*Sì*, old bread. Or, more specifically, *stampo per il pane*."

"Moldy bread? What would you need moldy bread for?" I was so confused. My head was swimming.

"Allow me to explain," said Natalia. She sat back in the chair and began to tell a story that started with doctors in ancient Egypt and ended with twelve stitches in my arm. One for each apostle, she said.

"You…you treated my fever with a bread-mold poultice?" I said, dumbfounded.

"Do not forget the *pepe nero*. That was an important *ingrediente*, too."

"Where did you learn all of this?"

"In my medical school in Scotland, of course! We were discussing homemade *antibiotica* preparation with our professor, and she told us how infections may have been treated long ago. With a little more research, I learned all about the active components in mold and pepper."

"I see," I replied after a long pause.

"I thought you might," Natalia said with a squinty look. "Interesting how you never batted an eye when I used the word *antibiotic* just now."

"I…I must have heard this somewhere before," I said with a puzzled look.

"Uh huh. I also said my professor was a 'she'. That did not strike you as odd, this being 1647, and all?"

"Um…ah, well…" I was grasping for words. What was Natalia doing?

"One more question, Dianora. *Where do you go to school?*"

"*I go to school in Ca…*" I stopped midsentence. Then I gulped. My face flushed.

Natalia had asked me that question in English.

I had answered her…in English.

"Your English is pretty good for someone who does not speak English," Natalie said in English, with arms crossed. "Now tell me, *Dianora*…what is this Gateway you were so insistent on going to when you were in your fever delirium?"

My lips were trembling. My mouth was moving, but nothing was coming out.

"And I'm curious to know who Jay is. You seemed very anxious to see him."

I didn't know what to say. So I said nothing. I just stared wide-eyed at Natalia. She uncrossed her arms and patted my hand.

"I'm sure this is very hard for you," she said. "Believe me, I *know* this is very hard for you. I would do exactly the same thing in your circumstance. Silence is golden, and all that. But you're going to have to trust me now…"

Natalia's English was different. *I'm*? *You're*? She was using contractions! And that proverb…*silence is golden*?

"I have something to tell you," she said. "Something you need to know." She looked directly into my eyes.

My body was shaking. Natalia was nervous, too, I could tell. I decided to tell her the truth about myself right then and there.

"Natalia, I…"

"It's Natalie. I'm Natalie."

"I *do* have something to explain to you, Natalie" I admitted. I struggled into a sitting position on the bed. "I'm not who you think I am."

"Oh, I think I know who you are."

"No, you couldn't possibly…"

"Oh, it's possible…"

"You see, I am not from here…"

"No, you're not."

"I am from a different place…"

"I'll say."

"From a different *time*, Natalie."

"Aren't we all?"

"No, no!" I exclaimed. "You don't understand!"

"Wanna bet?"

"Argh! You're talking back just like a child!"

"Truer words were never spoken, Michelle…"

"You better believe truer words were never…" I suddenly froze in place. Then my eyes got bigger and my shoulders dropped.

"Michelle? Why did you call me that?"

"It's your name, isn't it?"

"I…You must have heard me say this when I was in my delirium."

"No, actually. You never blurted out your real name the whole time. I was very impressed."

"Then how did you…when did you…Natalie who…who are you?"

Natalie took my hand into hers.

"My name is Natalie Campbell. I am…from the future."

I recoiled in alarm. "Wh…What?"

"Just like you are."

"WHAT?" I scampered away from her on the bed until I was pressed up against the wall. I was breathing hard.

"But…but how could you know my real name?"

"It's the name you gave me, Michelle Morel…I'm your daughter, Natalie."

Suddenly, the room got dark, and I slid down the wall onto the bed.

When Michelle started to stir five minutes later, I was again sitting over her in the sickbed chair. When she opened her eyes and saw me, it took about 6 seconds for her to come to her senses and overreact again.

"You're going to have to stop doing that," I said, as she tried to scoot away from me. "You're going to give me a complex."

"This can't be happening," she said with more amazement than alarm this time. "I don't have a daughter."

"You're technically correct, of course. You don't. Yet. But you will. And when you do…" I stretched out my arms. "Ta da!"

Michelle shook her head and sat up. "I can't be a mother! I don't even…I mean, I've never…"

"Well, you will. You and Dad will welcome me into the world in 2003, way after you get married. I've always wondered why it took you two so long to start a family."

"This is all too crazy! It's too much!" Michelle was sweating now. I passed her a cloth. "I'm just a university student!"

"Studying engineering, I know. What's your major?"

"Um…electrical."

"Two words for a better job prospect, Mom…" I interjected. "*Software*." I said that with a wink.

"That's not two words. And don't call me that!"

"What?"

"Mom!"

"But that's who you are!"

"Well, not yet I'm not!" Michelle took a deep breath to compose herself and looked at me with those Mom-eyes of hers. "Natalie…I'm sorry. This is just so much to process."

"Tell me about it. When I found out the truth, I went a little kooky myself."

"How did you find out? What gave it away?"

"It wasn't anything you said." I pointed at the closet. "It was the labels you cut out of your clothes, and your Arnold Churgin shoes."

"But I…"

"I licked off the black marker."

"I see," said Michelle. Then after a pause, she said, "You seem to have this time-travel stuff down pat, Natalie."

"Well, if it wasn't for Con…" I stopped abruptly in midsentence and gave an innocent smile. Michelle was having none of it.

"Con who? Conrad? Connor?"

My smile turned into the uneasy kind.

"Connor? Is that my son? You have a time-travelling brother?"

"In our family, we call it transtemporal trekking," I said.

"In our family? In our FAMILY!"

"Okay, I've said too much already."

Just then the door opened. Rita and Nerina burst in right on cue. They rushed over to the bed.

"Dianora you are awake!" Rita shouted, dropping onto the bed and throwing her arms around Michelle. "You have come back to us!" When Rita stood up, Nerina moved in to cup Michelle's face with her hands and plant a big kiss on her forehead.

"We were so worried," Nerina said. "But we knew you were in good hands."

"*Le mani di Dio!*" said Rita. "And Natalia's, too!"

"*Sì, sì,*" Nerina agreed. "We had confidence that the medicine Natalia prepared would heal you!"

"You must be *affamata*, Dianora!" Rita exclaimed, moving to the door. "We will get you something to eat right away! Would you like *la zuppa*?"

"That would be very nice," Michelle answered.

"And maybe some *panini*, too!" said Nerina. "With *antipasti*! *Vai avanti*, Rita!" The two of them scurried down the hall.

"It is so wonderful to have the other *sisters* in the house reunited at last!" Rita shouted from the stairs.

I looked at Michelle with a grin.

"Well, close enough," she said, returning the smile.

"Oh. Let me show you another 'tell' in ascertaining your true identity, Michelle Morel." I pushed her hair back and touched her pinched earlobe. Then I pulled back my hair and placed her hand on my pinched earlobe.

Tears welled up in Michelle eyes. And mine. We hugged each other for a long while.

"Oh my, I just thought of something," I said as we unlocked our embrace.

"What's that?"

"I know why you and Dad waited so long to start a family!"

"Oh?"

"It's because *I just told you* I was born in 2003! I'm the one who told you when I was going to be born!"

We both stared at each other in horror.

"AHHHH!"

Chapter 37

The embers in the kitchen stove were flickering as Michelle poured the second round of *caffè* of the morning. I got up from the table to place another log on the dying coals, but Michelle asked me to hold off on that since she was feeling quite warm now. I could tell she was starting to feel like herself again; it had been two days since she had awoken from her fever-sleep and her colour, responsiveness, and energy had mostly returned. So had her appetite, as evidenced by the half-eaten loaf of bread and almost-empty jar of honey on the table.

"How did you ever come up with the idea of using this on my bandage as an antiseptic treatment?" Michelle asked in English, pointing to the honey jar. With Rita and Nerina having gone to the market, Michelle and I were free to converse in any of our three languages. And we did – all at the same time, for the most part.

"That's an ancient-Egyptian trick, too," I answered, sitting back down at the table. "The science behind its use is pretty solid, given that the hypertonic sugar solution will kill any airborne cell on contact."

"And honey has a delicious post-antiseptic application, too!" she said, finishing her last bite of breakfast.

"*Oui*, but make sure there's enough left to continue the *protocollo*," I said with a nod at the jar. "We still need that honey for its pre-post-antiseptic efficacy."

"Can't we use something else in conjunction with it?"

"Not really. It's a mono-pre-post-antiseptic ointment," I said with a smirk.

"And here I thought it was a non-mono-pre-post-antiseptic balm," Michelle replied with a grin. "I wonder if you could use something else as a treatment, like oregano or thyme?"

"*Non*, it's all about the sugar content. Those herbs wouldn't work."

"So, oregano and thyme would be seen as pseudo-non-mono-pre-post-antiseptics, then?"

"*Exactamundo!*" I replied, in a language common to neither of us. "But if you added a bay leaf, at least you'd smell like *zuppa!*"

Michelle giggled. "Do we have inane conversations like this in the future?"

"All the time," I said after taking a sip of *caffè*. "It started when I was very young."

"Actually, it may have started right here," Michelle noted with unease.

"Yikes!" I exclaimed. "This TT stuff hurts my hippocampus!"

I pointed at Michelle's bandage. "Now, let me have a peek, okay?"

"Be my guest, Dr. Natalie," she said, offering me her right arm. I lifted the bandage, had a look, and gave a hmm.

"And that is diagnostic-speak for what exactly?" asked Michelle.

"That 'hmm' means 'a bit red and a little swollen, but much better than yesterday'. I'd say Mom is getting better."

"*Basta*, Natalia! You've got to stop calling me that!"

"Why? That's who you are!"

"Well, not *yet*, I'm not!"

"Not *yet*…and yet here I am as a testimony to your future fertility!"

"Ugh! You really have a way of putting things!"

"I got that from you. But my cute way of delivering a line comes from Dad."

"Don't go any farther! Blabbing away about my future could be dangerous!"

"But don't you think it could be kind of exciting to know about stuff that's going to happen in your world in the next thirty years? Don't you want to know about the flying cars?"

"There's going to be flying cars?" Michelle asked, eyes wide.

"*Non*, but wouldn't it be great to know some stuff ahead of time?"

"No, it wouldn't be rad at all."

"Rad?"

"Yes, rad. As in *radical*?"

"Ah, *sì*! Rad! As in, 'we don't say that anymore in the 21st century.'"

"Ack! See, now that's two more things I know about that I shouldn't!"

"Two?"

"*Oui*! Now I know that there *won't* be flying cars by 2023, and nothing will be *rad* anymore! I shouldn't know stuff like that ahead of time!"

"I don't know," I countered. "It could be fun. You could be at a dinner party where someone starts spouting off, predicting this and that about future travel. Everyone at the table is *sooo* impressed. And then you say, really smugly, 'Flying cars? Nah, not gonna happen.'"

Michelle paused, looking thoughtful. "You're right. That *could* actually be fun!"

We both smiled and drained the last of our *caffè*. Michelle was quiet for a moment, looking down at her cup and ringing her finger around the rim.

"I know you think that my spending four years here in Florence has been a bit, shall we say, excessive," Michelle said. "But there was a good reason for it."

"I know."

"You can see from everything that's happened that it was all meant to be, right?"

"*Sì*, I do see."

"I wasn't on some kind of extended sightseeing tour," Michelle averred. "I had work to do. Work that I was *sent* to do."

"I feel the same way," I replied. "I was sent to do a job. Perhaps a few jobs."

"*Oui, oui*. You set Francesco Redi back on the right path!"

"Well, that was nothing really," I said with a dismissive wave.

"And you helped return Luca Giordano to his family in Napoli!"

"Anyone could have done that, of course."

"You operated on the boy and saved his life!"

"I *did* do that, didn't I?" I responded with a blush. "But look at what you've accomplished, Michelle Morel! As Dianora Murelli you became Evangelista Torricelli's right-hand woman!"

"I suppose I was."

"You were there when he invented the barometer, right?"

"I did all the data recording, *sì*."

"You translated all his work for publication?"

"Into French, *oui*."

"And you edited his book, too!"

"*Opera Geometrica, si*."

"You were there through the microscopes and telescopes and that cycloid crisis with de Roberval, too." I reached over and held Michelle's hand. "And you were there the whole time when Evangelista needed you most, Michelle. You were there in his final hours."

"It was a blessing," she said.

"For all of us," I agreed, giving her hand a squeeze before letting it go.

"As long as The Gateway was still open, there was always a job to do," said Michelle.

"My brother and I call it The Portal."

"The Portal? I considered that as a name, but I didn't like it." Michelle got up from the table, taking the cups and saucers to the wash basin. "Way too sci-fi for me."

"Well, I'm sure you'll change your mind about that," I countered.

Michelle gave me a look. "Don't tell me…I call it The Portal in the future?"

"Uh huh. Probably because of this conversation, too."

"Ah! More TT mind-bending!" Michelle said as the cups clattered onto the counter. She turned to me. "As long as we're on the subject of open portals and jobs to be done, wait here. I'll be right back."

Michelle went up the stairs. I got up from the table and made myself busy with the dishes.

I was glad she didn't notice my pained expression when she mentioned *open* portals.

When I returned from the upstairs bedroom with the folder of papers and the strongbox, Natalie was sitting at the kitchen table looking pensive. I had noticed some discomfort creep in over the last part of our conversation. Maybe all this TT stuff made her feel uneasy, too. I placed the items on the table and sat down across from her.

"There were many times over the years that I thought the job in Florence might be done – after the barometer was finished, or after the textbook was published. But with The Gateway still open for business, it led me to believe that there was always one more thing to do. I think that this might be the 'one more thing to do'." I said this pointing at the folder.

"Torricelli's calculus papers," said Natalie.

"So, you recognized the notation when I showed these papers to you in the street last week?"

"I did," Natalie nodded. "I've seen enough dx and dy notation in my math courses over the years. But that squiggly *ess* really gave it away as being calculus."

"To me, too! So when I went home, after I did a microfiche search at the UofC library, I found…"

"A microfiche search?"

"Yes, a microfiche search," I said. "You know, the plastic film that you store information on?" Natalie looked puzzled. "It's a super-fast and convenient way to access facts and data."

"I'm sure it *was*," Natalie smirked.

"Your being clued into my future is getting to be a pain, girlfriend," I said. "So, how do you collect and store information in *your* day and age, Miss Sarah Connor?"

"Well, we don't go fiche-ing, but we do use a Net. And, by the way, I saw all the Terminator movies, too, just so you know."

"There's more than one?"

"Unfortunately."

"That movie was terrifying! I would never have allowed you to see it! Did you rent the tape behind my back?"

Natalie chuckled. "We streamed it at med school on a binge day. I couldn't sleep for a week."

"You use a Net, and stream movies? I don't think I'll ever understand your generation, Natalie." I was starting to sound a lot like a mom, now.

"Oh, I think you will. It was your generation that invented all of that."

"Fair point," I conceded. I patted the folder. "Now, back to the papers. I discovered something last time I was home – something astounding." I opened the folder, spun it around toward Natalie, and pointed at the first piece of paper. "A photo of this exact page was included in a book called *The History of Mathematics*."

"Ooh, a real page turner!" she quipped.

I gave her my patented side-eye. "Anyway, this page – this exact page - wasn't in a section devoted to Evangelista Torricelli. It was from an article written in 1684 by Gottfried…"

"Leibniz," Natalie interjected.

"Right!" I exclaimed, impressed. "I guess I didn't raise a mathphobe, after all."

"*Non*, but I'm no arithma-geek, either," Natalie said. "My brother is a real square when it comes to numbers, though." Natalie caught my pun-wince. "Hey, bad puns rule over our family, Future Mom. Get used to it."

"I'm not sure I'll be able to, Future Daughter." I pointed at the page again. "Now, I'm sure you can see the problem here, *oui*?"

"*Sì*, I can. This folder of papers has to find its way to Gottfried Leibniz so he can use it to 'invent' calculus." She said the word invent with added air quotes. "I suppose he's alive as we speak?"

"Barely," I replied. "He's 15 months old at the moment."

"Well, this folder will be better off in the possession of his father and mother than it would be with Lodovico Serenai."

"You think so, I think so, and Evangelista thought so. Which is why he gave these papers to me for safekeeping." I moved the folder over and slid the strongbox to the middle of the table. "And Evangelista gave me this, too."

"Don't tell me, let me guess," said Natalie. "That's the inheritance Torricelli left you."

"It is! How did you know?"

"I read that on the Net when I was looking you up. It said that Dianora, Torricelli's servant, would inherit a sum of money after his passing."

"Your Net called me a servant? Evangelista never even called me that!"

"You can't fully trust the Net because it's full of holes," said Natalie. "By the way, do you know the chimney sweep? He's going to inherit Torricelli's shoes and socks."

"Ha! That's a good one," I chortled. "Years ago, Ceccotto told Evangelista that he thought his leather shoes were too fancy to be comfortable. Evangelista said he would leave him his socks and shoes in his will so he could find out!"

"Ha! Good one!" Natalie said. She opened the strongbox. Her eyes grew large as she gawked at the trove of gold coins. "That looks like a lot of money. Is it a lot of money?"

"It's a lot of money," I replied. "More than enough to get the math folder to Leipzig."

"In Saxony," Natalie added. "Though you almost said Germany last time, didn't you?"

"You caught that, eh?"

"I did. But I didn't catch something that makes me embarrassed…your Italian surname, Murelli! How could I have not clued in that you turned Morel into Murelli? And where did you get Dianora from?"

"Diane is my middle name."

"Huh. News to me. Anyway, *sì*, that's plenty of money for the trip, I'm sure." Natalie put the lid back on the strongbox.

"So the question is, when will we be leaving?" I asked.

"It's not going to be we," Natalie said.

"You're not coming with me?"

"That's not what I meant."

"What? You think *you're* going to Leipzig without me?"

"I do."

"*Impossibile!*" I exclaimed with arms crossed.

"Just hear me out, Michelle. You've only just recovered from a near-death experience with typhoid. You've got a wound on your arm that looks good today, but could turn ugly very soon, despite our best efforts at staving off infection. If you take a turn for the worse on what is probably going to be a bumpy, cold, horrible trip to Saxony, it may cause a catastrophic relapse."

"But...but..." I weakly protested.

"Michelle Morel, your doctor is not allowing you to travel at this time, except back home to Canada through The Gateway."

I sat there quietly for a long moment, looking down at the table. Then I looked up at Natalie. The care and concern and love expressed on her face told me everything I needed to know.

"The Portal," I finally said. "It's called The Portal."

Natalie smiled at me. "Maybe the last leg of *our* journey to the past is for me to complete, Michelle. Maybe that's why *I'm* still here. There's one way to be sure that this is the way it's supposed to be, of course."

"I go through my portal back to Canada."

"Uh huh. And if you turn around and it's still there, we'll know your job here isn't finished, and you'll come back to Florence in a second."

"And if The Portal is gone," I said, hesitantly, "then we know you're the one to finish the job. But we could check with your portal first, to see if you can come back..."

"*Non, no,* uh-uh" Natalie snapped back. Her assertiveness caught me off-guard. "We'll check your portal first. Then we can check with mine if you come back." She stood up from the table as if a final pronouncement had just been made. "Agreed?"

I looked at her with tired eyes. She was right. I was in no shape to finish the work. The job of getting the papers to Leipzig was in Natalie's hands. Her capable, confident hands.

"Agreed," I nodded.

"Great. We can leave tomorrow! Whaddya say?"

"How will Rita and Nerina take all this?" I wondered aloud.

"Those ladies?" Natalie answered. "They'll take the news like the stout-hearted Italian women that they are!"

Chapter 38

Rita and Nerina were inconsolable, bawling in each other's arms on the front stoop of the house. Lucio and Giuseppe each carried a satchel to the carriage that was waiting in the street. Michelle and I stood awkwardly in the middle of the pathway, getting ready for another round of hugs. Rita and Nerina separated from each other, wiping the tears from each other's eyes. Then they both turned to look in our direction. They burst into tears again and ran down the steps to embrace us for the third time in two minutes. At this rate, Michelle and I would easily be on our way by mid-afternoon. Tomorrow.
"There, there. All will be *tutto bene*," Michelle said to Rita, giving her a reassuring pat on the back.
"I know it will, *infine*," Rita replied, between sobs. "I just cannot believe this day has finally *arrivato*."
"Your leaving makes my heart as heavy as a plate of Rita's *gnocchi*," Nerina said, giving me a squeeze.
We all uncoupled, changed partners, and repeated the embracing operation. The men returned from the street.
"Such *amore* on display!" Lucio exclaimed.
"*Sì*, how wonderful!" agreed Giuseppe. "You know what they say…*Amor che nasce tardi, tardi more!*"
We all turned and gave Giuseppe a befuddled look.
"How does this saying fit the occasion?" Lucio asked his friend. "A love that begins late, dies late?"
"Well…" Giuseppe began, his eyes searching the heavens for help. "The love these women have for each other, it began…ah, later in their lives, and now it is…um, dying, you see."
"I do *not* see," Lucio responded with a head shake. "You would have been far better off saying, *Amore vince sempre!*"
"And how does 'Love always conquers' work any better in this situation?" asked Giuseppe indignantly.

"It does not work any better, *mio amico*," replied Lucio. Then, shaking his fingers-collected hand in the air, he said, "It just *sounds* better."

"*Sì*, it does sound better," said Nerina. We all nodded in agreement.

"Come now, young lady," said Lucio, offering his arm to me. "Your *carrozza* awaits!"

The two men escorted me and Michelle to our one-horse carriage in the street, with Rita and Nerina standing in the path. The driver opened the door and we climbed aboard after receiving a kiss on the hand from both men. We sat next to each other facing forward.

"We will miss the two of you dearly," Giuseppe said.

"But pardon us, *per favore*, if we do not look as upset as we should," said Lucio. "For the two of us have decided to use this sad occasion for other ends."

Michelle and I gave each other a confused look.

"You see, Dianora, since you have been here in Florence living with the sisters, Giuseppe and I have not felt free to disturb the arrangement of the D'ambrosio household," Lucio explained. "But now that you are leaving, Rita and Nerina have become *accessibile*, as it were."

"*Sì, accessibile!*" Giuseppe agreed. Then he lowered his voice to a whisper. "Today is the day we propose *matrimonio!*"

"What?" Michelle cried out with surprise. The two men gave her a finger-to-the-lips shush.

"We shall be making our presentation this evening over roasted lamb dinner," said Lucio.

"But not until the *dolce* of pastries, of course," Giuseppe corrected.

"Congratulations to you both," I said. "You and Nerina will make a fine couple, Giuseppe."

"As will you and Rita, Lucio," Michelle added with a smile.

"*Grazie, grazie*," the two men said.

"So, we are sad to see you go, but not so sad, if you *capisci*?" said Lucio.

"*Capiamo completamente*," said Michelle.

"*Sì*," I said. "We completely get it!"

"*Meraviglioso!*" Giuseppe shouted. Then, with enthusiasm, he exclaimed, "*Arrivederci*, young ladies!" He nodded to the driver, who click-clicked to the horse and we were on our way.

"*Arrivederci*, Dianora!" Rita cried.

"*Dio vi benedica sempre entrambi!*" Nerina yelled.

"And God bless you all, too!" Michelle called out from down the road. "And *grazie ancora* for everything!"

We waved back at the two couples that were arm-in-arm at the top of the pathway. The women were crying and waving handkerchiefs.

The men were smiling and – was I seeing that right? - giving us a thumbs-up sign.

There was no real reason for us to take a carriage to the Duomo, since it was only a fifteen-minute walk from Casa D'ambrosio. But when Giuseppe had insisted and ordered one for a 10 am pick up, Michelle accepted the offer graciously. She told me that a horse-and-buggy ride would be a grand way to say goodbye to Florence. So, after we turned onto Via Romana, Michelle gave our driver, Signor Esposito – she called him Filippo, though I could have sworn it was Tonio – directions for a roundabout trip to *Cattedrale di Santa Maria del Fiore* that would take us the better part of the morning to accomplish. Filippo approved of the circuitous route and made a sightseeing suggestion or two of his own. No doubt he was being paid by the *ora* as opposed to a flat rate.

We passed by the Palazzo Pitti first. Michelle explained that this was the grand residence of the Medici family. It sure looked impressive, with its three-story stonework and seven-times-two, arched-window façade. Michelle said it wasn't even close to the most majestic of the Medici residences, but the garden – designed by the artist Nicolò Tribolo – was *stupefacènte*. She had accompanied Evangelista Torricelli to several outdoor parties there over the years, and had spent hours wandering through the orchards on the manicured pathways. We managed to catch a glimpse of the garden as we passed by it on the street. I told Michelle that using the word *stupefacènte* to describe it was an astounding understatement.

As we crossed the Arno River on the Ponte Vecchio, and after Signor Esposito pointed out the Vasari Corridor - the private passageway built for the Medicis – I asked our driver if it would be all right if his two passengers spoke in English for part of the morning, just for the sake of practice. Our driver replied that the only thing he would find offensive is if I continued to call him by his father's name instead of Filippo. He said that with a smile.

"So, Michelle," I said in my first language, "we need to go over a few things, in case this is your last day in Florence."

"I was thinking the same thing," she replied. "You want to start?"

"Sure. First, I want to tell you what a great job you did in concealing your adventure over the years of my growing up. I never had a clue you were at time traveller . I mean, not an inkling."

"Thank you."

"You're welcome. Now, in order to make sure that I remain your clueless daughter when you get back to Canada, you're going to have to drop your middle name."

"What?"

"You're going to have to get rid of the name Diane. My mother doesn't have a middle name."

"I don't? I mean…I won't? But I *do* have a middle name."

"Well, you can't have one in *your* future. Think about it. I told you that in this whole time in Florence, I didn't clue in on the fact you turned Morel into Murelli. But if my mother's name has *Diane Morel* in it, that sounds way too much like *Dianora Murelli* for me not to notice, right?"

Michelle sighed. "It does. And I'm going to raise a girl that's clever enough to see through that, I'm guessing. So, I have to legally change my name then?"

"Yep, because you also raised a snoop. If you have a birth certificate or an old driver's license lying around with the name Diane on it, I'm going to find it and call you on it, too."

"Okay, okay, I'll get rid of my middle name," Michelle said begrudgingly. "But I may change it back when you return from *your* TT. Agreed?"

"Knock yourself out, Mom."

"Cut that out, kid," said my mother. Michelle sat quietly as we turned right onto Via Vacchereccia. Then she said, "What are my parents going to say when they find out I've dropped Diane from my name?"

"Knowing *Grand-mère* and *Grand-papa adorè* the way I do, I think they'll understand," I said, carelessly.

"Why in the world would they understand? It was *Papa adorè* that gave me the name Di…wait a minute!" Michelle turned in the carriage seat to face me. "Oh, don't tell me…my parents are time travellers, too?"

"Well, it's possible one of them is, since TTing does run in the family. You haven't told us too much about all of it yet. You're going to explain everything to me and my brother this Christmas, when I come home from med school."

"This Christmas?"

"Well, *my* this Christmas, anyway. You can't believe how much I'm looking forward to the big family get-together on Boxing Day. It's going to be a crazy TT reveal! By the way, if you can remember, I could use a new rain jacket, with a liner in it, for my present this year."

"I'll make a mental note of that for 35 years from now."

"Well, 377 years from *right* now, actually. But who's counting?"

The carriage had to stop a few times to allow people to cross the busy street in front of the Piazza della Signoria. Michelle told me that this was the political centre of Florence. I told her that my date with Francesco Redi started right over there, near the palazzo. Filippo made a 180 after another block, and we headed back south. The morning was becoming warm; Michelle and I took off our shawls and put them into our satchels.

"Oh, yeah, another thing," I said, remembering another thing. "That wine-stain birthmark under your elbow. That's got to come off."

"Come off? Come on!"

"Look, I noticed it that one morning in the bedroom, remember? I told you I'd never seen one before. Obviously, then, my mother doesn't have a wine-stain birthmark."

"Ugh. How about I just hide my elbows from you for twenty-or-so years?"

"Good luck with that," I snickered.

"Okay, so how do I have this taken care of?"

"Laser therapy."

"Lasers? Who do I go to for that, aside from Dr. McCoy on the Starship Enterprise?"

"Settle down. Dermatologists are going to start getting really good at using them in your own day and age, Mom."

"Stop with the Mom thing, you brat."

We got to the Uffizi gallery 9 minutes later. Michelle told me all about the Leonardos and Michelangelos she had the pleasure of viewing in all their original vibrancy. She swore that she could still smell the paint on Raphael's *Madonna of the Goldfinch*! Her favourite painting in the gallery was *Bacchus*. She said that she once stood admiring it for over an hour. I told her I was surprised that she didn't run into Francesco Redi there. He likes Caravaggio the painter?, she asked. No, he likes Bacchus the wine guy, I replied. Michelle gave a knowing smile.

We swung north again, picked up the Via dei Calzaiuoli, and headed for the Duomo. But instead of turning right toward the cathedral, Filippo took a scenic-tour left at Giotti's Bell Tower. Michelle and I craned our necks to get a bottom-to-top view of the tall, square building with the double-stack of missile-shaped windows. Filippo told us that he had climbed the 414 steps to the top only last month, subsequently taking two days off of work to recover. He asked us to guess the height of the tower, minus the spire. I was about to say around 90 meters, but, thankfully, Michelle chimed in first with 190 *cubiti*. Filippo lauded the estimate, and said it was close enough to 186 *cubiti* to say she was perfectly correct. He then steered our steed east and headed for the Duomo.

"Oh, yeah, one last thing," I said. "In my future, for the whole time I've been on this TT, you and Dad are in the mountains on a canoe trip."

"That's good! I like canoeing! The fresh air, the warm summer breeze... "

"It'll be the end of October."

"...the ice on the water! Why did we choose a mountain canoe trip, for crying out loud! Why couldn't we have flown to Barbados, or something?"

"No cellphone coverage in the Rockies, or so you claimed. It was a pretty clever way to go incommunicado. You must have ignored a lot of my calls, because once I found The Portal and started TTing I texted you constantly."

"Texted?"

"You'll see."

Michelle nodded. "I understand the strategy behind the mountain trip. I was out of range and couldn't be reached, so I couldn't talk to you and influence any of your decisions. Makes sense."

"You stayed out of Connor's TT as well, and that turned out to be a good decision, too, as you'll see."

Michelle was quiet for a moment. Then she said, "I'm sorry."

"For what?"

"For not returning your calls."

"That's okay," I said. "You haven't really done that yet, so there's nothing to apologize for."

"I'm asking for forgiveness in advance."

"Granted," I replied. "Just don't do it again, okay? Oh wait, I think you have to!"

We both looked at each other and burst out laughing at the inanity of it all.

Filippo pulled to a stop at the front entrance to *Cattedrale di Santa Maria del Fiore*. He opened the carriage door and helped us out after removing the bags. When he steadied Michelle by placing a hand on her right arm, she exhaled and winced with discomfort. The bandaged wound under her sleeve was still tender to the touch.

"*Arrivederci, ragazze!*" Filippo said as he climbed into the driver's seat. "If I do not see you again, may your *futuri* be bright!" He clicked once, snapped the reins, and was off.

"Come," I said to Natalie, shaking off the sudden jolt of pain from my arm. "My portal is in the back of Brunelleschi's *cupola*."

We walked around the domed section of the cathedral to the quiet alcove at the back. I placed my bag down three meters from the outside wall that was next to the door.

"Well, there it is. There's my portal."

Natalie placed her bag down and joined me in facing the stonework. "Nice location. Easy access, not too much traffic. Does your entrance go right to the ground, or do you have to step in?"

"There's a step," I answered.

"Mine, too. My brother's portal was on the side of a hill, and he had to crawl through a tunnel to get to the light!"

"You're kidding! What a pain. But, you know, it kind of adds to the adventure of it all."

"I know, right? Time travelling through a tunnel seems more appropriate, don't you think? Way more sci-fi romantic. Do you want to check and see if it's all good?"

"Yes, please," I replied.

"I'll turn around."

Natalie spun in the opposite direction. In an instant, the Shimmering Light appeared on the wall in front of me.

"All good," I said. Natalie spun back around. The Shimmering Light disappeared as quickly as it had arrived.

"It's neat how it does that," she said with a smile, looking at the blank wall.

"*For your eyes only, only for you…*" I sang.

"I don't know that one," said Natalie.

"No? Sheena Easton. James Bond movie theme?"

"Nope."

"Huh. Well, maybe I'll play it for you sometime in the future."

"You can't, or this part of our conversation will never happen," Natalie noted. "Playing that song for me in the future could affect the past right now, which could then affect the future of the future."

"Okay, stop!" I said with an upturned hand and eye roll.

"In fact, now you have to *avoid* playing that song while I'm growing up."

"Ooh, that's going to be tough. I like that song. So, that means no Sheena Easton's Greatest Hits in the CD collection. Do we still have CDs in your future.

"Oh sure," said Natalie. "But Dad has a lot more music on vinyl."

"That's where I'm headed, you know," I said, pointing to the wall. "My portal comes out in the CJSW vinyl records room at the university."

"No way! That's so cool! The men in your life are going to love knowing that! My portal came out in a little second-floor conference room at the Byre Theatre."

"*Came* out?" I queried.

"Oh...sorry, duh," Natalie stumbled. "*Come* out! I meant come out! Sheesh!" She was looking as awkward as she sounded. I shrugged it off and moved on.

"So, here's the deal, Natalie. I go through The Portal. If I come back in one second, that means we go to Leipzig together."

"Check."

"If I don't come back in one second it's because I can't come back."

"Double check."

"And that means you're going to finish the job by going to Leipzig by yourself."

"You got it, Mama."

"For that last time, stop that!" I shouted. Natalie just smiled. "Okay, are we ready to do this?"

"I suppose it's time," Natalie said with some hesitance.

"Unless we walk to your portal first and check it out, just to make sure..."

"No!" Natalie said emphatically. "I mean, no. We're here, *your* portal is fine, it's time we do this."

I stood there looking at her. Natalie was uneasy. She looked nervous. I could tell something was wrong. I hadn't seen her look this way before, but I knew I was going to see this a lot more in the years to come.

"You're keeping something from me, Natalie. What is it?"

"I'm not. Really. I'm just…"

"Why did you say, 'My portal *came* out', past tense? Why did you say, '*Your* portal is fine', with a stress on the word 'your'? The implication is that there's something wrong with *your* own portal!"

"I'm sure it's nothing…"

"What's nothing? Natalie, what's going on?"

"It's probably just a temporary glitch…"

"A glitch? With The Portal? Natalie?..."

Her chin quivered as she tried to get the words out. "My portal… it's not there in the room at the Palazzo Medici anymore."

"WHAT?"

"It's gone," she said quietly, her head bowed.

I took Natalie by the arms. "What do you mean, 'It's gone'? Where is it?"

"I don't know. I looked everywhere. It's just disappeared."

"That can't be. Were other people around? Maybe they were looking in your direction when you were there!"

"No. No one was around to see me."

"Maybe if you went back to the room and…"

"The room's not even there. It's gone, too."

"Natalie, this can't be! Maybe if we…"

Natalie took my hands into hers and looked into my eyes. "Michelle. Listen to me. I know it looks bad, but I'm convinced there's a good reason for why this is all happening. When I discovered who you really were, when you were in your fever coma, I ran to the Palazzo Medici with the full intention of going back to the future to get you medicine. That's when The Portal disappeared and I went into panic mode."

"That must have been terrifying to go through."

"I have to admit, it wasn't pleasant. I felt pressure like I'd never felt before. But I stopped time to calm myself and…"

"You stopped time?"

"It's something I learned at med school. From my friends. I pictured a frozen clock, forgot about the future, and centred my thoughts on the 'now'. Then I let all the things I had learned about handling stressful situations come to the fore: I visualized, I remembered all the things I had practiced, and then I followed the advice of someone I respect very much…I committed the outcome of the situation to someone other than myself."

"You prayed."

"I prayed. And I received the clarity of thought that I needed to go forward, knowing that everything would work together for good."

I paused for a moment to contemplate. "That was good advice."

"That was the advice you gave me one of the last times we talked on the phone…" Natalie said with a smile, squeezing my hands. "…Mom."

I looked into the eyes of this young woman - this intelligent, sensitive, faithful young woman - and marvelled at her maturity and wisdom. She was teaching me so much.

We hugged each other long and hard. Time seemed to freeze.

"You're not that worried about your portal, then, are you?" I asked as we unlocked our embrace.

"No. I'm convinced I'll be able to return when the job is done and it's *time* to go home. I just know it, somehow."

"But…what if…"

"No, buts and ifs, Mom. I'll come home. I've got a big Immunology exam the day after I get back. You don't think I'll be allowed to miss that, do you?"

"No," I said, wiping a tear and smiling. "No, I suppose you couldn't get away with that."

"It's time for you to go, Michelle," said Natalie, turning her head toward the stone wall.

"Yes, I suppose it is," I replied. I picked up my satchel and handed it to her. "The calculus papers are in the folder on the bottom."

"Right."

"And the money box is on top of that. There's plenty to get you to Leipzig and back."

"Yes, I know."

"And I brought an extra scarf and wool stockings for your trip, in case it gets cold and…"

"Mom, I know! Chill!"

"Well, I might not be seeing you again, Natalie." I fixed that statement quickly. "For a while, I mean."

"For a while," Natalie said. She gave me a kiss on the cheek and then turned around. The Portal glistened into existence before me on the stone wall.

"Okay, I'm going to go now," I said. "I'll see you in one second, maybe."

"If not, you'll see me on my birth day!" she answered back as I stepped toward the light. "Literally!"

"I love you, Natalie."

"I love you too, Mom. Everything is going to be *rad*, you'll see."

I took a first step into The Portal. I glanced back to see Natalie my daughter, with satchels in hand, facing the opposite way towards an unknown future. The tears welled up in my eyes. As I took the next step into the Shimmering Light, I heard words come to me from the past…

My… father's… name… is… John…

I waited for thirty seconds before turning around, though only one was really necessary. Michelle was gone. She wasn't coming back.

I walked over to the cathedral alcove. I put the bags down on the ground and sat on the stone steps.

And I began to cry.

Michelle waited for thirty seconds before turning around, though she knew it wasn't necessary. The Portal was gone. She wasn't going back.

She dropped to her knees in the vinyl records room.

And she began to cry.

Michelle looked up when she heard the door open. "Are you all right, Michelle?" It was Jay.

"I...I'm fine," she said as she rose to her feet. She looked at Jay and saw the concern in his face. Then she shook her head.

"No. No, I'm not all right, Jay. I'm not." Michelle burst into tears again and moved toward him. He wrapped his arms around her and held her tight as she cried on his shoulder. She cried for a long time.

"Thank you," Michelle said as she moved away from the embrace. "Thank you for being here for me, Jay."

"When you just left a minute ago, when we were outside the studio, I could sense there was something bothering you. So I came after you."

Michelle's mind was racing. She felt such a strong pull to him, yet she now knew that it could never work, that there was no future for Michelle with someone named Jay. She placed a hand on his chest. "Oh, Jay. I can't..."

"Michelle," Jay interrupted gently. "Call me by my real name. Call me John."

Michelle pulled back, stunned. "Your...your name is John?"

"Yes. Jay is a nickname that Chase gave me years ago." John reached over and wiped a tear from Michelle's cheek. "He was adamant that I should have one. John is a short name already, I told him. But Chase said he could shorten it even more."

"So...so you're not Jay, J-A-Y?"

"No, I'm J, as in the letter J. For John. John Campbell."

The smile on Michelle's face grew until it reached both ears. Then she started to laugh. She threw her arms around John's neck.

"What's so funny?" John asked. He began to laugh, as well.

Just then, Michelle saw someone at the vinyl room door. It was Ken. A clean shaven, non-goatee sporting, vinyl-record carrying Ken.

"Is everything all right?" he asked the couple.

"It's perfect!" Michelle exclaimed. She stared into the eyes of the man who was holding her in his arms.

"I know now that it's all going to work out, John Campbell," she said. Michelle put her hand behind John's head, pulled him close, and gave him a long, heartfelt kiss. Then she placed a hand on his cheek and looked into his eyes.

"Everything is going to be *rad*, you'll see."

Chapter 39

I took a right turn off of Via de' Pucci and headed south on Via de' Martelli on my way to the Palazzo Medici. I wasn't about to embark on my big trip without one more check on the availability of The Portal. Michelle's satchel was a bit heavier than mine, what with the metal box of money weighing it down and all. I had to switch hands only once on the short walk to the palace. My heart was a lot heavier than the bag.

The garden door of the Palazzo Medici was open. I walked down the path, went through the short hallway, and entered the courtyard. There was no one around. Ladders and buckets and drop cloths were scattered about. The statues at either end of the floor were covered up. There was dust everywhere. The office that housed The Portal was still missing, as were the other rooms next to it on the first floor. They had been gutted for the renovation. I set my satchels down and had a seat on a bench in the middle of the courtyard. Resting my elbows on my knees, with my head in my hands, I stared straight ahead and tried to come up with a plan for the next part of my journey. I must have been hyper-focused in my contemplating, because the voice that came from behind startled me.

"*Mi scusi, signorina*, can I help you?"

I leapt up from the bench and abruptly turned. Standing before me was a sharply-dressed man wearing a stylish black hat that sported a long, blue feather. His upturned black moustache and triangle goatee gave away his identity in two heartbeats.

"Oh, Grand…Signor Excellency of…Duke," I stammered. My impromptu curtsey was so off-balance, I must have looked like an interpretive dancer in need of knee replacement surgery.

"Oh, you do not have to be so formal, Natalia Campo Bella! My friends just call me Ferdinando II de' Medici, Grand Duke of Tuscany, you know." He gave me a sly wink.

"You…you remember my name, Signor Ferdinando?" I gulped.

"But of course! You are the young lady that ignited my interest in the science of surgery! Do you know what I have done since I last saw you, Natalia? I have attended a blood-letting and a stone removal! Oh, and the two grisly amputations yesterday were such *divertimento*!"

My head was reeling: from the Grand Duke remembering my name, and from the words 'amputation' and 'fun' being used in the same sentence.

"I...I am very pleased for you, *signore*."

"Not nearly as pleased as I have been to have met *you, signorina*! How could I forget the young woman who helped introduce the *redicut* surgical procedure to the world!"

So, it was Ferdinando II de' Medici that was responsible for adding the word *redicut* to the medical lexicon. Go figure.

"Now, what brings you here today?" he asked. I hesitated in answering. Fortunately, Ferdinando filled the conversation gap. "Do you know someone here at the *palazzo*?"

"Why, *sì*. I know some of the people that work here. Andrea, Antonio, and Alfredo..."

"Ah, they were three sad souls, oh-me-oh-my!" Ferdinando chuckled. "No *cervelli*, no *cuore*, and much too *timida*! But never mind, that is all in the past."

"They say you are a great problem solver, Your Highness. A real *mago*."

"So nice to hear! Just like Osmano in the opera *L'Ormindo*, then! Have you seen it yet, Natalia?"

"*No*, but my friend Marianna has seen it."

"You should go! I just saw it again last evening!" The Grand Duke waved his hands excitedly in the air. "The captain of the army saves the day by his fast thinking. He is the hero of the opera! The *librettista*, Giovanni Faustini, wrote the role of Osmano based on me, you know?"

"I did not know that!" I said, impressed.

"*Sì*. Such a great honour, do you not think?"

"For the opera, Signor Ferdinando!" I said with a wink.

"Ah, Natalia! Well spoken, *mio caro!*" The Grand Duke of Tuscany then looked down at my satchels. "Are you going somewhere, Natalia?"

"*Sì, signore*. I am going on a trip. To Leipzig."

"Leipzig! Dear girl, why on earth would you go to Leipzig at this time of year?"

"I have to make a delivery, *signore*. A very important one."

"But this trip will take forever! And there are no passenger carriages through *Le Alpi* now. Only *traffico commerciale* would be venturing through the mountains, if it has not stopped already!"

"I see," I said in a dejected tone that was not lost on The Duke. We stood quietly for a quarter of a minute, Ferdinando scratching his goatee. Then he pointed his finger at the ceiling.

"I have it!" he exclaimed. "I have once again solved the problem! Let us sit and I shall explain it all to you!"

We sat on the bench and Ferdinando II de' Medici, Grand Duke of Tuscany outlined his plan. I was to come back to the palazzo later that afternoon where a carriage would be waiting for me. It would take me to Venice in two days. I would be given a letter of transit as well – stamped with The Grand Duke's seal - that would secure a ride on a commercial carriage for me from Venice all the way to Leipzig in Saxony. There would be many stops along the way, he noted. The trip would easily take an entire week, and that was with good weather all the way.

"Do you need money for lodging?" he asked.

"I have money," I said, pointing to the closest satchel. "A box of gold coins. Can I show you?" Ferdinando nodded. I opened the satchel and took out the strongbox. I removed the lid. Ferdinando picked up a coin.

"You certainly have enough money," he said with a smile. "Three of these will easily get you to Leipzig, with a pocket of change to spare!" He placed the coin back in the strongbox. I set the box back in the satchel.

"I will not be here for your departure this afternoon," Ferdinando said as he rose from the bench. "Vittoria has committed us to an appearance at the Uffizi. Apparently, Jacopo Vignali has done another portrait of me." He let out an exaggerated sigh. "I do hope it is better than the last one he did. I came across far too *severo*. Do I look stern to you, Natalia?"

"*No*, Signor Ferdinando. Not at all."

"How about now?" Ferdinando squinted his eyes and did something with his lip. He looked more disappointed than stern, like a squirrel that had forgotten the location of his acorn stash.

"A bit more *severo*, *sì*," I offered.

"I shall try to remember this face for later, when another disappointing portrait is unveiled before me. Speaking of art, have you had the pleasure of seeing the fresco in our chapel?" He pointed down the hall.

"The Journey of the Magi? *No*, not yet. But I hear it is *spettacolare!*"

"It is! But the whole area is under construction at the moment, so I cannot show it to you. The fresco is all covered up! Perhaps you shall see it in the near future!"

"I would very much like to, Grand Duke!" I replied.

"*Splendido!*" Ferdinando exclaimed, pointing a finger in the air. "Now, you must excuse me Natalia, I must be going." He kissed my hand and made his way to the courtyard exit.

"Oh, Signor Ferdinando!" I called out. He stopped and turned.

"*Sì?*"

"I think that Francesco Redi would be embarrassed to have the term *redicut* gain popularity."

"Not to worry, Natalia! I shall strike it from my memory this instant!" He turned to leave.

"Oh…and Grand Duke?"

"*Sì?*" he said, turning again.

"Do you remember that floral shirt you wore at my hearing? I think it was truly *favoloso!*"

"You did?" Ferdinando said with a huge grin. "Well, I shall tell Vittoria to have a dozen more made!" He turned to go and got only three more steps.

"Oh, and…"

"*Sì?*" he said, with a note of impatience and that squirrely face he was working on.

"*Grazie* for everything. You solved all my *problemi*! You are indeed a *mago*!"

Ferdinando II de' Medici, Grand Duke of Tuscany, gave me a big smile.

"The Wizard of Osmano, at your service!"

He took a deep bow and then he was off.

I knocked on the door of the stone house with the red roof. Cecilia Redi opened it. She grabbed me by the arm, yanked me into the vestibule, and gave me such a *grande abbraccio* that I was struggling for air.

"It is so lovely to see you, Natalia! Let me take those bags!" She snatched the satchels from my hand. "Where are you going with these? Have you come to stay with us? Are you and Ciccio going to…"

"I have come to say goodbye, Signora Redi."

"What?" said Cecilia, dropping the bags onto the floor.

"You are leaving us?" said Dr. Gregorio Redi, coming down the stairs. "Where are you going. Back to school in Scotland?"

"I am leaving for Leipzig this afternoon."

"Leipzig!" the Redis exclaimed in unison.

"*Sì*, Leipzig," I replied.

"Where the barbarians came from? That Leipzig?" Obviously, Cecilia was not impressed.

"The weather cannot be good for travelling," said Dr. Gregorio. "Who would take you on such a journey?"

"It is being arranged by the Grand Duke as we speak," I answered. "First to Venice, and then on to Leipzig."

"Duke Ferdinando is arranging your trip?" Cecilia was perplexed. "Is he banishing you to Saxony, then?"

"*No, no*, nothing like that," I said, supressing a smile. "I have a job that I must do there. I have been given a *responsabilità*. Something that I must perform."

"Something for Torricelli?" asked Dr. Gregorio. "Something that Signorina Murelli cannot fulfill at this time?"

"It is exactly that," I answered truthfully.

The three of us stood there in silence for a long moment. Cecilia then shook her head.

"Ciccio will be heartbroken," she said.

"May I see him, *per favore*?"

"*Sì*, of course," said Dr. Gregorio. He pointed down the hallway. "He is in his Room of Specimens."

I left the satchels in the vestibule with the Redis, walked down the hall, and knocked on the last door.

"*Entrare*," came the response.

I opened the door and stepped inside. Francesco was working at the far end of the room with his back turned. There were surgical tools scattered about the lab benches. I caught a whiff of a foul odor that was spreading throughout the room.

Francesco turned. His eyes grew wide with surprise.

"Natalia! Natalia! How wonderful that you are here!" he cried out. He dashed over, kissed my hand, and led me to his work station. "Come, I want you to see this."

There were over a dozen glass jars in the middle of the lab bench. A pile of 10x10 cm cheesecloths sat to the right. To the left, a slab of awful-looking meat sat at the ready.

"I am devising an investigation to see if living organisms arise from nonliving material. I wish to disprove *spontaneo generazione*!"

"Oh my!" I said, excitedly. "What is your experimental design?"

"Well, as you can see, I have collected many glass jars. I will place a piece of rotting meat in each. Some jars will be left uncovered, some I will cork-seal, and the rest I will close up with cheesecloth. Do you *comprendere* what I am doing here?"

"I think so. One set of jars is open to the air, one set is closed, and one set provides limited access."

"*Precisamente*! Limited access! The air can still pass through, but the flies cannot!"

"The flies?" I asked, though I knew exactly where he was going with his explanation.

"*Sì*! The flies! I believe them to be the true culprits of the crime and the future disprovers of *spontaneo generazione* all in one!"

"How so?"

Francesco cleared his throat. "As I am sure you are aware, Natalia, the current school of thought is that fly maggots arise directly from rotting material. I find this a preposterous *proposizione*! Maggots come from eggs laid by flies. I have seen this countless times in my studies! Everything here comes from eggs, Natalia!" Francesco waved his hand around his Room of Specimens. "Even Angelo the Asp!" He pointed at the snake in the terrarium.

"Maybe even you and me!" I offered.

"Ha! This is a funny joke that you make, Natalia! Human beings coming from eggs! How silly!"

Well, I suppose embryology *was* a few centuries away yet. Baby steps.

"Anyway, I think I have come up with a foolproof way to show that maggots come from fly eggs and not directly from rotting meat. In the open jar, I place a piece of meat..." He did this. "In another jar, I place a piece of meat and close it with this..." He placed a cork lid on top of the jar. "And in yet another jar, I place some meat and cover it with this..." On went the cheesecloth. "Now, can you see the purpose in all of this, Natalia?"

"I believe so. In the first jar, you have provided the flies free access to the meat. So there should be eggs laid and maggots produced on the meat. In the second jar, the flies have no access to the meat, so there will be no maggots produced at all."

"*Sì, sì*!" said Francesco. "And the third jar?"

"Perhaps some of your colleagues will claim that the sealed jar has no air for the maggots to breathe, so they cannot form. The jar with the cheesecloth allows for air but prevents flies from landing on the meat."

"This is exactly the idea! It is like you have read my mind!"

No, I just read the results of your wonderful experiment in the history books, Francesco Redi.

"It makes perfectly good sense, Francesco," I said instead, resisting the temptation to give away the big surprise: there *would* be maggots formed at the third jar…but on top of the cheesecloth itself! Bang! *Spontaneo generazione* bites the *polvere*!

"I am so happy you think so!" Francesco exclaimed. "As I said before, your undying belief in my abilities has spurred me on to greater heights, Natalia! This calls for a celebration! I shall open a bottle of 1642 Antinori Chianti! The grapes that year were particularly robust in…"

"Francesco, I need to tell you something," I interjected.

"What is it, dear Natalia?"

"I came here today…" I took a nervous breath. "I came to say goodbye."

"Goodbye?" he said with a stunned look on his face. "You…you are leaving?"

"*Sì*, Francesco."

"You are leaving…me?"

"It is not like that at all," I said. "I am not from here. It was only a matter of time before I left for home."

"But I thought…I thought, perhaps, that you would change your mind. That you would fall in love with Florence. That you would fall in love with…"

"Francesco," I said, taking his hand in mine. "I cannot stay here. I cannot be with…"

"There is someone else, is there not?" he said quietly.

"*No, no*, it is just…" Then a picture emerged in my mind. A picture of a young man smiling at me across the kitchen table, his eyes the colour of the water off our favourite Scottish beach.

I bowed my head. "*Sì*, Francesco, there *is* someone else. I am so sorry."

"Oh, Natalia, I have always known it. From our first meeting I knew that you were pledged to another. I could feel it." He squeezed my hand. "Who is this most fortunate man?"

"His name is Mark."

"Marco. This is a fine name. Is he a fine man, Natalia?"

"He is, Francesco."

"This is *buono*. I am *contento* for you, *mia cara*." He placed his finger under my chin and lifted my down-turned head. "I truly am *contento* for you."

"*Grazie, mio amico*," I replied. "*Grazie mille*."

"*Grazie mille*? Ha! I like this very much!" he said, trying to sound chipper. "Before you go, Natalia, I wish to give you something."

Francesco walked over to his desk and removed a piece of paper from the drawer.

"I wrote this for you. I hope you like it."

I took the paper and began reading aloud.

In Tuscan fields where vines entwine
Fair Natalia, divine, does shine.
Her eyes, like stars in evening's dance
Ignite a flame, a sweet romance.

Beneath the moon, her laughter spills
A symphony; passion instilled.
Her name, a melody in the air
Whispers love, beyond compare.

In softest hues of twilight's grace,
Natalia, a vision to embrace.
Her voice, the softest gentle stream
Flows through my heart, a tender dream.

With every gaze, a vintage wine,
Intoxicating, pure and fine.
In Tuscan nights, where dreams align,
Her cherished love, a sweet design.

I lowered the paper and looked at Francesco Redi.

"It is lovely, Ciccio. I will treasure this forever." I gave him a kiss on the cheek.

"I liked it, too," he said with a smile. "Though it could have used more wine, do you not think?"

"*No, no.* I like it the way it is!"

"Not in the poem itself, Natalia. In the *writing* of the poem!"

We both had a nice laugh over that one.

It was a tearful goodbye on the steps of the Redi house. Dr. Gregorio gave me a big hug and another thank you for assisting him with Luca Giordano's surgery. Cecilia embraced me, gave me a kiss on each cheek, and embraced me again. She stuffed two shawls and a blanket in my satchel. For the mountains, she said. Francesco and I, having already said our goodbyes, had one more hug and an exchange of heartfelt smiles. They waved to me all the way down the street, until I disappeared from sight.

In a few minutes, I arrived at my last stop before heading off to the Palazzo Medici. I walked through the front door of the *Ospedale degli Innocenti* and spotted Maria amongst the children playing in the central courtyard. She noticed me right away and scurried over.

"Signorina Natalia! It is so nice to see you again!" she said. "What brings you to the orphanage?"

"It is a pleasure to see you, too, Maria. I have come to speak with Signor Bartolomeo di…di…"

"di Antonio Canigiani?"

"*Sì*, that is him. Is he here?"

"*Sì, sì.* Come with me, *per favore.*"

Maria led me to an office just past the chapel. It was vacant.

"Ah, he must be in the *dormitorio. Un momento,* I will fetch him for you!"

I sat down in the chair across from the desk and opened Michelle's satchel. I took out the metal strongbox, opened it, and took out three gold coins. I placed the coins in my satchel. Then I put the lid back on the box and placed it on the desk.

Signor Bartolomeo entered two minutes later. I stood to greet him.

"Signor Bartolomeo," I smiled, extending my arm for a handshake.

"Ah, Signorina Natalia Campo Bella! The pleasure is mine!" He took my offered hand and kissed it instead. "What brings you here today?"

"I have come to give you something today," I said. I slid the strongbox toward him on the desk.

"Ah, have you come with a *trattare*, then?" he said, leaning forward.

"Something like that," I replied.

Bartolomeo lifted the lid. His eyes grew wide. His lips quivered. Then he said, "Signorina Natalia! This is too good to be true! But how…?"

"This is a gift to the orphanage from the estate of Evangelista Torricelli."

"It is a *bellissimo* gift, a *generoso* gift! I do not know what to say accept *grazie*." He looked at me with equal parts of gratitude and bewilderment.

"That is all that needs to be said, *signore*!" I said as I got up from the chair.

"Perhaps we will place this in trust," he said, rising from his seat.

"To be used to keep the orphanage as beautiful in the future as it is today," I offered.

"It is as good as done!" he replied with a big grin.

I made my way to the door.

"*Arrivederci*, Signor Bartolomeo di Antonio…ah…um…"

"Oh, it is *non importa*," he said. "Even my wife stops it short at Barto! *Arrivederci*, Dottore Campo Bella!"

When I got to the Palazzo Medici, there was an enormous two-horse carriage parked across from the main entrance. I recognized the driver right away.

"*Buon pomeriggio*, Filippo!" I called out.

"You are very close, *signorina*. It is Tonio at your service today!"

Darn those Esposito brothers! You were always on thin ice if you thought you could tell them apart!

"Let me take your bags, Signorina Natalia." he said, whisking them away. He stowed them on top of the carriage.

"Oh, Tonio, I may need those bags with me inside the carriage. They have clothes that I may need later to keep warm."

"I do not think so," said Tonio, dropping down from the driver's seat and opening the carriage door. "The Grand Duke has seen to your comfort."

To describe the inside of the carriage as luxurious would have been a gross understatement. The red velvet upholstery on the seats and walls was warm and inviting. There were wool blankets and over-stuffed pillows stacked in the corner of the rear bench. Two wooden boxes wrapped in blankets were sitting in the middle of the bench. A delicious aroma wafted out the door.

"The Grand Duchess insisted you have a hot dinner this evening: quail, I believe, with *asparago, pane,* and *torta di mele* for your *dolce*! A bottle of Chianti to wash it all down, too!"

"This is so lovely," I gushed. "I have never even met the Grand Duchess."

"A fine woman!" Tonio exclaimed. "Her financial advice to me has been life-changing! She makes me save everything that comes my way!"

I entered the carriage, Tonio closed the door, and in half a minute we were off.

I opened the shutter and looked out the glass window of the carriage as we passed by the Palazzo Medici, the Duomo, the Palazzo Vecchio, the Arno River, and all the other marvels that made up Florence in 1647.

I was going to miss this wonderful place.

Chapter 40

To say that the next two days of my life were a struggle would be like saying it's a small challenge to teach a cat to fetch. The royal carriage turned out to be a grand deception: the plush interior may have said 'The finest 1647 craftsmanship', but the solid wooden wheels and lack of suspension on the exterior cried out 'What did you expect for 1647!' Those reality survival shows on TV should think about including this type of travel in their Ultimate Endurance episode. It felt like I had made an intimate relationship with every pothole in Europe. The impression they left on me had to be massaged out at the end of every travel day.

The first leg from Florence to Rioveggio was the smoothest ride of the entire trip, though that wasn't saying much. But the fall colours of the Tuscan countryside more than made up for the discomfort, and the stops at the villages of Vaglia and Montecarelli were a welcome refreshment. We got into Rioveggio in the region of Romagna quite late in the day. We stayed overnight at Tonio's cousin's house. Marcella fed us well – *prosciutto*, *pane*, and pickled peppers - and I *dormito*'d like a log in the children's room.

The next day, in the late morning, we passed through Bologna. Tonio pointed out some highlights: the Asinelli and Garisenda towers; the University of Bologna that was founded in the 11th century; and the Fountain of Neptune at the Piazza Maggiore, which I got a good look at because of a traffic jam caused by a herd of sheep. The Italian carriage drivers were not impressed and let the shepherd, and even the sheep, know about it. The rest of the trip to Padua was uneventful but tiring, and by the time we got to the house of Tonio's second cousin by marriage, I ate quickly and then hit the hay. Literally, since my bed was in the loft of the barn.

Going from Padua to Venice took longer than expected due to some bridge maintenance at the River Brenta, but Tonio made good time on smooth-ish roads after that, and we got to our destination in Venice, just past St. Mark's Square, by early afternoon. The *Arsenale di Venezia* was a lively shipyard, with wagons and carts and carriages being loaded and unloaded from boats of all sizes docked at the harbor. Tonio parked under the west tower at the main gate.

"Wait here, Signorina Natalia. I shall be but a *momento*."

I wanted to get out of the carriage and have a stretch, but the decided absence of other females at the docks made me feel that I should just sit tight for that *momento*. Tonio returned a few minutes later accompanied by a tall, scruffy-looking man wearing a flat cap with a small brim. Tonio opened the carriage door and I stepped out.

"Signorina, I would like to introduce you to my good friend, Tobias Draisaitl. Tobias, this is Natalia Campo Bella of Florence, a personal friend of none other than The Grand Duke of Tuscany."

"It is a pleasure to meet you, *signorina*," Tobias Draisaitl said, with a deep bow. He spoke Italian, but with a decided German accent.

"It is nice to meet you, Signor Draisaitl," I replied with a head nod. "Or should I say, Herr Draisaitl?"

"Ha, ha! Herr Draisaitl is *correctto*, but certainly not *necessario*! Call me Tobias, *per favore*!"

"It is so very *fortunato* that Tobias is here today, *signorina*," said Tonio. "He is travelling back to Saxony this very day!"

"Well, as I mentioned to you, Tonio," said Tobias, "I do not have room in the *carro* for any passengers."

I took the opportunity to hand Tobias Draisaitl my letter of transit from The Grand Duke of Tuscany. He broke the seal, opened the letter, and read it carefully.

"But I would be honoured to escort *you* to Leipzig, Signorina Natalia!" he said, placing the letter in his coat pocket. "I have plenty of room for you in my *carro*, you know! The printer did not have his books ready for transport, so there is extra space. I hope you do not object to sitting alongside spices and salt for the entire trip north."

"An *aromatico* trip would be lovely!" I replied.

"Then come along, we will be leaving *subito*!"

Tonio carried my bags across the *Arsenale* and within a minute we stopped in front of a long, canvas-covered contraption, with big wheels in the back and big horses in the front. It appeared that the word '*carro*' in Italian not only meant 'carriage' but 'weather-beaten wagon' as well.

"It is far more *comodo* than it looks," said Tobias. "Behind my driver's seat there is a bench with blankets and pillows! We have water, dried meats and fruits, too! All the comforts of home!" He took my bags and placed them in the wagon. "Shall we go?"

I turned to Tonio. "Thank you for everything, Signor Esposito."

"My goal was to keep you well, *signorina*! And now, I pass you off to the trustworthy Tobias Draisaitl! *Arrivederci,* Natalia!"

I clambered aboard the wagon and took my seat on the bench behind the driver. I noticed the long-barreled musket lying underneath his seat.

"For our protection," Tobias said, noticing my noticing. "I have not had to use it often in my travels, but I would not pass up the opportunity to take a shot."

From Venice, it was a half-day backtrack to Padua and then on to Verona. Tobias was a fine travelling companion, which was a good thing considering the time we would be spending together. We arranged a daily travel schedule for the trip: we would leave at the crack of dawn each day after having breakfast at our overnight stop; we would have lessons in German - or, more specifically, *deutsche sprache* – starring Tobias Draisaitl as The Instructor (*Der Lehrer*), and Natalia Campo Bella as The Clueless Pupil (*Der Ahnungslose Student*); lunch; quiet time after lunch; mid-afternoon stop and stretch while attending to the needs of Wiener and Schnitz (no kidding), our two horses; find the next overnight stop; repeat as necessary until we pass through the Grimmaische Tor, the city gate of Leipzig.

There wasn't much to see in Verona since it was almost dark when we got there. I wasn't as exhausted as I thought I would be; the roads were good and the *carro* was surprisingly roadworthy. The inn we found in the city centre was nice and the food was even nicer. I got a good night's rest after a fairly pleasant day of travelling.

Before we left Verona the next morning at sunrise, Tobias took a slight detour before heading north on the main highway.

"Do you see that pink house on the left, Natalia?" Tobias asked, pointing.

"The one with the brown roof?"

"*Sì!* Do you know who lived there almost 100 years ago? Signorina Capulet!"

"I am sorry, I do not know her."

"Her first name was Juliet!"

"Juliet Capulet!" I exclaimed. "The love of Romeo?"

"*Sì, sì!* So you have read the play, *Romeo and Juliet*, then?

"I learned it in school," I replied.

"As did I!" Tobias exclaimed. "In *deutsche sprache*, we say *Romeo und Julia*. It is a marvelous play, *no*?

"*Sì*," I agreed. "I have even seen it performed on stage!" And in the movies. And I've got the soundtrack to *West Side Story* on my phone at home, etcetera, etcetera.

"There is the famous balcony on the second floor. Do you see it?"

"*Sì*, I do! But...O Romeo, Romeo! Wherefore art thou, Romeo?" I said that last part in English.

"Ha! I did not understand a word, yet I know what you said! *O Romeo, Romeo! Warum bist du Romeo*? Ha, ha!"

"I can see why the people in Verona have made this to be the Capulet house. It looks the part!"

"Dear girl, the Capulets still live there to this day," said Tobias, as he turned the *carro* back onto the main road.

Just as the sun rose in the cloudless sky, by late morning we were climbing, too. The rolling, forested foothills of the Alps were in full display with their vibrant red, orange, yellow, and even purple fall colours. The vineyards and agricultural lands were dormant, taking a well-deserved break before the arrival of another busy spring. There were no more cities now, and soon the towns that we passed through every few miles would give way to terraced villages that dotted the mountainscape. We got as far as Trento that day, and that was good enough, Tobias maintained. I was four days into my road trip and I was still in Italy.

I was expecting our next day to be one long ascent in the Alps, but it was relatively flat terrain all the way to Bolzano. That's right, Bolzano. Still in Italy! The highway ran along the Adige River through the Adige Valley. The route reminded me of the Crowsnest Pass through the Rocky Mountains back home in Alberta; mountains all around as you snaked your way in between. You could tell the lack of climbing was agreeable to Wiener and Schnitz; they were spirited and even frisky the whole day through.

The morning *deutsche sprache* lessons were going very well. Tobias was a good instructor and I told him so, though he said that anyone watching would be even more impressed with his student. Well look at me! As the Germans would say…*Achtung baby*! Or would they? In any case, I was learning the language. I could say all the major fruits and vegetables by our second lesson - my favourite being *blumenkohlblätterkraut* (cauliflower leaves), which is one of the crazy, mash-up words that the German language is great at creating – and I was moving on to simple words and expressions by lesson three. I had a collection of phrases that I wanted to memorize, and Tobias taught me how to say things like, "Good day, sir!" ("*Guten Tag, Herr!*"), "Can you tell me where to find a bathroom?" ("*Können Sie mir sagen, wo ich das Badezimmer finden kann?*"), "I have something to give you" ("*Ich muss dir etwas geben*"), and "Your baby is adorable!" ("*Dein Baby ist bezaubernd!*"). When I tried to piece together a new sentence from it all, *Dein Baby ist in bezaubernd Badezimmer*, Tobias just laughed and said, '*Das passt schon so!*', which I think means, 'Close enough for jazz."

I had a disappointing setback that afternoon as I rummaged through my satchel. I couldn't find the charcoal sketch of me that Luca Giordano had drawn, or the first poem that Francesco Redi had written for me. I checked the bag three times, and the other satchel twice. Nothing. I knew they couldn't go back home with me through The Portal, whenever that would be, but it still irked me that I had most likely left them on the dresser at Casa D'ambrosio.

The next day was a really cold one, and I had just enough layers on to stay warm. Tobias wore a fur coat in the morning and kept it on until dusk, when we reached our destination. I tried not to drape myself in blankets too early in the day, but by noon I was wrapped in a wool cocoon. Our cold meat and bread lunch was even colder today. I kept the water jug under the blankets with me, stirring it every half hour so it wouldn't freeze. It was frigid at the top of the Brenner Pass, but our hearts were soon warmed by the lights of a city as we crested the last hill. Innsbruck! Tyrol! As in, Austria! It finally felt like progress had been made in the journey.

On Sunday morning, Tobias informed me that today was going to be a long one, going from Innsbruck to Munich in Bavaria. I told him that as long as this day did not exceed 24 hours, that would be acceptable. He just gave a smirk and clicked the ponies into gear.

The sun was at our back for most of the morning, so it was a bit cool. We had to head west to go north, Tobias told me; following the Inn River was the only way through the rest of the Alps that would be easy on the horses and their passengers. And sure enough, there was little elevation change up until the noon hour. By the time we hit the halfway point of the day's journey, we had left the mountains behind and were loping over the rolling hills of Bavaria.

I spent the quiet time after lunch reading a good book. My little New Testament went with me everywhere now, finding a home in the pocket of my peasant dress. Sometimes I forgot it was even there, it was so unobtrusive. But when I rediscovered it after we had left Verona, I set up an afternoon reading schedule. First, I would read a portion aloud as requested by Tobias. He would say something like, 'Read the story of the blind man!', so I would turn to John 9, or, 'Find the one about the man in the sycamore tree!', and I would flip through Luke until I found the name Zacchaeus in chapter 19. Those readings took up a good part of the afternoon because I had to translate from English – this New Testament was the New Translation by J.N. Darby – into Italian, our common language. That wasn't easy if you were trying to do it right. I gained a whole new appreciation for the work of bible translators on this trip! After our reading time together, I would pick up where I had left off with my memory verses, which I had decided to turn into a memory chapter after we left Trento. I was up to verse 15 by the time we got to Holzkirchen and was able to recite Ephesians 1: 1-18 all the way through, with only one hiccup, by the time we got to Tobias' great uncle's place in the borough of Obergiesing in Munich that evening.

Tobias thought I should practice my *deutsche* in an immersive environment, so after I exchanged pleasantries with his extended family via translation he said that I was on my own for the rest of the evening. It was tough slogging, what with all the *na ja*'s, *wahnsinn*'s and *genau*'s being bandied about. But I thought, *oh well* this *craziness* was *exactly* what I needed. When Tobias' uncle asked me if I had *handschuhs* to keep me warm on the trip, I had to think for a moment before responding. I'd never been asked if I wore 'handshoes' before. Tobias helped me out by twiddling his fingers. Ah, *handschuhs* were gloves! That made sense. Kinda. At dinner, when Tobias' great aunt asked if I was going to see *Thomaskirche* when I got to Leipzig, I told her I would *tue mein bestes* to see it. She nodded – that was a good sign! – and said I should be *früh* to *vermeiden* a *warteschlange*. Um…I should be *early* so as to *avoid* a…*waitsnake*? *Waitsnake*? Oh, *warte* a minute! A queue! Ha! A long line-up is a 'wait snake'! I was starting to love this language.

After dinner, Tobias and his great uncle went to the barn and did some wheel repairs on the carriage late into the evening. I was fortunate enough to get to bed early.

The ride from Munich to Nuremberg was a picturesque journey through the charming villages of the Holy Roman Empire. Bavarian cottages, with their identical timber frames and thatched roofs, dotted the countryside. Their colourful window shutters – no rainbow hue left unrepresented - provided the accent for each dwelling. The rolling hills, the babbling brooks, the cultivated fields – it was all very *bukolisch*. Every stone bridge we passed over was rock solid, naturally, and built to last. German engineering for the win! The weather was beautiful, the trip uneventful, and the overnight stay at Tobias' cousin's *haus* was delightful. A great day.

When we left in the morning, Tobias asked me my opinion on today's travel plan. We were two days from Leipzig, he said: Would I like to split the rest of the trip evenly in distance, making two *gemütlich* days, or go as far as possible today – not so *gemütlich* - and arrive in Leipzig earlier the next day? I asked Tobias if he had a preference. He said that it might be better to stay the night with his younger first cousin twice removed in Eisenberg than his older second cousin once removed in Bad Berneck. Bad Berneck didn't sound like a good idea, so I said I was all for making this a not-so-serene travel day.

The day was long, yes, but it ended up rather rewarding. My *deutsche* lessons were in the semi-advanced stage now, and my instructor told me I was ready to *anpacken* any conversation in Leipzig with relative ease. It made me feel good to know I was ready to tackle some Saxons on their home field! In the afternoon, I finished memorizing the last verses of Ephesians 1, and recited the whole chapter to Tobias in English. He said he was impressed, and that it *sounded* wonderful, but he would have been even more *beeindruckt* if he knew what I was saying. I was going to tell him that J.N. Darby had a really good German translation of the New Testament that he would enjoy, but then I remembered that it wouldn't be written for another 200 years. So I refrained from the *bibelversion* advice for the time being.

It was dark when we got to Eisenberg, so I didn't see much of the city except for all the candlelight coming from the houses. Tobias' younger first cousin twice removed was a hoot. He played a mean harpsichord, and his children could sing in three-part harmony like little *éngels*! They taught me how to do an *allemande*, where you link arms and spin around the dance floor. It was an old-fashioned höedown in the old berg tonight, I tell you what!

The clock tower chimed for 12 noon when we pulled into the town square in Leipzig the next day. Tobias helped me out of the wagon, pulled out my two bags from the under the driver's seat and placed them on the ground.

"*Danke* for bringing me here to Leipzig *sano e salvo*," I said to him, accenting my German with a sprinkle of Italian.

"My dear, the pleasure was mine," Tobias answered with a bow. I reached into my pocket and took out the three gold coins.

"I would like to pay you with these…"

"Oh, no, signorina! I cannot accept this from you!"

"But I insist!" I countered, pushing the coins into his hand.

"*Nein, nein*! You do not understand!" Tobias exclaimed, reaching into his coat pocket. He gave me the letter of transit from The Grand Duke of Tuscany. I read it over.

"Now do you see?" he asked.

"I do," I replied, handing back the paper.

"Ferdinando de' Medici has made it very plain, has he not? I am to deliver you to Leipzig and have this document notarized by an official in the town hall to verify that you have arrived safely. Upon my return to Florence, I shall receive a *bella soma* of money for my trouble. And if he hears that I have taken money from you, he will have my head!"

"Actually, it says you will no longer be able to ply your trade in the *regione* of Tuscany."

"In the world of the Italian aristocracy this is mere s*emantica*, my dear girl. Now, shall we?" Tobias picked up my bags and we walked up the steps into the town hall.

You could tell the clerk in the office of the Bürgermeister had done this type of service before. He examined the letter, took oaths from us to verify our identities, and sped off to his higher-up to get a signature and an official stamp. When he returned, he placed a new wax seal on the folded letter and exchanged it with Tobias for a silver coin.

"Signorina Natalia, once again, it was my pleasure to assist you. Have a lovely stay in Leipzig! I pray that all your goals will be accomplished!" I gave him a big hug.

"*Arrivederci* and *danke*," I said to him. I pressed two gold coins into his hand. "Not for you. One each for Weiner and Schnitz!"

He smiled and pocketed the pieces. Then, with the tip of his flat cap, Tobias Draisaitl exited the town hall as I waved goodbye.

I turned around to the clerk and took a deep breath. It was time to put my *deutsche* into action.

"*Entschuldigen sie bitte,*" I said, excusing myself. "*Ich suche einen mann namens* Leibniz."

"There are many in Leipzig with this name," he answered somewhat dismissively. "You must be more *spezifisch*."

I thought for a moment. "He has a *sohn* that is close to one year *alt*, named Gottfried. Would that *helfen*?"

The clerk nodded and left. He returned in two minutes with an oversized, leather-bound book. He opened it to the middle and began a search, working backwards and using a ruler to skim the pages. In less than a minute he stopped, bent to have a closer look, and tapped his finger on the page.

"Here he is, Gottfried Wilhelm von Leibniz. You were quite *falsh, Fräulein*. The boy is sixteen months *alt*."

"I did say 'close' to one year *alt*."

"Close would have been one month on either side of the birthdate. You were four months *defizient* in your *schätzung*. If you had said 'around', it would have been more helpful. In the future, try and be more *exakt* in your *sprache*."

I suppressed an eye roll to remain *freundlich*. I looked at the clerk. He looked back at me.

"Well?" I asked him. "Can you tell me the *namen* of Herr Leibniz?"

"*Ja*, but this is not what you asked me. You asked if I knew a man named Leibniz with a one-year-*alt sohn*. And now I do."

I couldn't suppress the sigh. "May I have the *namen* and the *adresse* of Herr Leibniz, *bitte*?"

"Friedrich Leibniz is the *namen* of the *mann* you are looking for. The name of his *frau* is Catharina. He lives at *Rotes Haus* on Grimmaische Strasse, across from the University of Leipzig."

"*Danke*," I said, committing Red House on "Grim-i-sha" Street to memory, "even though your *informationen* was *über* what I asked for."

"Excuse me?" he said, affronted.

"I did not ask for the name of his *frau*. If I wanted this, I would have said as much. In the future, try and be less helpful. Though I am not sure that is possible."

I gave the clerk the good old Canadian side-eye, picked up my satchels, and was out the door in a *seckunde*.

The walk to Red House on Grimmaische Strasse took only 15 minutes, and I had to ask for directions only twice. It wasn't the house that was red, just the roof tiles. I had a mind to go back to the town hall and correct that clerk, but I let bygones be *vergangenheit*.

I knocked on the door, and a man wearing a blue jacket with matching knee-length breeches and white stockings answered.

"*Kann ich Ihnen helfen, junge dame?*" the man asked.

"*Ja*, you can help me if your name is Herr Friedrich Leibniz, the father of Gottfried Wilhelm," I replied.

"Ah…*ja*, this is *mein name*, and the *name* of *mein sohn*," Friedrich Leibniz said with a curious look.

I let out a sigh of relief and smiled. "*Guten tag, Herr*. My name is Natalie, and I have come from Italy."

"From *Italien*? Dear girl, *komm* into the house, *bitte!*"

Friedrich led me from the vestibule to an adjacent room where two comfortable-looking chairs on an area rug faced each other, separated by a table. The chairs were surrounded by bookshelves on all four sides, the only interruption to these being the window and door. There was barely a spot to park an extra text on the shelves. There are public libraries back home that would envy the volume of volumes in this den.

"*Setz dich bitte*," said Friedrich, motioning for me to take the near seat. I placed my satchels on the floor and sat down.

"*Danke* for your hospitality, Herr Leibniz. Your collection of *bücher* is very, um…*gross*?" I said this hoping that my word choice in *deutsche* sounded more appropriate than it did in English.

"*Danke*. It is a rather large collection, now. Most of these *bücher* are in Latin. They help me in my research and teaching at the university. Yet they are all *sekundär* to this, of course." He patted a bible that was sitting open on the table.

"Are you a *professor?*"

"*Ja bin ich.* I am a *professor* of Moral Philosophy, and I have been recently appointed as Dean of *Philosophie*. Have you come to Leipzig to work or to study?"

"Neither, *mein Herr*…"

"Call me Friedrich, *bitte.*"

"This is difficult for me to, ah, *erklären*, Friedrich," I erklären-ed.

"Because *deutsche* is not your first *sprache*?"

"*Ja*, and because I know this will sound *unglaublich.*"

"What could you say that would be so unbelievable, Fräulein Natalie?"

"I have come to deliver a folder of papers to you. But they are for your *sohn*, Gottfried."

"For my *sohn*? But he is only *ein baby.*"

I opened the closest satchel and removed the folder. I handed it to him.

"These are for Gottfried Leibniz," I said. "To be read by him when he is older. When he is *reif.*"

"When he is ready?" asked Friedrich, dumbfounded. "What does this mean?" He looked at the first page of notes and shook his head. "Truly, what does this *alle* mean?" I could tell he was befuddled by all the mathematical symbols.

"I cannot say, Herr Leibniz," I replied with an apologetic look. "I am only a messenger."

Friedrich Leibniz slowly lowered the papers onto his lap. His face became pale. I could see his hands beginning to shake.

"Friedrich?" I said.

He raised his head and looked at me. Then he reached over to the open bible on the table, turned it around to face me, and placed his finger down on the right-side page. I read the verse he was pointing to out loud.

"*Be not forgetful to entertain strangers, for thereby have some entertained angels unawares.*"

"*Hebräer, Kapitel* 13, *Vers* 2" he said, identifying the verse. "I have had this portion on my *herz* this past week. I have not been able *schüttle* it from my mind. I knew I was being told something, but what? And now, here you are!"

"But I am not an *engel*," I said.

"An *engel* is but a messenger, Natalie. *Und* a messenger delivers a message." He held up the folder. "Is this a message?"

"For Gottfried, *ja*." I said.

"Then I accept this message on his behalf and will give it to him when he is *reif*." Friedrich Leibniz stood up, went to the far bookcase and inserted the folder at the very end of the shelf.

"I do not know what all this means, but I believe in a Guiding Hand, Natalie. Do you?"

"I do, Friedrich. It has led me here to you, and it will lead me home again, I know." I got up from my seat. "Now, I must be going."

"But you only just arrived!" he exclaimed. "Must you leave?"

"I am sorry, Friedrich, but I must. I need to find my way home now."

I picked up the satchels and started for the front door. As Friedrich opened it for me, we were surprised by two people on the stoop.

"Oh!" said the lady who was holding a baby.

"Ah, Catharina!" Friedrich exclaimed. "You are home! I would like you to meet Fräulein Natalie. She is from *Italien*!"

We exchanged *guten tag*s. Friedrich reached out and lifted up his son, whose hands were outstretched toward him.

"Natalie, I would like to introduce you to Gottfried Wilhelm Leibniz. Gottfried, this is *die lady* who gave you a *wunderbar* gift today."

"*Ciao*, Gottfried!" I said, shaking the baby's tiny hand. His smile produced three more on the adults present. "The gift was from a lovely man from Florence. His name was Evangelista Torricelli."

"Do we know this man?" Catharina asked her husband.

"*Nein, meine liebste*, but I have a feeling that we will." Friedrich smiled at me.

"You can *count* on it!" I said, as I made my way down the path.

I put my satchels down and waved *auf wiedersehen* when I reached the end of the block. The Leibniz family waved back.

I picked up my bags, walked around the corner, and was soon out of sight.

"Oh, James, it's so good to have you home. If only for a short visit!"

"It's lovely to be back, Mum," said James, pouring the boiling water into the teapot. "It was nice of you to order up some lovely weather. I was expecting to be greeted by some good, old clouds and rain."

"Oh, stop! How much better can London be at this time of year?"

"Not much better, of course. But in Darjeeling last month, it was positively stifling! I don't think I've ever been so hot in my life!" James placed the teapot and cups on the kitchen table and sat down across from his mother.

"Brooke Bond certainly has kept you busy, sending you off to everywhere and sundry. Are you not getting tired of all the travel?"

"On the contrary, Mum, I'm finding it to be rather rewarding. India was an experience, let me tell you. And I think that this tea blend we've been working on is going to be wizard!" James poured warm milk into the cups.

"Wizard?"

"You know, as in top-hole, bang on…" James' mother still looked perplexed. "The bee's knees?"

"Ah, the bee's knees! It's really that good, is it?"

"Let's find out, shall we?" James said as he poured the tea. "You're the first person in the United Kingdom to try it." The two of them picked up their cups, blew on the top, and took a sip.

"I like this very much, James. Very much, indeed. I think it's very bold."

"It's made from only the tips of the tea plant," James noted. "I think the astringency is just enough to peek through the sweetness in the milk. Did you pick up the malty notes?

"I'm not sure," his mother replied after another sip. "But it does have a richness to it."

"Those are malty notes!" James took another sip and placed his cup in the saucer. "So what's new here in St Andrews, Mum?"

"Let's see...there's a new bakehouse on the high street, the Cunningham's bought a new car - well, not so new seeing that it's a year old – a 1929 Austin Seven. Oh, and you know that old cow byre on Abbey Street? It was bought by the local Play Club!"

"They're going to turn that old barn into a theatre?"

"They are! Charles Marford wants to call it the Byre Theatre!"

"How very cheeky of him!" said James. "Oh, I want to show you what I got for Dad." James reached into his pocket and took out a small, leather-bound book. He passed it to his mother.

"Oh, James! Wherever did you find it?"

"I bought it from a bookseller in Calcutta on the day we set sail. It's just the New Testament."

"Yes, and it's a JND! Your father will be so very pleased. He was just saying that he would like a small bible for his office at the university. This will do nicely!"

As she flipped the pages, a twice-folded piece of paper fell from the back of the book. James picked it up from the table and unfolded it once. He read the message, boldly written by a sure hand.

"Well, that seems very appropriate, don't you think, Mum?" He handed her the paper.

"It's like it was written just for him!" his mother said. She folded the paper and returned it to the back of the book. "What a lovely surprise that will be!"

She handed the New Testament back to her son and took another sip of tea.

"Does Brooke Bond have a name for this new blend yet?" she asked him.

"They want to sell it as a tea to be drunk before a meal. But naming it Pre-Digestive Tea isn't exactly market-friendly. So they're going with the fancy French equivalent, Pre-Gestee."

"Pre-Gestee?" said James's mother, unimpressed. She took the last sip from her cup and placed it into the saucer. "I'll just end up calling it PG Tips, I'm sure."

Chapter 41

I spent hours wandering around Leipzig carrying my satchels. I didn't know what else to do. What was I going to do now? I had one gold coin left. I suppose it was enough money to get me back to Florence. But what would I do there when I returned? Wait for the renos to be done at the Palazzo Medici and hope that The Portal pops back up? What if it didn't? I suppose I could get a job with Rita and Nerina and keep up the search for the way to get home. Maybe I could get a job here in Saxony for a while. I could work in a bakery. I'm pretty good at baking stuff. I could audition by making a German version of *Schiacciata Fiorentina*. Maybe call it *Leipzigtorte*, or something. Or I could help out in a hospital somewhere and put my training to use. Well, maybe that's not such a good idea; I don't need to introduce any more medical procedures to 1647. The 'redicut' was bad enough. No one in the 17th century needs a 'nataliaplasty' just yet. At least I don't think they do.

After walking past the market square for the second time and drawing some suspicious looks from the vendors, I turned left on Thomasgrasse. At the end of the block, an understated tower with a small gold spire caught my attention. Its black dome and white plaster walls stood out against the blue sky. That must be *Thomaskirche*, the church that Tobias' great aunt told me about. I walked up the street to the front door. There was no one else around. Where was the *warteschlange*? I was hoping to a see my first waitsnake! I shrugged, climbed the steps, and went inside.

I passed through the darkened apse and stepped around the central pillar of the archway. I stood slack-jawed at the impressive sight before me. The arched nave of the cathedral had a honeycomb pattern of red-painted support beams that were in stark contrast to the white ceiling and white columns. In the centre section, four long rows of ornate, wooden pews faced another four rows across the aisle. The raised pulpit at the far end had gold-painted beams and colourful stained glass adorning a semicircular recess. I turned around and walked backwards five paces to get a better look at the church organ above my head. The polished silvery pipes that stood tall in the detailed wooden casework were simply breathtaking. I set my bags down in the aisle and sat in the first pew seat at the rear. I was suddenly very tired.

Absently looking at the pew across the aisle brought up a mental-picture of the 'church-pew' bench at Jannettas Gelateria in St Andrews. A wave of sadness passed over me as my memory took me back to my table of friends and our Anatomy Lab celebration. I closed my eyes and I saw Holly crunching her cone, telling me how I was clutch like Bobby Nystrom in the lab room. And there was Marianna, licking her Vanilla and Tayberry gelato, and saying, no, I was more 'Bobby Osmano clutch'. And Mark…oh Mark. It felt so great when he told me how impressed he was with me that day. He always makes me feel great.

I looked at the pew across from me again and I saw Filip plonking himself down on the bench in the gelateria. I closed my eyes again as I recalled our conversation about Dorothy Gale: about a miraculous occurrence; about ending up in a foreign place; about being a catalyst to help new friends find their hidden potential; about getting to return home when the job was done…'Dorothy Gale isn't a lost little girl! She's a woman on a mission!'…'We're all Dorothys, charged with the responsibility to help our friends fulfill their dreams and aspirations!'…'Her energy…her selfless actions…Dorothy's grace under pressure'…'The reward will be there in the end'… 'That reward was always with her'… 'Always with her…' Always…'

I opened my eyes and looked around the cathedral. Then I reached into my dress pocket and pulled out the little New Testament. I turned to Romans 8:28, read it, and took a deep breath. There was no doubt about it. This whole circumstance would work together for good, because there was a purpose behind it. I just needed to have confidence and faith in the process.

Just then, something fell to the floor from the back of the book. I picked up the twice-folded paper and opened it up carefully because it had that yellow look of being very old. The writing on the paper wasn't faded though. It looked to have been written boldly by a sure hand. I read the message. It felt like it had been written just for me.

I unfolded the paper one more time to see the whole page and I read the words. I began to tremble and my heart raced.

It *had* been written just for me.

I placed the New Testament back in my pocket. I stood up from the pew with the unfolded paper in my hand. The wood-floor aisle leading to the front of the cathedral was interrupted by brass-coloured square plates every three metres. The plates glistened from the window light. I left the satchels on the floor and followed the yellow-brick aisle toward the pulpit. I turned right at the pulpit stairs and came to a stop when the bricks did - at a door that was slightly ajar. I pushed on the door and it creaked open. I stepped inside.

The 4x4m room was illuminated by a semicircular window that was fixed into a stone wall on the right. The wall on the left had an off-white, textured-plaster appearance. There were two straight-back wooden chairs and one fancier chair with armrests set around a rectangular table that was occupying the middle of the room.

It couldn't be. Could it?

The light from the window was shining on a painting that was hanging from a peg in the plastered wall. I walked over and looked at it. It was a depiction of a young nobleman on horseback with an entourage of serious-looking old men in tow. There were deer jumping, horses prancing, and birds flying this way and that.

It was The Journey of the Magi, the painting that hung in the office that had housed The Portal.

I looked around the room again. There was no mistaking it. This was the same office that had disappeared in the Palazzo Medici in Florence. And now it had reappeared in Thomaskirche in Leipzig.

I looked back at the painting and I heard the words, 'Perhaps you shall see it in the near future!' rise up from my memory. The words that The Grand Duke said to me when I last saw him at the Palazzo Medici. I now saw a familiar face in the young nobleman in the painting - it was the face of a Medici. The face of Ferdinando II de' Medici, and he was smiling at me from the picture. He knew I'd see the painting soon enough. I smiled back at the young nobleman, the magi on the horse. He was truly the Wizard of Osmano.

I walked around the table to the back wall of the room. I pressed the unfolded paper on the stone wall. It began to glow. I let go of it and stepped back. The paper held its place and began to sparkle. Then it dissolved into the stone wall and spread out as an opaque film. A Shimmering Light emerged from the fuzzy opening. It was the most beautiful light I had ever seen.

The Portal had returned. And just like Dorothy, I always had the power with me. I just had to learn it for myself.

Now I was going home.

Natalie stepped into the quiet room at the Byre Theatre and let out an enormous sigh of relief. She patted herself up and down, just to make sure everything was all right. And it was. She was back in Scotland, back in the 21st century. She was home.

Emotions began to well up inside her in the darkened room, but they were supressed in an instant as the sound of shuffling feet grew louder outside the door. Before Natalie could think about what to do, the doorknob turned and the door creaked open. A hand reached out and flipped the light switch. Two figures in hoodies stood in the doorway, wearing sunglasses. Indoors. On a cloudy day.

The figure nearest to Natalie – a woman - took off her glasses and removed her hood.

"Mom!" Natalie cried out. She ran over and dove into Michelle Morel's arms.

"Oh, Natalie!" said Michelle. "My girl!"

They hugged for a long time. Like they hadn't seen each other for hundreds of years.

"But…but how did you know when I was coming back?" asked Natalie, wiping away tears after they had unlocked their embrace.

"On the day I left you at the Duomo in Florence, you told me not to worry," Michelle replied, stroking her daughter's hair. "You said you had to come back because you had an Immunology exam the next day. And last week on the phone, you told me the exam was on the 27th. Today is October 26."

"I accused you of fishing for information, didn't I?" said Natalie sniffing and smiling all at once.

"Your mother's good at that," said John Campbell, taking off his sunglasses. "Much better than fishing for actual fish."

"The day I came out of the fever coma, you told me you were curious to know who Jay was," said Michelle. She turned to her husband and held out her hand. "Natalia Campo Bella, I would like you to meet Jay."

Natalie gave her dad a hug. He kissed the top of his daughter's head.

"I had to give up a pretty good nickname because of you, kiddo," John said.

"Was it worth it?" asked Natalie as the hug came to an end.

"I'm still debating that."

John Campbell got a punch in the arm from the med student. Then he said, "Come on. Let's go get a coffee at that BrewCo place and we can have a ridiculously convoluted time-travel conversation." He picked up Natalie's bookbag from the table and the three Campbells made their way to the door.

"So, how was the canoe trip?" Natalie asked.

"Oh, we abandoned that trip the morning we video chatted with you from the mountains," Michelle replied.

"Canoeing at the end of October!" John exclaimed as he closed the door behind him. "Who's bright idea was that, anyway?"

The two women pointed at each other, then broke out into laughter.

As they walked down the hallway together to the sound of a Bobby McFerrin tune coming from downstairs, Natalie stopped.

"Wait just a second, okay?"

She dashed back to the quiet room and opened the door. The Portal was no longer there.

"*Tout bon?*" asked Michelle.

Her TTing daughter closed the quiet room door and returned to her parents once again.

"*Sì, sì,*" Natalia answered. "*È tutto bellissimo, amica mia.*"

Chapter 42

The Boxing Day crowd at the Campbell house was abuzz with chatter. Transtemporal Trekking chatter. All the TTers in the family showed up first to the get-together as per tradition, before the non-TT relatives on the Campbell side and the not-as-of-yet TT relatives of the Morel clan. There was excitement in the air with the news that two more family members had recently come back from their journeys to the past.

Connor was called upon to give a summary of his trip to Paris in 1771, which was documented in short-hand by Uncle François who was designated by the family as Chief Record Keeper. No computers, no recordings on phones, just notes on paper to be transcribed later into the family Transtemporal Trekking Journal. Uncle Laurent asked some pointed questions regarding time discrepancies, he being the Chronologist Designate for the group. When Connor got to the part in his story where the time lapse on the France-side of The Portal went from less than one second to one whole week, it created a stir in the audience and drew an audible gasp from Aunt Camille. Uncle Laurent, sporting a huge grin on his face, turned to his brother, Alexandre, who was sitting on the sofa. Alexandre nodded, pointed his finger at his brother, and gave him a wink; their 'PET' theory of Portal Elasticity of Time now had some solid evidence. Connor concluded his presentation in 20 minutes, and the floor was opened for more questions. Auntie Amandine asked Connor if he had a 'stepping on a butterfly' moment that could have altered the future. She needed to know this since she was the Aberrations and Incongruities Officer. He answered that aside from the letter he wrote to Éleuthère Dupont, he couldn't think of one. Oh, and maybe he had invented the word *restaurant*, too, he admitted sheepishly.

Then it was Natalie's turn. Her 1647 story was very well received by the family until she got to the part where Dianora's true identity was revealed. Uncle François dropped his pen, Uncle Laurent dropped his jaw, and Auntie Camille dropped another audible gasp.

The room erupted with chatter that was equal parts incredulity and indignance. Why did Michelle not explain this in her own TT story back in 1989, when she recounted it for the family? How could she have kept this us from us? But cooler heads prevailed after Michelle's father, Charles - her *Papa adorè* – addressed the relatives under the theme of 'And what would *you* have done under similar circumstances?' That got everyone thinking, and soon there was general agreement that Michelle's past story omission concerning the true identity of Natalia was not only wise but necessary. The Chief Record-Keeper and the Chronologist Designate both shrugged their shoulders in acceptance; it was a good story, but it was going to be a nightmare to chronicle for posterity. When Natalie was asked by the Aberrations and Incongruities department about any potential glitches from the past, she asked her brother Connor about the word 'redicut'. Connor looked puzzled and said that he'd never heard that word before. Natalie looked at Auntie Amandine and said that there were no glitches to report.

After Natalie was finished her talk, she and Connor received an ovation from the audience and lots of hugs and kisses. Everyone went back to eating and socializing. Natalie's *Schiacciata Fiorentina* was a big hit on the buffet table.

Natalie heard a knock on her bedroom door. Before she could say, 'Come in', Connor came in.

"Hey, I found you!" he said. "Whatcha doin' upstairs? Hiding?" He plonked himself down on the bed next to his sister.

"No, nothing like that. I just needed to wrap one more present." A bag decorated with Snoopy in a Santa hat lying on his Christmas-lighted doghouse sat next to her.

"For me? Aw, you shouldn't have!"

"I didn't. You got yours yesterday. This is for someone *special*."

"Ouch!" said Connor, with hand over heart. "Anyway, you did a nice job with your story down there. Even Great Uncle Claude was smiling, though I think he was asleep."

"Major victory for me, for sure. I liked hearing your story again, bro. But the description of your carriage ride to the north brought back some painful memories." Natalie massaged her backside.

"We both had a bad experiences with German engineering, didn't we?"

"At least by 1771 they had suspension on those buggies! You got off lucky, Connor!"

Her brother chuckled. "We need to go downstairs, Nat. Grand-Papa Charles wants to tell the two of us about his TT before the rest of the non-TTers arrive later. He seemed pretty excited."

"He's been waiting a long time to share it with us, that's for sure. Has Dad come back from the airport yet?"

"Not yet. Who's he picking up again?"

"He just said 'a particular someone'."

"Oh, that narrows it down, doesn't it?" Connor smirked.

There was a knock at the door. Before Natalie could say, 'Who is it?', her mother came in, a present bag dangling from her wrist and two mugs of tea in her hands.

"Another present for me?" said Connor. "Oh, Mom, you shouldn't have!"

"I didn't. This is for someone *special*, son." She placed the bag and mugs on the desk.

"Strike two," Connor replied, getting up from the bed. "And three's a crowd, so I'm off to find my Grand-papa."

"He's watching the Canada/Slovakia World Junior hockey game in the living room," Michelle informed her son.

"Cool. Hey, is Uncle Chase calling the game?"

"As always," said Michelle.

"Are he and Auntie Gilliana coming here for their annual visit next month?" Natalie asked.

"They wouldn't miss it for all the tea in Colombia," Michelle said with a sly grin. Natalie and Connor gave each other a confused look, not getting their mother's inside joke.

Connor turned to leave, then turned around again. "Oh, one thing, Mom."

"What's that, son?"

"This came to me when I was retelling my TT to the family just now. Remember when I came clean about my time travelling to you and Dad at our family meeting?"

"Sure," Mom replied. "Our conversation in the den, with Natalie on the laptop from Scotland."

"Right. You and Dad knew all along I'd been time travelling, because Natalie told you about my adventure when you two were together in 1647. So your surprised reaction to my story that evening was just a big put-on!"

"Well, we had to act like we didn't really know you were TTing to keep your sister in the dark. If we would have said to you, 'Oh, yes, Connor, we knew all along that you were time travelling', you and Natalie would have wondered how we got the information."

"Yeah, okay. But once Natalie was offline, you and Dad could have told me the whole story about her TT adventure, couldn't you?"

"Well, yes…"

"But you didn't."

"Well, no…"

"Because you think I would have been bad at keeping the secret from my own sister."

Michelle didn't say a word.

"You think I would have eventually told her everything I knew and would compromise her TT."

Michelle just looked at her son.

"You think that I'm still not old enough yet to handle the fallout from all of this time-travel business."

Crickets.

"You know, Mom," said Connor, a smile emerging on his face, "you're probably right." He gave the two women a wink and left for the party.

"That was actually a pretty mature assessment from someone who's not old enough yet," Natalie said to her mother.

"The truth is, Dad and I didn't even trust *ourselves* not to compromise your TT, which is why we left on our canoe trip. I'll remind your brother of that, later." Michelle passed a mug of tea to her daughter.

"PG Tips, I hope," said Natalie, taking a sip.

"*Bien sûr*!" Michelle replied.

"Thanks for the present yesterday," said Natalie. "I can't believe you remembered that I needed a rain jacket with a liner."

"Well, you only told me that 35 years ago," Michelle smiled.

"Technically, it was 377 years ago, but when it comes to time travel, who's counting. I need to tell you, though, Mom…that jacket is not exactly stylish."

"I bought it on sale," said Michelle. "Back in 1995."

Natalie laughed. "Speaking of back in the day, that dermatologist you saw did a great job taking off your wine-stain birthmark."

"She did, didn't she," said Michelle, looking at her elbow. "Isn't it odd that I was left with the floor-nail scar on my arm, though? I really thought that when I went through The Portal for the last time it would have disappeared like my typhoid symptoms did."

"Well, at least you got to bring back a souvenir. That can't be said for every TTer."

"So true!" Michelle replied with a chuckle.

"I talked to Grand-mère Juliette," said Natalie. "She's going to sit down with us after dinner and show all of the pictures of you from when you were growing up. And your wedding pictures, too! So they weren't all lost in a house move, were they?"

"My mother would never have let that happen, of course," said Michelle. "But we couldn't let you see pictures of me when I was a teenager, now could we?"

"I probably would have seen through your Dianora persona pretty quickly if I had seen pics of you as a young woman. Oh yeah, and Dianora's colour was brown." Natalie touched her mother's hair. "How long have you been dying it?"

"Ever since my wedding."

"And the wearing of coloured contact lenses?"

"Not for very long. I think my eyes turned a bit bluer from hazel as I got older. Does that sound right, doctor?"

"It's a pretty rare occurrence," Natalie answered. "But I don't think I would have made a direct connection between my mom's and Dianora's eye colour, anyway."

"I wasn't going to take that chance, though. You're a very perceptive young lady, Natalia Campo Bella." Michelle stroked her daughter's cheek. "*Merci, encore,* my darling girl. For everything."

"Aw, Mom," Natalie said, bashfully.

"Well, I've waited a very long time to be able to thank you for your act of love in Florence."

"Your typhoid vaccine did the heavy lifting," Natalie noted. "I was just spotting for you with some supplemental care."

"We can agree to disagree about that, *ma chérie.* You saved my life, plain and simple." Michelle kissed her daughter's forehead.

"Well, I saved *my* life, too, of course," said Natalie. "There's a wacky, time-travel self-preservation aspect to our story."

"I try not to think about it."

"If you never made it home from Florence…"

"Don't go there…"

"…then there's no Natalie…"

"Stop it…"

"…and no, Connor. John Campbell marries a civil engineer…"

"Oh, no, not a *civil* major!"

"…and two of their kids are named Konrad and Natalka."

"Do they time travel?"

"Only in their minds."

The women laughed and smacked each other on the leg.

"Well, everything worked out in our timeline, anyway," said Michelle. "I got home from Florence, I married my university sweetheart, and we had two annoyingly delightful children."

"And speaking of all things working out in our timeline," added Natalie, pointing at the calculus book on the bedroom shelf. "Leibniz became the Father of Calculus and credits the notes in his father's library and Evangelista Torricelli for the inspiration!"

"A job well done, Natalia."

"A job well done, Dianora."

Michelle and Natalie clinked their tea mugs and took sips.

"Oh, I almost forgot," Michelle said as she reached over to the desk, picked up the present bag, and passed it to Natalie. "A little something else. For Natalia."

Natalie opened the bag and removed the framed picture. Her mouth started moving, but nothing was coming out.

"Oh, my…Mom…but…how?" she managed to say. She gazed in wonder at the charcoal sketch on the yellowed paper. It was a drawing of a young woman in left profile, looking rather melancholy, with just the slightest upturn on the corner of her mouth. It was the sketch of Natalia drawn by Luca Giordano.

"You left it on the dresser in our room at Casa D'ambrosio."

"Um, yeah, I know. But it couldn't come back through The Portal. So how did you get this?"

"When I spotted it on the dresser, I was going to take it, but I knew it couldn't come back with either of us. So before I came down stairs the day we left Rita and Nerina's, I made a slight detour and went up to the attic."

"You put this in the attic?" said Natalie in amazement. "And it survived all these years?"

"Along with Casa D'ambrosio!"

"But that doesn't explain…"

"Your father and I were there last week. We didn't go on any canoe trip, as you know. After we video chatted with you on the phone, we left the mountains in a hurry. And before we flew to St Andrews, we made a stop in Florence. There was an open house at Casa D'ambrosio because it's up for sale!"

"So you went upstairs to the attic and found this?"

"Pretty much where I had left them!"

"Them?"

"Look at the back."

Natalie turned the frame around and read the first stanza of a poem that was attached to the back.

> *In Tuscan lands, where Bacchus reigns,*
> *A lady fair, Natalia by name,*
> *Her smile, a burst of sunshine's rays*
> *A flower in bloom, her beauty aflame.*

Her eyes welled up. She looked at her mother and saw the smile of her best friend from long ago. Natalie threw her arms around her.

"The first poem Ciccio wrote for me! This is the best present ever. Thank you, Dianora. Thank you so much."

"*Prego, mia amica, Natalia. Mia più vecchia e cara amica.*"

After the hug was spent, Natalie reached over, picked up the Snoopy present bag, and gave it to her mother.

"This is for you."

Michelle opened the bag and lifted out a 6"x 9" picture frame. She gazed at the black and white, high-resolution photo.

"Is this a crater?" she asked.

"Uh huh. It's a lunar impact crater on the far side of the Moon. Those are its coordinates." Natalie pointed to the 4.6°S 28.5°E on the bottom right of the picture. "The name of the crater is *Torricelli*."

A sad smile came over Michelle's face. She traced her finger around the rim of the teardrop-shaped crater, and wiped away a droplet from her cheek.

"*Grazie, Natalia.*"

"*Prego*, my dear old friend."

Just then, the doorbell rang.

"Oh! That will be your father!" said Michelle.

"Why would he ring the doorbell?" asked a confused Natalie.

"To make sure that *you* were in the room when he comes in with our guest! *Allez!*"

Michelle grabbed Natalie's hand and whisked her down the stairs to the vestibule. All the TT guest conversations in the house were put on hold. Michelle opened the door, and her husband John stepped in from the cold carrying a small suitcase.

"It isn't a fit night out for man nor beast!" he said, stamping his boots on the doormat. "Here's the man, and here's the…well…here's Mark!"

John Campbell stepped aside and Mark Munroe entered the house.

"A Blithe Yule to all!" he announced in his Scottish brogue.

"Mark!" Natalie exclaimed. "Mark!"

Natalie ran to the door and jumped into Mark's arms. They hugged each other for 14 seconds before unlocking their embrace. They looked at each other awkwardly, realizing in the moment that all eyes in the living room and kitchen area were fixed on them. Connor broke the silence.

"Ahem," he remarked, pointing at the mistletoe hanging from the light fixture over their heads. Natalie put her hand behind Mark's head, pulled him close, and gave him a long, heartfelt kiss. Long enough that everyone in the living room and kitchen took a turn at feeling awkward. When the kiss was over, the audience applauded and returned to chatting, but the TT conversations were now officially ended.

"That was a surprise," Mark said to Natalie. "A very welcome one, at that."

"One surprise deserves another," Natalie replied. "I can't believe you're here!"

"I asked your dad if I could fly in on Boxing Day to see you and meet your family."

"I told him I'd put a big X on top of the house for a landing target, just like I do with Santa," said John, hanging his coat on a peg. "And you know what? He laughed at my humour!" John patted Mark on the back. "I'm going to like this boy, I tells ya!"

"Come in, Mark," said Michelle. "Let me make you up a plate of treats and nice cup of tea."

"Thank you, Mrs. Campbell," Mark replied. "I could use a tassie of tea right now."

Mark took off his coat, revealing a Santa-in-a-grass-skirt studded Aloha shirt. Natalie let out a sigh of pleasure mixed with relief, and gave Ferdinando II de' Medici a big, silent thank you. She took Mark's hand and led him toward the kitchen.

"Let's join the game at the table," she said to him. "Have you ever played *briscola*?"

"Not yet, but I get a feeling it's in the cards," Mark said with a wink. "Is it easy enough to learn?"

"Just watch me," Natalie said, reassuringly. "I've been playing it for *ages*."

They walked into the kitchen through the living room, where a 7-1 final score was being displayed on the TV.

"Well, Chase, that was another great, first-inaugural victory for Team Canada, wouldn't you say?"

"Um, no I wouldn't, Ray, because saying 'first-inaugural' is redundant. Boy, if Danny Gallivan were alive today, he'd be rolling over in his grave!"

Klaus called out to his fellow caretaker, who was busy polishing the brass floor tiles in the centre aisle of the church.

"These satchels have been here all day, Carl! No one has returned to claim them!"

"Perhaps they should be placed in the Vórzimmer, until the owner comes back, ja?"

"Ja, ja!"

Klaus picked up the two bags and walked up the aisle, turning right just before the pulpit stairs. He pushed open the creaky door of the anteroom and stepped inside. He placed the satchels on the table at the back. As he turned to go, Klaus noticed a twice-folded piece of paper lying on the floor. He picked it up with the intention of placing it into the garbage container, but his curiosity got the best of him. He held the paper up into the window light and unfolded it once. He read the message. A message that was written boldly, by a sure hand.

Klaus began to tremble. Beads of perspiration formed on his brow. He looked around in a panic, at a loss for what to do next. He dropped the paper into one of the satchels, as if he were ridding himself of a venomous serpent, and quickly left the room.

He hoped – he prayed - that the message had not been written for him.

Interior of Thomaskirche in Leipzig, Germany,
with its 'yellow-brick' aisle, by Tobias Reich

Acknowledgements

Again, love and thanks to my two favourite teachers: my wife, Christine and daughter Hannah. They are my inspiration and constant blessing.

Thanks to the Krusche family for being my biggest supporters. Konrad, Natalka, and Filip are the most wonderful of friends.

And, finally, a big shout out to all the talking heads on the sports radio broadcasts that I've ~~endured~~ enjoyed over the years. They're the ones that are responsible for every malaprop, mixed metaphor, mondegreen, and Spoonerism that our man Chase employs in this book. The only sad part - all those linguistic faux pas were collected in the span of about one week.

About the Author

Rob Lederer taught senior level Chemistry in both public and private high schools for 35 years. He lives in a tiny hamlet outside of a big city. He still enjoys running down the highway, looking for treasures in the ditch.

Also by the author…

Connect Online

www.roblederer.ca

@robledererwrites

chemguy1

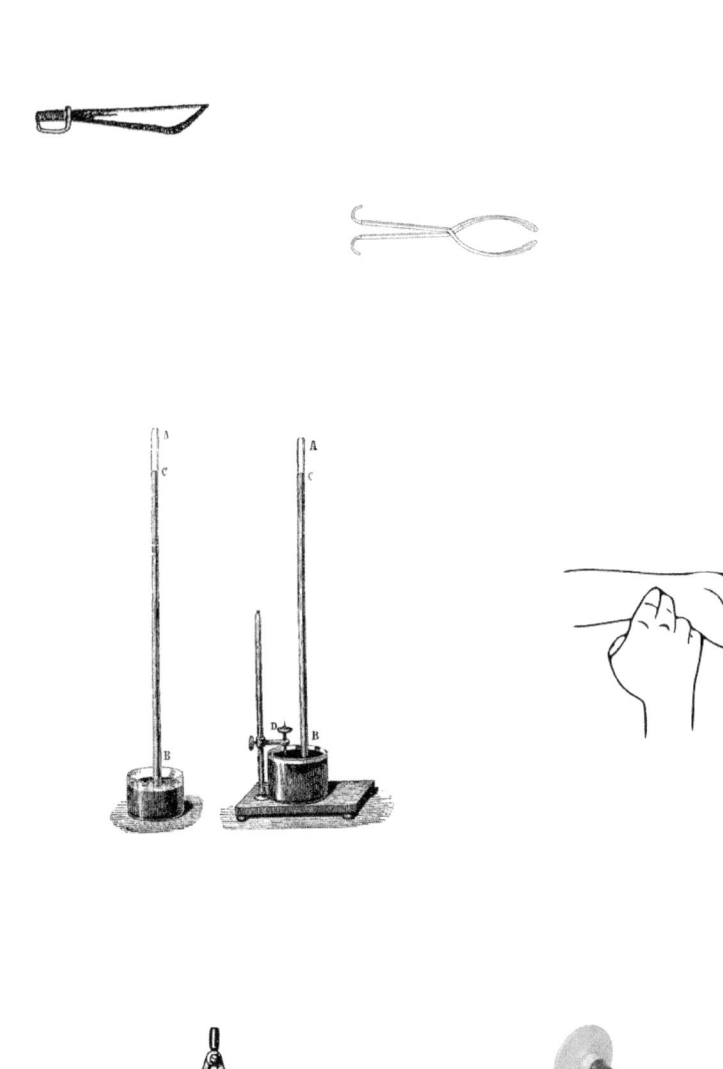

Printed in Great Britain
by Amazon